Praise for Basil Sands

"Sands is fearless in his storytelling, and tireless in his quest to connect directly with his audience."

—Scott Sigler, *NYT* Bestselling Author

"Basil Sands is one awesome writer, penning stories pumped with enough adrenaline that you'll suffer from insomnia until you read the last word. This is one writer not to be missed."

—Jeremy Robinson, International Bestselling Author

"Basil Sands has a knack for blending action and intrigue in an all-too realistic setting.... I just hope there are heroes like Basil's heroes fighting on our side."

—Evo Terra, founder of Podiobooks.com

Also by Basil Sands

65 Below
Karl's Last Flight

Ice Hammer series
Invasion
Insurgent

FAITHFUL WARRIOR

BASIL SANDS

PERMUTED
PRESS

A PERMUTED PRESS BOOK

ISBN: 978-1-68261-697-0
ISBN (eBook): 978-1-68261-863-9

Faithful Warrior
© 2018 by Basil Sands
All Rights Reserved

Cover art by Christian Bentulan

PERMUTED
PRESS

Permuted Press, LLC
New York • Nashville
permutedpress.com

Published in the United States of America

CHAPTER 1

Khat Village
Thirty miles west of Mogadishu, Somalia
March 3rd, 1995

Doctor Clara Bailey crossed her arms and refused to budge. A shock of her tousled red hair dangled angrily across her brow, having escaped from its rubber band.

"Captain, I am not leaving these people behind." she said with an Irish brogue.

"Ahmet's militia is coming, this is your last chance to accept my help." Captain Farris pointed to the bullet scarred door of the clinic. "Me and my men are leaving in one minute."

"Then you'd better get going. My assistants are free to go, but I am not abandoning my patients."

Farris's Marines knelt in a circle around the small medical missionary clinic, weapons pointed outward in every direction. The sour odor of panic permeated the atmosphere of the place.

As the forces of the United Nations Peacekeeping mission prepared for the final pull out of Somalia, Farris's company from the US Marines Special Operations Force had been sent back in to find and evacuate foreign non-government-organization workers like Doctor Bailey and her aids from the health clinic. The Marine's orders were to get as many civilian workers as would go to leave with the UN personnel. It would be their last chance for escape before their protectors left the country for good. Soon the forces of militia leader Alef Muhammad bin Ahmet would descend upon every non-Muslim man and woman to exact the full price for the supposed apostasy of the village's Christians.

Captain Farris opened his mouth to make one final plea. Half-formed words hung in his throat when Dr. Bailey's chest blossomed bright red and a pink mist expanded around her torso. Her eyes stretched wide with shock as the sniper's bullet caught her square through the center of her sternum. The young woman next to her shrieked in terror as a second shot tore the Doctor's forehead apart spraying brain matter across the face of the Somali aid. The doctor's body wavered then fell straight back, lifeless arms still at her sides. Farris grabbed the aid and made a dash for the back of the clinic shoving chairs and tables aside. Bullets ripped into the building smashing glass fronted cabinets and splintering furniture. A puff of white fuzz exploded from an examining table mattress filling the air with a blizzard of cotton that floated around Farris and the girl. A rocket propelled grenade crashed through a window and exploded in the medical office's lobby. Half a dozen people, young women and clinic workers stuck in the panic, were killed instantly.

Militia soldiers poured from alleys and houses in the crowded village. From the first shots, the group of thirty Marines encircling the clinic fired back with disciplined precision, holding off the oncoming militia while the clinic staff and a dozen other civilians ran. Once the civilians were out, the signal was passed to withdraw. The Marines rose, one three-man fire team at a time, and retreated a few yards under cover of their mate's fire. Then they dropped, turned, and provided cover for the next team to withdraw. The leap frog pattern repeated for several blocks through the small town as the warlord's men pressed their advance leaving a trail of bodies strewn in their wake. The soldiers, if they could be called that, were neither well trained nor disciplined. Some wore partial military style uniforms of various styles, but most just wore slacks or jeans and t-shirts. There were old men and boys as young as eight or nine mixed into the horde, many of whom seemed barely strong enough to hold their AK-47s up, let alone shoot them.

Like armed sheep dogs the Marines herded the people toward two oncoming rescue helicopters. Bullets zinged by them close enough for them to feel the air as the bullets passed their heads. Ricochets bounced from the stony ground spraying them with rocks and hot bits of metal. As if hit with a giant hammer, a young Somali civilian suddenly toppled forward and skidded to a halt in the dusty street. The terrified mass passed him without slowing to help him up. One Marine ran to the man and without breaking stride hefted him from the ground one handed and swung him over a shoulder and kept running. His team mates followed, running backwards and firing into the crowd of armed militiamen.

Running in front of Farris, Dr. Bailey's aid stumbled and fell hitting her head on the bumper of a surprisingly-clean cream-colored Mercedes parked on the street. Geysers of dirt erupted around them. Eyes wide with terror she tried desperately to get back on her feet, using the car to help her stand. She screamed and went back down, grabbing her leg. Farris grabbed her by the arm and dragged her around to the front of the car for cover. Her ankle was a bloody mess, dangling by shreds of skin and broken bone. Bullets thunked into the car like someone rattling a snare drum. A stream of fuel ran from under the car. One of Farris's Marines ran toward them, armed with a short-barreled, drum-fed M-249 machine gun. He dropped to a knee half way and fired a storm of brass jacketed lead into the mass of charging men. A dozen Somalis collapsed in the stream of 5.56 caliber bullets. Captain Farris rose and as he reached to grasp the woman's waistband and heave her over his shoulder a rocket propelled grenade hissed from behind the fallen men in the street. The rocket struck the car and exploded, tearing Captain Farris's grip from the woman and flinging him like a rag doll toward a nearby building.

He slammed into the building so hard his helmet flew off. Ribs cracked beneath his armored vest. A team of Marines ran toward him only to be raked with machine gun fire that forced them back behind a wall. A shadow moved over him. He felt himself being tugged along the street. He glanced up in time to see the butt of a rifle descend toward his face before everything went dark.

Mike's head spun in a dizzy whir. His jaw ached. It was swollen and stiff. He tried to take a deep breath but was cut short by an intense stabbing pain in his left side, reminding him of the broken ribs. He forced himself to relax and stifle the apprehension that threatened to morph into fear as the realization of his circumstance dawned on him. He was in a situation few Marines found themselves in: prisoner.

He had no idea where he was, or how long he had been there. The last memory he could conjure was the image of the young Somali woman's body torn in half by the exploding car. He closed his eyes and searched for more, but there was nothing. He leaned back and studied the ceiling above his head. Strips of fibrous bark stretched across wooden poles were laid in a conical pattern above the small round room. Beams of sunlight shot through holes and cracks between the ceiling's bark sheets and the loose slats that made the thin walls of the hut.

Not much protection against rain. Of course, that's not likely to happen anyhow.

During the months Captain Mike Farris had been in country, the temperature hovered at one hundred degrees or higher every single day. He often wondered how a society could possibly have existed for so many thousands of years in such a miserable, desolate place. That held particularly true from where he sat on the dirt floor in the sweltering heat of the bark-roofed hut. He stared out between the cracks in the wall in front of him. Heat waves squirmed from the fiery red dust like an army of serpents dancing to a rhythm unheard by human ears, emanating from the bowels of hell. The heat beat mercilessly against the arid landscape, driving the desire to live out of the earth itself. His hands were lashed behind his back by rough cords of rope that cut into his wrists. The wounds burned as salty sweat ran over the raw, split skin.

Captain Farris closed his eyes and whispered a prayer that he would be able to get out alive. If survival was not his God-given destiny, he prayed to die quickly and without having his body dragged through the streets for his parents to see on the news back home. They had been excited when they learned the morning after receiving orders for Somalia, that their son had been accepted to the Graduate School at Fuller Theological Seminary for a Master of Divinity degree. On account of his numerous combat deployments, his paper-work to transfer back to the reserves for the completion of his eight-year officer's commission had readily been accepted.

He would follow the footsteps of his father and grand-father, both former Marines and pastors. In a matter of forty-eight hours, everything had spiraled in an uncontrol-lable vortex of violence at the end of which he found himself bound in a bark covered shack baking in the oven-like hell of Somalia. Farris still wasn't ready to give up hope.

His eyes focused on the bright blue door of the rickety hut which stood in stark contrast to everything else around him. It was a real six-paneled residential wooden door like one might find in suburban America, except for the leather straps that acted as hinges. As he stared it burst open with a jolt, startling him. The thin bark walls quivered as the door slammed back. A menacing shadow loomed above him, black in the noonday sun. The tall, thin, dark-skinned figure stalked into the makeshift cell and kicked the bound captain in the chest with a sandaled foot. Farris grunted from the impact. He screwed up his eyes in pain. The broken ribs pulsed white-hot as if shot through with lightning. He clenched his teeth, refusing to cry out. The man leaned down and looked into Farris's face. A demonic glint flashed across the man's eyes. His mouth opened in a grotesque smile.

"Get up, pig!" the man hissed through rotted green teeth. A spray of white spittle leaped out from between his lips on the thickly accented words. "The commander wants to see you, pig!"

He reached down and grasped Farris by the back of his shirt collar and yanked him to his feet. The Marine's head swam with sudden dizziness as he was jerked upright, flashing lights sparkled in his eyes. The lieutenant shoved him, and Farris stumbled out the door.

Hands tied behind his back, Captain Farris was unable to control his balance. He toppled forward and fell face down in the hot, hard dust. He grunted from the impact. The pain of the broken ribs washed over him anew with blinding force. Farris lay in the dusty red dirt gasping for breath.

Akbar kicked him in the ribs where he lay. Farris curled into a fetal position to protect his internal organs from the assault. A malevolent grin stretched across Usein's lips. He again grabbed the back of the Marine's collar and once more lifted him up. The man let Farris hang in his grip half way off the ground. Mike choked against the collar that closed around his neck. His full body weight pressed against his trachea until his face turned blue. Only when he drifted to the edge of consciousness did the Somali slowly lift him back to his feet.

"I hope he lets me torture you to a long, slow death, American." He put his lips close to Farris's ear, hot breath hissed across his skin. The fetid odor of khat weed floated into his nostrils on the man's exhaled breath making Mike's nose curl. "Your people should never have come here. You should not ever have set foot in our country."

Akbar pushed the Marine across a wide dirt courtyard. Red dust swirled around their feet in puffs that looked like miniature explosions. The dry heat sucked away the little moisture that remained in his mouth. Farris's feet scuffed wearily across the parched land. The dust rose in clouds and stuck to the sheen of sweat that covered his body. It caked on his skin in thick, dry layers that made his movements feel rusty.

The man led him to a large mud brick building and shoved him into the gaping black hole of an open door. Although the interior of the building was completely shaded from the sun, it was no cooler inside than it was in the blinding sun outside.

It took several seconds for Farris's pupils to expand and adjust to the darkness. He gradually became aware of the shapes of several men with AK-47's standing behind a seated figure. The seated man carried himself with a regal air, like a tribal emperor.

The warlord General Alef Muhammad bin Ahmet was a tall muscular man in his mid-thirties. Ahmet's ebony skin glimmered with an oily sheen of sweat that beaded across his broad face. His features were intense with self-satisfaction and puffed-up pride. He leaned back in a large wooden chair that vaguely resembled a throne. The edges of a leopard skin drooped over its back and sides. Thick lips curled into the beginning of a snarl at one side as the American stood before him. General Ahmet was a rival of the more well-known warlord General Mohamed Farrah Aidid, who had been the instigator of the perceived defeat of American forces during the first battle of Mogadishu.

Ahmet's ego was bigger than reality. The General felt slighted when the Americans had chosen to go after Aidid instead of him. It had really pissed him off when his rival had caused such an impact with the world media, propelling Aidid into hero status throughout the Muslim extremist world. Ahmet felt it should have been him that slaughtered the Americans.

Since that day, nearly two years earlier, General Ahmet had gone out of his way to make every effort to poke his finger in the eye of the "Great Satan" in retribution for not recognizing him as the worthier opponent. Finally, he was going to get his chance to send a message to the cursed Americans, and the entire world would see what happens to those who cross the Great General Alef Muhammad bin Ahmet.

"What is your name?" grunted Ahmet.

"Farris, Michael, Captain USMC," replied the Marine officer.

"Captain Farris, your people have humiliated me too many times, and now you are going to pay the price. Does this frighten you?" asked the General.

"No," came the blunt reply from Farris.

The General flipped his long fingers toward the tall man who had dragged Mike from his cell. He reared back and drove his bony fist into Farris's kidneys. The captain collapsed to his knees. Blood and saliva spurted like a fountain from his mouth. He nearly fainted from the pain. Farris strained, clinging desperately to consciousness. The man held him upright.

"The price I will charge your country will be paid slowly. I will exact it one layer of skin at a time, and I will put it all on videotape to send out to all the news agencies in the world, so that they can watch a warrior of the Great Satan scream for my mercy. I will make sure a copy of the tape is sent to your pig of a father and whore of a mother so that they can see their son scream like a little girl."

Ahmet flicked his finger again and the man pounded the side of Farris's head with his knee. The Marine thudded to the ground like a sack of iron weights. A two-inch gash opened on his cheek. Blood streamed from his face and mouth onto the dirt floor.

"Take him out into the sun and tie him to the post," ordered Ahmet. "Lieutenant Usein, what is your record thus far?"

The man holding Farris nodded, his eyes narrowing to slits. "Eight days, General."

"If you keep him alive for ten, I will give you my youngest daughter Kezia as your next wife."

"I would be most honored to be your son-in-law, General," Usein replied.

"Show me your skill and you will enjoy the girl in two weeks, on her thirteenth birthday," said Ahmet. He motioned with his hand and two men stepped out from behind the general's throne. They rushed towards Farris like death angels coming to collect a soul and snatched him by his still bound arms. They yanked him to his feet, nearly dislocating his shoulders. They dragged him, head drooping, back outside. His bare feet drew a serpentine trail in the dirt as they moved out into the courtyard in the center of the small village.

The two men stood him up and then unbound his hands. They moved them from the back of his body and retied them in front. Once his hands were tightly bound again, they pulled his arms above his head, hoisted his body up, and attached his ropes to a hook that jutted out from high up on the wooden torture post. Bits of dried gore hung from the hook. Reddish brown spatters of blood and shriveled flesh discolored the length of the post. Farris's toes barely touched the ground as he hung, suspended like a slab of meat in the hot sun.

They shredded the fabric of his uniform with knives then ripped the clothes from his body until he was totally naked. His bare white skin reflected like a snowy pillar in the sunlight. His thick muscular chest heaved with every labored breath. The entire left side of his torso was a deep purple bruise. The sharp edge of two ribs jutted grotesquely beneath his skin.

Rays of unfiltered solar energy burned into his flesh. He felt like he was being roasted alive. The two men backed away. Usein stepped close. He held his face inches from Farris. Eye to eye. Nose to nose. His body odor filled the air around the captain's head. When exhalIng, his stench was overpowered by breath that stunk of the khat weed. The evergreen shrub, when chewed, produced a powerful narcotic high similar to cocaine. Criminalized in most of the world, Khat is a staple crop throughout the Horn of Africa. In spite of the fact that the Muslim regime of Southern Somalia had outlawed it, most of the militias' ignored the ban. The drug for which the home village of Ahmet's army was named after fueled their armies.

Usein was pumping hard on the substance. A crooked smile spread across his face, parted lips revealing green khat stained teeth and diseased orange gums. A large ragged starburst shaped scar stretched across his right temple to the edge of his forehead. The African lieutenant's pulse pounded in the blood vessels around the scar. The whole mass of tissue throbbed in a heavy rhythm as if it had life of its own, a living creature attached to Usein's head. It looked like an alien being that controlled the man.

Two of the men in the crowd finished setting up a video camera on a tripod. One peered through the eyepiece of the camera then raised his hand and pointed like a movie director creating a summer blockbuster.

Usein saw the cue and leaned even closer to the captain before he abruptly reared back and smashed his forehead onto the bridge of Farris's nose. Mike grunted as bright lights exploded across his vision. Blood spattered across his chest; it dripped from Usein's face. His crooked smile widened in derisive pleasure.

The gang of men encircling them burst into a cheer. They laughed and urged Akbar on to more. The tall, thin lieutenant drove his fists into Farris's abdomen, alternating blows rapidly as if the naked Marine were a punching bag. He paused, and the captain gasped for air. Blood and saliva streamed from his mouth and smashed nose. He controlled the urge to cry out, steeling himself against the pain and comforted himself with the thought of death ending the torture.

Usein turned towards the circle of cheering men and raised his hands in a vain, glorious gesture. Facing the camera, he stretched his mouth in an evil smile then spun around and rammed his knee into the captain's testicles.

Farris's eyes squeezed shut, so tight it felt as if his eyelids were going to burst. Undulating waves of nausea washed over his entire body. The young captain wretched, then vomited what little contents were in his stomach onto the ground between him and Usein.

Captain Farris began anew in silent prayer. He asked God to grant him a quick death. He asked for strength so that he would not cry out. He prayed that in dying delirium he would not satisfy these beasts by begging for mercy.

Usein backed away from his victim. He reached behind his back in a slow, dramatic movement and drew a long knife from a leather sheath on his belt. He raised it high above his head letting the steel blade catch the glint of the bright afternoon sun. He stepped close again. The circle of men fell silent, their cheers fading in weighted expectation as he lowered the knife and held its razor edge to Farris's throat.

"Now, Marine," growled Usein, "I am going to skin you alive. I am going to take your skin from head to toe, and while you are still alive, I am going to wear it like a shirt. I will not be fast. I will take my time, and the entire world will see you scream like a little virgin. They will witness you beg for mercy when they watch the video tape of it."

Farris could not reply with anything more than a grunt. His face was unrecognizable, a mass of swollen purple flesh and shattered bone.

The two men with the video camera picked up their tripod and moved closer. They argued between them as to the best set up and the angles of the sunlight. It was imperative that they get a good, clear, close-in shot of the process.

Farris looked hard into Usein's eyes and prayed again. This time instead of asking for mercy from God, he asked for revenge.

Father God, his lips moved in silent prayer, *whether I live or die, I ask that you kill this man.*

As if Usein could read Mike's mind and heard his supplications, the African smacked him hard across the cheek with the back of his free hand. White-hot lightning shot through the shattered framework of Farris's face. A stream of blood shot skyward. It spattered on the camera lens. One of the cameramen reached up with a piece of cloth and wiped it clean then stuffed the cloth into his back pocket.

Akbar Usein pressed the blade of the knife into the top of Farris chest then slowly dragged it across the top of his pectorals. He sliced into the outermost layers of skin with excruciating languor as the Marine braced himself against the searing pain of the steel's razor edge.

Captain Farris clenched his teeth and squeezed his lips shut. He forced his thoughts to another time and place. He pictured being in his father's church on a beautiful autumn day. He conjured the memory of clean mid-western air and picture red, yellow, and brown leaves drifting to the cool ground in lazy fluttering spirals. As the blade slid over his body from right to left across his collarbone he was forced back to reality. He stifled the cries that welled up inside his lungs. A thin stream of bright red blood flowed in an even sheet from the wound and flowed over his quivering pectorals.

Usein grabbed Farris's chin in an iron grip and forced his face straight. "Look into my eyes, Captain Farris. Remember my name. I am Akbar Usein, Allah's avenger. If Allah wills that you not burn in hell, then you will be bound to me as my slave in paradise."

Commotion rose among the encircling men. A thunderous sound exploded around them, reverberating off the walls and ground. The *WHUP WHUP WHUP* of two Cobra attack helicopters split the air. It drowned out all other sounds. Before the militia soldiers could react the high-speed rip of 20-millimeter chain-guns erupted from the nose of the helicopters, spitting hundreds of bullets, each the size of a man's index finger, into the circle of men who stood around Akbar and his victim. Their bodies danced like marionettes whose strings were being jerked by a child in a temper tantrum. The firing abruptly stopped, and their torn bodies crumpled to the ground.

Smoke trailed from the multi-barreled Vulcan nose guns as the Cobras' rose from the scene of destruction. The pair of blood-satiated beasts tilted and droned away. Two Blackhawk helicopters zoomed in fifty feet above the buildings and hovered at the edge of the courtyard. Black ropes dropped like tentacles from the open side doors followed by a rapid discharge of armed men. Like a platoon of grim reapers they floated to the ground, weapons blazing. Long yellow flames stretched from AK-47 muzzles on the ground trying to force them back up their ropes, but torrents of death rained down as they swooped from the sky.

Usein turned to look at the action and his tall frame convulsed spasmodically as several rounds of 5.56 mm ammunition punched into his chest. Blood fountained into the air as the bullets stitched across his frame and out his back. Usein staggered, then spun back towards Farris. He lurched toward the captain who dangled helpless on the pole, intent that the prisoner would die before he could be rescued. He hesitated then raised his knife. Blood spattered from his mouth, and he dropped to his knees in the hot red dirt. The African lieutenant toppled face first onto the ground, the arc of the blade barely missing Farris. Akbar Usein lay still, blood pooling around his body.

A stocky Marine staff sergeant ran forward and cut the captain's bonds. A corpsman joined him and unfolded a metal framed litter into which they lay the barely conscious captain. He directed a helicopter to land nearby, and the two men hoisted the litter and started for the helicopter. Half a dozen other Marines formed a ring around them firing into clusters of militia that rushed at them from the buildings as the rescue force made their retreat.

"We're getting you out of here, sir," shouted the staff sergeant, "Don't you worry about nothing. Hogan and Company is on the job!"

CHAPTER 2

Present Day
Sunday, October 16th
Faith Presbyterian Church
Picktown, Ohio
12:30 Hours

Pastor Michael Farris stepped down from the tall wooden pulpit on the stage of Faith Presbyterian Church at twelve thirty on a crisp mid-October Sunday afternoon. Sunlight streamed in through the vaulted windows of the large church's sanctuary and shone in warm streaks that lay invitingly across the red cloth covered pews. It was an extraordinarily bright and cheerful day.

Through the windows Mike could see the early onset of fall colors as the leaves of the beech changed, seemingly before his eyes, from green to yellow and the oak and hickory leaves to red. The stalks of harvested corn lay across the land like a dusky brown blanket over the fifty-acre field next to the church. Above the horizon at the edge of the tree lined field, a flock of geese flew in V-formation. They cut a southward swath through a sky that shimmered overhead in a shade of blue that fell somewhere between turquoise and sapphire.

He made his way through the milling crowd and out the front doors of the church, stopping on the step so he could greet his congregants as they left the service. Outside, he inhaled deeply, filling his senses with aromas of damp earth, forest, and sunshine. Peace flooded his soul.

The morning message Pastor Farris had delivered to the five-hundred-plus members of the congregation of Faith Presbyterian Church had been well prepared and intentional. If the comments of the congregates as they passed by shaking his hand on their way out were an accurate indication, he had hit his mark straight on.

His sermon had been on reaching out to others in need of help regardless of their present appearance or their past sins. The topic was amplified by the presence of two former gang members whom he had been working with for some time. Both were young men in their late-twenties, who had recently completed training as ministers and were working with Columbus' inner-city gang community. One of the young men, LeRon Davis, was especially enthusiastic about his newfound calling.

LeRon had been a major player in a lot of the gang related crime that plagued the city of Columbus a couple of years earlier. He had been in and out of jail since fourteen and at sixteen had killed a rival gangster in a fight. By the age of twenty-two, LeRon had worked his way up the gang-land chain of command until he was the leader of a drug ring that held control of the markets for cocaine, ecstasy, methamphetamine, and heroin in several neighborhoods of Columbus, Ohio. It was in that scenario that Pastor Mike Farris and LeRon Davis met.

Pastor Mike and a couple of men from the church had taken to doing street ministry in the hardest sections of the city. Mike had taken a position on a corner in LeRon's own neighborhood, a mecca of drug deals and prostitution. He had boldly preached his religion out loud to everyone in ear-shot, which in Mike's case was nearly two city blocks. LeRon quickly grew tired of the preacher breaking up his business. He confronted Pastor Mike with three of his street thugs as back up.

After leaving the marines, Pastor Mike had stayed fit, and he carried himself with the air of confidence that comes from the kind of training and experience he had received in that career. LeRon was accustomed to bullying anyone that came between him and his desires. He had definitely not expected the preacher to stand his ground and appeared shocked when Mike would not leave.

One of the thugs, a short skinny man known as Li'l Mac, blurted out, "Do him LeRon; just do him and shut this crazy fool up!"

"Good idea Li'l Mac. I think he is done."

With a light metallic click, a switchblade knife flicked open in LeRon's left hand. By the time two police cars sped around the corner, emergency lights flashing and sirens blaring, LeRon and one of his men lay unconscious on the ground. Li'l Mac and the other man took off on foot. Li'l Mac was caught. The fourth gang member was killed when he ran into traffic trying to escape from the police.

Pastor Mike visited them in jail regularly and over time developed a friendship that became deep and strong. To LeRon, Mike's consistency and legitimate kindness endeared him like a big brother. Li'l Mac grew to respect the preacher as well. Both men eventually committed themselves to the down to earth realistic Christian faith that Pastor Mike preached.

In time, the three of them developed a ministry in the prison that became quite successful. LeRon and Li'l Mac got out of prison a little over a year later. They both became members of Mike's church and eventually, leaders of one of the most effective anti-gang ministry in the city.

Later that evening, the church leaders joined Pastor Mike and his wife for dinner at the two-story parsonage across the street from the church. It was a nice house, designed for entertaining and comfortable for fairly large groups.

Built in 1986, the Victorian style two-story with a wide wrap-around porch was owned by the church and had been the living quarters for last two senior-pastors and their families before Mike took the job. It had replaced the original parsonage, circa 1860, that had been, along with the church building, severely damaged by a tornado twenty-five years earlier.

Mike married late in life. He turned forty the day of his wedding to Janelle who was ten years younger. They had met at a denominational conference. She was the daughter of a seminary professor and had just returned from a three-year missionary assignment to Kazakhstan. They married within six months of meeting.

Janelle was both attractive and energetic. She had a shapely feminine figure. Her long and straight sandy-blond hair hung to the middle of her shoulder blades, shimmering like sheets of silk that framed her pretty oval face and glittering hazel eyes beautifully. Narrow shoulders sloped gently above small breasts that were set above a slim waist. Her gently rounded hips were perfectly proportionate to the rest of her slender body.

Her physical features were definitely eye catching, but her personality struck Mike more than anything else. Janelle was lively and fun. She emanated an optimism and bubbling joy that positively infected everyone who came in contact with her. Mike enjoyed every moment he spent with his wife.

Eighteen-month-old Mike Junior, dubbed Mini-Mike by the teens in the church, was born a little less than a year after their marriage. The boy had his mother's bubbly personality, with the same sparkle in his eyes and a smile that never seemed to fade.

Mini-Mike was the center of attention in the kitchen where Janelle chatted and laughed with the deacons' wives to the accompaniment of clinking china and silverware while cleaning up after the meal. The men cleared the table then returned to discuss the business of the church over the smoky scent that floated on steam rising from mugs of freshly brewed dark roasted coffee.

LeRon leaned forward on the table and laid out plans for a new outreach to the University Heights neighborhood near the Ohio State University campus.

"The way I see it, we can easily and relatively safely get a youth program started in the area right away," he said. "I have already made an agreement with the guys at the boxing gym to use their facility for two hours every day after school to get the kids involved in activities and keep them off the streets."

Deacon Andrew Phelps sipped his coffee as he listened to LeRon.

"What about the gangs in the area?" asked Deacon Phelps who was in charge of the hospitality ministries of the church. His wife Lenora was the church secretary. "I am sure they have heard of it. How are they reacting to the plan?"

Li'l Mac answered. "They don't like it. They've heard of LeRon's success in the other neighborhoods and have actually made a threat against him, but that's been the case with most of the neighborhoods we've worked in and nothing ever came of any of them. God has always protected us so far. Just in case though, we've worked out a deal with the Guardian Angels to have a half-dozen of their guys stationed outside the gym and also to escort any guest speakers we might bring in."

Elder Harry Johnson, an eighty-year-old retired antiques dealer who had been a member of the church since the late sixties, spoke up. "Is it wise to go into an area that requires us to have protection and body guards? I don't want to be endangering any of the members of our church who want to help with this mission."

"Don't worry about that, sir," replied LeRon. "Li'l Mac and myself will be the only ones from the church going into this neighborhood for a while; at least, until we get it all set up and smoothed out."

LeRon turned and gestured to Pastor Mike. "We're not even gonna let the Preaching Marine in there. He has Mini-Mike to take care of."

"And," added Mike, "we've let the city police know what we are doing. The success of our work in other neighborhoods where we set up similar programs has impressed them. They said they'll add a couple of extra patrols through the area while we are there."

Elder Johnson leaned away from the table and rubbed his fingertips on his forehead. Concern lay heavy on his expression.

"I don't want to put a damper on this whole thing. I think you men have been doing a great job, a really effective work, but…"

He paused and shifted uncomfortably in his seat.

"I don't know how this is going to sound to you," he took a deep breath, "but I have been having a bad feeling lately, a feeling like something terrible is going to happen. I can't exactly explain it, but…well…"

Elder Johnson hesitated again, carefully considering the next few words. At length he blurted it out.

"I've been having some bad dreams. Dreams like I have never had before."

There was silence around the table. Harry Johnson was the least likely person they expected to hear such a statement from. Elder Johnson was known as a serious pragmatist and generally quite boring.

Of the men at the table, only Pastor Mike was aware of the elder's further past. Harry Johnson had spent most of his younger life as a covert CIA field agent spying against the Soviet Union at the height of the Cold War. He had made an entire career of actively confronting America's enemies, often with extreme "violence of action," while the other men at the table were still in diapers or not even born yet. Johnson and Farris shared a common bond for the similarities their lives had shared. The elder had let Farris know much of his past. Johnson likewise was the only person to whom Mike confided his own military past.

Elder Johnson continued. "Back in fifty-three, when I got home from the Korean War the army psychiatrists warned me that my experience there might give me bad dreams and such. Well, it never did. That whole part of my life, three years in that awful war, was behind me. I committed it to God and he took it off my shoulders. I never had a bad feeling against any of those North Koreans or Chinese, because I figured they were just like me, you know, just doing their job, obeying orders. I never dreamed about that war and the terrible things we all did to each other there. That is, until the last couple of weeks."

"Two weeks ago Friday, I had a dream. I was in Seoul, running through the streets trying to get a man who killed my friends and who I knew was planning to kill more of them. Then I heard a big explosion and a baby crying, and I woke up. Now the funny thing was I knew the dream wasn't about my own experience, because I had never fought in the battle of Seoul."

"Now, you all know I am not the kind of person who puts much merit in all that wishy-washy dream stuff, but I have had this dream repeated almost every night since then, and I've got to be honest with you. It has me concerned. I just don't know what else it could be but a warning from God."

The men around the table, some of whom had known Harry for decades, nodded their heads quietly. The statements were so out of character for Harry Johnson, they had no choice but to take him seriously.

After a long silence, Pastor Mike spoke, "Well Harry, it sounds like this is something we will all have to spend some time in prayer about and see what comes of it. We have a couple of weeks before we will be ready to start. Gentlemen, let's take this time to pray and think about what Elder Johnson has brought up. In the meantime, LeRon, continue with your arrangements, but keep in mind we may have to stop before it actually goes live."

"I understand," replied LeRon. "Elder Johnson, thanks for letting us know about those dreams. Even though I may seem all fired up to get in there and do this thing, one thing I've learned since coming to the Lord is that patience is golden."

Janelle poked her head into the dining room and signaled her husband with raised eyebrows. Mike rose from his chair at the table.

"All right, gents. Sorry to break up this party, but my wife needs to put Mini-Mike to bed pretty soon, and Big Mike is getting tired too. Sunday's sure are taxing on me these days."

The men rose from the table as their wives entered the room. They collected their jackets and shuffled to the door as a group. Mini-Mike stood like a sentinel in the foyer and demanded a good-bye hug from each of them as they left.

Elder Johnson was the last to leave. He stopped at the door and hugged the little boy. Then stood up and turned back to Mike.

Mini-Mike toddled across the floor to his mother's arms.

"Mommy, juice?" he asked.

"Where is your sippy cup?"

"In duh chicken." He answered and pointed to the kitchen.

"No silly, that's the kitchen, not the chicken."

28

The three adults chuckled at the boy's error. Janelle took Mini-Mike into the kitchen to get his sippy cup.

When she left, Elder Johnson spoke softly.

"Mike, I am telling you, as a fellow warrior, watch out. Somethings got my radar up, and I just don't know what."

"Thank you, sir, I understand, and I'll keep my eyes open." Mike said, "I appreciate all you have done for me and the church. I will take your warning seriously."

Elder Johnson turned and walked out and down from the porch to the immaculately kept 1982 Cadillac Eldorado parked in the driveway. When he fired up the engine, it purred to life with a gentle quietness that belied the serious power under the hood. He pulled out and a moment later the house was empty except for the Farris family.

Janelle ascended the steps towards the bedrooms. Mini-Mike held her hand as he slowly walked up one step at a time.

She called out from half way up the staircase, "I'm going upstairs to put your son in the tub, honey."

"Alright," came the response from Mike as he entered the small downstairs bathroom to relieve himself. It had been a large dinner, and after several hours holding it in, he couldn't wait any longer.

Just as he sat down on the toilet the doorbell rang.

"Oh man!" he declared. Mike cracked the door open and shouted into the hallway, "Honey! Janelle! Could you get that?"

Janelle had just reached the top of the stairs. Mini-Mike smiled up at her in triumph, having walked up the whole staircase on his own feet.

She sighed and said, "Yes, I'll get it."

She picked up the grinning toddler, turned and went back down the stairs to the front door. Janelle opened it to find LeRon standing there, an apologetic smile on his face.

"Sorry to bother you Mrs. Farris, but I forgot my cell phone in the dining room," he said.

"No problem, LeRon," she answered, "If you know where you left it, go ahead and get it."

"Thanks," he replied as he went in. LeRon retrieved the small phone from the dining room table and put it in his pocket.

Janelle and Mini-Mike stepped out onto the porch and waved at Li'l Mac who sat waiting in LeRon's car on the street in front of the house.

LeRon returned and walked outside. As he stepped out the door onto the front porch, Mini-Mike called out to him.

"Bye, unka Newon!"

His cute, stubby, little toddler hand waved up and down as he smiled to his daddy's friend.

LeRon turned and smiled brightly back at the baby.

"Bye-bye, Mini-Mike." The reformed gangster raised his hand and wiggled his fingers in return. He scrunched his face into a silly expression that elicited a musical giggle from the child. Mini-Mike's eyes sparkled with childish joy. Li'l Mac glanced up to the house and waved towards them.

Fast moving tires squealed on the street pavement. An engine roared in acceleration. LeRon and Janelle both instinctively turned towards the noise. The baby smiled playfully at LeRon, oblivious to what the adults were looking at.

A loud burst of staccato pops erupted like the rattling of a snare drum. A long white flame burst from the rear passenger side window of a speeding car bright white in the dusky evening twilight. The sharp crack of shattering glass cut through the air and Li'l Mac let out a yelp as bullets slammed through LeRon's car and into his body. LeRon abruptly tumbled forward onto the porch his arms flinging outward, grasping for something to catch himself. His eyes blinked in wild confusion.

Janelle wrapped her arms tightly around her baby then buckled and dropped to her knees. A loud thump echoed from the wooden surface of the porch as she fell face down, Mini-Mike under her chest, the stillness of their bodies framed by a pool of rapidly spreading blood.

CHAPTER 3

Sunday, October 16th
Faith Presbyterian Church
Picktown, Ohio
21:57 Hours

Columbus Police Detective Dan Martin sat on the edge of the couch. Across from him Pastor Mike Farris slumped in his wing-back recliner. The chair looked like it was meant to be the most comfortable place in the house. Mike sat at the edge of it, rejecting the plush cushions behind him, face planted in his hands.

Detective Martin touched the tips of his fingers against each other and looked at the floor. After more than a decade as a homicide investigator he loathed working these kinds of cases. Even more than the deaths of apparently innocent bystanders, he hated the dismay of the survivors as they felt that their god had abandoned them. They had put their trust in some mythological idea of a benevolent being who would protect them from evil, only to have it shattered by a devastating random act of violence.

There was only one part of the christian doctrine Martin heard of which he thought touched on reality. Men are inherently evil. He had seen more than enough to demonstrate that concept in twenty years as a cop. Unlike the christian view though, he saw no hope of redemption.

Men killed each other for the stupidest reasons. Sometimes they killed each other for no reason at all. Detective Martin had seen so much evil in his life, much of it perpetrated by people who claimed to hear the "Voice of God", that there was no room in his heart to believe in any benevolent being. If there was a god, Dan Martin hated him.

"Pastor Farris," he said, "I am really sorry about your wife and son. We will do everything we can to track down these killers and get them off the streets."

Mike's hands dropped from his face and landed with a soft slap on his lap. His eyes were red and puffy, his gaze distant. Martin wasn't sure if the pastor heard his words. He stared towards some point in the middle of the room as if searching to find an image of his family to grasp hold of before it faded away. Martin had seen this type of reaction a hundred times as the survivor rewound a mental recording of the day's events, trying in vain to undo the scene, to wake from the hellish nightmare.

"Thank you, Detective," Mike responded in a low voice, his gaze focusing back on Martin. "I know you will do everything you can for us."

"Did you see anything at all that could help us?" said Martin.

"No, I was not in a position to see anything until it was over," said Mike.

"Can you tell us," asked the detective, "Who may have wanted to kill LeRon?"

"It could be about half the gangs in Columbus for all I know," replied the pastor. "We have youth missions in eight different neighborhoods, and basketball outreaches in a dozen more. Every one of them has been drawing kids away from the drugs and gang scene for the past two years. LeRon was good at reaching out to the kids."

Martin looked down, staring at the pattern in the carpet. "But do you know if anyone in particular had put out a threat on LeRon? Anything specific?"

"No," Mike answered, "I don't know of any specific threats. There have been many general threats over the years, but never anything specific that made us really look into it."

"Nothing at all?" said Martin.

"Detective," replied Pastor Mike, "I manage the ministries of my church from an executive level. I let the ministers who work under me run their own work in a manner that best fits them. To do that I use a hands-off approach and let them have maximum control over their work so that they can reach their maximum efficiency. I have never micromanaged the programs here. LeRon and Li'l Mac have had almost free reign ever since they took that ministry over. I don't know the specifics of the threats that may have been made against them. Perhaps you should wait at the hospital and ask Li'l Mac. He may be able to tell you more."

"He is in a coma. There is a bullet lodged in his brain. The doctors are not sure that he'll survive the night," replied the detective. "Is anyone else close to their ministry that may know something more?"

"No," replied the pastor. Exhaustion ebbed through his muscles and joints. It rumbled beneath the sound his voice.

Detective Martin rose from the couch, straightened his brown cloth tie and pulled at the bottom edge his brown wool tweed sport coat. He stretched out his hand towards Mike. The pastor stood and shook the hand.

"Thanks for all you are doing," said Pastor Mike, "I am sure you will do everything possible."

Detective Martin pursed his lips and stared intently at Mike's face. At length he nodded his head.

"Yes sir. We will get it done."

They released their handshake and Martin walked to the door.

"Pastor Farris, you have my card. Call me if anything comes up or you remember something that will help, OK?"

"I will."

After Martin left, it was still another three hours before the crime scene unit was done. They took scores of pictures, measured trajectories, and gathered information. Just before two in the morning, Mike Farris locked the door to the house and forced his weary body up the stairs to his bedroom. Detective Martin and a police chaplain had suggested he stay somewhere else, but Mike insisted on remaining in his house. He did not want to be away from the last place he had seen his wife and son.

He collapsed on the mattress of the gigantic king size bed. Engulfed by the silky softness of the thick comforter Janelle had bought at a sale just a few days earlier Mike curled up in a fetal position. Convulsive sobbing waves overcame him, and he mourned from the depth of his being. In a moment, a blink of an eye he had lost his wife and his only child. He was a trained warrior, but had been unable to save his own family.

The week followed in a blur of visitors offering their condolences. The following Saturday, a memorial service and funerals were held for all three of the dead. The ceremonies were presided over by Mike's friend Don Mallory, the pastor of the Methodist church that stood a mile and a half from Grace.

Li'l Mac was still in the hospital where he struggled to hold on to the thin thread that kept him on the mortal side of life. He was still in a coma. The doctors told his family that he was not expected to last much longer.

After the funeral Mike called the church leaders to meet at the parsonage. Mike asked them to let him leave his assistant pastor in charge and take a month-long leave of absence. He needed to sort things out, to decide what direction to take next. They said that he could have that month and more, if needed.

They did not stay long after the discussion. When the last car left his driveway, Mike closed and locked the door.

Mike slowly walked through the house. He made sure every picture was straight. He dusted the flat surfaces, washed the few dishes in the sink, did the single load of laundry, and vacuumed the carpets. The cleaning itself did not take long. The ladies of the church had come in a couple of times since the shooting to tidy up. They had even made some meals for him and put them in plastic containers in the refrigerator so that he'd just have to microwave them.

He went through the entire house as if he were inspecting a barracks in the Marines. He made sure it was, as they said in the Corps, "Squared Away." The cleaning spree was a formality, a sign of finality—closure.

Once he was finished he climbed the stairs with the laundry basket and put the clothes in their proper places in the drawers and the walk-in closet. Then he went to the window of the bedroom and looked out across the street to the church that had been his for the past ten years. He stared for a long moment, then twisted the long plastic rod that hung along the side of the window. The mini-blinds rotated down until they blocked out the image before him.

He pulled the curtain from the retaining hooks at either side of the window and let it close. The thick cloth completely obscured the view from the outside. Not even a shadow was visible.

Mike turned from the curtained window. He looked up to the ceiling. A tear ran down his cheek.

He glanced at the floor. Another tear rose from his eye, slid across the length of his eyelash, hung for a moment at the end of the fine hair, and then released its grip. It dropped silently though the space between his face and floor and vanished into fibers of the carpet without a sound.

He closed his eyes. A whisper floated from his lips.

"Father, please forgive me."

Mike wiped the moisture from his eyes and walked across the room to the master bathroom. A door stood open just inside. He walked through into a room-sized closet with a dressing area. Inside the closet he took off the pastoral khaki Dockers and white dress shirt he had worn through the evening and replaced them with loose fitting black denim jeans and a dark blue polo shirt.

Against the wall, behind the multi-colored, crisply-pressed shirts and neatly-hung slacks stood the cubic bulk of a heavy black steel gun safe. A combination lock keypad protruded from the center of the door above a three-pronged handle.

Mike punched in the numbered code, twisted the locking lever and pulled the heavy gauge door open. He reached inside and pulled out an immaculate and well-oiled custom-made MEU/SOC M1911A1 .45 caliber pistol.

Almost never were Marines allowed to keep their issued weapon from their time in service. The Marine Corps, under order of the Commandant, made an exception for Major Mike Farris. At his farewell reception he had been presented with the weapon he had carried on covert missions throughout his twenty-plus year career.

While the world will never know how many lives you have saved, or wars you have averted, we will always remember. The words of the Commandant of the Marine Corps echoed in the chambers of his mind.

From a shelf at the top of the cabinet he took a loaded magazine and slid it into the well in the handle of the weapon. He pulled the receiver back then let go and let it slam a round into the chamber. He dropped the magazine back out, and slid a fresh round into the top of magazine then reinserted it into the pistol.

"Forgive me," he whispered again.

CHAPTER 4

Sarajevo, Bosnia-Herzegovina
September, 1998

Captain Farris stepped into the Legion Bridge Hotel in southern Sarajevo wearing the rumpled white polo shirt and khaki dockers he had put on nearly twenty-four hours earlier when he got out of bed in Pasadena, California. The century old hotel had recently become home to the Sarajevo Military Headquarters of the United Nations Special Operations Command, UNSOCOM. He made his way up to the reception desk and presented his ID and a set of stamped orders to a red-haired British army sergeant. The young man studied the ID and the documents thoroughly while the exhausted US Marine captain stood before him.

It was nearly the end of summer break in Mike's seminary studies. When he left his west coast apartment he told his landlord he'd be gone for a while on his annual two-week reserve duty with the Marines and to keep an eye on the place. The post office had been notified to hold his mail while he was away.

When he walked through the gate at LAX and boarded the fully booked American Airlines 747, Mike Farris had not looked forward to the next twenty plus hours of international air travel. His discomfort was significantly amplified when he found himself squeezed between two inhumanly large professional power lifters traveling to Holland for the "Met Rx World's Strongest Man" competition. By the time he arrived in Amsterdam, and transferred to a flight to Frankfurt, he felt as if he'd been stuffed in a suitcase in the baggage compartment. He still had only partially recovered when he touched down in Sarajevo.

"Mike!" A voice called from down the hall. "You look like crap!"

Captain Farris wheeled to the left and snapped to attention. He winced at the pain in his stiff joints.

"I feel like crap, sir. Is there a place I can take a shower?"

"Of course," replied Lieutenant Colonel Cecil Hardwick, commander of UNSOCOM Bosnia. "You are bunking down the hall in a semi-private room. Sorry to say that you have to share a bathroom with the enlisted guy next door, but I believe you know him, so it shouldn't be too bad."

"I know him?" asked Mike.

"Staff Sergeant Paul Hogan, from your last command."

"Hogan's here?" Captain Farris got visibly excited. "I haven't seen that guy since he literally saved my skin in Somalia."

"You'll appreciate the fact that he's going to be your NCOIC for this operation," answered Lieutenant Colonel Hardwick.

"Outstanding!" Mike said. Excitement rose in his voice but dissipated as travel exhaustion ebbed back into his bones. "But sir, I have to ask for permission to take that shower soon, the air conditioning on the plane wasn't working too well and almost the whole way, I was stuffed between two three-hundred-pound gorillas headed to the 'World's Strongest Man' competition. My funk is pretty ripe after nearly twenty hours in that can."

"No problem, Captain. It's o-nine-fortyfive now," said Hardwick looking at his watch, "you have until fourteen-hundred to get cleaned up and maybe get some rest. I'll send a runner to pick you up at that time and have you to the briefing room by fourteen-thirty. Be in civilian attire and ready to fill your brain, we'll take care of all of the other logistics as needed later on."

"Aye aye, sir."

"Carry on, Marine," said Hardwick. He handed Mike a room key then turned and walked away. His heels clicked against the centuries old marble floor of the grand hotel.

Captain Farris walked to the room that matched the number on the key Lieutenant Colonel Hardwick had given him. Luckily for his worn-out body, it was only a short distance away at the end of the hall on the main floor.

Mike went in to his temporary quarters, dropped his bag by the door, and peeled off his clothes like shedding a layer of sweat crusted skin. The partially updated bathroom was shared between his room and the next. Some of the fixtures had been replaced, apparently as the old ones broke down. The sink looked like it had been installed in the forties, as did the shower head and handles, but the toilet and bidet were both eighties as was the wall paper. The tub itself was a cheap plastic insert while the curtain looked like something designed in the twenties. The look created a sense of time confusion for him, as if he were caught between eras, pre-communist, communist, and post-communist all jumbled together in the bathroom. Whatever epoch this place was in, the long, hot shower rinsed away all of the travel grime he had built up in the long journey from Los Angeles.

After the shower, Farris wrapped himself in a clean white bathrobe that hung on a hook on his room's side of the bathroom door. Barely conscious, he stumbled across the room and collapsed onto the thick soft mattress of the comfortably wide queen-sized bed. He immediately drifted into a deep sleep. His senses blacked out: no sight, no sound, not even the feeling of the blanket under him. It seemed like only a few minutes. At precisely 1400 hours there was a loud rap on the door, the signal that his nap was over. It was now time to get to the business portion of his trip.

He opened the door to find the runner, a lance corporal in a "Charlie" service uniform of short-sleeve khaki shirt, green wool-blend trousers and black shoes shined to a glass-like sheen. The trim young warrior, who looked like he couldn't have been a day over nineteen, stood at attention two feet away. The black plastic name tag on his left breast pocket read "Phelps" in stamped white letters.

"Sir, Lieutenant Colonel Hardwick requires your presence at the briefing room in thirty minutes."

"Alright, Lance Corporal, take a seat and wait while I get dressed. I'll be about five minutes. You'll need to take me to the nearest coffee pot on the way."

"Aye aye, Captain," replied the young man.

Five minutes later Mike Farris exited the room. Lance Corporal Phelps rose from a black leather lobby chair against the wall opposite his door.

"Lead the way, Marine." Farris said as the door clicked shut behind him.

Phelps walked fast. Captain Farris followed the young Marine down the hall and past a wide stairway bounded by a beautiful wrought iron balustrade topped by an ornate decorated rail of dark wood. The rail reflected their shapes as they walked past, its surface shined to a high gloss by more than a century of oil and polish.

After they passed the staircase Lance Corporal Phelps turned and entered a small room filled with tables and chairs. Along the far wall a neat row of vending machines stood like a formation of robots. The first machine in the row had a brightly lit front panel depicting a four-foot tall cup of steaming coffee surrounded by glossy mounds of black and brown coffee beans.

The Lance Corporal pointed to it and said, "This machine is without a doubt the best cup of coffee in the building. It actually grinds the beans fresh for each cup and makes it according to how strong you want it. Just choose what kind of coffee you want from the menu then press the star button here in the corner to increase the strength. One press equals about one teaspoon of coffee grounds. Select your grind style, from coarse to espresso, and hit the 'Go' button here." The young man spoke as if he was trying to sell the machine to Farris.

"You got stake in a franchise for these things, Marine?"

"No sir, I just get to show it to a lot of people," answered the young man. He grinned then added, "But once I get my promotion to full corporal, I am going to take the pay difference and invest it in the contractor who has our vending business, this company is making a killing!"

Mike pressed the buttons to make a cup of straight-up black coffee then hit the star button four times and pressed the espresso grind button. He needed it to be as strong as he could stand. The machine whirred for several seconds. That sound was followed by a grinding noise as the beans were pulverized into a fine powder.

After the grinding stopped, a cup dropped from inside the machine onto a grate where it was held by a spring-loaded arm while steaming hot water ran through the grounds and into the waiting container. When Mike pulled the cup out of the machine he put it to his nose and inhaled its steam. The scent was invigorating all by itself. He took a sip. The lance corporal was right. It was one of the best cups of coffee he had ever tasted.

They moved back out of the room into the hallway and climbed the decorative flight of stairs, then ascended three more flights just like it. Phelps led the captain down several corridors until they finally came to a room where the lance corporal opened the door and motioned for Captain Farris to enter. Once he was inside the young Marine closed the door and left Farris alone. It was twenty minutes past two. The meeting was to begin in ten minutes.

Mike crossed the room to the large flat window and looked out. He scanned the remains of Sarajevo that stretched before him to the east. Memories flooded his mind from the last journey he had made to this once lovely city. He had spent six months in Bosnia-Herzegovina as a NATO Observer at the outbreak of hostilities in 1992. The general landscape and layout of the city was the same, but the beautiful buildings that had made the Yugoslavian city a jewel of the Balkans for hundreds of years were now mostly hollow, burned out shells of their former glory.

Beneath him the brown water of the slow running Miljacka River moved in its perpetual course parallel to the stone bounded road. From his vantage point on the fifth floor of the hotel he could see the reconstruction of the Unis Towers, newly renamed as the Unitic Towers, to the northeast. At ninety meters the twin towers symbolized the prosperity of the eighties in the former Yugoslavia. Both had been almost destroyed during the height of the war that had tenuously ended in 1995. Although every window in both towers had been shattered the buildings themselves somehow had structurally survived. The long arm of a tall derrick slowly turned towards the towers. A heavy bundle of building materials swung gently at the end of a thick cable as the machine lifted it to workers on a floor about half way up the building. Everywhere he looked, reconstruction was under way. The people of Bosnia were digging out of the ashes of the bitter civil war that had split their once great nation.

His thoughts were interrupted when the door abruptly opened. Through it walked half a dozen men in an assortment of uniforms. Behind them entered a heavyset and balding, older white man followed by a thirty-something Asian woman. They both wore casual civilian attire. Lieutenant Colonel Hardwick entered last.

"Mike!" Lieutenant Colonel Hardwick called out with the characteristic smile that creased the corners of his eyes. "Good to see you looking more like your normal self."

He gestured to the rest of the group as they filed in around the table.

"Let me introduce you to the coaching staff of our fine institution."

Hardwick began the introductions in ranking order, starting with a mustachioed British general in his mid-fifties.

"This is Brigadier Charles Fender from the British Special Air Service. Next, we have Colonel Harold Blake from the US Army Special Operations Command. I believe you have met Lieutenant Colonel Kevin Arlington US Marine Corps Special Operations. Finally, this is Lieutenant Colonel John Jacoby, Commander of the US Army Ranger detachment in Bosnia."

The officers each nodded or otherwise acknowledged Captain Farris with various greetings as the introductions proceeded.

"Next we have our civilian representatives. This is Mark Clark, CIA station chief, and Margaret Chung MI-6 area supervisor. They will be briefing you on your mission details."

Hardwick finished with the introductions and motioned everyone to their seats.

"Let's get this started."

Clark and Chung went to one end of the table. Chung set up a laptop computer and plugged it in to a large, boxy LCD projector. She dimmed the lights in the front half of the room then turned on the projector. It threw a bright display onto a white screen that hung from the ceiling at the end of the room.

Chung was an attractive woman who appeared to be of Korean descent. She bore an uncanny resemblance to a woman who attended one of Mike's seminary classes. She touched a couple of computer keys and clicked the mouse button. The screen flashed with the first slide of a Power Point presentation. A ten-foot-wide rendition of both of the spy agencies logos glowed on the screen. The title "Operation Anarchist" stood out against a bright white background.

Clark, a portly gray-haired man in his late fifties, moved toward the screen, cleared his throat and began to talk. He had the thick, gravelly voice of a heavy smoker.

"Captain Farris, you come highly recommended for the job we need done. I understand that you're personally familiar with at least one of the targets. That is why we asked for you specifically."

Clark grunted to clear his throat and took a sip of water from a bottle he had brought in.

"Excuse me gentlemen, it seems I've developed a bit of laryngitis or something over the past couple of days."

He took another sip of water and continued.

"As you all know the war here in Bosnia officially ended a little more than two years ago. Apparently, not everyone is happy with that arrangement. Margaret, go to the next slide, please."

He took another sip of water as she transitioned the slide to a picture of several people standing on a city street corner.

"Three weeks ago, we received a coded message from one of our deep cover agents in Syria that something was being planned against a high official here in Bosnia."

He directed everyone's attention to the picture with the beam of a laser pointer.

"This was taken two weeks ago by one of Margaret's operatives in the city of Jajce, a rather pretty little town situated at the confluence of two rivers in the hill country northwest of Sarajevo. Most of the men in the picture are known members of the Sons of the Sword organization, a militant Islamist group with general ties to international Jihad movements. This particular organization is one of the most extreme groups. The bastard's standard operating procedure is basically to kill all non-Muslims, or even better, to get us all to kill each other."

Margaret tapped a key on the keyboard and the image zoomed in on the faces of the men.

"This," Mark aimed the red dot of the laser pointer at one of the men, "is the one we are most concerned about. Do you recognize him, Captain Farris?"

Mike's expression darkened.

"Of course. Brett Mathis. Is he a Muslim now?"

"No." answered Margaret, "he's still as godless as ever—and still a mercenary."

Her smooth, upper-class British accent surprised Farris. Because of the familiarity of her facial features, he had subconsciously expected her to speak with a Korean accent, like the woman in his class.

"This time though," added Mark. He took another sip from his water and cleared his throat again before continuing, "he's been hired by the Sons of the Sword. Based on what they are paying him, they have gotten some good funding from somewhere, too."

The water bottle rose to the CIA chief's lips again.

"How much would that be?" Lieutenant Colonel Arlington asked.

"Two and a half million British pounds," said Margaret.

"Dear God!" said Brigadier Fender, his expression aghast. "How does your source know this? Can he, or she, be relied upon?"

"Unequivocally," replied the British spy boss, "he is one of America's best agents. You may have heard of him. His name is Kharzai."

Colonel Blake, a powerfully built yet quiet looking man with both a Ranger and a Special Forces tab on his uniform sleeve, nodded.

"I can vouch for what she is saying." Blake said. "I know Kharzai. He has an uncanny knack for getting very high up in the enemy's camp. He's one of the spookiest spooks I've ever known."

"This is the real deal." Margaret said, "We verified that the money is already in Mathis's Suisse Banc account."

"What on earth is Mathis being paid that much to do," Fender grunted, "kill the Pope?"

"No, sir," replied Mark. He coughed, then cleared his throat yet again before continuing. "We believe he is being asked to repeat history on a grand scale."

Colonel Blake leaned back in his chair and said, "How?"

Mark Clark coughed again. He cleared his throat and tried to speak. As soon as he tried, he broke into a hacking fit of harsh dry coughing. The CIA station chief motioned to his MI-6 counterpart to take over the presentation. He sat down and sipped at his water as Margaret picked up where he left off.

"In nineteen-fourteen a Serbian dissident named Gavrilo Princip assassinated Austrian Archduke Franz Ferdinand. Princip was part of the nationalist Serbian movement called the Young Bosnians. This somewhat small-scale local event sparked a war between Austria and Serbia, which, as I am sure you are all aware, became World War One. Five years and nine million lives later the world wondered how it got so far so fast."

Brigadier Fender spoke up, "We all know the history of what happened there. I assume by what you are saying that this Mathis intends to assassinate someone and start another world war, but, the question of the moment is whom does he plan to kill? To my knowledge there are no sufficiently high-ranking officials here that could ignite such a war."

Clark raised a finger and tried to speak. He broke into another hacking fit. He surrendered to the cough and motioned to his British counterpart. Margaret Chung tapped an arrow key on the laptop and changed slides on the screen. The face of Russian President, Boris Yeltsin, appeared on the screen.

"We didn't know at first either," Margaret said, "but just yesterday President Yeltsin's staff let us know that he was planning to make an unannounced visit to the Russian troops stationed here as part of the Multi-National Force. We believe that Mathis has been hired to assassinate Yeltsin. Most likely he will be disguised as an American or British soldier in order to throw the blame our way and attempt to spark a new world war."

Silence hung in the room. Mike read the expressions of the men around the table as they pondered the ramifications of such an event.

Lieutenant Colonel Jacoby took a sip of his coffee. He set the cup down and said, "How much time do we have?"

"Three days." Mark said holding up his fingers to illustrate the number. He coughed harshly again after the two short words.

"That is why we called in Captain Farris, gentlemen," said Lieutenant Colonel Alexander. "With his personal knowledge of Mathis, we figured he would be the fastest route to track him down and end this thing before it takes off."

Colonel Blake looked at Farris and said, "How do you know Mathis?"

"We met originally at scout sniper school in eighty-seven when I was an enlisted reservist. He was one of my instructors. Later, I was his shooting partner on half a dozen missions. He had a falling out with several senior officers a few years later and resigned from the Corps in ninety-one. He took off to work freelance as a mercenary. Mathis became a contract operative and we used him on black ops several times in the early nineties with no problems. His issues at the time seemed to be personal with a couple of specific officers at Quantico and not with the Corps or the US government. I met him last in Indonesia in December of nineteen-ninety-four when my team was sent in to rescue some US civilians who were being held hostage by local guerrillas. Mathis led us into a trap that killed two of my men. We managed to get out, but he got away from us. I haven't seen or heard anything about him since then."

"Gentlemen," said Lieutenant Colonel Alexander, "Captain Farris knows the way Mathis thinks and moves. If anyone can catch up to him, it is going to be Mike."

"The clock is running," said Blake. "Let's get this thing going."

CHAPTER 5

Mike slid the pistol into a smooth brown leather paddle holster tucked discreetly inside the back of his trousers. He pulled on a black North Face jacket and stuffed two more loaded magazines into the right pocket. He put a third into the left to balance the weight.

He reached into the black metal gun safe and moved three hunting rifles from one side to the other. Then he bent down and pulled up the floor panel of the steel cabinet revealing a shallow hidden chamber. Mike put his hand into the space and wrapped his fingers around the object he was looking for. He pulled his hand back up, the weight of the object pressed in to his palm. He held the round metal tube in front of his face for a moment then placed it in the left pocket of his jacket with the single loaded magazine. If he were caught he would have to ditch the silencer quickly. While he did have a legal concealed carry permit for handguns, there was no such permit for silencers. They were simply illegal for everyone.

He had kept both items, holdovers from his days in special operations, through the years since he had left the Corps. Janelle had known about the pistol, but she hadn't known about the silencer. He closed the safe and locked it then walked out of the closet back into his bedroom.

Mike left the bedroom and went back downstairs. He entered the study and sat down at his desk. A black and silver Hewlett Packard mini tower computer hummed next to a wide screen LCD monitor. He pulled the keyboard tray out, slid the mouse pointer to an icon on the screen, and clicked the button. Microsoft Word opened the document file. Mike clicked the printer icon button at the top of the menu bar. The laser printer hummed to life from its perch on a shelf above the monitor. Sheets of paper slid through the wheels and rollers of the machine with a quiet whispery sound.

Once the printer stopped its whirring, Mike picked up the pages from the output tray. He turned from the printer to a nearby fax machine. He programmed the machine to send the two sheets to their intended recipient at eight o'clock the following morning. The fax machine quickly scanned the documents and put the image of them in its memory for delivery at the scheduled time.

After both of the pages had run through, Mike took them from the fax machine, neatly folded them and stuffed them into an envelope as he walked to the kitchen. He set the envelope on the island in the center of the room, picked up a pen and wrote "Detective Dan Martin" in large black letters across the front. Then he stood the envelope up and leaned it against a coffee mug. Anyone who walked into the kitchen would immediately see it. The note he had programmed into the fax machine and had left on the kitchen island for Detective Martin contained the general details. It also held instructions for his burial in the event he was killed.

Detective Martin,

I feel it necessary at this time to inform you, as you may have already guessed, that I lied when you asked me about any specific threats against LeRon. In reality, there was a very specific threat not only against him and Li'l Mac but against me and my family. I honestly did not think they would go through with it; at least, not as quickly as they did.

The gang that made the threat was the Uni-Thugz from the University Heights neighborhood. Their leader, who calls himself "Cold-Bones," said that if we tried to put a youth mission in his neighborhood, he would kill LeRon and rape my wife in front of my eyes. I guess his gunners read the instructions wrong and ended up killing my family instead.

LeRon had discovered where the Uni-Thugz hideout was and told me the day before the shootings. That is where I have gone. God willing there will be several fewer of these murderers breathing our atmosphere by the time you read this. I have left a map and directions in the envelope at my home as well as burial instructions in the event I am not successful.

I am sorry for the extra work this may cause you, but I know that if you were to arrest these men it would be tied up in a trial for a long time, and they would most likely get out of prison in only a few years to return to the streets and continue their crimes. I cannot allow that to happen and am willing to face the consequences with a clear conscience.

Mike Farris

Mike walked from the kitchen, through the dining room, and into the living room. He slowly and calmly made his way towards the front door. As he passed through the living room, Mike stopped in front of the fireplace mantle and stared at the neat row of framed pictures of his wife and son on the white marble shelf. His eyes rested on a happy looking photo taken only a week before their murders. In the picture Janelle held their cherub-like child on her left hip. She and Mini-Mike waved towards the camera. The spotlight of the bright autumn sun lit their faces with an almost heavenly glow. Their wide, shining smiles seemed to jump right out of the picture.

"Baby, I love you. Please forgive me for what I am about to do. I hope you will understand."

Mike stroked the tips of his fingers gently across the image of his family, then turned and walked out the front door of the house. He locked the door behind himself and strode over to his car. In his driveway sat a very used looking '99 Chevy Lumina with tinted windows. He got in and habitually buckled the seatbelt. His face transformed as the vehicle started. His expression grew cold as granite, his eyes hard like steel. Farris's mind became singularly focused. Every thought vanished save the goal set before him. Mike looked back over his shoulder, put the car in reverse, then backed out of the driveway and sped quietly off into the darkness.

The night was dark and heavy. A low layer of clouds obscured the moon and dulled the noise of the city. It was a perfect setting for the work Mike planned. Brisk autumn air flowed in through the partially open window of the Lumina. It was twenty-five miles from the suburban community he called home to his destination. The route took him through a jungle of strip malls and office complexes. Those gradually gave way to tall high-rise buildings as he moved through downtown Columbus. Near the OSU campus area, the scenery shifted from steel and concrete high rises to two story single-family homes. From that, the scene moved to symmetrical rows of boxy post World War II era houses, then to Victorian style town homes and finally to the architecture of red brick and mortar duplexes and four-story government housing projects.

The city pulsed with the boom of hip-hop music that thumped from doorways and passing cars. The sound provided a rhythmic musical score to the night, lending a movie like quality to his mission. Men and women stood on most of the street corners. Some stared at his car out of curiosity as it passed. Others instantly turned away to hide whatever it was they were doing. Gangs of youths milled around in groups of five or six, restlessly wandering, not caring, or not aware, that tomorrow was a school day.

Mike was familiar with this part of the city. When he came to these neighborhoods he drove the beat-up Lumina as opposed to the newer Denali SUV his wife had used. The Lumina did not stand out when he was doing street ministry. Therefore, it was not as likely to become a target for thieves or vandals. Tonight, the beat-up, old car served as good camouflage as he passed through one of the most crime-ridden districts of Central Ohio.

Clusters of people huddled on the front stoops of houses where they sipped at forty-ounce bottles of malt liquor. A few times someone looked up as he drove by, only to turn back to their drinking partners as he passed. Twice hookers called to him proclaiming how handsome he was, in spite of the fact that they couldn't see him through the tinted glass in the dark, and were insistent that he needed a friend for the evening.

A pale white whore in a tight red leather miniskirt and black silky blouse stepped into the street and shouted.

"Hey baby! Love is on sale tonight!"

Dark rings circled the woman's sunken eyes rendering her face with a skull like appearance. From the top of the skull-woman's head burst a tangled, frizzy mass of orange hair. It looked like she hadn't brushed it after her last several clients.

Her companion, a medium toned black woman with a wide mouth and manic looking eyes wore painted on jeans and a partially unzipped jacket which revealed a long slit of tightly squeezed cleavage that threatened to pop from the pressure of the constrictive push-up bra. She put an arm over the skull woman's shoulder and added, "Yeah, baby doll! Buy one get the second for half off!"

"Blue light special!" the skull faced hooker added. "Better than K-Mart, honey!"

The two prostitutes exploded into laughter. He continued two more blocks on Fifth Avenue then slowed as he came to King Street and turned left. A little further, he pulled into a dark alley between two rows of red brick town homes and drove another block. As he came out of the alley he switched off the vehicle's headlamps, turned right and drove to Ninth Avenue. He made two quick left turns and came to a stop in another alley. He parked the Lumina behind a dumpster and shut off the engine.

Mike Farris sat in silent darkness with the windows down. He listened intently, allowing his senses to adjust to the environment. The sounds and the rhythms of the neighborhood slowly rose on the air. Distant angry voices, an argument between a man and a woman, floated from several houses down. At another house, someone was washing dishes near an open window. A chorus of crickets chirped in time to each other; a smaller number of their kind echoed on the offbeat. Barely audible through the walls above him, a mother calmed a crying child. Life, families, love, but none of it his.

Mike opened the door and rose from the vehicle in silence. He pulled up the collar of his jacket and donned a

black knit balaclava. He rolled the end of it up to his forehead like a stocking cap and walked the rest of the length of
the alley staying hidden in the dark shadows. At the end of
the block, Mike turned right and proceeded half a block to
Loyal Street. He turned into the shadows between the rows
of houses and positioned himself in a dark space between
two duplexes. He leaned against the rough red brick wall and
pulled the balaclava down over his face. He waited in silence
watching and listening to the sounds of this part of the neighborhood. They were different sounds. No one talked on this
street. No sounds of home life floated on the air. No mothers
cooed their babies. There was almost no motion along this
entire block. No hookers walked the corners. No men sat on
their porches drinking forties. A couple of times someone
stepped out of a house to only go right back in or to get in a
car and leave. The entire neighborhood seemed to be aware
that there was something dangerous in the air.

Across the street and four houses down stood 1639 Loyal,
a duplex house converted to a single residence that LeRon
had said functioned as Cold Bones headquarters. Lights were
on in the first-floor windows. Shadows drifted back and
forth behind thin yellow curtains. A young man sat on the
porch in a lawn chair. He looked like a guard. He blocked the
entrance with his body, probably watching for rival gangs or
to warn of police.

Mike watched the guard for several minutes. The young
man appeared alert and observant, like a Doberman Pincer.
His eyes followed the few vehicles that passed. From his seat
he peered into the shadows and scanned the surrounding
street and buildings. He was slow, careful, and methodical.
It was obvious that this guy was not one of the drug addicts
fed by Cold Bones' business. He might even be a military vet-
eran. He was no dummy. His presence would make entering
the house a little more difficult, but only a little.

After fifteen minutes waiting in the shadow, Mike backed up and slinked through the shadows behind several houses until he had passed 1639 and moved behind four more buildings to the south. A deep shadow beneath a broken street lamp provided the cover he needed to cross the street.

When the guard's gaze scanned away from him Mike moved quietly, with catlike grace. He crossed the street with smooth fluid motion. He carefully kept his upper body from bouncing as he slid over the pavement high on the balls of his feet, a dark shadow within a shadow. Mike seemed to float over the pavement to the other side then disappear between the houses. Once across he made his way through several backyards until he stood in the darkness behind the stoop of the home next door to the residence in which he hoped to find Cold Bones and his crew.

He had done this more times than he wished to remember in his past career. It was a job then. He had been under orders to "Render Harmless." It was just names and pictures on a sheet of paper, he had never done it for personal reasons. He had never hated his targets—until tonight.

Mike waited in the shadows for several more minutes warily observing the guard at the front of the house. Every sense in his body was awake. He felt rather than heard every sound. The rhythmic chirp of the crickets echoed in the distance; even they were not close to this house. Mike's vision sharpened and came into clear focus. He could see the details of the guard's face, the light fixture that jutted out beside the front door of the house, the railing around the porch, the brand of the man's sneakers. A gentle breeze rustled through the dry leaves. They crackled as they clung to their last days of life on the graying branches of the trees.

His mind was calm, his thoughts purposeful and defined. His perception of the world seemed clearer than he had experienced in years. He slid the pistol out of the holster in the small of his back, reached into his left jacket pocket and pulled out the black metallic tube. He rotated the silencer in his hand as he screwed it onto the end of the pistol. His heartbeat no longer thudded in his ears. His breathing made no sound. The world slowed, and the fabric of time ceased to flutter. His muscles tensed as he slowly rose from the shadow. The crickets fell silent.

Mike brought the pistol up and aimed. The top of the guard's head rested unwittingly just above the cold steel at the end of Mike's pistol. The five-millimeter-tall sight post sat squarely, unwavering, inside the notch of the rear sight.

Mike leaned his body forward. He braced his shoulders against the shot. He tensed his thighs, his calves, his toes to rush the house at the moment the first bullet left the muzzle. By the time the guard's body hit the floor Mike would be past him and inside the house. The job would be completed within less than sixty seconds if everything went right. If it went wrong, he would be reunited with Janelle and Mini-Mike very soon.

The front door of the house suddenly sprung open. The motion startled him. He froze for a split second then slinked back into the depth of the shadow as Cold Bones walked outside. Behind him another man came out the door. The second man was Middle Eastern looking with dark, tan skin and an incredibly thick bush of curly black hair covering his head. An equally thick beard covered his face and neck all the way down to the open collar of his white button-down shirt from which burst an explosion of long black chest hair. His eyes were lit with an insane sparkle as they flitted back and forth, taking in the scene of the neighborhood. He reminded Mike of a jackal, scanning not so much for defense, but as if searching for prey.

Cold Bones muttered something to the guard where he sat in the chair. The young man nodded and spoke a reply that Mike couldn't hear then pointed up the street opposite Mike.

The hairy Middle Eastern man turned towards the deep darkness of the shadow in which Mike stood motionless in a half crouch. The man's gaze froze. He stared into the dark space around Mike with animal intensity. His eyes met Mike's. Mike's heart fluttered. The man's smile widened. Then the hairy Middle Eastern man winked his right eye.

Mike tensed. He expected to be revealed and have to fight his way out. The Middle Eastern man with the thick hairy face turned away and joined the conversation with Cold Bones and the guard. Mike was confused, a flutter of uncertainty fell over him. He was certain the man had seen him. Certain the man had winked at him. It didn't matter. Before any attack came his way, Mike was going to take them all out.

The hairy man moved back across the porch towards Cold Bones. A third man came out the door. He was tall and thin, and his skin was extremely dark, an almost bluish tint reflected from his smoothly shaved head. His back was to Mike. Four quick shots and he would be done.

Mike focused on his primary target and exhaled. The hairy man moved across the porch. His walking pattern and physical movements had a manic kind of quality about them. Mike was certain the man was either insane or on psyche-delic drugs. He was unpredictable. Mike might miss him. The crazy man might get him. He prayed that if he died he would join his wife and son in the next few minutes. A feel-ing in his gut quivered nauseatingly as the thought struck him. Was this murder? What if God didn't forgive him. He pushed the thought aside and pulled the hammer back on the .45 caliber pistol and raised it. He carefully took aim at Cold Bones' head.

He leaned in. Tensed for the shot. The bullet would blow half of the gangster's head off when the hollow point lead projectile exploded into his skull. Mike's finger slowly curled around the trigger. He would take out Cold Bones, then the hairy one, the guard, and tall dark-skinned man in that order.

Cold Bones and the hairy man turned around to face the third man. The tall blue-black man carried himself with graceful confidence like a cheetah stalking through the grass of a Savannah. His muscles slid smoothly beneath the skin of his arms, shoulders, and back visible through the fitted sweater he wore in the cool autumn air. He was a predator. He was doomed just the same.

Mike focused his attention and tracked the movement of the man who ordered the killing of his family. He aligned the pistol's sight post tight above Cold Bones' left ear. The tall thin dark-skinned man turned and glanced at the guard who had risen from his lawn chair. His face came fully into view. Mike's heart suddenly pounded in chest, the sound echoed in his body. He froze, dumbstruck.

The dark-skinned man's crooked smile creased the inky blackness of the night. Akbar Usein. The man who sixteen years earlier had attempted to skin Captain Mike Farris alive now stood only yards away. A man whom Mike had thought long dead was clearly still alive.

Farris blinked trying desperately to clear the vision from before his eyes. Half hoping it was a hallucination. Despite the impossibility of what he saw, there was no mistake as to Akbar's identity. The starburst shaped scar on his right temple was clearly visible even in the twenty-yards distance between them. Usein had not visibly aged at all over the years. His eyes glinted in the light of the porch.

A sleek dark-blue Lincoln Navigator pulled up to the curb in front of the house. Usein, Cold Bones, and the hairy man crossed the lawn and got in. The vehicle quietly pulled away from the curb and took them away.

Mike waited in the shadow until they were gone before he attempted to move. As the guard watched the Navigator roll out of sight, Mike crept back through the neighborhood. In a mental haze, he made his way through shadowed alleys and yards until he returned to the car in the alley behind the dumpster. His mind spun as he tried to get a grasp on what he had seen.

A shiver rattled through his body.

Did he come back to find me and finish the job? Did he spend all these years tracking me down?

Mike drove back through the city robotically. He cruised unaware of scenery or the passing of time until the headlights of the beat up old Lumina flashed across the garage door and he found himself back in his own driveway.

Home. Reality. Maybe none of this had actually happened. Maybe he would walk in and wake from the nightmare and find it all was just a dream.

Mike walked into the house in a daze. It was not a dream. He couldn't process the facts of what he had seen, but he knew it was not a dream. The sight of Usein after all these years rocked his world onto its side and threatened to tip him off the edge.

He went back downstairs and sat in the wing-back recliner in his living room. He propped his feet up and lay back as he tried to sort it all out.

Sometime after six thirty am he slipped into a deep, exhausted sleep.

CHAPTER 6

The Lincoln Navigator, its windows nearly completely shaded, rolled quietly through the dark streets of the city. The semi-notorious small-time drug lord Reginald Whorly, known on the streets by his gang name Cold Bones, sat in the darkness of the back seat with his newest business partner Akbar Usein. Usein's associate, Seirim Al Gul, sat in the front with the driver. Al Gul's name, Cold Bones had been told, translated literally from Arabic and Aramaic as "Hairy Demon." In Cold Bones' opinion, the name fit. The man emanated an unnerving, borderline psychopathic aura of unpredictability and violence. Cold Bones fearfully respected Usein. He was freaked by Al Gul.

The driver, a very large, very muscular black man with a shaved head skillfully maneuvered the large vehicle over the streets of the city like the pilot of a yacht through the sea. His shoulders filled more than half the space that would normally fit three typical adults. He made Al Gul look like a stick in the seat next to him as he guided them to the riverside warehouse district. They were on the way to a clandestine appointment with Ohio's newest kingpin of drugs and crime, a man known on the streets as Mister White.

"Mister White is pretty cool as a boss." Cold Bones said, "I mean, he is seriously organized and even put the dealers that work in his corporation into a profit sharing and 401k plan. But let me warn you in advance, he's a little strange at first."

Akbar glanced over to Al Gul who had turned in his seat, so he could see the two in the back. He turned back to Cold Bones and spoke in a deep, accented voice.

"How do you mean that he is strange."

"Well," answered the gangster, "for one thing, you won't never see his face, or for that matter his whole body. He keeps himself all locked up somewhere and don't let nobody but his bodyguards in. When we get to the warehouse we'll actually be going to a conference room on the main floor and talking to him through a video teleconference system. His voice is disguised too. I don't actually think he's even in the same building. Hell, he probably ain't even in the same part of the city. It's pretty hot technology and all, but still kinda creepy, if you ask me. He keeps his face covered with some kind of hood and wears gloves the whole time, so you can't even tell if he's white or black."

"He must be an important man then, to keep such security." Akbar said in response.

"Yeah, he's pretty big stuff." answered Cold Bones.

"Or maybe he thinks he's hunted," said Al Gul.

Al Gul grinned mischievously. He spoke with an accent that was between Arabic and British. His voice had a tremulous undertone that set Cold Bones on edge.

"To be hunted indicates that one is important. If he were not a dangerous man, he would have nothing to worry about."

"Whatever," said Cold Bones, with a shrug, "as long as he and I keep each other's pockets lined, I don't care if he is

Satan himself, 'cause he's the hottest boss in town. You know what I mean?"

The drive across Columbus took about fifteen minutes. The driver stopped the Navigator in an empty parking lot in front of a nondescript gray steel building. The paint was flecked off in various places, and random patches of rust shone through. Dry dead clusters of tangled weeds jutted up through cracks in the asphalt.

The building was situated in an old warehouse area on the western bank of the slow moving Sciota River. Many of the structures, most of which seemed abandoned, were of nineteenth century architecture and bore faded signs por traying names of long-gone, unfamiliar companies.

The driver stayed with the SUV as Cold Bones led the others towards the building. Al Gul surveyed the area. He slowly spun three-hundred-sixty degrees as he walked. A cool autumn breeze moved through them. It caused the thick mass of Al Gul's curly hair to wave as he observed his surroundings. He ran his gaze across the moonlit faces of the buildings around them. The dim yellow lamps of the parking lot cast a pale glow that reflected off windows and were absorbed into the dark shadowed recesses between the buildings.

They approached a battle-ship-gray metal door in the building. The pale, cold illumination of a single mercury lamp washed over the area from a pole that hung on the wall ten feet above. Everything looked flat and lifeless.

Cold Bones grasped the handle, twisted, and pulled the heavy door open. The hinges screeched in loud protest as they spun on their pins. The sound echoed in the cool night air.

The men stepped in to pitch-blackness. They paused just inside the door. Shadowy shapes gradually appeared as their eyes adjusted to the darkness. In the distance a narrow, vertical bar of light came into focus from behind a barely open door. Other than the room from which the light shone, the giant warehouse was completely empty.

"That's the room over there." Cold Bones voice echoed off the metal walls. He pointed towards the light in the distance, and they walked towards it. The sound of their footsteps resounded against the concrete and steel, amplified by the cavernous room.

When they reached it, Cold Bones pushed open the door to reveal a sparsely furnished room about twenty feet by twenty feet in dimension. A table and four old-looking wooden office chairs sat in stark silence in the center of the room. A waist high wooden cabinet, worn and ancient looking, leaned against one wall. A fluorescent light fixture hung from two long metal shafts bolted to the white sheet metal frame of the ceiling. The cold light lent the room the aura of a torture chamber.

Usein and Cold Bones each sat on a chair behind the table opposite the cabinet. Al Gul paced slowly around the room, suspiciously scanning the walls and ceiling.

The battered wooden cabinet suddenly came to life. A gentle whir vibrated from within and its top opened slowly. Al Gul spun towards it. He cocked his head in curiosity as out of it raised a wide flat-screen television monitor.

The "Hairy Demon" slid his hand behind the cabinet and swept it up and down between the wooden surface and the wall. There were no wires or controls to be seen. He knelt down at the side of the cabinet staring at the space behind it in apparent awe at the technology. Cold Bones thought he looked like a caveman discovering something akin to fire. He almost laughed at the scene but dared not to.

The screen flickered then gradually brightened. On it appeared the shadowy image of a broad-shouldered man sitting in a tall chair. The man on the screen wore a large gray hooded robe. The robe looked like something worn by the members of a monastic order. Its hood extended far enough that it cast a deep shadow across his face. Anyone who looked at him from any angle would not make out even the slightest feature that could identify him. At the end of the long, wide sleeves the man's black leather gloved hands were clasped in front of him as if praying.

"Mister White, sir. We can see you on this end." said Cold Bones. He spoke in a respectful tone and straightened in his chair as his benefactor's image became clear on the screen.

"Yes, thank you, Mister Bones. Introduce me to your new friends." The voice of the hooded figure on the screen was digitally altered to sound like an impression of Darth Vader. Depending on the perspective of the listener this made his overall appearance either more sinister or laughably comical.

"Yes, sir." Bones motioned towards Usein and said. "This is Mister Akbar Usein. He represents a major organization in Central Asia that wants to partner with us."

Al Gul moved into view of the screen and stared wide eyed at the image before him.

"Is this for real?" he said in a mocking tone.

"And this, Mister White, is Seirim Al Gul. He is Mister Usein's associate."

Al Gul moved closer to the video screen.

"You look like the bloody emperor from Star Wars. Are we to take you seriously?"

Mister White appeared unfazed by Al Gul's mockery.

"Mister Al Gul, exactly what is your function with Mister Usein?"

"I am the demon on his shoulder," he said in a hoarse whisper.

Al Gul widened his eyes and stared into the camera aperture at the top of the screen. He put his hands up in a claw like gesture, bugged his eyes wide, opened his mouth and flicked his tongue out like a Maori Haka dancer.

Usein called out, "Al Gul, sit down. We are here to offer business, not to frighten them."

The hairy man nodded to his superior and put his hands up in apology. He grabbed one of the chairs next to the table and backed himself to the wall beside the door, out of view of the camera on the television monitor. Al Gul stood the chair against the wall and squatted, knees bent to his chest, on the seat. He looked like a gargoyle. His gaze alternated from the monitor to Cold Bones and back. The hooded figure on the screen showed no reaction to Al Gul's behavior. He spoke directly to Usein.

"Mister Usein, I understand you come to me with a business proposal from your associates in Central Asia. Please explain your offer."

Usein stood, bowed politely towards the screen then sat back down. His thick lips spread wide with something resembling a smile that stretched across green stained teeth. The mental image of a serpent negotiating with a bird over her eggs crossed Cold Bones mind.

"Thank you for seeing me on such short notice, Mister White. I trust it will not be an inconvenience to you." He paused for a moment then continued. "I represent a large faction in the Central Asian Republics that has access to massive quantities both of raw opium and processed heroin as well as a good supply of extremely potent marijuana and methamphetamine. We are looking for a buyer who can take our product into the market of Midwest America. And we are offering a very good price for mass purchases, nearly thirty percent below wholesale value. Are you interested?"

The shadowy figure of Mister White answered back, "Why do you bring this offer to me, and why the American Midwest?"

"Why you?" Usein asked, "Mister White, we have already heard of your rather amazing abilities and your incredible business savvy. In just a few short years you have risen to the top of one of the largest drug markets in the world. You have outpaced all of your competitors and even taken territory from them. There was no doubt among my superiors that you are the best person for them to approach with this deal."

Akbar Usein paused, letting the flattery sink in.

"And why the Midwest? Quite simply, the Midwest is very profitable, even more profitable than the coasts because, due to the lower cost of living, more people have greater amounts of disposable income. I am sure you understand that, or, being the wise business man you are, you would not have opened shop here."

White's posture straightened even more at Usein's ingratiating language, which seemed very well studied for a foreigner.

"To facilitate delivery, we have recently organized a strong transportation chain that can easily deliver our product to you and your associates."

"I see you have done your research," replied White. "Why are your prices so low?"

"Because there is a caveat to this offer," answered Akbar.

"And what may that be?"

"I need four couriers you can trust here in Columbus to do some work for me." Akbar said. "They must be men you would trust with your own life. Intelligent. Not drug users."

"For what do you need these couriers?" asked White.

"That is my own business." Akbar replied. "I am reducing the price of my product to a point as to allow you to make as much as an extra million dollars in a single shipment. I am also including at no charge two-hundred kilograms of fine cocaine as a gift to buy your confidence. If this offer will not suffice, then we have no business. I will report to my superiors that we must have been mistaken about your operation, and I will go elsewhere."

Mister White sat in silence. He made no move for several seconds. Cold Bones opened his mouth and was about to ask if his boss had heard Usein's last lines when the hooded figure broke the silence.

"Will my drivers be returned to me alive at the end of your business?" White asked. The voice modulator removed all emotion from his voice, rendering it with a funeral parlor tone.

"That will be up to them," answered Akbar.

"Wait," said White.

The video screen abruptly went blank. Cold Bones quietly contemplated what Akbar had asked for. Al Gul glared at him from his perch next to the door. The staring maniac made him very uncomfortable. He turned to face away from the crazy man and was about to speak to Akbar when the image of the hooded crime boss came back on the screen.

"Mister Bones." said Mister White. "Provide three of your best drivers to Akbar. I will provide the fourth from my own headquarters. I will reimburse you for the time lost with a generous portion of the product Mister Usein provides to us."

"Yes sir, Mister White." Cold Bones replied.

"I know I can trust you, Mister Bones," replied the hooded figure, "and I believe I can trust you too, Mister Usein, but let me make one thing clear to you: if for any reason I think you are going to cross me, you and everyone associated with you will be killed."

Al Gul barely suppressed breaking into laughter at the threat. Usein held a warning hand up to his associate.

"You have nothing to worry about, Mister White." Akbar said. "I will make sure you profit well, and everything will be in our mutual interest."

CHAPTER 7

Pastor Mike nearly jumped out of his skin at the high-pitched screech that exploded out of the fax machine in his office.

"Oh, dear God! No! No! No!"

He leaped from the wing-backed recliner in which he had fallen asleep and ran towards the office. Still groggy, his foot caught the edge of the couch as he tried to round past it. He stumbled and nearly lost his balance. His fax machine had obediently followed the command he had programmed into it for transmission at eight o'clock in the morning. He burst into the office and looked first at the status blocks at the bottom of the fax machine's LCD display. The first page of the message was already partially received by the fax machine at the other end.

Mike frantically punched the cancel button with the tip of his index finger. No reaction from the machine. In desperation he reached behind the device and pulled the power cable from the wall. The digital display went blank and the screeching halted. He disconnected the telephone cord from the back of the fax machine and plugged the power cord back into the wall. As soon as it cycled through the power-on sequence he went through the menus and printed a report of sent items.

Last Send: Failed at 30%
Reason: Unexpected Power outage
Total Errors: 001

A high-pitched tweedling sound rose from the phone on his desk. Mike sighed and squeezed his eyes closed in resignation then lifted the handset. He glanced at the small LCD above the dial pad. A tremor of dread rolled over him when he read the name on the caller ID.

"Hello?"

"Alright Pastor, what the hell is going on?" Growled the agitated voice of Detective Dan Martin.

"How much of the letter did you get?"

"You identified Cold Bones."

"Come over, let's talk."

"I'm on the way, don't go anywhere."

"Don't worry. Do you like coffee?"

"I'm a cop."

"There'll be a fresh pot when you get here."

"Twenty minutes."

Mike ran upstairs and took a quick shower. Ten minutes later he returned downstairs in fresh clothes and went to the kitchen. He filled the coffee maker half way with water, scooped a couple tablespoons of fine black grounds into the filter, and pressed the brew button. Just as the last few drops of the black liquid fell from the filter basket into the pot, the doorbell chimed. He opened the door and Detective Martin stormed in, his brow furrowed. An angry scowl covered his face. He walked into the living room and waited for Farris to follow him.

Martin spun towards the pastor and glared at him with blood shot eyes. His face was red with barely controlled rage.

"Alright, Pastor," Martin grunted, "give me the whole story. Don't leave anything out this time."

They sat down in the same places they had sat the night of Mike's family's murders—Mike on his chair, Martin on the couch.

Pastor Farris explained to Martin all that had happened. He included a brief description of how he met Akbar Usein in Somalia. He gave Martin only the most basic details of his military past. He did not mention that he owned a silencer for his pistol.

Detective Martin fidgeted with his fingers as he listened. His face grew deeper red. Anger boiled inside him. Martin ran his fingers through his hair.

"And you are absolutely certain this is the same guy who tortured you in Somalia in ninety-five?" Martin said in a low voice.

"Yes, beyond a doubt," replied the pastor.

"Do you realize how many laws you broke, and nearly broke, just by going out there?" said Martin. He stared into Mike's face, not concealing his contempt for being lied to. "And I want you to know that I am more than a little pissed that you didn't tell me about Cold Bones when I asked you last week."

"I figured you would be." Mike spoke without emotion. He had no remorse for what he had planned to do. He felt no guilt. "I hope you also understand my reason for not telling you."

"Isn't revenge one of those things the Bible forbids?" asked Martin.

"Tell me where and in what context the Bible says that." replied the pastor.

"Didn't Jesus say to 'turn the other cheek' and 'vengeance is mine says the Lord?' How do you reconcile being a Pastor and a self-appointed executioner at the same time? That just seems to be rather hypocritical to me."

"Look Detective," said Mike, "there's a lot you probably don't know on that subject; perhaps you should sign up for one of my Bible History classes when I get back to work at the church. In the mean time, I did not call you to talk about my theological positions, and I don't have to justify myself to you."

Martin bolted up from the couch.

"Like hell you don't!" He shouted and jabbed his finger in Mike's direction. "You are flat wrong about that! You do have to justify your position to me, or I am going to put your ass in jail! You understand? You are a pastor, not a detective, not a sheriff, not even a god damned meter maid! You do not have the authority to be running around in the shadows with a gun trying to assassinate someone you think deserves it. Just because your family was killed, does not give you the right to take another man's life. Especially without a trial!"

"Look detective!" boomed Mike in return.

He rose from his chair and met Martin eye to eye. His voice was forceful and clear. Martin was surprised by the unexpectedly strong personality that confronted him as Mike allowed the Marine officer side of himself to come out.

"Akbar Usein is a terrorist. I know that for sure. He is either working for Al Qaeda or for a similar organization that is probably allied with them. You had better do something about it, and fast, or a whole lot of civilians in this city are going to be dead! That much I know."

The intensity with which Pastor Farris spoke stunned Martin. The detective ran the fingers of both of his hands through thinning strands of brown hair that swept back from his high forehead and held in place with hairspray. The style accentuated the front of his balding scalp which was currently glowing bright red with anger. He turned from Farris, took a cell phone from his jacket pocket and thumbed through the contacts list. Once he found the number he was looking for he pressed the dial button and put the phone to his ear. It rang once then a female voice answered. Mike heard the voice on the other end over the small phone's speaker. The volume was very high.

"FBI, Ohio Valley Anti-Terrorism Unit."

"This is Detective Dan Martin with CPD. I need to talk to the task force chief."

A brief pause, then a male voice spoke in the distance on the other end.

"What can I do for you Dan?"

"Paul, I have a serious situation on my hands and need your immediate attention. Can you spare a few hours?"

"What's it about?"

"Can't say on the phone."

"As it happens, my whole morning schedule just got clear. Your place or mine?"

"Can you come to this address? I have someone you need to talk to."

He gave agent Hogan the address for Mike Farris's house then pressed the disconnect button on his phone and stuffed it back into his pocket.

"He will be here in about an hour," said the detective. "In the meantime, I am not letting you out of my sight."

"Don't worry. I'm not going anywhere, Detective," replied Pastor Mike.

Detective Martin paced slowly around the outside of the room, behind the couches and the chair. He squeezed his hands into tight fists that he pounded rhythmically into each other as he paced. Half way around his second lap of the room Martin spun back around towards Mike and spoke in a low growl.

"I should have you arrested for obstructing an investigation, conspiracy to commit murder, vigilantism, and half a dozen other charges, and you had better believe it when I say that if things are not exactly as you say when we get this all together, that is just what is going to happen."

The tension between the two men was palpable. Mike sat quietly in his wing-back recliner as Martin paced several more laps around the room. Eventually, Martin returned to his seat on the couch. He spent the rest of the wait going over emails on his Blackberry. Farris extended the footrest up on the recliner and drifted into a heavy power nap.

A little less than an hour after Martin's phone call, tires crunched up the pavement in front of the house as a vehicle pulled into the driveway. Farris snapped awake and walked to the window. He peered out and watched a tan Ford Expedition with US government license plates roll into his driveway. A man in a dark suit and tie got out from the driver's side door and walked around the front of the SUV. Dark sunglasses obscured his eyes. As he strode towards the front step he put a cell phone into an inside pocket of his suit jacket.

The man was average height, but quite stocky. He wore a very short military-style tapered haircut. Thick arm, shoulder, and chest muscles bulged beneath his custom-tailored suit. As he approached the house he carried himself with an upright and confident stride, exuding a strong yet relaxed aura. There was a sense of purpose in his body language as he mounted the steps to the porch.

Mike opened the door to welcome the FBI agent as he approached. When the stocky man reached the open door, he stopped in front of Mike. He did not enter or offer greeting. He just stood there and grinned.

"Come on in, sir." Pastor Mike offered, motioning with his hand, but the FBI agent stayed where he was in front of him, staring from behind his sunglasses. The FBI agent's smile broadened. Mike looked at him uncomfortably.

"Is there a problem?"

"Nope, just making sure it really is you…Major Farris."

"How do you know…."

The FBI agent took off his sunglasses.

"Don't you worry sir…Hogan and company are on the job!"

"Paul Hogan!" shouted Mike as he reached out his hand to the FBI agent formerly known as Gunnery Sergeant Paul Hogan USMC, the man who had pulled him off a pole in Somalia when he was about to be skinned alive.

"Paul! What in the world are you doing here?" asked his former commander.

"Well," replied Hogan, "it's like this. I'm the SAC, that's Special Agent in Charge, of the FBI's Ohio Valley Anti-Terrorist Unit. When I heard what happened a couple weeks ago, I thought it might be you and inquired of Detective Martin, but he had no idea of your past and couldn't verify. I asked him that if anything came up with your case that might possibly involve us, to call me directly, and what do you know, it really is you."

"Yeah, it is." said Mike patting the muscular man on the shoulder. He motioned for Hogan to come into the house and closed the door behind his old friend. "Man, it's been years since we last saw each other."

"Yes, sir. Bosnia as I recall. I lost track of you when you went back to seminary."

"Well, come in and have a seat." Mike pointed to the recliner in the living room. Detective Martin stood up as the two men entered.

"Agent Hogan." Martin reached out his hand to shake the FBI agent's. "You two know each other?"

"Yes, we do," Hogan answered. "He was my boss during the several years we spent fighting bad guys together in the Corps. Major Farris, US Marine Corps Force Recon, was one tough hombre, and to imagine that he became a pastor."

"Major? You didn't tell me you were a Major, pastor," said Martin. He looked irritated again.

"You didn't ask," replied Mike. He turned to Hogan and said, "Paul, you want some coffee? I'll brew some fresh real quick."

"Sure, love some."

Mike walked into the kitchen and the other two men sat down in the living room.

"Hogan," asked Martin. "What is up with this guy?"

"What do you mean?"

"First off, he lied to me about threats against his family. Then he kept back evidence as to who did it. Then he goes out in the middle of the freaking night and tries to assassinate the guy. Now, I am finding out that he is some kind of Special Forces operative in addition to pastoring a flock of five hundred souls in the middle of the Ohio cornfields. That's what I mean."

Hogan nodded and said. "Well, yeah. He is all of those things, and as far as lying to you, well...I'll wait till he comes back in to explain this together. Let me just say that Mike Farris is probably not what you think he is, but he is one of the best good guys walking around this little blue marble today."

Hogan leaned forward and grinned as he added, "I will also say this; you'd better chill before you have a stroke. You don't have a high enough clearance to know everything about Mike Farris, so get used to being a little confused...and keeping your mouth shut. Understood?"

Detective Martin was about to protest when Mike walked back into the room carrying a steaming mug for Hogan in one hand and the pot of coffee in the other. He handed the hot cup to the FBI agent and refilled Martin's and his own mug on the coffee table.

Mike went over the short version of the details of his discovery. As he listened again, Martin's stress level rose exponentially. The pupils of his eyes constricted to tiny dots. The whites pulsed red with bulging bloodshot veins. Tight wrinkles crunched in a tense bundle between his eyebrows. He did not like this kind of stress. He hated to not be in control of what was going on around him. He especially despised being told that he was not in charge of his own investigation.

Nineteen years as a cop, twelve of those as a detective, had surely been enough to earn him the right to be able to run an investigation without being ordered around by some muscle-bound FBI agent. Mike finished his retelling of the story.

Hogan said, "Alright then, we'll get started on it right away and see what we can come up with."

Martin's head snapped towards Hogan.

"Look, Agent Hogan," Martin's voice brimmed with barely suppressed rage as he spoke. "I don't care if Farris here is Colonel Ollie North and you are the President himself, this is my city and my investigation. I've been running it from day one, and I expect to be told everything, and we'll start with," he turned to Mike, "who the hell are you for real, Pastor Farris?"

"Martin, I'll humor you for the time being," said Hogan, "but be advised, once we verify that Akbar Usein is present in the area and involved in any way with these gangs, this becomes completely an FBI investigation. That being said, you might want to try and make friends with us so that I don't end up leaving you out of the whole thing. Go ahead Mike, tell him what you can."

"Alright," answered the pastor, "Michael Farris is my real name. I really am a fully ordained pastor and the senior pastor of Faith Presbyterian Church. I can also tell you that after my initial tour of duty as a Marine officer, I did not leave the Corps. I stayed in the reserves and only retired after I met my wife. During the years of reserve duty, I was frequently called up to run covert operations against assorted terrorist targets all over the world. Once I was fully ordained and became a senior pastor, I no longer directly participated in operations, but managed them from a point of command. My church members were aware that I was doing my required drill time with the reserves, they just didn't know the details."

"So you deceived your congregation just like you deceived me. So much for 'thou shalt not lie.'" Martin retorted.

"I did not lie to them. I just didn't tell them the specifics of what I was doing," Mike replied. "One of the members of the church did know what I did. He had been a member of the CIA in the fifties and sixties and figured it out pretty quick. If anyone else asked, I would simply tell them it was classified work, and that would be enough. No one really questioned it, and the ex-CIA agent never told."

Martin stood and paced around the room as he tried to digest what he was hearing. "So just exactly what did you do during these 'missions?'"

"Kill people," Mike said flatly.

"Excuse me?" Martin stammered. A shocked expression replaced his rage.

"I killed people who threatened the security of the citizens of the United States or directed those who did so."

"Like who?" Martin asked incredulously.

Hogan interrupted, a smile on his face, "That's the part that you aren't allowed to know, Danny boy."

"Don't worry," added Mike, "I committed no crimes against the US, its allies, or its legal residents."

"Whatever happened to 'thou shalt not kill?'" grumbled Martin, "That makes two of the commandments that you seem to think unimportant, pastor."

"Actually," answered the pastor, "In the original language, the commandment says, 'You will not murder.' I am sure you know the legal difference between killing and murder, Detective."

"How can you call yourself a man of God?" Martin retorted, "You're no different than those nut jobs who blow kids up for Allah."

"All right. Let's get this back on track," Hogan interrupted again. "We are not here to debate theology or the Ten Commandments gents, we are here to find and render harmless a real-life terrorist named Akbar Usein and his cronies."

CHAPTER 8

Tuesday, October 25th
FBI Regional Headquarters
Office of the Ohio Valley Anti-Terrorist Task Force
15:00 Hours

Agent Hogan led Martin and Farris through the outer security doors, past multiple guard stations and through more security doors until they reached a small windowless conference room.

"Welcome to the bowels of the FBI." Hogan said. "Agent Rottbruck will be here in a few minutes. She will be in charge of surveillance and intelligence gathering on this operation. She's one of the best signals intelligence specialists in the FBI."

"Rottbruck?" questioned Martin, "What kind of a name is that?"

"You think that's something?" asked Hogan. "Her first name is Hildegarde. She's of good stout German stock."

He flexed his arms and made fists with both hands bringing to mind the image of a stocky German beer frau.

"Oh Jeez," Exclaimed Martin, "What is she, one of those hairy East German wrestler dykes or something?"

"What can I say? The FBI is an equal opportunity employer, we hire...."

Hogan's description was cut short as the conference room door slowly opened.

"Well, speak of the devil. Here she is."

The view from the angle at which Farris and Martin sat was obscured by the door, which opened from the opposite side. Someone pushed a heavy metal cart into the room. A metallic "whang" resounded as the cart's wheels crashed over the threshold of the door accompanied by an effeminate, yet male sounding, grunt.

A flurry of pleated red cloth billowed into view from the lower half of the door. Two thin, yet decidedly not feminine, hands appeared from behind the door and dropped a heavy box onto the table. The hands hesitated there just long enough for thick dark hair to come into focus on the back of the knuckles. The hands pulled out and the empty metal cart banged even louder as it was wheeled away.

A raspy voice called out, "Thanks, Hank."

A woman backed into the room and let the door shut. Her back to the men, she coughed and cleared her throat. Then she turned around. Martin's jaw fell open. He stared in stupefied shock as he laid his eyes on the form and face of Hildegarde Rottbruck.

Hogan's smile widened at Martin's expression. Farris glanced at the woman and nodded politely. Hildegarde regarded the two new men in the room and gave a modest smile of greeting. Martin kept staring. Hildegarde's expression turned quizzical, then sardonic. She cleared her throat again then spoke to them in a clean sounding alto voice.

"Hello, I am Agent Rottbruck. Judging by your expression, I am going to assume that Agent Hogan has taken the liberty, once again, of trying to build an image of me ahead of time."

"I only said your name, and that you were German, Hilde. Whatever they thought was up to them," said Hogan.

"Yeah, right. You know, Paul, one of these days I'm going to turn you in for harassment," she said. There was not a hint of humor in her voice. Then she abruptly allowed a wide sarcastic smile to spread across her face. "But the expression on some men's faces when their jaw drops and they drool like dogs is priceless." She looked at Martin and said, "Close your mouth detective, you look like an idiot."

Hildegarde Rottbruck was somewhere in her thirties. She was about five feet four inches tall. Shoulder length straight auburn hair cascaded in a thick silken flow from her head across her long smooth neck to where it hung loose over her shoulders.

Her skin was smooth. She had a lightly tanned creamy complexion. Deep green eyes sparkled like polished emeralds above high cheekbones and a narrow Nordic nose. Her lips, full but not puffy, were touched by only a modest amount of lipstick. Her body was too-perfectly proportionate. Slender but not thin. Full figured but not overly buxom. A loose fitted white linen blouse lay pleasantly over her very feminine shape. The pleated red skirt spilled like a short waterfall from her waist over rounded hips to where it swished loosely just below her knees when she walked. Hildegarde Rottbruck could certainly be described as beautiful, perhaps even stunning.

"You must be Mike Farris." Hilde reached out to him in greeting.

"Yes ma'am." He rose from his chair and took her hand.

When he stood up Mike looked directly into her face. His eyes immediately grabbed Hildegarde's attention. They were warm and comforting. His eyes carried in them a depth of gentleness unlike any she had seen in other men. And yet there simmered within those eyes, those windows to his soul, a powerful undercurrent of strength. Hidden in the depths of his being lay a beast. It lurked dangerously at the edge of his consciousness. Not a beast to be feared. A good beast. She felt, as she looked at him, that she could unequivocally trust this man with the deepest secrets of her heart. She felt that he would give his life to protect her. She felt safe with him in the room. Her face grew warm, and she felt her cheeks flush. Her breath felt shallow. Her heart raced. Embarrassed and confused by the sudden rush of emotion, she pulled her hand away.

"Sorry about your loss," she said, trying to focus. "We'll do everything we can to get this guy."

"Thanks." He smiled meekly and sat back in his chair.

Hogan pointed to the box Hilde had brought in. "What you got in the box, Fraulein Rottbruck?"

Hilde grabbed the handle on the side of the file box and pulled it to the center of the table. Its white cardboard sides bulged at the seams from the mass of papers and file folders stuffed into it. Hilde pulled out a couple of paper folders and laid them on the table.

"Before I start, are these guys cleared to see this information?" she asked, looking at Hogan.

"Farris is for sure," Hogan answered, then turned to Mike and said. "You are still good on your Alpha clearance, right?"

"Yeah, it was just renewed a few months ago, actually."

"Martin," Hogan asked, "Have you ever had a federal top-secret clearance?"

"Are you telling me that I have to leave the room?" Martin's eyes snapped back from Hilde, and his voice returned to irritated indignation.

Rottbruck looked at him with a cold expression and said matter-of-factly, "You may be asked to leave, if we come up to certain types of material."

Martin tightened his expression. "I am a senior detective with CPD. I've been to the national academy and all of that crap. If you can't share your evidence with me, I am going to have to go over your head."

"That won't do you much good, unless you are best buddies with the President," replied Rottbruck. "Some of this material is Top Secret Alpha. They used to call it 'Presidential Eyes Only.' That means there are only a few dozen people in the country that can legally look at it. If you have at least a Top-Secret level, I can let you see everything else though."

"What?" Martin exploded up from his chair in a barely controlled rage, a disgusted snarl across his face. "You mean to tell me that this preacher has this Top Secret Alpha clearance, or whatever, and that gives him access to stuff that I can't even see? That is just bullshit!"

Hogan let an amused grin spread on his face.

"Yes, Danny Boy, as a matter of fact this preacher just happens to be on a first name basis with the past several Commanders in Chief, including the current one. And what you term a bullshit clearance happens to be what he carries. For your information, it is also known in the field as a 'terminal clearance.'"

"What the hell is that?"

"Well, basically, if you see the data and it is later discovered that you made any part of it known to anyone without that same or higher level of clearance, you will be terminated… no trial…no questions…no evidence…no chance to escape. That's what Pastor Mike's clearance is. As are both Hilde's and mine, so there is simply no way you will see this specific material and then walk out of here alive. Understood?"

Martin's eyes narrowed. He muttered an expletive under his breath and slumped back into his chair like a rebellious fourteen-year old.

"Like I said earlier, detective," Hogan continued, "be nice to us. Make friends and this will go a whole lot smoother."

Rottbruck said, "While we are all here let us go over what we can. We will save the highly-classified stuff for later. Are you ready, Detective Martin?"

Martin grunted his begrudging approval and leaned towards the table. He glared sideways at Mike out of the corner of his eye, trying to read whatever else he didn't know about the man. Hilde opened the folder in front of her and spread out a couple of photos. One of them showed a candid shot of Usein in a mountainous desert region with several men wearing Taliban-style black turbans and carrying weapons.

"This is Akbar Usein. He was last seen in Uzbekistan trading drugs for weapons for the various Al Qaeda allies in the region. He dropped off the CIA's radar sometime in December last year and hadn't been seen since—until this morning, that is.

"Right after you called me this morning Paul, I ran a digital facial recognition scan against INS and DEA databases on him with a couple of file photos and within less than thirty minutes got two hits. This picture was taken at Miami International Airport last Friday coming in on a flight from Barbados. We don't know where he came from before there though, but we suspect he was smuggled in with a drug shipment. This next one was taken at Ohio Stadium on Sunday."

Hogan raised his eyebrows. "Sunday? He just got into town this weekend?"

"We actually just got the download of that particular camera this morning. The system had logged a dozen or so potential tangos over the weekend and automatically sent them in. His was one of those suspected faces that the database caught."

"We have that technology?" asked Martin. "I thought that was illegal in America. I thought only the British had that stuff."

"Actually, we've had it and been using it since the late nineties. This is confidential information though, so I expect you will not be telling your friends, Detective," said Hogan, his humorous tone gone.

Martin shook his head in disbelief then looked down at the photos laid on the table. Farris picked up the Ohio Stadium photo. The date and time stamp in the lower right corner showed that it had been taken at three in the afternoon. It was a perfect shot, full face with good afternoon sunlight. By the look in his eyes there appeared to be no doubt in his mind. Hildegarde Rottbruck looked down at Mike Farris. The expression on Mike's face was cold and far away. An appearance of hardness slowly took over where there had been soft friendliness only a few minutes before. A lifetime of pain etched itself in the corners of his eyes as he squinted at the picture.

"It is him, isn't it?" She asked. "You can verify his identity?"

"Unless he has a twin brother with the same scar on his right temple," answered Mike, his voice low and gravelly. "This is definitely him."

"Well, then," said Hogan, "what else have you got in that there box, Hilde, my dear?"

"Mostly tons of file items related to where he has been over the past twelve years since we started keeping tabs on him," she said. "Some of it may be relevant, most of it is pretty general. But..."

She reached for a couple of photos that were in the pile from which Farris took the one of Usein.

"...this one is a panned-out image taken just a few seconds before the one that caught his facial profile. It shows several other people around him, a couple of whom seem to be with him. These others are zooms I did on four of the men standing closest to him."

She handed the pictures to Farris. He looked at the first one, a massive looking white man in his late twenties or early thirties. He handed it to Martin who in turn passed it to Hogan. Mike did likewise with the second and third picture, both of twenty something black men; one with a cocky attitude and the other with an intelligent look in his eyes.

"That first picture, the white guy, I don't know him." Mike said, "Never seen him before. The second one is Cold Bones, Reginald Whorley by birth, leader of the Uni-Thugz gang. He's the one who had my family killed. The third one looks vaguely familiar. I may have seen him on the street or something, but I'm not sure."

Mike held the fourth photo in his hand as he spoke. He studied it closely. It was the hair covered face of Seirim Al Gul. Al Gul glared out the corner of his eyes towards something in the distance.

"This guy." Mike tapped the picture. "He...I feel like I know him from somewhere. I just can't place where it is that I know him from though. Seems like something in the fairly distant past but maybe not."

He looked at it a moment longer then handed the last picture to Hogan, who held it in his hand and studied the image.

"Yeah..." Paul Hogan drew the word out with thought. "He does look familiar. Maybe I..." Hogan stopped mid-thought. "No...I don't know him. I probably just saw his face in a file somewhere."

He handed the picture to Martin who glanced at it and shook his head. "I don't know the hairy guy, but you are right about Cold Bones. That is definitely him in the second picture. The white guy in the first picture though, I have seen him. His name is Lucas Ring. They call him Ringmaster. He used to be a bouncer at a couple of nightclubs on the west side. He was pretty aggressive and kept hurting customers.

That energy got him fired and blacklisted after a couple of assault charges put him in jail. No one wanted to have him around their clubs anymore. He dropped out of sight about six or eight months ago. The guys in the third and fourth, I don't know, never seen them."

"Does Ring have any known associates?" asked Hogan.

"What? You want me to share information with you?" said Martin. His lips curled in a sneer. "Maybe you'd better treat me nicely, huh? If, that is, you want this information I've got."

"Don't think so highly of yourself, Detective Martin. I've got plenty of friends in the West side precinct who can answer any questions I've got. If you want to stay on this case and see it through, you'll mind your manners."

Hogan wasn't laughing this time. His humor had dried up as they looked at the photos of Akbar Usein. He too remembered that day in Somalia. He remembered coming in on the Blackhawk in the furnace of the African desert, looking across the radiating heat waves toward the tiny collection of huts.

In his mind's eye Hogan saw the whole scene again. A nineteen-year-old Marine private first class seated next to him in the helicopter pointed to a circle of men. Two figures were in the center. When they hit the ground, the only thing on Hogan's mind as the other Marines mercilessly killed the thugs in the circle, was rescuing his commander, his friend. Farris was barely recognizable. Blood oozed from a slice across the skin of his chest. It ran down his torso in a thin sheet that covered his upper body. He wasn't moving. He didn't seem to be breathing. When Hogan lifted him onto his shoulder, Farris's body was totally limp. Desperate to verify that his Captain was still alive he shouted his signature slogan.

"Hogan and Company is on the job!"

"This is pretty one sided, don't you think?" Martin's question jerked Hogan's thoughts back to the present.

"Yes, it is," retorted Hogan. "Deal with it. You're in over your head already. If you stick with us in this, you're going to see things that may make you reconsider your chosen profession."

Martin's face turned an angry shade of deep red again. Thick veins pulsed along the sides of his forehead. He rose from his chair.

"You keep talking to me like I don't know what I am doing. I have been a cop for almost twenty god-damned years! I think I can handle it!"

"How many men have you killed, detective?" said Farris. His voice was barely audible.

"What?" snapped Martin.

"I said, how many men have you killed?" the preacher looked up from the picture in his hand and amplified his voice.

"What does that have to do with anything?" Martin said. "I can handle myself in a fight just fine!"

"I'm not talking about taking down a drunk in a fight, or breaking up a brawl between a couple of neighbors," said Farris. "I'm talking about sneaking up behind a man in the dark and slitting his throat. I'm talking about holding your hand over his mouth as he bleeds out. Holding him until he goes limp in your arms. I'm talking about snapping a man's neck with your bare hands or shooting him and watching his guts spill out in a steaming mess onto the ground."

Farris looked directly into Martin's eyes and continued, "Have you ever looked into a mass grave filled with the freshly-dead bodies of dozens of women and children massacred because they refused to convert their religion?"

Martin stared blankly at him.

"Have you ever sat in a shadow until someone stepped outside to piss in the dirt? Then in the most private of moments, when he is unaware of anything but the peaceful feeling of relieving himself, while he is standing there thinking who knows what, you take aim at the back of his head, pull the trigger, and blow his brains out? Have you ever had to decide on firing your weapon into a crowd of civilians because that's where your target had hidden himself, behind innocent children in a schoolyard or behind a bunch of little girls in a market? And you had to risk hitting one or even several of those kids, because if you didn't, that evil man in there was going to launch a rocket that would kill more civilians than you might have to while trying to get him."

Martin's expression sagged. His gaze moved to the floor.

"Because if you have never done those things, if you have never had to make that decision, Detective Dan Martin, then you don't know what you are up against. These guys are not psychopathic serial killers leaving a body here and there for the cops to find. These men we are up against, Usein and his kind, are warriors on a mission. They are not in it for money or for pleasure or for any motive men like you would really understand. Their sole purpose is to utterly destroy western civilization, at any cost, even the loss of their own life. It is that simple. They want to kill you and rape your wife and enslave your children. I have seen it with my own eyes in Somalia, Sudan, Bosnia, Indonesia, and a dozen other places on this planet. I have fought it face to face for longer than you have been a cop."

Martin looked with an almost timid expression at the preacher. When he finally responded there was a slight quiver in his voice.

"Look, I may not have been to those kinds of places in my lifetime, and I may not have seen or done the things you and Hogan have, but I have put myself on the line for the safety of the people of this city for my entire adult life. I am ready for whatever comes. Just don't cut me out of it. I want to catch these guys just as much as you do."

"Then maybe we can work together peacefully," said Hogan.

Hildegarde breathed a sigh and said in an almost whispered voice, "Well, now that we've cleared the air of that formality, can we get back to the pictures?"

"Let's," replied Hogan. He turned back to the table.

The information that lay before them was sketchy at best. Detective Martin opened up and told them everything he knew about Cold Bones operation, which was admittedly very little. The Uni-Thugz were not in his precinct; therefore, he did not have firsthand knowledge of their methods of operation.

"Basically, gentlemen and ma'am, all I can say is that Cold Bones and the Uni-Thugz are a mid-sized gang with only a two or three neighborhood reach, all of those neighborhoods within a mile or so of the OSU Campus."

"Thanks, Detective," said Agent Rottbruck. "My people are working on setting up surveillance at 1639 Loyal and the immediate surrounding area. We are also going to start tracking his vehicles as soon as we can get a device attached."

Martin rung his hands together nervously and leaned forward in his seat. "I hate to come back to questioning your tactics, but is that legal? Tracking him with a homing device, I mean? I'd really hate to capture everyone then have them set loose on a legal technicality in court."

"I understand your concern," Hogan responded, "but because of the presence of Usein, a known international terrorist, we are not bound by domestic laws on this case. Cold Bones and his crew have just become terrorism suspects due to their association with the wonderful Mister Usein."

"Under what authority can you do that?" Martin said. "The Patriot Act was repealed."

"They may have repealed the law in name," replied Hogan, "but they replaced it with new ones that the media never heard of. Don't worry, what we are doing will definitely hold up in court."

Paul Hogan clapped his hands together and smiled, adding, "Mister Reginald 'Cold Bones' Whorley et al. have just waived their collective rights as US citizens, and that, my friends, makes our job much easier."

"If I can add something about Mister Whorley," said Mike Farris. "I do not know his full area of operation, but I do know that the word on the street is that he has recently become a franchisee of a much bigger player. Before the hit on my house, LeRon had mentioned hearing about some guy called Mister White who may be controlling several of the gangs in the city."

Martin looked at him quizzically and asked, "Mister White? I've never heard of him, but I will check into it. You say he is trying to take things over on the city level?"

"Yeah, well, LeRon told me about it almost with a bit of humor." Mike continued. "It seems that Mister White is offering salaries, rather lucrative ones at that, as well as benefits packages including profit sharing, health insurance, 401[k], and stock options. It's as if the new neighborhood godfather is trying to legitimize the drug trade."

"Wow," said Hilde, "sounds like a good place to work."

"I'll look into that with the west-side precinct." said Martin. "This Mister White sounds like an odd cookie though."

"He's probably an MBA looking to make big dollars fast or perhaps even a legitimate businessman using his company as a front while working into the drug market," said Hogan. "Let's look into it that way regarding Mister White. In the meantime, we need to figure out just what it is that Akbar is up to in the quaint little city of Columbus. Hilde? What have you got going on?"

"Like I said," she answered, "I've got surveillance teams working the address you gave us, Mister Farris. Paul, do you want me to send out an APB to the local police stations?"

"No." Hogan answered. "Usein is the kind of guy who could have moles just about anywhere. Let's keep it tight for the moment. If we don't have any information in twenty-four hours or so, we'll release it to the local police. You gonna work with us on this Dan?"

"No problem," replied Martin, "I think I can keep my mouth shut for a day or two, but pretty soon my boss is going to ask what's going on. He saw the fax from Farris."

"Stall him for the moment." Hogan said. "I don't want it leaking out that a known international terrorist is plotting something in Columbus, Ohio."

Hogan turned to Mike and said, "Pastor Farris. Are you ready to go all in?"

"I'm already in," said Farris, "Let's just bring this guy down."

CHAPTER 9

Detective Martin left the FBI building at six o'clock. Hilde had shown him everything he was legally allowed to see. After he was gone, Hogan, Farris, and Rottbruck continued to go over the more highly classified files that she had brought in related to the history of Akbar Usein.

"Jeez," remarked Hogan, "This guy has been all over the map in the past few years. Look at this."

He picked up a printed copy of an email memo from a CIA field agent. It listed actions Usein was known to have had a lead role in.

"From 2006 to 2010, Akbar Usein, aka Alef Ahmet, Mohamet Sulliah, Khan Ayalah, and Joseph Sonniman, has been directly involved in no less than seventeen direct actions against the forces, agencies, citizens, or allies of the United States to include:

1. *Commanded insurgent militia in western Baghdad April-November 2006*
2. *Directed civilian kidnapping raids in Fallujah, Kirkuk, Tikrit, and Baghdad late 2006 to mid-2007.*
3. *Personally conducted torture and execution of civilians captured in above listed raids*
4. *Kazakhstan 2008, witnessed buying arms and ammunition in exchange for cash and drugs with Kazakh*

military commanders. These arms later ended up in San Diego and Los Angeles in the hands of several gangs that were involved in the border conflict; 223 Mexican and 236 American civilians were killed during armed assaults on border security stations and commuter train depots.

5. *Turkmenistan 2008, destruction of US Embassy via truck bomb, killed 132 embassy personnel and civilian passersby.*

6. *Pakistan March 2009, took elementary school hostage to coerce US military to release two of Osama bin Laden's generals from prison. When his demands were not met, Usein ordered the burning of the school with 350 children and teachers still inside; only two children managed to escape; one later died of her burns.*

7. *February 2010 commanded coordinated rocket and sniper assault on Egyptian consulate in Spain in retaliation for Egyptian government's support of US troop movements. 43 dead, over 100 injured.*

Mister Usein is deemed a deep security threat to the United States and this office requests permission to render him harmless at first available opportunity.

B. Caldwell
Station Chief
B2/7-A4

Hildegarde raised her eyebrows and said, "Well, he certainly is not a candidate for the Mister Rogers award, now is he?"

"How the hell did he get through INS is what I want to know." Hogan replied.

"Same way we always got into places we weren't supposed to, Paul," answered Mike. "Right under their noses. No matter how tight you make your ship, the rats will always find a way to get in."

By the time they looked up from the mass of files on the table it was nearly eight o'clock. Hogan rubbed his stomach.

"I don't know about you folks, but my tummy is in serious need of something yummy."

"Agreed," answered Mike. He pushed back from the table and rose to his feet. "Are you going to join us, Agent Rottbruck?"

"Of course," Hilde answered. She put the documents back into their folders and returned the folders to the box. "If one of you is buying."

"Gotcha covered, Hilde," Hogan said. "I owe you one anyway, this is good information."

Hilde called down for an armed escort to return the evidence cart back to the secure storage area in the basement. Five minutes later, the box was picked up, signed for, and wheeled away by two armed officers.

The three of them left the building together. Each drove their own vehicle as Hogan led the way to the Blue Loon Downtown Bistro. It was a popular place for quiet meals. It was filled with nearly sound-proof high-backed booths covered in supple red-brown leather seat backs and cushions.

The elegant booths curled around tables topped with smooth white linen. The lighting was low. A shallow, water-filled bowl with three floating candles shaped like small round flowers sat in the middle of the table. The dancing flames showered a sparkling cascade of glimmering light on the table top. Its light reflected from the water in the bowl and cast a warm glow to the faces of those sitting around it. Thanks to its layout and atmosphere, the Blue Loon was a preferred location for both business meetings and romantic liaisons.

"The meals are a bit expensive, but not unreasonable. At least they're not unreasonable for me these days. Between a

GS-15 salary and my disability pension from the Corps, I'm making some pretty good money. A whole lot better than a Marine master sergeant's paycheck, at least," Hogan told Mike. "Anyway, the food here is simply amazing."

The maître d' sat them in a quiet back corner. They had a wide view across the dining room, which was full of couples and business people in various stages of conversation and dining. Most of the couples in the room were in their thirties and older. While there were several wait staff in their twenties, the lack of youth at the tables was indicative of the menu prices.

On a pastor's salary, Mike seldom got to dine in such fine surroundings. Entrees at the Blue Loon started at thirty-two dollars. He had taken Janelle to similar fancy restaurants only three times since they had married. Once on their honeymoon and then again on each of their anniversaries.

A very courteous waiter took their orders of medium rare New York steak, lobster thermidor, and poached fish. They sipped at glasses of fine French Burgundy and chatted while they waited for the food to arrive.

"So," started Hilde, "you two go back a ways, I understand?"

"Yes, ma'am, we do," answered Mike. "Paul here, quite literally saved my skin from this Usein guy in Somalia about sixteen years ago. If it wasn't for him, I'd just be the deceased star of a torture video being passed around on the Internet. I owe him my life."

"Yeah well, you repaid that debt a long time ago, preacher man," replied Hogan. He turned to Hilde and continued, "Twice this guy's superman-like vision and reflexes kept me from getting capped."

"Sounds pretty even then," she said.

"Yeah, I'd say we're pretty much even," said Hogan. He raised his glass and saluted Mike.

"So Paul," said Mike, "Now that you've got a good-paying career and all that, what have you been up to? Have you started to settle down, get married, and started a family yet?"

"Settle down?" he replied, "I got medically retired from the Corps in '04 after a Taliban RPG left a cart load of metal and gravel in my legs and shoulder. I was just two years short of full retirement too, been working for the bureau since."

"So you came straight into the FBI from the Marines?" asked Hilde. She lifted a large bulbous wine glass and took a sip of the deep-red burgundy. Her lips glistened in the candle light from the wetness of the wine as she set the glass back on the table. Hilde glanced over at Mike. His eyes turned towards Paul just as hers found his face. He was remarkably handsome, she thought.

"Pretty much," Hogan answered, "I had finally finished college with an international law degree in the summer of two-thousand-one then nine-eleven came up, and off I went to hunt for Bin Laden. After the injuries, the Corps told me I wasn't allowed to play anymore, so I figured I'd put that law degree to work. The Bureau actually approached me in oh-three just a couple months before my final salute, and the rest is history. I worked my way up and have been here in Ohio since oh-nine. I took over Task Force Tango, as I like to call it, back in January of this year."

"So you still haven't answered my question. You have no significant other?" asked Mike, "No romantic companions, no hot chicks waiting at home?"

"Nope," said Hogan. His smile stiffened. It was slight but noticeable, "don't have the time."

Mike sensed his old friend's growing discomfort and shifted the conversation to Hildegarde Rottbruck.

"So Hilde, if you don't mind me calling you that, what about you? What do you do outside the bureau?"

"While it is a bit early in our relationship," she smiled coyly, "I suppose I can let you call me Hilde."

"And you can call me Mike." He bowed his head politely.

"OK, you seem like a relatively safe type." Her eyes glimmered with a friendly, almost mischievous gleam. Her full lips glistened in the sparkling candlelight, and her eyes flickered happily. "I pretty much just work. No boyfriends or ex-husbands or anything like that. What little time I have to myself I tend to spend either at the gym or at my computer."

"At your computer?" asked Hogan, "Don't you get enough of that at work? I guess you techno-geeks just can't stay away from those machines, eh?"

"Actually, it is not techno-geek work," she answered. "I'm just playing around."

"You're a gamer?" Quipped Mike. "I never would have placed you as being a computer gamer."

"Oh yeah…sure…Counter Strike, Sonic the Hedgehog… that's me," she said, sarcasm in her tone.

"Sonic the Hedgehog?" replied Mike. "That's so… nineties."

"OK, so I am obviously not a gamer," she said. Hilde put her hands flat on the table cloth and smoothed out a couple of wrinkles they found in it. Then she said with a modest, almost embarrassed voice. "I am actually working on a novel."

"A writer." Mike nodded his head. "I can picture that. What kind of book?"

"Don't laugh, OK?"

"No, of course not," said Mike.

"I might," said Hogan, as he set down his glass.

"If you do, I'll kick you." Hilde replied. She glared at him with a stern expression of warning.

"Mike," Hogan turned to the preacher, "can I trade seats with you? Hilde kicks like a donkey."

"I do not." Hilde said. Her foot shot out under the table, the toe of her shoe catching Hogan square on the shin.

"Ow!" Hogan yelped. "See? She's dangerous."

They all laughed as Hogan raised his leg and rubbed the sore shin.

Mike said. "OK, so what is this great American novel you are writing all about?"

"It's a romantic thriller about a secret agent who falls in love with an attractive but fairly ordinary farm girl from Pennsylvania."

Hogan put his leg back down. His expression hung in silent expectation of the rest of the description. When more of the story summary didn't come he said, "That's it?"

"Well, there's secret agent stuff, too. I mean, you can figure out the rest, can't you? You are one yourself after all." Hilde said in a defensive tone.

"I see," said Mike reassuringly. "The main part of the story is these two falling in love and trying to make it happen while in the middle of a dangerous situation that draws them closer together, yet the danger may drive them apart. Right?"

"Yeah, something like that," she answered.

"Something like that?" Hogan said in a sarcastic tone. "That's like the premise to almost every thriller out there. What's the catch? What'll make me go buy it?"

Hilde pursed her lips defiantly at his questioning and went on.

"Well, part of it is that the girl is totally in love with the agent, but he is resisting falling in love with the her, or at least letting her know that he is in love with her too, because his last girlfriend was killed by his enemies, and that sent him off the deep end for a while. Then…"

Hilde suddenly stopped mid-sentence.

"Oh God," she stopped abruptly. Her cheeks blushed a darker red than her lipstick. The outline of her lips seemed pale by comparison. "I am so sorry Mike. I didn't mean to bring something like that up. I…oh God…I am so sorry."

Mike smiled at her comfortingly and said, "Don't worry about it. There's nothing to feel bad about. Life goes on."

Hogan's smile faded as he tried clumsily to change the subject, as if nothing had happened. "So Hilde, have you done any other writing? Gotten anything published yet?"

"No," Hilde replied quietly, "this one is only a draft still. I don't even know how to end it."

"Don't worry, I am sure you will come up with something," Mike told her. "You seem like a pretty smart woman. Besides, life has a way of providing us with endings for every story."

"More wine?" asked Hogan, picking up the bottle of Burgundy the waiter had left at the edge of the table.

"Yes, please," replied Hilde. She lifted her glass and pushed it towards Hogan's offering hand.

"Just a little for me," answered Mike. He scooted his glass forward.

The food came. It was delicious, just as Hogan had said. The conversation meandered about each person's child-hood and the past adventures of the two Marines, but Hilde couldn't really get into it. She smiled politely and nodded on cue. Her reactions were almost robotic. As she listened to them, she beat herself up inside. How could she have been so thoughtless.

CHAPTER 10

Sarajevo, Bosnia-Herzegovina
September 1998

"Captain Farris." said Staff Sergeant Hogan. He snapped to attention then relaxed and reached out his hand and smiled in greeting. "It is seriously good to see you again, sir. How's seminary going?"

"Pretty good, Paul." Mike smiled widely at the sight of his good friend. "Man, are you a sight for sore eyes. Glad to see you are still alive, Devil Dog."

"Likewise, Captain," answered the staff sergeant. "Our gear is waiting for us. We'd better get over there and pick it up before the armory closes."

Hogan motioned Captain Farris on with his hand. He led the Captain down the hall to the UNSOCOM supplies warehouse, which was housed in the space of three hotel rooms that had been remodeled to include reinforced walls and bullet proof glass.

As they walked, Hogan said, "Say, do you remember Gunnery Sergeant Marcus Johnson from Second Force Recon?"

"Gunny Mojo? The Warrior Poet? Heck yeah!" said Farris, "Hard to forget that guy. What's he up to?"

"Actually," said Hogan, "he's here in Sarajevo."

The previous spring Mojo, as his closest friends called Johnson, had been assigned to a British royal marines unit on an international exchange duty. Such exchanges were a common practice between the US and its allies. While serving with them they, along with Johnson, had been sent on a peacekeeping mission in the war-torn nation of Sierra Leone. During an attempt to rescue the British staff of an orphanage, the unit was ambushed and massacred.

Mojo was the sole survivor and had only barely survived at that. A local pastor had found and cared for him for several months until he was able to make it out of the country on his own. In the process, Mojo helped the pastor's village escape the war zone to safety in a refugee camp in Guinea.

"I assumed he'd be on a long R&R after Sierra Leone? Is he already back on assignment over here?"

"No," answered Hogan. "He's on leave and decided to come this way and visit the SAS guys he had been stationed with here before the Sierra Leone incident. He is still pretty torn up about those Royal Marines he was with. He had become close friends with a couple of them, and then every one of them was killed. On top of that, when he finally escaped that God forsaken hellhole he finds out his fiancé thought he was dead and had started boinking some civilian. She got impregnated while he was trying to get out of the jungle. The whole time he was focused on surviving, so he could marry her."

"Man," said Mike, "poor guy. How's he handling it?"

"Good enough, I guess. You know Mojo. He's the personification of Mister Cool: calm and collected," replied Hogan, "but I tell you what, I would not want to be on the receiving end when he gets back in action. That's going to be some serious rage working out of him."

"I imagine so." Captain Farris took a few steps without talking then said, "Can I meet with him? Is he still here in the area?"

"Yes, sir," answered Hogan. "He was hoping to see you, if we had time. He's actually here in town, staying at the Star Hotel just down the street. It's where the SAS guys are billeted. We're going to take a couple of the SAS blokes to Jajce with us; hopefully, Mojo will be home when we come calling. He really wanted to see you. By the way, he knows that Mathis is in Bosnia and may want to play with us. Your call though, Captain."

They reached the supplies room and entered through a heavy wooden door. The door was inlaid with crisscrossed strips of metal. Inside there was a small window in the center of a wall protected by a thick layer of bullet-proof Plexiglas. A US army corporal on the other side of the window smiled up at them as they approached. The name tape on his uniform was embroidered with the rather unusual name Happyman. The soldier's attitude seemed to do the name justice.

"Good afternoon, gentlemen, what can I do for you?"

The soldier smiled like a Wal-Mart greeter.

"This is Captain Farris, and I am Staff Sergeant Hogan, Marine Special Operations. I was told we had a consignment of gear waiting for us in there."

"Yes, you do, Sergeant. I just need to see your stamped orders and some ID for verification before I let you back here."

Hogan produced a piece of paper and slid it through the slot at the bottom of the window. He and Farris also held up their military ID cards and the UNSOCOM badges they had received in the building. After scanning the document and their ID's, Corporal Happyman let them into the secretive chamber filled with the weapons and equipment used by the US and British Special Operations forces in Bosnia.

"Right over here, gents." The Corporal led them across the room to a table that contained neat stacks of gear. Happyman grinned like a circus hawker. He pointed to the piles and went into what sounded like a well-practiced spiel.

"Here we have your mostly standard-issue death-and-destruction kits for the Bosnian Theater of Operations. I have included for your killing pleasure a pair of fully-functional night-vision goggles for each of you, one standard issue M40A1 7.62-millimeter rifle with high power scope, one precision tuned M-4 carbine, and your own SOCOM M1911 pistols with screw on sound suppressors. If you're wondering, Captain, your armory in Pendleton overnighted your personal one when you left California. We also have assorted camo gear, black pajama and ninja mask outfits, encrypted radio headsets, encrypted satellite phones, and a few other typically useful items. I looked at your previous requisition lists from other missions and tried to personalize your issue based on what you had each used in the past to the best I could. If you have any questions or find anything missing, please let me know, and I will see what we can do. Otherwise, look it over, sign your collective lives away on these forms, and have a wonderful day."

He smiled at the two men like an overly excited maître d' then stepped back and excused himself as they inventoried the equipment and signed the forms. The equipment was locked up in a personal locker in the storage room, and each man put his own lock on it. Once done, they left the building and headed down the block to the Star Hotel to meet up with their team members and hopefully see Mojo Johnson.

At the hotel Hogan went to the front counter. He asked the clerk to notify Mister Oliver Hardt that Paul Hogan was in the lounge. Hogan and Farris walked over to the lounge, sat down, and ordered drinks. Within five minutes, four ordinary looking men in civilian clothes came off the elevator and walked across to the lounge. As they entered the room Hogan signaled to Captain Farris and the two of them stood in greeting. One of those men, directly in front of the Captain, was a handsome, light skinned black man, with almost Asian looking features.

"Gunny Johnson." Farris held out his hand to the man. "Good to see you again, Mojo."

"Likewise, Captain," Mojo answered in a calm voice.

Hogan swept his hand in a wide gesture of introduction towards the other three men.

"Mike Farris, these men are with the local maintenance service contractor from London. Oliver Hardt, Aaron Smythe, and Martin Flynn."

The men that Hogan introduced to Farris as "maintenance service contractors" were undercover operatives in the highly regarded British special air service. As members one of the world's preeminent commando forces, they held the ranks in order of their introductions, of captain, lieutenant, and sergeant.

Farris took each man's hand in his and shook it firmly. All three of the British soldiers were very average looking men. Their hair was cut to a neat civilian length, their clothing was generic, and their mannerisms were not overtly military. In a crowd all of them, including Johnson, would go by unnoticed for the most part. Which, of course, was what they wanted. These men were intelligence gatherers, and as needed, exterminators. The group sat down at their table, and Hogan ordered a round of beer for the four new companions.

"So," started Hardt pointing with his thumb to Johnson, "you know ol' Mojo here, eh Mike?"

"Yep," replied Farris, "we go back a ways."

The waiter arrived at that moment with six-pint mugs of a hazy-looking yellow ale that carried a thick white foamy head. The beer had the look of being freshly brewed. Its taste was heavy on the hops and very strong, probably topping out at eight or nine percent alcohol. Mike sipped the strong brew set before him and immediately decided he would not be finishing the whole thing. He waited for the server to leave before continuing.

"Marcus here was instructing at sniper school when I took my recon team through a couple courses in ninety-two. Then he was in Indonesia in ninety-four when my team was sent in on a search and rescue. Mojo and his boys were sent to find my team when our radios went dead in an ambush that Mathis led us into. We both have a common desire to see him brought in."

"I see," answered Hardt. "Small world, isn't it? First thing in the morning, then, we'll be taking off to fulfill that desire."

"How do we get up there?" asked Hogan.

Smythe set his glass down and said, "I've got us two vehicles. One VW Minibus and a Ford Escort. They have non-matching plates, one Bosnian the other from Montenegro. Registrations and travel permits are in the glove box."

Hardt continued laying out the plan. "Smythe and Flynn will take off first in the minibus, with one of your men, at four-thirty in the morning. They should be in Jajce about eight a.m., depending on road conditions and checkpoints. I've got a motorbike that I'll take on my own. Mike, you and your other man should leave here by no later than seven. That'll put you there at about eleven or so."

"My other man?" asked Farris, "Does this mean you want to play, Mojo?"

"Yes, Captain, I do," replied Johnson. "You may be needing your back watched, and I've got nothing to do for a few days, so if you don't mind the company, I'll ride up with you in the morning."

"No problem," answered Farris. "Other than Hogan here, I can't think of anyone else I'd trust as much as you. You need gear?"

"I'm set, sir. The Brits had a stash of unsigned gear."

"That's right Cap'n," chimed in Flynn in a clipped Belfast Irish brogue, "No need for worrying about paper work that way. He is on holiday, after all."

Oliver Hardt passed envelopes to each man with directions to where the specific teams would arrive and how they would meet up in Jajce. After they talked over a few other details, the group all rose from the table.

"Well gentlemen, it's time for the leprechaun to be getting to bed." said Flynn, "Either that, or we'll end up in a ditch, or half way down a Balkan mountainside before we get to the lovely little place we're headed at oh-four-thirty in the dark, dark morning."

Hogan smiled at the Irishman and said, "I'm with you Marty. Mike, we'd better be heading back. Marty, Aaron… I'll meet up with you two on the sidewalk out front at that dark, dark hour."

"Goodnight all," said Hardt.

Smythe waved his farewell as they walked out. The others all followed behind.

At six thirty the next morning, Johnson arrived in a blue Ford Escort to pick up Farris at the UNSOCOM building. They loaded Mike's gear in the trunk with the gear that Johnson had already put in there. Both men wore their side arms in concealed shoulder holsters that hung tight against their rib cages beneath the thin fall jackets that covered them.

Farris had taken the liberty to grab some food for both of them at the Legion Bridge Hotel before Marcus arrived. They ate it as Johnson started the drive north in the darkness. Few vehicles were on the road yet. The sound of the tires quietly rumbled beneath the car on the smooth new pavement.

"So," said Farris, "How are you handling yourself after Sierra Leone?"

"It's hard." Johnson replied.

"I figure it would be."

"I've seen a lot of men killed in the past twelve years, but never my entire unit." Johnson pressed his back and shoulders into the top of his seat. His arms stretched towards the steering wheel. "I'm a professional. It shouldn't hurt this bad, but it does. All I can think of is revenge, but I got the revenge. I killed the one who did it, a rogue KGB bastard and a couple dozen of his men, and still I want to get more. It's as if I want to dig him up and kill him again."

"I understand you had also lost your girl while you were MIA."

Johnson was quiet.

"You think she's the one you're really mad at, Mojo?"

He stared ahead through the windshield.

"Look, Captain. Are we off the record? I mean no rank, man to man?"

"Yes, we are."

"I know you're trained as a pastor, and you are also one of the finest officers and Marines I have ever known." Johnson paused. "How do we compartmentalize the things we do?"

"What exactly do you mean?" asked Farris.

"You are a preacher, yet in your spare time, you travel the globe and kill bad guys. I have no problem with that. Weird as it sounds I think the two jobs are actually similar, so I'm not asking about the theological questions that others may ask."

He paused for a second to gather his thoughts and choose his words carefully and then continued.

"When you get up in the pulpit, and you look out at your congregation, and as you are preaching the good news to them, telling them how to love each other, you notice a guy out there who you can just tell by the way his body moves, or the way his eyes shift around when he's listening that he's a scumbag. The dude may even be a pedophile or a rapist, and you know in your heart that he may commit a crime, perhaps even that very night. What keeps you from sneaking out in the middle of the night to get rid of him? What keeps you from taking this side of your life into that one?"

Farris answered without hesitation.

"Context."

"Sir?"

"Context," Farris repeated. "You see. When I am under orders to kill someone, there is a specific target, for a specific purpose. I am wiping out a particular threat, not of my own choosing, but as selected and ordered by the officers above me and authorized by the commander in chief. It is not under the guidance of my own emotions, or my hatred of the individual, it is directly for the protection of the people of my country. The fate of the individual, or individuals, I am ordered to take out has already been sealed; they have run out of chances to change their ways."

Farris leaned back in the seat and squinted out the window then continued. "On the other hand, in public or in a congregation, that same person, prior to the order to render him harmless, still has another chance, the option to repent, to change his ways."

"You say it as if you are simply acting out God's will in what you are doing," Johnson said.

"That is what I believe it is," Farris replied. "If at any time I step over the boundary, or take matters into my own hands and decide to make the judgment call without orders from above, I firmly believe that I will end up running out of chances. The reason I have no remorse for what I have done, or what I will do, is that I have never taken an innocent life. Given the opportunity, I would rather have taken some of these same individuals and seen them change their ways and become good guys instead of me putting a bullet in them. So outside of actually catching one of those scumbags you mentioned in the act, I would have no justification for taking him out."

"So, Mojo, that is how we keep our heads in this game." He turned and looked towards the man next to him. "What you need to do is stop hating this guy that took your woman, scumbag or not. After all, she thought you were dead. She had no evidence otherwise until it was too late, and the dude, well, if your woman is half as beautiful as I think she is, he was just acting naturally."

"In other words," Johnson said, "forgive them, and keep my mind in the work."

"Pretty much." Farris looked hard into Johnson's eyes. "And whatever you do, don't put that guy's face on your enemies. Let him go, let them live their life, and let your real enemies be the ones you deal with. If God wants you to have a wife, he will make it happen in his own time."

"I think I understand," said Johnson. "Thank you, sir."

CHAPTER 11

The three finished dinner at ten thirty. They would meet at Paul Hogan's office at one the next afternoon.

Mike was exhausted. He needed to get some sleep. Except for the pair of interrupted naps after getting home that morning he hadn't closed his eyes to sleep in nearly forty-eight hours.

He pulled into the driveway at his home and wearily dragged himself into the house. He climbed the stairs to the bathroom and slid out of his clothes. Exhaustion seeped through his pores as he dropped the disheveled garments in a heap on the bathroom floor.

Mike looked at himself in the mirror as he brushed his teeth. He was a mess. It wasn't that he looked unkempt. He had showered and shaved that morning before Martin arrived. He looked hollow. Every facet of his life had dulled at once. The loss and stress chipped away at his physical being. The mirror reflected back a ghostly appearance. His eyes were sunken and circled with dark rings. His cheeks looked thin skinned. He was pale and gaunt. His life was in limbo.

No, not limbo...a coma. The thought careened through his mind. *Spiritual vacuum.*

Mike was not sure if he would ever be able to return to his pastoral life, even after everything was cleared up. He had kept the details of his military past hidden from his friends and family for so long only to have it rear its ugly head. The violence he had participated in years ago refused to recede into the past, and he had no one to turn to.

Janelle and Mini-Mike were gone; the best chapter of his life closed in a few seconds of rage. His parents had both died not long after the birth of his son. He had a sister, but had no idea where she was. She had practically disowned him when he joined the military. They hadn't spoken in more than a decade, and her last contact information was no good anymore.

The only real friends he'd had beyond his family, ones that he could confide in, were in the Corps, and they, with the exception of Hogan, were all either dead or scattered to the corners of the earth in the final years of their careers or in their own retirements. He wondered if any of them suffered from a similar predicament as he. Mike would have liked to know where they were and what they were doing. Would they have to unravel the ghosts of the past or face demons that had haunted them relentlessly through their violent lives?

Mike remembered Elder Harry Johnson.

Yes, Harry. He's the only one I can really talk to. I'll make a point to sit and chat with him. To see how he would handle this.

White steam billowed from around the rich-looking French-patterned shower curtain. Janelle had bought the fancy looking curtain, made of tan fabric laced with gold threads, because she said it looked like "autumn in a palace." She had always liked to decorate the house based on the season. Mike's heart twisted within him. The mental image of his wife hanging the curtain coursed through his mind. The two of them had laughed as Mini-Mike acted silly by putting the curtain hooks, shaped like golden roses, on his head. The toddler giggled uncontrollably as the gold-painted resin flowers tumbled from his head to the floor, clattering loudly in the tiled room.

He rubbed his eyes to push the memory away. He did not want to let his life be lived in the past. Pools of tears obscured his vision. The mirror clouded over with steam and he felt like he was walking inside a cloud.

Mike stepped into the shower and let the hot jets of water stream over his body and rinse away the topmost layers of stress. He switched the shower head to pulse mode and let the rhythmic bursts of hot water pound at the tensed muscles at the base of his skull, along his neck, and across his shoulders.

As the sweat and tears of the day ran down the drain of the tub, physical exhaustion pulled at him. Mike got out of the shower, grabbed a thick white terry cloth towel, and dried off. He hung it over the shower curtain rod to dry it for the next time he showered. He crossed out of the master bath to the bedroom, slipped into a fresh pair of cotton boxers and a clean white t-shirt, and lay down on the cool sheets of the wide king-sized bed.

His thoughts drifted back in time.

September 1998.

The town of Jajce in Bosnia-Herzegovina. Captain Mike Farris and Gunnery Sergeant Marcus "Mojo" Johnson lay silently in an abandoned house waiting for evil to show its face. Waiting to kill. Was this all fate's retribution? Had he brought this pain on himself?

He pushed the memory from his mind and shifted his body to lay on the far-left side of the bed, the side on which he had lain every night since marrying Janelle. His body was nearly at the edge of the mattress. Janelle had often let Mini-Mike sleep with them for at least the first part of the night.

Mike had slept at the edge to make sure they had enough room, since the slumbering boy seemed to move constantly in an ever-shifting attempt to stay as closely snuggled to mommy as possible.

As he drifted quietly into the periphery of consciousness, Mike instinctively reached over to the space Janelle had filled for the past two years. In his near dream state, part of him expected to find her there. To touch her warm skin, for her to react to his loving caress. Mike's hand found nothing but cold, empty sheets. His heart ached with an emptiness that ate at him deeper than mere emotions. A heavy, almost tangible, darkness overcame him and brought him once again to the edge of weeping as it had every time he lay down for the past two weeks. In his heaviness, he slowly drifted off to a restless sleep. Then it happened. At some point after a couple hours of deep sleep the dream visited him. The nightmare started slowly, as it had nearly every night since the shooting.

He was in a small room with the door locked. His pulse began racing, picking up speed, and pounding in his head as he realized he couldn't get out. The room suddenly went dark. He heard shooting. It chattered fast and high pitched like the rattle of a snare drum outside the walls of the cell-like room. Running footsteps thumped outside the suffocating walls. The door burst open. Screams. Distant, pleading screams. His son crying.

"Daddy! Daddy!"

Janelle and Mini-Mike lay in a pool of blood in front of him. Then Akbar Usein stood before him smiling, snarling.

"I'm going to wear your skin like a shirt."

The sound of Usein's laughter echoed around his head. His face faded and was replaced by that of Mike's training sergeant from sniper school, Brett Mathis. Sergeant Mathis was wearing a black tactical suit. Mathis's face glimmered with thick red blood that oozed across his skin and dripped from his nose and chin.

"I'm sorry, Mike, but you know how this stuff goes."

The ground in front of Mike opened up and he fell in, tumbling past images of children clutching their mother's limp forms. Falling past burned bodies into the darkness beneath him. Usein's insane laughter echoed in the abyss through which Mike fell. He tried to scream, but there was no sound in his throat. A bright flash exploded before his eyes. Mike shot straight up in the bed.

The blankets were soaked with sweat. His pulse throbbed explosively in his neck. His heart pounded against his rib cage. He looked desperately around the dark room, struggling to see through the black void. He was awake. He was in his own house, and everything was where he left it. He was back in reality.

"Oh, dear God!" he panted. "Please get me through this. Please don't let me lose my mind!"

Sleep did not return easily. Once it did arrive, his prayer was answered, and he did not dream again that night.

CHAPTER 12

The living room of the house at 1639 Loyal was surprisingly clean, almost sterile. Seirim Al Gul stood in a corner of the room. He stared at the four men, three seated on the couch and one on a chair across from Akbar Usein. The men made an effort to maintain their thuggish cool. The hard look in their faces seemed natural, but the presence of the hairy, wild man unsettled them. His eyes bore into them and an insane smile stayed on his lips. His body was tense, ready to pounce. From time to time, Al Gul's tongue slid out and over his lips as if he were thinking of food. One of the men had earlier commented to the others that he thought Al Gul was a cannibal. They all believed that to be possible.

Lucas Ring stood behind the drivers, a menacing figure that hovered over them. At well over six-feet tall and with a nearly sixty-inch chest the Ringmaster's three-hundred-plus-pound frame was enough to intimidate most men without him having to utter a word. It was hard to tell if he was there to lead them or to push them into the job.

119

Al Gul showed no sign of fear of Ring. That pissed him off. Lucas Ring didn't like the thought of someone not being afraid of him. The two men traded hateful glances at each other as Usein laid out the orders for the task to the drivers. Usein leaned forward in the large leather chair. His long arms rested on his knees as he scanned the faces of the four men before him. The scar on his temple pulsed with every beat of his heart.

"You four have been chosen by Mister White to drive for me."

Usein rose from the chair.

"You were chosen because he thinks you can be trusted. You must prove him right."

He strode around to the back of the brown leather chair he had been sitting in. Usein leaned his palms against the back of the chair and continued speaking.

"You are being sent to retrieve certain packages for me. You will follow my instructions precisely. If you do, you will be rewarded very generously; I swear it, but if you fail to obey me to the exact detail, you will be more formally introduced to my associate, Al Gul."

He motioned with a slow sweep of his hand towards Al Gul who responded with a guttural chuckle and licked his lips. The men on the couch looked at the hairy, mad man warily. Ring turned up the corner of his lip. He refused to be intimidated by the lunatic.

"What's the stuff that we are picking up?" asked one of the young men.

"None of your business," replied Usein.

"Bullshit!" said another man. His fingers were covered with gold rings. Several gold chains hung around his neck. He wore a wide-brimmed baseball cap low over his eyes. The brim of the hat, which was too big for his head, was cocked at an angle towards his right ear.

"'Das right," said one of the others.

"I did not get up this early in the morning to be doing no damn puzzles, and I sure as hell ain't driving around with some shit I don't know what it is. Shit might get my ass the death penalty for all I know."

"Then don't get caught," replied Usein.

The young man moved to get up from the couch.

"I'm out."

As he stood, his right hand grasped the buckle of the belt that held his baggy pants up. Ring unfolded his arms. He leaned forward to put a hand on the young man and make him sit back down. Halfway up from the seat cushion the man's left hand moved behind his back to shove himself up from the couch. In the corner of the room there was a flash of motion. A thunderous explosion blasted in the morning quiet. The group of four drivers convulsed with surprise.

Shouted curses filled the air. The defiant driver's hat fluttered across the room and landed against the wall ten feet away. A neat ten-millimeter hole had appeared through the brim.

"Next one's in your face," growled Al Gul, a smoking Glock 10mm pistol in his outstretched hand. "Left nostril, I think."

The crazy man's head tilted forward. He glared intensely at the man. A spark of insanity flickered from his eyes as his mouth spread in a toothy grin. A wild shock of his thick, curly black hair fell over one eye. Al Gul let out a slow rhythmic grunt of a laugh.

Usein, who had not flinched at the shot, said, "Sit down and do not ask questions."

Ring pursed his lips and narrowed his eyes. His face boiled red as hatred for the lunatic seethed through him. Al Gul had taken it upon himself to discipline one of Ring's own men. By the expression on his face, it was clear that that action was unacceptable.

Usein continued. "You were chosen by Mister White because he trusts you. There is no option to leave. You must now follow my orders. They are not bullshit."

Usein pointed to four envelopes on the coffee table in front of the drivers.

"These are your instructions. Follow them precisely. There is a GPS on the seat of each vehicle. Follow its directions and do not vary from the route. Once you arrive at your first location a text message will appear on the GPS. Do what it says, and you will find yourselves a great reward. Stray from it and no one will ever find your body."

"If there's anything left of it," mumbled Al Gul.

"Now go. There are four vans waiting outside. The gas is full in each and here is one thousand dollars for more gas and food as you need it."

He handed each man a bundle of twenty-dollar bills. They took the cash and pocketed it. The four men rose and walked across the room to the front door. They stepped outside into the predawn darkness at just before six o'clock in the morning. The horizon to the east glowed with the pale gray light of early morning as the sun made its way past the eastern United States on its daily route to the west. Usein followed them with Al Gul behind him. Ring blocked Al Gul's path. His body completely filled the door frame. He glowered down at Al Gul whose head only came up to the middle of Ring's chest.

"Don't ever school my men like that again, asshole. I will take care of them."

"Really?" the smaller man looked up at Ring. His eyes flickered, and he started to laugh and mutter to himself again.

"He thinks he's safe because he's big."

"Heh, heh. Let him think that."

"Yes, of course, we will."

"He could last a long time."

"No…we'd need a freezer to keep him fresh. Besides… he'd be tough to chew."

"Hahahaha…yes…heheh…too tough to chew."

As he spoke he kept his eyes focused on Ring's. Ring looked down on him like he was contemplating shooting the man before he did anything crazier. Usein called out.

"Al Gul, now is not the time."

Ring turned and Al Gul zipped past him through a tiny space Ring had allowed to open. He heeled behind Usein like a dog behind its master and glared back over his shoulder at Ring. Al Gul turned his attention towards the vans. Ring walked past Al Gul and Usein, bumping the hairy man's shoulder as he passed and walked off the porch. He crossed the yard towards his own car parked at the side of the street. The van's engines fired up and the men sat in the running vehicles for several minutes as the heaters slowly warmed the cool interiors.

Al Gul swayed on his feet next to Usein. The African looked sideways at him with a quizzical expression on his face as he took on a trance-like appearance. Seirim Al Gul grunted rhythmically beside him. He made hand signs in front of his midsection, holding his long bony fingers in odd patterns that he changed every few seconds. His mouth moved in wide spoken words, but the sound came out only as a whisper.

"Kah-zah-yeeee."

He repeated the whole sequence twice more saying the same phrase over and over as his hands moved in the patterns in front of his belly.

"Kah-zah-yeeee. Kah-zah-yeeee. Kah-zah-yeeee."

He continued the odd mantra until the vans pulled away and rounded the distant corner at the end of the block. Usein looked at him sternly.

"What was that about?"

"Scaring away the demons who would try to stop us," replied Al Gul, "I learned it from a great mullah who had been a witch doctor before coming to the light of Islam."

Usein turned and walked back into the house. Al Gul followed Usein into the house. Once the door closed behind them, Usein grabbed Al Gul by the shoulders of his shirt and shoved the madman against the wall. He leaned close and growled under his breath.

"I warn you only once, do not overact your part. I only brought you here because the Sheik required it. You are not under his protection in this country. I do not like having a lunatic with me. If you cannot control your demons, I will be rid of you. Do not threaten Mister White's men unless I specifically tell you to."

"Please forgive me, Akbar Aga." Al Gul used the Arabic term of respect. "I was only helping press your point forward. Quelling rebellion before it starts."

"I will control the men myself."

"Of course, Akbar Aga." Al Gul bowed his head in exaggerated humility, "Even the Sheik is not fully aware of what you are doing here. Perhaps, if you let me in on the full plan, I will be better able to serve you."

"You will know when the time is right, not before."

"Yes, Akbar Aga. If only I may be of service to the Sheik and to you, and if Allah has mercy on me, to kill the infidel."

"Do not play me for a fool," Usein growled. "I know you were sent to watch me; I am not avowed to the Sheik. I am not here for his pleasure. I do not serve your Brotherhood of the Sword. If it is the infidel you wish to kill, your time will come, but only when I say."

"Yes, Akbar Aga, of course."

CHAPTER 13

Wednesday, October 26th
FBI Regional Headquarters
Office of the Ohio Valley Anti-Terrorist Task Force
12:45 Hours

Hildegarde Rottbruck had just finished her lunch: a cold chicken salad purchased in the downstairs cafeteria. She turned in her chair and stretched to put the black plastic container in the trash can under her desk. The phone suddenly bleated its loud electronic ring tone on her desk. The sudden noise startled her. The plastic salad container slipped out of her grasp and landed next to the trash can. It fell upside down. The remnants of shredded carrots and purple cabbage splashed across the dark blue carpet, outlined by a pink splatter of Thousand Island dressing.

The phone bleated again like a lost and miserable techno-sheep. Hilde hated that sound but had never been able to figure out how to change the ring tone. She was too embarrassed to ask for help, since she was one of the senior IT people in the building. She usually just tried to answer the thing before it rang twice. Flustered, she sat upright and snatched the receiver from the set.

"Hello?"

"Ms. Rottbruck, this is Andy Fleiss in tac-ops."

Fleiss was the tech she had assigned to monitor the Usein case.

"Yes, Andy. Did you find something?"

"Yes, ma'am. I believe we definitely have something. Can you come down here and take a look?"

"I'll be right there, Andy. Give me a couple of minutes."

She hung up and rose from her chair. She made a mental note to send an email to the housekeeping staff to clean up the carpet when they came through that night. She walked out of her office into the hallway. In ten quick steps, Hilde was down the hall and pressing the button for the elevator. It arrived a few seconds later and the doors swished open. She got in and tapped the number on the floor listing to take her down to the second basement level where the "listening room" was located.

As the door slid shut Paul Hogan passed into view in the hall. He was on the way to his office with a large latte in his hand. Hilde jutted her hand between the elevator doors causing them to slide back open when the sensor detected something in the way.

"Paul!" she shouted to him. "Come take a ride with me."

At the urgent sound of her voice, he turned and took three jogging steps to elevator.

"Whatcha got?" Hogan said as he jumped in. A drop of the latte splashed out of the cup onto his thumb. He winced at the hot liquid, reached up the hand and licked it off then blew on the reddening skin.

"The listening room just called. Andy Fleiss said they have something but didn't say what."

"Well," he replied with a smile, "Let's go check it out then."

Hogan pulled a cell phone from his pocket and called the security front desk. He told the officer who answered to bring Mike Farris down to the listening room when he came in. Less than a minute later Hogan and Rottbruck approached the door of the FBI's Tactical Operations, Signals Intelligence Group. Hilde punched an eight-digit code into the cipher lock on the handle then put her hand on the white scan plate affixed to the wall to the right of the entry. A high-pitched beep signaled that she was cleared to enter. She turned the handle and opened the door that lead into one of the most technologically advanced communications centers in North America.

The room and most of the furniture was bright white, contrasted by shades of gray and black, and strands and coils of bright yellow, blue and green cables. It was also cold, kept at a constant sixty-five degrees Fahrenheit twenty-four hours a day, all year long. The room was maintained at such a low temperature to ensure the smooth operation of the wall to wall banks of rack mounted servers, routers, switches, network storage arrays, and fiber optic cabling that seemed to cover every square foot.

"Agent Rottbruck, Agent Hogan, come take a look at this." Andy Fleiss motioned to them from a bank of LCD monitors.

Fleiss was a man of average height and fairly athletic build. His head was topped with a mop of tousled brown hair. He wore thick glasses that made his eyes seem twice as large they really were. His short-sleeved button-down shirt sported a pocket protector brimming with a variety of pens, screwdrivers and a laser pointer, and he looked every bit the part of the computer nerd who worked in a sub-basement of a secret government facility.

Despite the look, it was not really his style. After "Bill Gatesing" his wardrobe a couple of times as a practical joke, he discovered that it was actually very practical work attire. He continued to dress that way for the past several years. And the glasses did not dry his eyes out as much as contacts in the constant blowing of the air-conditioned atmosphere.

Off duty he was quite a fashion-conscious guy. When he went to clubs the glasses gave way to contacts and the wardrobe was Abercrombie, Hilfiger, and Armani. When properly attired he had a look that reminded people of a young Hugh Grant, the quintessential English heart throb of the nineties. His male friends liked it when he came along to the clubs with them because he was what they called a "high-tech chick magnet." At work though, no one would have guessed as the Gatesified Andy Fleiss was all business.

The two agents moved over to Fleiss' workspace and looked at the monitors that lay in two rows of six each above his desk. Several of them displayed what looked like the same scenes at different points in time. He pointed to the two on the bottom row farthest to his left and explained what they were looking at.

"These two monitors are displaying the camera's live shot at 1639 Loyal. Cold Bones' house. One at the front and one at the rear."

He pointed to two different monitors on a shelf directly above the live shots.

"These two are the same shot at about four o'clock this morning."

In the recorded shot, four light blue minivans were parked in front of the house. A man sat on the porch, like a sentry.

"Now, in just a second watch the area behind the house, in the alley." Fleiss said.

As they watched the second monitor on the top shelf two vehicles entered the camera's view and pulled up to the back of the house. Two men got out and went in the back door. In the shadows cast by the street lamps the men's faces and details could not be seen, but one of them, the only white man, was very large.

"Can you zoom in on those guys?" Hogan asked.

"Already did sir. I also brightened the picture. Screen three is the brightened zoom."

On screen three on the bottom row of monitors they could make out the side of the face of Lucas Ring as he entered the back of the house. The other man, a thin built black man, never turned towards the camera. His build reminded Hogan of the unidentified man in the photos from Ohio Stadium they had looked at the day before.

Hogan's cell phone rang inside his sport coat. He reached into his pocket, pulled it out and pressed the answer button.

"Agent Hogan, this is Officer Clark at the front desk. Just letting you know that Officer Jakeman is bringing Mister Farris down to you, he should be there in a couple of minutes."

"Thanks," answered Hogan. He clicked the phone off then turned to Rottbruck. "Mike is on the way down. Fleiss, hold those pictures until he gets here, I want him to see them."

Hilde's stomach fluttered at the mention of Mike's name. She was surprised by the subconscious reaction of her own body and hoped that her face hadn't flushed. She tried to focus on the screens and asked the specialist, "I see on the live shot that the vans are gone. What time did they leave there?"

Fleiss looked down at a notepad on his desk covered with numbers and scribbled words. He found the one he was looking for and clicked his mouse to open a list of images in the center screen of his panel of monitors. He scrolled through the list until he found the lines he sought.

"All of them left at six a.m. this morning," he replied.

"Did we get tracer chips on them?" she asked.

"Three of the four, yes. We had a man on scene that shot the chips onto the vehicles. Three of them stuck fast on the bumpers of the vans, but on the fourth, the adhesive malfunctioned, and it fell from the vehicle as they took off."

"Where'd the three head off to?" asked Hogan.

"That's the funny thing," said Fleiss. "The ones we are tracking all headed in different directions and seem to be stopping at random locations along the way to wherever they are heading. It's been almost like they are making deliveries or something."

"Or pickups," added Rottbruck. "Maybe they are trying to do a street magician's cup and ball trick on us."

There was a knock at the door. Hogan walked across the room and opened it. Mike Farris stood in the hall with Officer Jakeman. The uniformed federal police officer held out a clip board to Hogan.

"Agent Hogan, please sign here to take responsibility for him being in this area."

"Hey Mike, I guess this means you belong to me now!" Hogan quipped.

Mike raised an eyebrow.

"Good day to you too, Agent Hogan."

Jakeman took the clipboard back and turned to walk away. Farris stepped into the room and followed Hogan. The door clicked shut behind them as they walked over to the bank of monitors. Hilde turned towards them.

"Hi, Mister Farris." Hilde smiled in greeting. Her abdomen fluttered again, and she felt warmth in the skin of her face. She hoped she wasn't blushing. She held out her hand to his, and he took it in an old fashioned gentlemanly greeting. Mike smiled back at her as he released her hand. Hilde was certain that she was blushing then. She turned away and introduced Fleiss.

"Mike, this is Andy Fleiss. He's one of our star techies down here in the 'Cave of Wonders' as we like to call it."

Fleiss looked up from his chair and got right to the point.

"Hi, Mister Farris. I understand you gave us the address and stuff of this Cold Bones guy. Well, we've already seen some good activity, as these monitors here show. These two," he pointed to the ones showing the recorded images of the vans, "are from about four thirty-ish this morning. I was just showing them some enhanced images of the people when you came down."

Hogan walked back to the group and said. "The big guy is definitely Lucas Ring. That was Martin on the phone. He said that he just got word from the west-side precinct that the Ringmaster has recently taken up work with the new kingpin Mister White. They also said that they have an inside man in the gang. He's been there a few months and is working his way up to the top to find out who Mister White is. Martin said they wouldn't tell him who the undercover agent is."

Rottbruck asked, "Can we get directly informed by their man inside?"

"Negative. I asked," answered Hogan. "It seems this guy only trusts one person in the west-side precinct and that he will only pass info to that one officer, a detective name Mellon. Mellon in turn will pass information to Martin and him to us."

"What if it comes to shooting?" asked Rottbruck. "We don't want to hit the informant."

"We'll play that as it goes, Hilde," replied Hogan. "If the bullets start to fly, hopefully their man'll be outta there already. If not, I imagine he knows the rules of the game that he got himself into by now."

"Uh, Agent Hogan," Fleiss said, "check this freak out."

Hogan and the others turned back to the monitors. On the center display, Fleiss zoomed in on a dark, hairy man standing on the porch moving his hands in a rhythmic pattern and moving his mouth in wide gestures.

Hogan raised his eyebrows. "What is that guy doing? Is he supposed to be some kind of witch doctor?"

"I don't know," answered Hilde, "but I have never seen anything like it."

Fleiss watched the movements closely. "Wait a minute, there's a pattern to it. He's starting the pattern again, and there's audio."

They looked closely at the motions as Fleiss unplugged the headphones from the computer and turned on the speaker. At first all they could hear was the vans. Then the agent operating the camera zoomed the video and the microphone in closer. A series of weird rhythmic grunts could be heard from the strange man.

"That's just creepy," said Hilde.

The pattern of four hand symbols repeated four times in succession.

"Wait a minute," Hogan said. "Back up and play those hand signs again."

Hogan stared at the man with the wild hair and thick beard as he made the signs again. Fleiss slowed it to half speed. An expression of disbelief spread across Hogan's face as he watched.

The man on the screen formed his two hands into the shape the letter "U" in front of his belly. Then he took his two hands and pointed the fingers toward each other spreading them apart into a version of the "Vulcan" peace sign from the old Star Trek TV show. He put the top two fingers of the left hand into the space between the two pairs of fingers of the right without touching them. The bottom two fingers of the left were below the fingers of the right without touching the fingers. The combination left a space between the fingers that looked like a letter "S." He then manipulated his hands so that the fingers of each joined to make a letter "M." Finally, the hair-covered madman made a letter "C" with each hand. He held this sign and nodded his head up and down several times.

Hogan blinked and rubbed his eyes. He stared at the screen, mesmerized.

"Zoom up to his face," Hogan commanded.

He watched the man closely as he mouthed something. The microphone picked up the sound of the man's whispered phrase being repeated.

"Kah-zah-yee."

Hogan's jaw dropped open.

"Kharzai."

CHAPTER 14

I-70
West of Dayton Ohio
Wednesday, October 26th
09:50 Hours

The non-descript blue Dodge delivery van pulled up to the New Paris Sun Gas & Quick-mart station. The driver parked in a space near the door. The building looked as though it had been built in the 1940s. While the gas pumps were modern, everything else about the place looked to be original. What had once been two bays for mechanic work had been converted on the inside into a convenience store. William Coffee, known on the street as Billy Z, got out of the van and walked into the station as he had been instructed.

The interior was decorated with vintage signs and advertisements for Coke and Pepsi, Prince Albert tobacco and some brand of bread Billy had never heard of. He glanced towards the clerk behind the counter. The young woman was distracted ringing up another customer's Gatorade and candy bars. She didn't seem to notice him come in. Billy passed them and headed to the men's room at the rear of the store.

Once inside, he closed and locked the door. He put down the toilet seat, letting it drop with a loud smack. Then Billy walked to an ancient looking hand cranked paper towel dispenser that jutted from the wall and felt carefully around the edges where it sealed to the cracked tile. His fingers felt the smooth hard caulk around the edge until he scraped against something sharp. A barely visible piece of paper jutted out from the space between the dispenser and the wall.

Billy Z pulled out a Gerber multi-tool and flipped open the needle nose pliers from the end. He pinched the tiny edge of paper with the narrow tip of the plier and gave it a tug. Out came a small folded square of yellowed paper. He opened it up and read the words scrawled in faded ink.

482 Stouderman High

This was the tenth stop he had made. The previous nine had been mini-marts, restaurants, gas stations, and a hardware store. At each of those he had simply waited in the parking lot and a pre-programmed text message appeared on the GPS loading a new map with directions to another place. Those directions lead to a very specific location in a seemingly random direction. This was the first time there had been a paper note to pick up.

He committed the text to memory then, as instructed in the text message, tore the paper into small pieces and dropped it into the toilet. He pulled off a couple strips of toilet paper, wadded them up and dropped them in the bowl on top of the bits of note that floated in the water. He flushed the mass of soaked paper down the toilet, the weight of the shredded toilet paper ensured that all of the note fragments went down the drain in one clump. Billy left the restroom and went back into the store. He picked up a bag of corn chips and bottle of tangerine flavored Gatorade, paid at the counter, and left.

He drove the van back onto I-70 and headed west. According to the map, there was a road called Stouderman about eighteen miles inside the Indiana border. It lay in rural farm country just beyond the city of Richmond where it snaked through fields and woods north from the freeway.

Within fifteen minutes of crossing the border Billy took the exit that headed into the low green hills and wound back along the border of northwest Ohio and northeast Indiana. The first house he passed had the number 11623 in crisp white letters stenciled on a new black mail box. Half a mile later the next mailbox was labeled 11514. Each of the houses was separated by several acres of forest and field. Runs of barbed wire fence topped by an electrical line outlined expanses of pasture land where black and brown cows lazily grazed on the final remnants of grass and fresh greens that poked up through the cold ground.

"Damn! four-eighty-two is going to be a long ways north from here."

He was right. After nearly an hour of driving along the fairly straight country road the numbers got down to three digits. Just after number 596, the chip and tar pavement ended abruptly. It gave way to a rough gravel road pocked with holes. Some sections were corrugated by ruts that jarred his whole body if he hit them too fast. It meandered through an unpredictable sequence of twists and curves along the course of a narrow stream that gurgled over rocks and around old fallen trees.

The autumn colored woods became thicker and the houses more difficult to spot from the road. He passed a mailbox with the number 490 painted on the side and slowed a bit. He did not want to miss the driveway and get lost this far out in the boonies.

He'd heard many bad stories in the past of being a black man found alone in a backwoods like this one by men who hadn't accepted the civil-rights laws of fifty years earlier. Billy had been in many scary places and survived a lot of violent altercations. His only fear though, one that had even crept into his nightmares, was being kidnapped by a bunch of neo-

Nazi militia nuts with a mind to lynch him. He pressed the accelerator and forced himself on.

A mile further, he slowed. A dingy, faded plywood sign hung from a tree. He made out large but barely legible numbers: 482. The sign looked ancient, like a leftover from prohibition. The lane that turned off Stouderman had tall grass growing up from its center, bounded by hard packed ruts, from which nothing grew, worn smooth by years of vehicles and tractors making their way back to the farm.

Billy drove up the road, through thick trees and past long abandoned fields. It was the kind of place he imagined some hillbilly types in blue coveralls might be working a still and sipping moonshine from mason jars with long double-barreled shotguns across their laps.

At the end of the winding driveway the property opened up to a wide expanse at one side of which stood a tall, very old looking barn. The wood of its walls was a faded, lifeless-looking gray. The structure canted unsteadily to one side like the Leaning Tower of Pisa. It definitely looked unsafe to enter.

Billy sat in the van and assessed the area. He turned off the engine, rolled down the window, and listened in silence. He made mental notes of the details of the surroundings before getting out. A pile of rotted and molding firewood stood next to the barn. Weeds burst out from between the logs like shocks of wild hair. Behind that lay a stack of old planks. The grass around the barn and along the boundaries of the drive way stood straight and tall, unbroken. There were no overturned leaves, no broken soil, no signs of human presence that he could make out. No one had been here in a long time.

He listened to the birds settle back into the songs. A squirrel chirped loudly at the end of the dried, grassy field as a woodpecker noisily drummed its food from a tree somewhere in the distance. A rabbit darted out of a stack of warped gray lumber near the barn. The creature moved with awe inspiring speed and dexterity as it sprinted halfway across the field, faded to the left like a pro-football player then shot into the woods where it vanished into the brush. The natural movement and sound of the animals was enough to satisfy him that he was alone. They did not sense danger in the air; there was nobody moving around in the area; at least, no one the animals knew of. He was certain he had not been followed, but Billy always went on the side of caution. That was what had kept him alive for more than ten years in this business.

Billy got out of the van and walked up to the large open door at the front of the barn. He cautiously entered the unsound structure and stood just inside the entrance. It was probably a remnant of a pre-Civil War farm and seemed not to have been used in at least twenty years. The barn reeked with the musty odor of old wet hay and a hint of diesel fuel that emanated from four rusting metal drums on the floor in a far corner. A long work table ran the length of one side. A small assortment of old tools were scattered about it, the metal rusted and the wooden handles dried and cracked. Dust covered every surface.

In the back of the barn a hay loft stretched between the upper most wall beams. Its thick wooden floor stood twenty feet above the ground. The note had said "High." It probably meant that whatever he was looking for was up in that loft. He'd have to check it out. A wooden ladder ascended from the ground level to the loft surface. From the center of the barn roof hung a rope suspended on a pulley. One end of the rope was tied to the railing of the loft; the other end had a rusty metal hook that grasped the banister.

Billy walked over to the ladder, took hold of it, and gave a couple of hard jerks against its side rails. Once he was satisfied that it seemed sturdy enough to hold his body weight, he took a deep breath and climbed gingerly to the top. He reached to the top of the ladder and clambered onto the surface of the loft.

The space was mostly empty. In the far corner was a four-foot-high pile of molded hay. In the center, against the back wall a filthy canvas tarp lay in a wrinkled heap on top of some mass. A long pitch fork rested against the wall near him. The rest of the loft was just covered in dust and bits of hay and animal droppings.

Billy approached the tarp. The shape beneath it was about the size of a small suitcase or courier bag of some kind. Large enough to hold a decent amount of drugs. He reached down and grabbed a corner of the tarp. He pulled up on it.

The silent stillness of the barn was shattered by an ear-splitting scream. His heart leaped into his throat as he stumbled back towards the ladder. Before he realized he had grabbed hold of it, his pistol was flying up towards a dark shape that moved rapidly towards him, screaming like a banshee.

Before he could fire, the creature flew past him and started for the ladder. It reached the steps and deftly ran face first to the surface below. It stopped at the ground beneath him, turned, and screeched back up toward the loft.

"Shit!" Billy exclaimed, eyes wide with terror. "A raccoon! A stupid raccoon!"

The raccoon looked back up at him and barked its protest like a retort at being called stupid. If raccoons had language, this one was probably cussing his best at the inconsiderate human that had woken it from its comfortable home.

Billy caught his breath and forced himself to relax. He laughed at himself for having been so frightened. He was glad he was alone, because he was certain that the look on his face when the beast had jumped out did not look very cool. Pistol still in his right hand, he turned back and grabbed the pitch fork that leaned against the wall. He walked to the far corner of the loft. He shouted out loud towards the pile of hay. When there was no movement he jammed the pitch fork in several times, keeping his weapon ready in case something else jumped out at him.

Satisfied that nothing else was alive in the loft, he pushed the hay aside with the pitch fork. His nose curled in disgust as the disturbed mold spores puffed into the air. Beneath the foul-smelling hay, he found what he was looking for. A medium-sized black plastic-coated suitcase sat on the floor. He grabbed its handle and pulled it out. Billy was surprised by how heavy the suitcase was. Although it was only about eighteen inches tall and twenty-four inches wide he estimated its weight at nearly eighty pounds. Oddly, the majority of the weight seemed to be concentrated in a mass at the center of the case. Three metal combination roller locks were set in the edge near the handle.

He tugged and dragged it to the edge of the loft, where the rope that hung from the ceiling was tied. He grabbed hold of both ends of the rope and tugged hard against it to make sure the pulley in the ceiling was strong enough to hold the cases mass. Satisfied, he untied the rope and attached the hooked end to the handle of the suitcase. He held the other end of the rope and let the case swing out from the loft then he lowered it hand over hand, slowly, until it came to rest on the dirt floor.

Once the case was down Billy descended the ladder and walked over to it. He studied the case cautiously. It was old. It looked as if it had been sitting in its corner of the barn for a long time. Stains from the hay under which it had been buried were embedded into the plastic coated outer shell. The exterior did not give in when he pressed against it. It was very solid. A metal suitcase.

"There ain't no way this thing is full of cocaine or any other drug. Not with that much weight in such a little space and not for as long as this has been sitting here."

With much effort, he carried it to the van and put it in the back in a hidden storage compartment under the rear bench seat. He got back into the driver's seat, started the van and followed the driveway back to Stouderman Road. Instead of returning the way he came, he followed the road north until it came to a "T" at state route 27. This route would take him back to Dayton without the locals seeing him pass by a second time. He would be back in Columbus by four o'clock at the outside.

Billy took out his cell phone and pressed an auto dial number. The initials "JZ" appeared on the screen. A voice came on the other line.

"Sup."

"It's me."

"Man, where you been?"

"Me? I tried to get a hold of you yesterday, but you didn't answer."

"Hmm. Phone must've been on silent. Anyhow, what's going on?"

"Somethin's goin' down. Ring got me and three other guys together with that African dude and his hairy attack-dog friend. They sent the four of us out in different directions in delivery vans to get something that was hidden in different places. He gave us all kinds of crazy directions that are being automatically downloaded to a GPS each time we arrive at a checkpoint. It's like putting together a puzzle but he doesn't want us to see each piece ahead of time. I ended up in an old barn in eastern Indiana where I found a suitcase to bring back. The crazy thing weighs a ton, too. I thought it was going to be drugs, but it doesn't seem like it, unless someone found a way to process lead into a narcotic. This thing must weigh about eighty pounds and…"

The digital signal to the phone suddenly scrambled and made a wild array of electronic noises for a few seconds.

"Hello?" Billy called out, "Hello?"

"Yeah, I'm here," the voice replied. "You were saying the cases were heavy."

"Yeah, damn heavy. It's a custom metal case with three locks on the top. I don't think its drugs," said Billy.

"Where are you?"

"On S.R. twenty-seven, headed…damn!" The phone screeched loudly in Billy's ear. Its signal broke up again. After a couple more seconds of interference, the phone went completely out. Billy looked at the display on the phone and saw a red flashing stop sign that read "No Signal."

CHAPTER 15

Jajce, Bosnia-Herzegovina
September 1998

The picturesque city of Jajce is home to about 40,000 residents. It is situated among the beautiful hills and valleys at the confluence of the Pliva and Vrbas Rivers. Before the war, tourists and families on holiday frequented the point where the Pliva flows powerfully over a twenty-meter high water fall into the Vrbas. It is considered one of the jewels of the Balkans, a lovely place.

Despite its beauty the city of Jajce did not fare too well during the war. The quaint town in the beautiful setting was bombed senseless by both sides. Massive damage was inflicted to buildings and bridges throughout. Postwar reconstruction was under way, but the effort was off to a difficult start at best. Tensions between Bosnian Muslims, Croatian Catholics, and Orthodox Serbs still divided the region.

The slightest spark could easily start the war afresh, but this time there were large numbers of Russian troops in the area who had supported the Serbs. American and NATO troops were also there to support the Bosnians and Croats. Any fighting in this parklike setting almost certainly would get those troops caught in the crossfire and could potentially ignite another world war.

Johnson pulled the escort up in front of a small stucco plastered house. Most of the other homes around it were in various stages of repair and dilapidation. Hardt's motorbike was parked in a narrow space beside the house. The minivan that contained Smythe, Flynn, and Hogan was nowhere to be seen.

The two men got out of the car and walked up to the door. Johnson reached up to rap his knuckles on it, but before he could knock, the door swung open and an attractive brown-haired woman in her early twenties motioned to them.

"Come in, quickly," she whispered in English.

Hardt stood in a room that was off the hall just inside the door.

"Gentlemen, welcome to my humble abode in scenic Jajce." He greeted them and put his arm around the young woman.

"Let me introduce to you my wife, Jasna. "

"Nice to see you again, ma'am," said Johnson.

"My pleasure," said Farris.

"Mojo, it is good to see you again too, and you must be Mike Farris," Jasna replied in a smooth British accent.

Johnson glanced back and forth between the two of them. "So is this an operational marriage or the real thing, Hardt?"

Hardt motioned to a couple of couches in the room and explained as they sat down.

"Jasna really is my wife, not just part of the operation."

"Wow, when did this happen?" Johnson asked.

"We have been married for about a year now, since just after you left us last time." Hardt went on. "Her father was a Bosnian Muslim who worked with us extensively during the war to gather intelligence against both sides. He vanished last summer. About the same time her mother, a Bosnian Serb, was killed by a renegade group of Croats."

Jasna looked at Farris and said, "I am very tired of this fighting. Every time we start to get back to a normal way of life, someone comes out of the woodwork and tries to blow up our chances for peace. I want it to end. If there is anything you need from me, or the network of associates I work with, please do not hesitate to let me know."

"Well, thank you, ma'am," said Farris. "Your accent, or lack of one, is somewhat surprising. Did you go to school in England?"

"As a matter of fact, I did," she replied. "Ollie and I actually met at school there, where we both attended Queens College, Cambridge University. He was a graduate student in social sciences, and I was only an impressionable first-year fresher when we met. Just before the war, I graduated and returned home to Jajce. About two years ago he showed up here as an SAS operative, and through a strange series of coincidences we ended up like this: married and trying to avert World War Three."

"Wow, that's quite a story." Farris said.

"Yes, it is quite romantic, except for the part about people killing each other in the middle of it all." Hardt said. "Now, let's get down to business. We've only got two good working days to get to Mathis before President Yeltsin arrives."

Johnson asked, "Where are the other three men?"

"Already on the ground. Jasna's informants in the Croat section said that they saw Mathis with two other men in a café near the American military checkpoint this morning. Those three went to check on the claim. They should be back here anytime soon, unless they are onto something."

"In the meantime," asked Farris, "do we have an idea of the itinerary of the Russian President?"

"Right here," answered Jasna as she spread a topographic map of the city on the table. "He is arriving the morning after tomorrow, in a convoy driving from Banja Luka."

"He's driving from Banja Luka?" Johnson asked with a tone of surprise in his voice. "Is his protective staff insane?"

"I know. The logic doesn't click for me either, guys, but that is what our mole on his staff told us," Jasna said. "I thought it sounded crazy too, but the President wants to visit the Jajce outpost, and the airfield here is still a mess; even helicopter traffic is closed for the next few weeks."

"What is so important about Jajce that the Russian President is insisting on coming here?" asked Johnson.

"It seems," answered Hardt, "that the commander of the Russian-army observers unit in the area is his nephew."

"Why not tell them that there is a threat and let them deal with it?" asked Farris.

"Because," Hardt replied, "they would then realize that we have a mole in their operation, otherwise we could not have known that Yeltsin was coming here."

"Understood," Farris said. "Do we know who our enemies on the ground are, locally I mean?"

"We don't know just which local group the Sons of the Sword are working with," Jasna said. "Bosnian Muslims, Kosovar Albanians, or one of the many splinter militias running around, but we do know that their main goal is to reignite a religious war, and they are working overtime at getting us and the Russians to start shooting at each other."

"Alright then, let's get a look at this map and see if we can second guess Mathis."

"You are the expert on him, Mike," said Hardt, "so I will defer to you on the best probable way to find him."

Jasna traced her finger along a blue line on the map that followed the main road, E761 from Banja Luka to Jajce.

"He is coming in on the main highway, up to this point. The Russian observers have got this checkpoint manned for the next week, it is their scheduled turn among the UN forces there."

"It's pretty crowded in that area. He'd probably want to be in the nearby buildings, you think?" Hardt said.

Farris scratched at his scalp for a second and said, "Don't be sure of that. Mathis loves distance. I was his spotter once when he took out a Columbian drug smuggler from more than a mile away. No distance is safe from Mathis."

"A mile away is pretty good, but this is fairly hilly country. He will be lucky to have three seconds to get a sight picture and pull the trigger in most spots along this highway before the target is behind cover again," replied Hardt.

"He can do it. That smuggler was on a boat moving in the waves of the Caribbean. He was a mile out to sea, and Mathis got him from a hide on shore." Farris said.

"OK," said Hardt, "where do you think he will strike?"

"Biggest audience." Farris said, "If the point of this is to start a world war he will do it where people can see Yeltsin go down, and the best way to start a war would be to do it in the area under US or UK observation in order to point the finger at us."

"It is possible that he may break his own preferences and do the shot from close up," Johnson said, "but I think he'll probably have a patsy standing nearby in American or British uniform and holding a smoking gun while he takes the shot from a safer distance."

Hardt outlined the areas on the map that were under US and UK observation. Farris and Johnson stared contemplatively at the map for some time then came up with four possible locations they thought suited for the type of attack Mathis would try. Of those, two stood out as preferred choices with best field of fire and cover, as well as plausible escape routes. They agreed that they would stake out those spots with two-man teams and have a couple of other men check the secondary spots.

The door swung open. Smythe, Flynn, and Hogan, who had been checking out the lead on Mathis at the café, came into the house.

"Gents, Mrs. Hardt," greeted Smythe. "He wasn't there by the time we arrived, but we did see two men we recognized from the Sons of the Sword there, and they were both in American uniforms."

"They were just sitting back and enjoying a beer while the crowd milled around them," Hogan said. "Several real American soldiers were in the area too, and they had made friendly conversation with them. I overheard them say that they were up here on liberty to see the waterfall. They spoke with perfect American accents. One said he was from Baltimore, the other from the Midwest."

"They are either his security team or they may be the fall guys," Farris said. "Keep an eye on those two and see where they frequent. That will probably be the area Mathis will try for the shot."

CHAPTER 16

Wednesday, October 26th
FBI Regional Headquarters
Office of the Ohio Valley Anti-Terrorist Task Force
15:30 Hours

Farris, Hogan, Hilde, and Fleiss carefully studied the surveillance videos. They poured over the details of the vehicles and as much as they could see of the men's faces. Fleiss put the hairy man's hand motion sequence in a loop that repeated itself on one of the monitors.

"That guy is the same one I saw on the porch the evening I went to turn off Cold Bones' lights," said Farris. "At that time, I thought it was crazy, but I could've sworn he saw me, and he winked."

"That'd be Kharzai alright." Hogan said.

"So who is he?" Hilde asked.

"I knew him in Iraq." Hogan answered. "He was a deep cover CIA operative who had penetrated several insurgent cells. He somehow managed to get into a junior leadership position and lead a company sized element of them in a pretty big attack against a regiment of Marines in An Nassiriya. The thing is, he called us ahead of time and said where, when, and how many they would be. Our commander wouldn't believe him when he offered to lead us to the soft flanks of the bad

149

guys, so in the middle of the battle he hooked up with some British royal marine's buddies of his and led them right into the soft underbelly of the insurgents and their republican guard backup. Thousands of tangos went to their virgins that day, all thanks to that insane madman. He was the sole survivor of the group he brought in to us."

"Wow," said Fleiss. "Sounds like a movie or something."

"Yeah well, after the battle I got to know Kharzai pretty well. He gave us a lot of really good intel, including Saddam and his generals' locations on several occasions."

Hogan slowly shook his head side to side as the memory of the man flooded back in.

"Kharzai was more like a movie...no...I take that back. He was more like a comic book character, than a real person. Somehow, after the slaughter in An Nassiriya, he not only survived, but returned to the insurgent group he supposedly served and got promoted. They called him Seirim Al Gul. The Hairy Demon. He managed to convince them that he had survived by some kind of miracle. He proved it by bringing back battlefield souvenirs. The heads of a couple of the British officers and Iraqi turncoats. As well as the head and testicles of the man he told them had led the British to their positions."

"He brought them British officer's heads?" Farris asked.

"No, not really. He told me later that it was just some poor Iraqi blokes he found dead by the road. They looked vaguely western: one had blue-green eyes, and the other had light hair. He cut off their heads and let the sun swell them up a bit."

"Gross," said Hilde.

"Yeah, well, that's war for you." Hogan replied. "The guy that he said was the traitor was actually the commander of the republican guard detachment we had fought against. Saddam had the guy's whole family killed for the supposed betrayal."

"Dear God!" said Hilde.

"And you are sure this is the same guy?"

"Unmistakable. That thing he was doing with the hand signs, that was a thing a bunch of us made up for a brigade talent show on our second tour around Christmas of o-three. He showed up out of the blue and joined us. It spelled out USMC and also involved a Haka dance, or at least our sloppy variation of one. The Kiwis and Australians who were serving with us laughed their asses off at the crazy man with the full head of hair."

"Do you think Kharzai is Martin's inside man?" asked Mike.

"Doubtful," answered Hogan. "Kharzai doesn't work for locals, especially not cops. He doesn't trust them. Based on the signs he was giving, I'm under the impression he knew or assumed that I would be watching that video."

"Should we tell Martin?" asked Hilde.

"No," Hogan said, "not yet."

A woman's voice suddenly screamed.

"Phone!"

Everyone except Andy jumped at the sound. Hilde yelped, and Farris and Hogan both spun towards the door, hands reaching to the pistols in their shoulder holsters. Andy grinned and rose from his chair.

"Chill, folks. Man, you guys are tense."

The voice screamed again.

"Phone!"

"Holy Crap!" Paul Hogan said as the tone made him jump again. "That's a freakin' scary ring tone, Andy."

"Sorry, that's my sister's voice. I set it loud enough to hear if I have earphones on."

Fleiss answered the phone just as the voice started into a third scream.

"Yeah, he's here. Who's calling for him?"

He listened.

"Oh, OK. Agent Hogan, it's for you. Detective Martin."

Hogan took the handset from Fleiss and spoke into the phone.

"Hogan here."

"Paul, this is Dan Martin."

"Yeah, how'd you get this number?"

"I didn't. I called the front desk, and they transferred me. Cell phones are down all over the place right now. Some kind of solar flare killed the satellites."

"Did you find something?"

"Maybe, the inside man we've got on Cold Bones just called his controller. He said that the call died mid-conversation, but the guy told him, and I quote, *'Ring got me and three other guys together with that African dude and his hairy attack dog friend. They sent the four of us out in different directions in delivery vans to get something that was hidden in different places. He gave us all kinds of crazy directions that are being automatically downloaded to a GPS when we arrive at a series of checkpoints. It's like putting together a puzzle, but he doesn't want us to see each piece ahead of time. I ended up in an old barn in eastern Indiana where I found a suitcase to bring back. The crazy thing ways a ton, too. I thought it was going to be drugs, but it doesn't seem like it, unless someone found a way to process lead into a narcotic. This thing must weigh about eighty pounds.'"*

"An eighty-pound suitcase, huh?" Hogan asked.

"Yeah, and there are four of them."

"Potentially."

"What?"

"Potentially there are four of them; the other vans may have been decoys."

"Yeah, maybe."

"Do you want to come down to my office and join us for a brain storming session?"

"I'll be there in twenty minutes."

"Don't speed."

"I'm a cop."

"Then use your flashy light thing."

Hogan hung up the phone then turned to the others. "What is eighty pounds, fits in a suitcase, and may have been stored in an old barn in eastern Indiana?"

"What?" asked Hilde.

"What is eighty pounds, fits in a suitcase, and may have been stored in an old barn in eastern Indiana?" He repeated.

"Is this a rhetorical question or a joke?" asked Farris.

"Shit!" Fleiss shouted, "Oh, Man...shit...shit...shit!" Fleiss slammed his fist onto the desk.

"What?" demanded Hilde, surprised by his outburst.

"The damned satellite just dropped our tracers!" Fleiss jumped from his chair and paced frantically and pressed his fingers into his stress wrinkled forehead and then on through his hair. "The signal was there, went fuzzy, came back, then blamo! It dropped totally, and now the computer is giving me an error!"

Farris looked at the screens. An error message scrolled in continuously repeated lines up the LCD display.

"What's wrong with it?"

"I think it was a solar flare, and hopefully its only temporary, but I'm going to have to reboot the computer to get the satellite back online."

"That was Martin on the phone just now; he said the cell phone network is down due to a solar flare as well. Must have been the same thing. See what you can do."

"Damn it!" said Fleiss, red faced with frustration. "NOAA is supposed to warn us of those things! I mean they get like four freaking days warning before they hit! Man, I hope someone's head rolls for this."

"Chill, Andy," said Hilde. "Just chill a bit, ok? I never knew you had such a temper."

"Aren't you concerned about finding that van?" Fleiss replied, flustered.

"Of course, I am," she answered, "but we don't even know what's in it yet. They may just be a diversion."

"Diversion? Yeah maybe one or two of them, but at least one of them has a nuclear device on it!"

"What are you talking about? We never said that," said Hogan. "How do you know?"

"I don't know, but I can assume, and I make my living based on my assumptions."

Farris looked at the young man and said, "Explain your assumption."

Fleiss inhaled deeply and let the breath come in a calming whoosh from pursed lips.

"In nineteen-ninety-one, a Russian KGB colonel named Stanislav Lunev defected to the US. He gave the CIA a list of about thirty potential sites on US soil where Soviet spies may have placed suitcase nuclear devices in the mid to late eighties. He did not know which sites were used, but he knew the exact location of each site and that there were to be twelve weapons stashed here for retrieval in the event of war. Each one of these weapons is basically a ball of radioactive material surrounded by a detonator and shielding. It weighs between sixty and eighty pounds and fits in a regular-sized suitcase."

"How do you know all of that?" Hogan asked. "You were only in elementary school in 1991."

"Middle school actually, and my dad was an officer in the Ohio militia back then, he kept all of these books around, and I happened to read some of them. One of them was a book by Colonel Lunev written just before he died of cancer in nineteen-ninety-five. He was frustrated that the CIA didn't act on his warning. I checked into the story later as an adult, after I got my clearance, and found out that the documents he had turned in got lost in nineteen-ninety-eight. Someone stole them from the CIA's files. I would be surprised if they didn't turn up in Al Qaeda hands pretty soon after disappearing."

"Dear God," said Hilde, "let's put traces on that radiation then, and get that thing tracked down."

"We can't; it's in a sealed case," said Fleiss. "The only time that radiation will be visible is when they open the case to arm the bomb. Then you've got about fifteen or twenty minutes to find the radiation signature and get to the bomb before it goes off."

Farris nodded pensively. "And it could be anywhere in the country by then."

Hogan let out a sigh. He stretched his neck side to side and squeezed his fingers into tight fists then released them and stretched the fingers out again.

"Work on that computer signal, Andy. See if you can get the satellite back online."

"You two," he pointed at Mike and Hilde, "let's get up to my office and think this thing out. Martin's on the way. He should be here in about ten minutes. Let's try to figure out what they are planning to do with this thing. If Fleiss is right, we don't have much time."

CHAPTER 17

Wednesday, October 26th
FBI Regional Headquarters
Office of the Ohio Valley Anti-Terrorist Task Force
16:25 Hours

Dan Martin entered Hogan's office harried and flustered.

"Sorry it took so long. Traffic is totally snarled on the beltway. I tried to call, but the cell phones are still out."

Hogan looked up from his desk and said, "No problem, Danny boy, come on in. We've got more worries than phones being out. Take a chair."

Detective Martin sat in a simple brown leather armchair next to Farris. Rottbruck sat in a third chair on the other side of Mike. One more chair was empty next to her.

"This thing is through the roof, Dan." Hogan said.

"Like how?" asked Martin.

"Usein may have a nuclear device," answered Hogan.

"Holy shit," mumbled Martin. A shocked look spread across his face.

"That's not all," said Hilde. "We lost the signal on all of our tracking devices when the solar flares hit the satellites."

"You were tracking them?" asked Martin.

"Yeah, our onsite surveillance team saw the vans leave this morning. They managed to get tracking chips on them before they pulled out," Hilde replied.

"But it's not doing us any good right now with the communications satellites down," Hogan said.

"Can't you follow them by radio signals or something?" Martin asked.

"No," Hilde replied, "too weak and mobile, we'd have to have our own vehicle within line of sight at all times to track them properly."

"So what does this mean then?" Martin asked in a hushed voice.

Hilde looked down at the carpeted floor.

"We have no idea where these vans may be."

"So," said Hogan, "we need to figure out what potential targets Usein would hit with a small nuclear device in the immediate future."

There was a sharp knock at the door. Before Hogan could reply, it suddenly swung open. Andy Fleiss stepped quickly in.

"Agent Hogan, I've got bad news. The signal on those vans is not coming back. The flare damaged a board on the satellite. When the board blew, it was in communication with the chips and probably sent a high voltage signal that must've blown them. I managed to commandeer a different satellite signal, but can't find the chips."

"Ok," said Hogan, "we'll need to do this the old-fashioned way then."

Farris turned to look up at Fleiss, "How powerful is one of those suitcase nukes?"

"Between one and five kilotons. Enough to utterly destroy two city blocks, damage six to eight mor,e and spread enough radiation to make a fifty-square mile area uninhabitable for a long time."

Hilde crunched her eyebrows as she looked at Fleiss and asked, "Andy, how in the world do you know so much about these things? I thought you were a computer science major."

"I had a dual major," he responded, "computer science and nuclear physics."

"You're a nuclear physicist?" Martin asked. "What in the world are you doing working here?"

"I found out that an IT Specialist with the FBI makes almost the same salary as a nuclear physicist, but here, I get to play with a lot more cool toys and hang out with people who don't wear pocket protectors when they go to the clubs at night. For that matter, I get to hang out with people who go to clubs at night instead of working on physics problems until oh-dark-thirty."

"Oh," said Hogan, "that makes sense. At any rate, I'm glad you're here. Why don't you stay and sit with us for a bit. Maybe you can be of more use here, since your satellite's broken anyway."

Fleiss sat in the last available chair and joined the conversation.

"Ok, folks," said Hogan, "based on the presence of Usein and Whorley on Sunday, we know that Ohio Stadium is a possible target. If that was their target, when would it be?"

"Saturday," Fleiss said bluntly.

"Saturday?" asked Hilde. "You mean this weekend?"

"Of course! The OSU-Michigan game," Martin said. "Dear God! There will be over two-hundred-thousand people in the OSU stadium area; what a perfect target!"

"That's not for two more weeks," said Hogan. "The admin office sent out a notice of a ticket raffle."

"Yeah, I saw that email too. November twelfth is the game," Hilde said.

Martin looked at them wide eyed, "Your email is wrong. The past several years it has been the second Saturday of

November, but this year there was some conflict on the Michigan schedule, and they moved it to October twenty-ninth, this Saturday."

"Yeah," Fleiss added, "I got tickets."

"If a nuke was set off in that stadium it would make 9/11 seem like a tea party," said Farris.

"Before we conclude that this is their target, as obvious as it sounds," Hogan said, "could there be any other possible targets in the area? And let's not just keep it to Ohio, let's look at everything. They could transport this thing almost anywhere in the country in three days."

"Well, at least we have phone contact with one of the drivers," Farris said. "He can keep us up to date on the location of his device."

"You think there may be multiple devices?" asked Martin. "They've got four vehicles running."

"Not likely," said Fleiss. "There were only a handful of those devices hidden here according to Lunev. They'd be scattered all around the country."

"Let's figure it out folks."

"I'll get some analysts on it right away, Paul," Hilde said. She rose from her chair and headed to the door. "They're not going to like working late at such last-minute notice, though."

"Too bad," Hogan said flatly. She walked out of the room and briskly moved down the hallway towards her office.

Fleiss got up and followed her.

"I'm going to check on those chips," he said as he walked out the door.

Hogan continued, "Danny, can you notify the university area precincts and the highway patrol to be on extra high alert for those vans? We need to find them ASAP."

"Will do," Martin replied.

"But," added Hogan, "don't mention nukes. I don't want this info to leak to the press; it would cause a massive panic that would make it almost impossible to find this thing."

"Got it. I'll only tell them to put out an APB on the blue vans," Martin said as he rose to leave.

"Danny," Hogan called to him one more time, "thanks for the help. You're a good cop."

Martin turned to face him and nodded as he walked out the door. When it closed behind him Hogan looked over to Farris. His eyes flickered with excitement.

"Mike, do you feel like doing some recon tonight?"

"Sure, what've you got in mind?" Farris answered.

"Let's see if we can make Usein show himself a little early, make him start looking over his shoulder."

CHAPTER 18

Chrissie Fine was five-feet tall, blond haired, hazel eyed, and very petite. The twenty-one-year-old college student at Ohio State University was the leader of the teen girls group at Faith Presbyterian Church. She was also a member of the OSU Campus Evangelism Team of Youth for Christ.

Chrissie had grown up in Faith church and loved Pastor Farris like a treasured uncle. When he first came to the church she had even fantasized, as twelve-year-old girls sometimes do, that the muscular, handsome, and very single pastor was like a knight in shining armor, a heroic Lancelot riding up to save her from the dragons of the day.

His preaching was fiery, his personality engaging, and unlike the stereotype of most Presbyterian pastors he knew how to have fun. Whenever the youth group was out playing soccer or volleyball, he made time to be there and often joined in the game. He loved to play with the little children of the congregation, and those little children seemed completely at ease, safe, and secure when he was near. Pastor Mike was compassionate without effort. He always took time

161

to listen to the fears and concerns of anyone who asked for his attention and was wise in dispensing advice.

When Chrissie was eighteen, she, like most of the single women in the church, had her heart broken when Pastor Mike introduced his new sweetheart Janelle. The heartbreak was very short lived though as Janelle turned out to be just as fun and engaging as her husband, and when Mini-Mike was born, he became the center of attention. Never was the tike without companionship at church or any other function. Anytime Mike and Janelle wanted to go out for a date, there was no shortage of willing and available babysitters among the two-dozen teenage girls and college-age women of the church.

All of that came crashing down when a car full of gangsters shot up the pastor's house, killing Janelle and Mini-Mike in an instant along with LeRon and putting poor Li'l Mac in the coma in which he still suffered.

Chrissie had seen it all happen. She had just finished a late meeting with her teen girls group. The last students had left the parking lot by the time she headed out. She had stopped to make sure the door was locked. The car came screeching around the corner and opened fire on the Farris's house in the hazy twilight of early dusk. Fear had completely immobilized her. Her body was frozen in shock. She had found herself unable to move or scream or even blink. The whole world stopped its rotation. The wind stopped moving. Time ceased to pass.

No one saw her there in the dark vestibule of the church where she hid and watched as the police and ambulances arrived. After the scene cleared, she made her way out the side door and left quietly from a rear exit of the parking lot. Chrissie told no one that she had been a witness to the murder of Janelle Farris and her toddler son, Mike Jr.

The guilt of her own silence had eaten Chrissie up since that horrible nightmare had passed. She reasoned within herself that there was nothing more could she have told them but the obvious. The sun was just below the horizon. It was dark and shadowy. She didn't know what kind of car it was. She hadn't seen the license plate. She had no information to give them anyway. She was just a silly girl shocked by the horror of what she had been forced to witness. She had seen nothing of value. Nothing that is, except the face of one of the shooters. She didn't know how she saw it across the distance. It had been more than fifty-yards away.

After the shooting stopped, the gunman in the back seat of the car had turned and looked directly at her as they drove off. He couldn't have seen her in the shadows of the church entrance. At least, she hoped that he didn't, but she saw him. Every detail of his face stayed fresh in her mind. It stared at her when she closed her eyes to sleep at night no matter how hard she willed it away.

Chrissie thought about going to the police with the description, but the overwhelming fear of being found by those cold-blooded killers froze her will to say anything. Her parents were away in Argentina on a missionary trip for the next six months. She was all alone in their big house with no protection. She did not want to be caught by herself by the kind of thugs that may come after her. No, she would keep quiet and hope that the police would find those terrible men soon.

Chrissie drove to the OSU campus to meet with her friends, Maria and Song Yi. The University Arts department was hosting a big hip-hop concert featuring local bands and singers at the arena. The girls thought it would be a perfect field to spread the word of God's love to the masses of spiritually-hungry youth that would be there.

The plan was to pass out gospel tracts and flyers at the Saint John's Arena parking lot and hopefully strike up some good conversation that could lead to one-on-one evangelism. Those kinds of personal contacts always had a good measure of success in inviting new people hungry for a sense of belonging and tired of the drugs and booze of college culture to their campus Bible study.

She arrived just after 7:30 and parked her old Honda Civic, its hatch back covered with more than two-dozen gospel bumper stickers and christian band stickers, in the Tuttle Parking Garage between the arena and the Ohio Stadium. She called Maria on her cell phone.

"Me and Song Yi are already at the arena talking with some people in line. Hurry up, we've got a pretty good conversation going on here."

"OK, I'll meet you there in a few minutes."

Chrissie smiled at the news of such a good start to the night's outreach. She locked her car and headed out of the garage. Half way between the garage and the arena, she crossed Woody Hayes Drive. As she stepped up from the road onto the curb of the sidewalk a cluster of men ahead glanced her way. A flutter of terror raced through her abdomen.

There he stood. Under a streetlight talking to three other men. The gunman who killed Janelle and Mini-Mike. He glanced in her direction. She froze in fear, staring wide eyed at this man who ended the happy life of the family she most looked up to.

"What you looking at, bitch?" He shouted at her. "Ain't you never seen a black man before?"

"Oh, I uh, I'm sorry." Her voice shook out the reply. She turned away, her pace quick and nervous, like a small animal trapped by a carnivore.

"I asked you a question, bitch!" His voice called angrily after her. "Don't you walk away from me, you white whore!"

Chrissie heard a rush of footsteps. She turned and found the killer and his three friends coming up behind her. She tried to run, but it was too late. The killer grabbed her hair from behind before she took two more steps.

She screamed. Her body trembled in pain and fear.

"Please, let me go!" she begged. "I thought you were someone else, that's all! Please let me go!"

She began to sob uncontrollably.

"Oh! You thought I was someone else, did you?" he said slowly. He pulled her tiny body close against his own and spoke in a deep soft voice. "Now, who did you think I was… baby? Hmmm?"

"I know who she thinks you are, G-man." said a skinny, young white man with a shaved head and dark sunken eyes. "She thinks you're her lover. She thought you was the one who made her do the black snake moan."

All three of G-man's friends laughed like fiends.

"Oh yeah?" G-man looked lustfully down her blouse, "You like the black snake, don't you, blondie?"

"Please," she whimpered, "just let me go. Please?"

"Yeah, baby, but you gotta do me a favor first." He reached around her with his free hand and groped at her small breast. Her nipples were hard but not with excitement. Her body quivered like a small tree being shaken at its roots. A terrified whimper escaped her lips.

He snickered, "There ain't much there, but I'm sure you got plenty to share between me and my friends."

"Oh God! Please, no!"

G-man signaled to the others, and one of them grabbed her other arm firmly. The two of them lifted her small frame off the ground and quickly carried her to the shadows in a dark recess behind Schoenbaum Hall.

Chrissie struggled to make a noise, to call for help, but her voice was caught in her throat. Finally, she let out a high-pitched scream. It was immediately met with a hard slap across her face. Her head spun. She nearly lost consciousness. Two of the men held her down to the ground by her arms as G-man grabbed roughly at her body.

The skinny white man reached down to pull her slacks off. She suddenly exploded with a burst of primal energy and jammed her foot into his groin. Her shin made solid contact with his testicles. The blow sent the skinhead to the ground with a guttural grunt, eyes tightly squeezed against the excruciating pain. G-man laughed at his friend's predicament. Still laughing he looked back at Chrissie.

"You shouldn't have done that."

Then he drew back his fist and punched her in the stomach. The force of the blow sent the wind out of her lungs in an audible wheeze. Her face turned deep purple as she struggled to force her lungs to draw in a breath.

"You stupid bitch!" screamed the white man, still doubled over. "You stupid bitch! I'm gonna kill you for that!"

"Shut up, Allie! Shut up or you'll get us all caught!" whispered one of the other men hoarsely.

A voice called out from the darkness behind them. "Now, what do we have here, Major?"

"Well, Gunny," came the reply, "it looks to me like we have an unfair advantage. Don't you think?"

"I do think."

G-man's head shot up towards the source of the voices.

"Who the hell are you?" he blurted.

The men holding Chrissie down spun around, still gripping her arms. G-Man squinted at the shadows of two men approaching him.

"Mind your own business, if you know what's good for you."

"But this is my business, friend," said the taller shadow.

"Get off the girl," said the short, stocky shadow.

They continued walking forward.

"Get'em boys!" replied G-man. "Ain't no hero gonna ruin my party!"

The men who had been holding Chrissie's arms down rose and charged toward the two shadows. Allie tried to stand, but his balls throbbed, and he remained hunched over in pain.

As the thugs drew closer, Mike Farris suddenly lunged forward and drove his fist into the throat of the man nearest him. The impact made a thick-sounding audible crunch, like chicken bones being crushed in a vise. The man instantly dropped to his knees clasping his hands on this throat and gasping for air through his shattered windpipe.

The other man took a running step towards Hogan only to have his feet taken out from under him as the FBI agent dropped low and swept a straight leg in an arc over the ground and into the man's ankles. The young man hit the ground with a heavy thud. Hogan deftly stood back up and kicked him on the side the head. The man's jaw shattered with a sickening crack. He made no move to get up. His body lay in a limp pile on the pavement.

The two shadows moved towards G-man and Allie.

"Shit!" exclaimed Allie. He pulled up his shirt and reached into his waistband for the pistol he had kept hidden there. Before the young gangster could pull his weapon out Hogan took three swift steps and had his forty-five out and pointed at Allie's pale shaved head.

"Put your hands up where I can see them," Hogan said in a quiet yet firm voice, "or I will kill you here."

"Who are you?" stammered G-man, "Cops?"

"What difference does that make?" asked Hogan.

"I got rights!" said G-man, "You'd better show me some badges, cops!"

"You've only got the rights I say you've got," said Farris, "and at the moment, I'm debating taking away your right to breathe."

"This is shit," said Allie, "we pay you guys enough to keep off our backs!"

"Excuse me?" asked Hogan.

"Shut the hell up, Allie," shouted G-man, "You stupid ass!"

G-man turned towards the two men in front of him, "You ain't cops, are you?"

"Worse," said Farris, "we're Marines."

G-man dropped his head and mumbled, "Mister White ain't gonna like this shit!"

Farris and Hogan both turned their eyes to G-man.

"What did you say?" asked Mike Farris.

"If you do anything to me, Mister White will have your balls for dinner before you can blink."

"Really?"

"Yeah, really," added Allie. "You fools don't know who you're messing with, coming in on Mister White's territory. I don't care what gang you say you're from. He's bigger than the Mafia, and your balls are his!"

Hogan stepped in closer to Allie whose hands were still in the air. The young thug stood in a partially crouched position, his groin obviously still in a serious state of discomfort. Hogan swiftly moved his left knee up and made contact with Allie's already tender private parts. The young man collapsed to the ground with a cry of pain. He balled up in a fetal position and puked what little contents his stomach contained onto the cement.

Farris went over to G-man who stood defiantly with his arms across his chest. As Mike came close G-man slowly took his arms down, expecting Farris to make a move. Before he could be ready Mike's fist slammed into the rapist's stomach. G-man doubled over, gasping for air.

"How does it feel, girly man?" Farris asked. "Since you like beating up little girls, how about if I give you a dose of your own medicine?"

Farris dragged the gasping G-man over to the girl. She had caught her breath and was sitting up on the ground, watching the scene around her in confusion. The girl was darkened by the shadows of the building cast by the distant lights that glowed brightly in the distance behind her. Mike was not able to see the details of her face. From Chrissie's perspective, she could clearly see him.

"Pastor Mike?"

"Who are you?" Farris was surprised by the sound of his own name.

"Its me! Chrissie Fine!" she started to sob uncontrollably. "Oh, Pastor Mike! Thank God! Thank God it's you!"

"Chrissie?" his voice sounded with alarm. "Chrissie, what are you doing here?"

She spoke rapidly.

"We were doing evangelism, me and some friends from the Campus Evangelism Team, and…and…this guy tried to rape me!"

Her sobs choked the words. She tried to catch her breath.

Mike looked down at G-man's face. He twisted the back of the thug's shirt tightly, pulling it against his throat.

"You tried to rape one of my church members? Things are looking pretty bad for you, punk."

Mike's voice was low and terrifying. Panic widened in G-man's eyes. He tried to pull away to run. At the rearward jerk Farris reacted by swiftly reaching up with his other hand and grabbing G-man's trachea with the tips of his fingers. His ironlike grip nearly crushed the man's windpipe.

"Don't move!"

G-man's eyes bulged, and his tongue stretched out of his mouth as he tried in vain to breath.

"Pastor Mike," Chrissie cried out, "there's more! He's the one who killed Janelle and Mini-Mike and LeRon! He's the one who shot them! I saw him do it!"

Farris froze. He stared into G-man's terrified eyes. Hatred boiled inside him. He released his grip just enough for the man to suck a lung full of air. Mike's fingers slid up into base of G-man's jaw. He squeezed, slowly crushing the man's tonsils inward.

In the moment of silence, Hogan finished cuffing the moaning Allie where he lay on the hard pavement. He rose and walked toward Farris and the others.

"How do you know this, ma'am?" Hogan asked.

"I saw it the night that it happened, but I thought he saw me too, and I was too afraid to say anything, because I thought the gang would come after me."

She wept the words, nearly hysterical, as she tried to get it all out in a fast stream without spaces between them.

"I am so sorry, Pastor Mike. I am sorry I didn't say anything that night, but I was too scared. Then I saw him tonight as I crossed the street, and when I stared at him, he attacked me, and I thought it was because he recognized me."

"Alright, Chrissie," Mike said, in a calm pastoral voice, his grip still tight on G-man's throat. His face was only inches from G-man's. He stared into his panic-stricken eyes. Mike spoke with a voice that sounded detached. G-man thought that the gentle sounding, comforting voice could not be coming from the killer that now held him in a death grip. "Calm down. It's alright now; we have it under control."

Hogan knelt down to Chrissie. She collapsed into his arms, and she wept uncontrollably onto his shoulder. He whispered to her gently.

"It's alright ma'am. We'll take care of it. You're safe now."

"Bitch is lying!" G-man squeaked from his constricted throat. "I ain't killed no preacher's wife!"

"How do you know she was a preacher's wife?" Farris muttered in a low rumble.

"I was ordered to!" G-man said in desperation. "Let me go and I'll tell you everything!"

Farris felt around G-man's waistband until he found a pistol tucked in the small of the gangsters back. He pulled the nine-millimeter handgun out with his left hand, clicked the hammer back, and put it to the side of G-man's head.

"You killed my wife and my son and my friend."

He whispered in a harsh raspy voice. The young man in his grip trembled.

"Why should I let you live?"

"I was ordered to! Mister White and Cold Bones ordered me to!" he choked the words out. "Please don't kill me and I'll tell you everything!"

"You will tell," Farris said, "or I will kill you."

A puddle suddenly pooled around G-man's knees. The acrid odor of fresh urine rose to their nostrils.

CHAPTER 19

Thursday, October 27th
Mister White's warehouse
Columbus, Ohio
08:45 Hours

The image on the TV screen stayed motionless for what seemed like an eternity. Allie fidgeted nervously. His palms scrubbed against his thighs, and he scratched at random itches that came up all over his body. His right knee bounced up and down spastically as he stared at the floor.

"So, Allie," Mister White began. The Darth Vader voice filter sounded ominously melodramatic. "Tell me again what G-man said to those two men."

"He said that if they didn't kill him, he would tell them everything." Allie muttered.

He slouched in the chair. Exhaustion from walking halfway across the city after having his balls crushed, twice, ebbed from his body as he spoke to his boss.

"Speak Up!" Mister White shouted.

Allie flinched, his body jumping in the chair.

"Show some self-respect and don't mumble!"

"I said," Allie raised his head in weak defiance and spoke louder, looking up at the camera, "that G-man said he would tell them everything if they didn't kill him!"

"Better. Speak with self-confidence and you will go much farther in life, Mister Allie," Mister White replied. "Those men, were they police officers?"

"No, sir," said Allie. "They said they wasn't cops, but they was from some other gang. From California, I think. They said they was Marins. Ain't there a Marin County?"

"Marins?" White asked. "Are you sure that's what they said?"

"That's what they said, but they pronounced it funny. I ain't never heard of that gang though. Maybe they was Mexican, but they looked white."

"Marines?"

"Yeah, that's how they said it. 'Marines' was what they called their selves."

"Of course, Allie," Mister White replied in a reassuring tone. "Tell me more."

"When the tall guy was about to bust up G-man, the girl suddenly recognized him and called him Pastor Mike. Then she said that G-man was the one who killed some bitch and her kid, and the tall guy got really pissed. He started to strangle G-man then put a gun to his head, said something to him I couldn't hear, and then G-man pissed in his pants. Dude really had him scared."

"The girl called him Pastor Mike?" asked Mister White.

"Yes, sir," Allie replied. "Then they cuffed up G and let me go. When the short guy took off my cuffs, he told me to tell you what happened, or he would find me and kill me too."

"Are you afraid that they may come back for you, Allie?" Mister White asked.

"Those dudes was tough, sir. They busted up Markie and Theo so fast those guys didn't know what hit them. Whoever they are, they are seriously bad ass," replied the trembling gangster.

"Don't worry, my son," Mister White said in a calm even voice, "you work for me, and I always take care of my people. Sit tight; we will have you under protection in a short time. Don't leave the building, I am sending a car to come for you and take you to a safe place until this all blows over."

"Yes, sir," replied Allie. "Thank you, sir. I really want to get those two assholes back. I owe them."

"Of course, you do, Allie," said Mister White. "You will have your day."

The screen went blank, and the monitor descended back into the wooden cabinet. Allie waited patiently in the room for fifteen minutes. He jerked with surprise when his cell phone rang in his pocket. He took it out, flipped it open, and spoke into the microphone.

"What?"

"Come outside," said a deep voice on the other end.

The wiry white gangster picked himself up from the chair. He struggled to force his legs to stop trembling as he walked to the outer door of the warehouse. As he opened it, he saw the massive form of Lucas Ring waiting for him beside a long blue Lincoln.

"Ringmaster!" he said with a relieved smile. "You are a sight, man. Let's get out of here."

"You sure know how to get yourself into trouble, don't you, little man?" Ring said grinning.

Lucas reached out to shake Allie's hand. Allie accepted it. The smaller man had no chance to cry out as the Ringmaster grasped his bony hand and deftly spun him into a headlock. Lucas snapped Allie's neck in a single motion. It took almost no effort. The young man instantly went limp like a rag doll. Lucas Ring hoisted Allie's lifeless form onto his shoulder with little effort and tossed the body into the trunk of his car. He closed the lid and drove off to dispose of the scrawny punk in a distant wooded area.

CHAPTER 20

Jajce, Bosnia-Herzegovina
September 1998

The hot summer sun hung at its late-in-the-afternoon spot in the clear blue sky. Waves of heat danced off the asphalt pavement of highway E761. Johnson drove the blue Ford Escort along the route they had been told President Yeltsin would take. As he drove, they discussed with each other every vulnerable position along the route from Banja Luka to Jajce.

There were too many vulnerabilities to count. On their side though, was the fact that the Sons of the Sword wanted to get a lot of media coverage. They wanted to spark a world war. Therefore, Johnson and Farris both agreed that the hit would most likely be in the city, where the whole world would see it.

They made their way back into the city of Jajce and wound through its narrow streets. Within a few minutes they were at the checkpoint nearest the café where Hogan and the others had seen the two terrorists that morning. It was a crowded square with soldiers of several nations milling around among locals who enjoyed their daily business.

Johnson parked the Escort at the curb about twenty meters from the coffee shop. He and Farris, both dressed in civilian attire, got out of their vehicle and walked into the café. They ordered two coffees and sat down at a table on the sidewalk from which they could observe the surrounding neighborhood.

"So Mojo," Farris said, "what do you think? Could this be the place?"

"Could be," Johnson replied. He pointed a finger towards the sloping hillside opposite them. Houses were built all the way up the hill, most with good visibility into the street in front of them. "There's a lot of good positions all over that hillside and up there for a half mile or more. Whoever chose this spot for a checkpoint needs to be spanked…hard. This is practically indefensible against sniper attacks."

"Agreed," replied the Captain. "So if you were him, where would you put yourself up there?"

The pair quietly scanned the area for several minutes as they sipped at the strong dark roasted coffee.

Johnson then replied, "Well, sir, it looks to me like the best possible locations up there, at least from this vantage point. That cluster of houses over there to the left seems likely. There seem to be few people milling around up there who might see something, and no children who might stumble into the hide and make a scene. Otherwise, that office building straight ahead, the one with the broken windows may be a likely place. Everything else seems to have too many people to make a safe retreat."

"And with as much money as he has been paid," said Farris, "we can be certain that Mathis wants to make a good retreat."

"Here is how I see it then," said Johnson. "The two guys Smythe, Hogan, and Flynn watched this morning will be in the square, either for sight verification that the target is dead or maybe as fall guys who'll go to martyrdom to make the mission work. Mathis fires from up there somewhere, waits for the signal from his guys down here then splits, Or maybe just splits and doesn't wait around."

"That sounds about right," Farris said. "Let's get the rest of the team up and into that area to scout around and see if we can find where Mathis might be setting up. We've got less than thirty-six hours to shut this thing down."

They finished their coffee and then went out to the car. Once inside, Farris took the encrypted cellular phone from his pocket and called back to Hardt's house. He told the SAS Captain his plan and asked to have the whole team come out to this side of town right away.

"Sorry, Mike, I can't," Hardt replied. "There was a disturbance at the mosque on this side of town and all roads in and out of the area are shut down. Even I can't get out at the moment without raising a whole lot of suspicion."

"How about the others?" Farris asked. "I tried their cell phone number but got no answer."

"I'll see if I can get a hold of them and have them head your way, but at the moment I have no idea where they are."

"Mojo and I are staying on this side of town tonight," said Farris. "Ring me at this number if you need to."

"Roger that, Mike. By the way, check in with Clark and Chung to let them know what you're doing," Hardt said and then clicked the line off.

"OK, Mojo, we're on our own for a while," Farris said. "Hardt said there's some kind of disturbance on the other side of town and they have all the roads closed at the moment. He's going to try to connect with the others and get over here as soon as possible."

"Well then, boss, how's about we take a little tour of that hilly side of town while the sun is still up?"

"You're driving, Gunny. Take us wherever you wish. I'm going to check in with Clark and give him the lowdown."

While Johnson drove through the city, Farris dialed the number for Mark Clark's office in the UNSOCOM HQ in Sarajevo. The CIA agent answered his own phone.

"Clark here," he coughed softly after the words. His voice sounded very hoarse.

"This is Farris. Hardt wanted me to give you a status of what we're doing."

"Good," Clark cleared his throat and said in a quiet gravelly voice. "Damn cold. Well, I can't talk much, but I can listen, go ahead."

"We're pretty sure Mathis is going to hit at the central checkpoint where all of the services have troops located. With that in mind, we're going to lay up near some good locations we saw up in the hills on the south side of the town that have a clear view of the square."

Clark cleared his throat and muttered, "Sounds good. Are the others there too?"

"No, Hardt is stuck on the other side of Jajce. Traffic is blocked in all directions due to some kind of disturbance. I haven't been able to contact Hogan's team. Their cell phone must be dead, or they're out of range."

"Well," said Clark. "Keep in touch. Let me give you my cell phone number. I've got a doctor's appointment in the morning to get this throat thing cleared up. Call me if you find anything."

Clark told Farris the number then signed off the call. Johnson found a small restaurant where they ate a delicious light meal of the local cuisine. Just after seven o'clock they left the aroma of fresh food and steaming coffee, and Johnson drove the Ford up the hillside.

Mojo wound the vehicle up narrow streets among the closely built, brightly colored houses and buildings. Many of the structures were still pockmarked by bullet scars and holes left by rocket impacts. Windows were boarded up in many, and one of the houses had its entire roof caved in. Miraculously, there were a handful of other homes in the midst of the destruction, which looked as if they hadn't been touched at all.

Very little human traffic moved through the areas. In their place, packs of mangy dogs roamed the streets prowling for anything to eat. Through the course of the war, in its desperate days when families were running for their lives, thousands of domesticated animals had been left behind by their owners. With no one to take care of their needs for them, the creatures had quickly succumbed to natural animal instinct, and now they survived the only way they knew how: by terrorizing the neighborhoods in search of food.

The houses Mike and Mojo had spotted from below appeared before them as they rounded a corner. Johnson parked the car in an alley between two houses. From the alley they had a view of the buildings and the town square. He shut off the engine and they sat in silence in the early evening twilight.

They scanned the buildings and the street for a quarter of an hour before they got out of the car and walked along the sidewalk. The block contained several houses and one apartment building. All of which had only suffered minimal damage in the fighting but were nonetheless completely empty. There was no one on the street in the whole area. No sounds of living people came from the houses or buildings. No pots jangled; no radios or televisions crackled with noise. No children talked in hushed voices to parents. Even the breeze seemed too quiet as it passed between the walls and moved down the street.

"Well, the people are all either hiding from us," said Farris, "or this block is a ghost town."

"I wonder," said Johnson, "if this neighborhood had been inhabited by people of the opposite religion of the surrounding neighbors, and the owners are afraid to come home."

"Good point," Farris said. He pointed to a deserted-looking two-story house with a flat roof. "Let's get up on that roof and have a better look around."

They walked over to the house and climbed up a flight of stairs built around the outside running all the way to the top. From there, they could clearly see down into the town square below. It was less than a kilometer to the checkpoint that was currently manned by American soldiers. In two days' time the checkpoint would be manned by the Russian Army, commanded by one Captain Illyich Yeltsin, the Russian President's nephew. The unobstructed field of fire from this vantage point was amazing. The town center in its entirety lay open beneath them.

"Man," said Johnson, "this town is a wide open killing field!"

"No kidding." Farris nudged Johnson's arm and pointed up the road in the direction they had come from. "Look over there; the office building we saw from below."

Johnson glanced in that direction. The five-story office building had the most commanding view of the entire area. What they had seen from below though, was only a façade. The entire back side of the building had crumbled to the ground. Only one wall of offices remained and access to that section would be precarious at best. What still stood of that building seemed as if it would probably topple over if someone yelled loud enough.

"Well, I guess that rules out that building, unless he's Spiderman," Johnson said.

The sound of a small vehicle engine drew their attention. A moment later, a two-door Nissan pickup puttered up the street. The rattle of the oil starved engine echoed off the walls of the silent houses around them. It stopped a few houses over between their position and the decrepit office building.

Both men lowered themselves behind the parapet of the roof and moved to the edge to peer at the vehicle.

Two men got out of the small pickup truck. From the back they picked up what looked like bags of cement. They carried them into a house with a peaked roof that made it the tallest in the neighborhood. The pair made several trips back and forth into the house with a couple dozen of these bags and then left.

Mike and Mojo waited ten minutes, then descended from the roof and made their way over to the other house. The door was unlocked. They let themselves in, drawing pistols as they entered.

The inside of the house was caked with a layer of gray-white dust. A broken table leaned at an odd angle against the hallway wall just inside the entrance. It was obvious that no one currently lived there. The two men may have been workers dropping off supplies for some necessary remodeling, but the condition of the interior did not look like it was in any state of repair.

They followed the men's shoe prints in the layers of dust that covered the floor, and cautiously climbed a flight of stairs to the second story. They followed the dusty trail through the upstairs hall to another set of stairs. These led to an attic. At the top of those steps was an open room with a gabled window that jutted from the rooftop and looked down to the checkpoint in the square below. Just inside this window stood a table ringed about its edges with cement bags. Bags were piled on the floor beneath the table like a protective wall.

"Jeez, Captain," whispered Johnson. "This looks like a textbook defensive sniper position."

"Yeah it does, doesn't it," Farris answered, "but why would he set up a protected position like this for a hit that he wants to fire a single shot from then escape?"

"This isn't logical for Mathis," Johnson said.

"Unless he has some other deception in mind," Farris added. "We'd best get out of here for the moment and set up an observation point somewhere nearby."

CHAPTER 21

Thursday, October 27th
FBI Regional HQ
Columbus, Ohio
Interrogation Room
10:30 Hours

Mike Farris tried to sleep a few hours in Paul Hogan's office. His attempts were futile. The dream kept coming back.

The sound of gunshots echoed in his mind like a snare drum. Janelle and Mike Jr. lay in a pool of blood. Usein's twisted smile glared at him. Brett Mathis's voice.

"I'm sorry, Mike, you know how this business is."

Falling. Falling past the image of a dying child clutching his mother's bloody corpse.

Eventually he gave up trying to sleep and walked downstairs to the chamber where Hogan had left the gangster overnight. Paul had restarted the questioning about half an hour earlier. Mike watched from behind the one-way mirrored window in the adjoining room.

"Where's my lawyer?" demanded G-man, aka Damon Clark. "I ain't talking to you no more without a lawyer!"

"You've already said enough, Damon." Hogan answered. "You told us that Bones and White ordered you to kill the good pastor and his friend LeRon, but instead of the pastor you killed his wife and son. You've also said that you had delivered a van to Cold Bones house for some guys who were being sent to pick up a stash of drugs for an African guy named Usein. Last night you confessed these things in tears, but now you are saying none of it is true?"

"Nothing I said last night counts, I was being tortured by that preacher dude!"

"Tortured?"

"He kept choking me until I talked!" Damon replied, "Then he put a gun to my head!"

"Really?" Hogan said. "Did he do that?"

"You saw it! He threatened to kill me, if I didn't talk!" shouted Damon. "That's torture! I know my rights! Nothing I said last night will hold up in court!"

"You know," said Hogan, "you're right. It won't hold up at all. As a matter of fact, I think we may have stepped over the line in your case. With that in mind, I guess we will have to let you go."

"What?" asked Damon. "You're going to let me go?"

"Yup."

"Just like that?"

"Yup."

Hogan grinned.

"I'll even give you a ride back to Cold Bones' house."

"What?"

"Yeah, free taxi. Just for you."

"Uh," Damon hesitated, "I don't want to go back there. Just let me go from here."

"Nope," replied Hogan, "we can't do that. You see, it is policy that we have to return an illegally detained individual to their last known place of residence once the error has been realized. I'll make sure you have the right forms to file a lawsuit against us for reparations for your inconvenience over the past night."

Hogan reached into his pocket and grabbed his cell phone. He flipped it open and dialed a number.

"Yeah, Phil? This is Paul. We're going to let the suspect go. Is there a ride ready to deliver him to the address I gave you earlier?"

He smiled down at Damon whose eyes were brimming over with fear.

"Good, thanks. Five minutes and I'll have him at the front door."

Damon looked up at the FBI agent. "You can't do this!"

"Oh?"

"They'll kill me!" his voice squeaked.

Hogan tilted his head and scrunched his eyes in mock contemplation.

"Hmmm...that certainly is a possibility, isn't it?" He leaned onto the table and pressed his palms into its surface. "Didn't Mister White lay out the risks involved in this kind of job when he hired you?"

"Look! You're a government dude! You can't do stuff like this!" Damon's voice squeaked in desperation.

"Well, Damon, here's how it is. You have confessed to committing multiple murders, trafficking drugs, committing assault with the intent to rape, and associating with, for that matter taking orders from, a known international terrorist. You will most likely get life even if you plea-bargain. If you don't, you'll almost certainly get the death penalty in our care. At least this way, you have a chance to run...right?"

Damon quietly looked down at the floor.

"Well? Come on," Hogan said, "Let's get you back to your crib."

"Wait!"

Hogan stood staring at the young man. Damon Clark's eyes were moist with tears. His lower lip trembled as he spoke.

"I'll talk on the record," the gangster said. "Maybe we can make a deal. Just don't send me back there and get that death penalty off me, and I'll tell you everything."

"OK," replied Hogan as he sat down across the table from Clark, "the tape is rolling."

Damon retold everything in great detail. How he and two other men, including Allie, had gone to Pastor Farris's house with orders to gun him down, and to kill LeRon and Li'l Mac too. When they drove up to the house, they unexpectedly saw LeRon and Li'l Mac there and opened fire on the whole group.

"Shooting the woman and baby was a mistake," he said. "Allie was zoomin' on meth and kept shouting at me as we drove up, and so it threw off my aim, and they got hit by accident."

"You hit Mrs. Farris twelve times Damon and the baby four times."

"I was using an Uzi! They shoot fast, man. I couldn't control it with stupid Allie shouting at me!"

"Alright, so you need some firearms training then."

Paul Hogan leaned back in his chair. He struggled to keep his face from turning dark red as he tried to control an explosive rage that churned deep inside him. He barely managed to retain an air of emotional indifference to what he was hearing and keep suppressed the desire to take out his weapon put a bullet between the eyes of this two-bit thug. He motioned with his fingers to continue.

"Tell me about Mister White. Who is he?"

"Don't nobody know Mister White except for the ones who work right next to him, and except for the Ringmaster, we don't even know who that is," Damon said. "He only meets us through a flat screen TV set in a big, empty warehouse up by the river."

"Can you take us there?"

"I can give you directions, but I ain't going there," replied the young man.

"Yes, you are going with us," said Hogan. "You are going to take us there, and walk us into the building. Don't worry. There'll be plenty of protection for you, but you are going to take us there."

CHAPTER 22

The GPS coordinates had been fairly easy to program. Akbar Usein had told Al Gul to make sure to keep the drivers off their guard and fairly lost long enough that they could not tell someone else where they were going. The four men sent out had been told to follow the explicit instructions, and he knew they would do so. They had also been instructed not to open the containers they picked up. The containers themselves were sealed with locks and tamper proof wax tape. Of the four containers, there was nothing truly incriminating in three of them. At least nothing more than a police officer would expect to find in a van being driven by a man who may be a known drug dealer.

Three of the packages the men picked up contained about eighty pounds of various drugs. One of heroin, one oxycontin, and one of cocaine. Al Gul knew this because he loaded the cases himself and hid them in various strange locations around the state. Al Gul had no idea what was in the fourth case, nor did he know where it was hidden. That he had to find out.

The reputation of Akbar Usein was well established in terrorist circles. He was known to be one of the most ruthless murderers in the world. The most virulent Sheiks and Mullahs walked in fear of him and dared not speak against him. Major governments had been humiliated by his vicious tactics, in some cases paying the price in hundreds of lives when they refused to grant his requests.

Seirim Al Gul, whose real name was Kharzai Ghiassi, did not believe for a moment that Usein was in the US to set up a drug trafficking operation. Usein had traded drugs for weapons before, including chemical weapons and spent uranium munitions, but he had never tried to set up a regular trade business for his drugs. He only used them to help advance his violent rampage against the west. Usein was in America to perpetrate violence, this much Kharzai knew, and he was going to find out what it was.

Kharzai Ghiassi was the American-born son of Persian immigrants who had come to the US in the 1970s. His parents had been close friends and supporters of the Shah and had barely escaped the wrath of the Islamic Revolution that eventually ousted the government they were part of. After a rather boring life growing up in Indiana, Kharzai found a home in the CIA.

In time, he became one of their most valuable deep cover assets, working throughout the Middle East and Central Asia. Several years ago, his value became very clear to the clandestine services when he was directly involved in the prevention of a nuclear holocaust set in motion by the government of his parent's native land.

After debriefing out of that mission, it was a fairly-short period of time before he found himself back in deep cover, breaking into the group that had given him the name he now carried, Seirim Al Gul: the Hairy Demon. Much to the surprise of his CIA handlers, Kharzai had managed to get himself promoted up the ranks of the Sons of the Sword, a rival organization to Al Qaeda.

Kharzai's tactics and methods were, as his file at Langley stated, unorthodox. More than once a stuffed shirt puzzle palace bureaucrat had labeled him unfit for duty due to psychological reasons. They had recommended him taken out of the field and tested for a range of issues from Attention Deficit Disorder to Schizophrenia. The recommendations were never followed up on. Kharzai Ghiassi got results. He got results every time.

The "Hairy Demon" had managed to stop dozens of major terrorist attacks, often by personally killing the perpetrators. Somehow, through methods no one could figure out, he always survived and deepened the trust of his terrorist masters. Those CIA officers placed in charge of his operations had realized long ago that they were handlers, not controllers of the man. No one could control Kharzai.

This talent was how he found himself, under orders of Sheik Aboud bin Salaam, head of the Sons of the Sword, tasked with finding out what Usein was doing and making sure that their organization got the credit for any major attack, or to get rid of Usein if he deemed necessary. Missions like that were what Kharzai loved the most about his job. Helping the enemy kill each other.

Al Gul sat in the comfy leather executive chair in the small office of Cold Bones' house. Usein was out with Cold Bones somewhere. He had not said where he was going nor had he mentioned when he would return. Al Gul had not been invited and was not happy about that.

Usein had done one thing that Al Gul liked though. In an apparent oversight he had left his laptop on the desk powered on and logged in to his account. Kharzai sat down at it, opened up a game of Solitaire and played until the game was about half done. Then he stopped and opened the My Documents folder.

He quickly scrolled through the My Documents list and randomly picked files with Arabic names that looked as though they may lead somewhere. Some opened, but they bore no information that would help him. Most of them were locked with strong 256-bit encrypted password protection. The files were stubbornly refusing to submit to his attempts at reading their contents.

Hmmm…I should've paid more attention in Hacking 301 back in the day.

As he browsed through the files on the laptop, a tiny image flashed in the bottom right corner of the screen. A small box with Arabic script briefly rose from the bottom of the screen then vanished after two seconds. It was quick but long enough for Kharzai to see what it said.

New Email: 1

Kharzai's smile widened. He opened Microsoft Outlook. It glided up from the bottom menu and opened to a list of messages received. At the top of the list was an email header in bold, indicating it had not been read yet. The text was not in Arabic like most of the others. It was in the Cyrillic letters of Russian.

He opened the message. A text box expanded in the center of the screen stating that the message he was about to view was encrypted and asking if he wished to continue. He clicked OK and the message used an existing encryption algorithm that Usein had stored on the email system. Much to Kharzai's delight, while the encryption was strong, the message was not password protected. It opened right away.

Fluent in Russian, he grinned with satisfaction as he read the text.

Your agent picked up the package yesterday.
Eyes verified.

Price increase 500k.

Deposit 24hr or no code.

"My, my, my," muttered Kharzai under his breath, "it really isn't drugs. Hmmm…how am I going to get this juicy bit of info to the Gunny?"

He clicked on the forward button in the email and typed in the address of the man he hoped was already on the case.

Before leaving Syria, once he knew of his destination with Usein, Kharzai had checked into who was in charge of the FBI Anti-Terrorism unit there, in case he found a need for back up. Much to his surprise he discovered that it was none other than a man with whom he had served alongside in Iraq several years earlier: former Gunnery Sergeant Paul Hogan, USMC.

That old friendship would certainly prove useful if he could get a hold of him. The Voodoo hand signs the previous night had been an attempt to alert Hogan of his presence. He had caught a glimpse of a shadowy figure he assumed to be either a government agent or an assassin at Cold Bones' house earlier in the week. He signaled with a wink, but wasn't sure the man caught it. He hoped that the FBI already had surveillance set up at the house but had no way of knowing. Now, he had a chance to do something more direct.

Kharzai clicked the send button. The message flashed off. A status bar crawled across the bottom of the screen as the message was sent. It only took a couple of seconds, then it disappeared from the outbox and sped onto the information superhighway on its way to the FBI agent.

Send Complete

Kharzai moved the mouse to put the cursor on the title of the message and clicked the right mouse button. A menu slid down and he chose the item "Mark as Unread." The message header darkened to a bold font as it had been before he opened it. He then moved the mouse pointer down towards the "Sent Items" folder so he could delete the record of having forwarded the message.

A door slammed open and heavy footsteps headed his way. Usein's voice echoed clearly through the house.

"We will see when he arrives," he stopped briefly in the hallway as he spoke into a cell phone.

"I expect everything to move ahead with no problems." Usein said in response to the person on the other end.

The front door of the house was only fifteen feet from the office. In five steps the African would be in the room. Kharzai clicked the red "X" in the top right corner of Outlook and the program closed. He quickly closed the My Documents folder and maximized the Solitaire game he had left open. The familiar green background of Windows Solitaire filled the screen and Kharzai dragged a King to a blank space at the top row of cards.

Usein walked into the office and stopped in the doorway, staring with hate filled eyes at the hairy Persian sitting at the desk.

"Al Gul! What are you doing on my computer?" he demanded angrily.

"Playing cards," Al Gul replied in a mocking sing-song manner. "Duh!"

"How did you get into that computer?" Usein demanded.

"Uh…you left it on. Why? Do you have top-secret stuff on here?" replied Al Gul.

Usein stormed over behind the desk and slammed the lid of the laptop shut. Al Gul yanked his fingers back, barely avoiding getting them smashed in the machine. He feigned surprise then dramatically glared back at Usein.

"If it is important information you are hiding from me, you had best not leave your precious machine turned on, Akbar Aga," He heavily pronounced the terrorist's name.

"Do not touch what is mine, crazy man, or I will have you killed."

"If you are hiding something from the Sheik, you had better know I will find out, and then I will dine on African cuisine." Al Gul curled the edge of his lip and stared with a glimmer of insanity into Usein's eyes. He snapped his jaws at him then let out an unsettling guttural chuckle.

"Stay out of my way, Al Gul," Usein growled back.

Al Gul walked past Usein and slowly stepped to the door keeping his body facing toward Usein as he moved. He kept glaring eye contact with the man. He smiled manically and licked his teeth as he backed out of the door then walked down the hallway and outside.

Once on the porch he laughed out loud and shouted a banshee cry.

"Kazzaayeee!!"

CHAPTER 23

Damon Clark's hand trembled as he pointed to the warehouse by the river.

"There it is," he said.

His eyes darted back and forth. He swiveled his head and glanced across the length of the parking lot. Damp autumn clouds hung low over the city, casting flat, pale shadows over the old buildings. Deep darkness in the few windows and the alleys between the buildings could hide any number of violent things. Damon shrugged his body down, reducing his profile in the car's windows. Hogan looked in the direction Damon had pointed.

"That's the place, huh?"

"Yeah," Damon replied nervously. He raised himself just high enough in the seat to look over it and pointed to a door in the side of the building.

"You go in that door there. The TV is in a room at the end of the hall in a cabinet. It only opens up when he starts a meeting. He must control it on his side or something because there's no remote control or anything in the room."

"Let's go inside." Hogan said.

"Are you crazy?" Damon replied.

"Probably, but that's beside the point," Hogan replied. "You are still going inside."

Mike Farris and Hildegarde Rottbruck got out of the front seat of the vehicle.

Hogan, who sat in the back with Damon, pointed to the door and said, "Get out G-man. Show the way."

Damon opened the door with a trembling hand and got out of the car. He led them towards the door of the warehouse. He put his hand on the handle, turned it, and pushed, but the door didn't open.

"What the hell?" he said. "It ain't never been locked before."

Hildegarde tried the handle. The bolt moved easily but the door was held firm in place by something at the top.

"Magnetic locking plate," she said, "There must be a camera somewhere, so they can see who is at the door and send the signal to unlock it remotely."

As she spoke, there was a click. The door unlocked, released from the tension of the electro-magnet that had held it. She tried the handle again, and it opened.

Mike said, "Looks like Mister White is inviting us in."

He and the two agents took out their weapons and scanned the interior of the warehouse, pupils widening to adjust to the inky darkness. Farris reached into his pocket, took out a small night vision monocle and scanned the inside.

"I don't see anything unusual," he said.

"You go first, Damon," Hogan said. He grabbed Damon's shirt sleeve and tugged him towards the dark room. "Lead the way."

Damon "G-man" Clark's body shook visibly as he entered the warehouse. His feet shuffled into the door. Once inside he paused and tensed his body in anticipation of something bad happening. When nothing happened to him he relaxed only a little and took a few more small steps then moved ahead. The others followed behind him, weapons up, eyes alert.

Hilde took a small palm computer out of her pocket and turned it on as they moved inside. Its three-inch by four-inch screen glowed blue and cast an eerie pallor onto her face in the unlit interior of the cavernous building.

Damon led them to the end of the warehouse room, where a door stood open. The lights were on as if they had been expected. When they entered the room the large wide flat screen television was already on, protruding from the worn wooden cabinet, patiently waiting for them.

The hooded image of a man filled the center of the screen. Its face obscured by the shadows deep within the hood. Mister White looked every bit the part of a comic book villain.

"Mister Clark. You have been a very naughty boy." Mister White's modulated voice called out, attempting to sound sinister. Hogan thought that he sounded more like the farcical character Dark Helmet from the eighties comic parody movie "Space Balls" than evil Darth Vader from "Star Wars."

"Mister White," he said with a shaking voice, "I had no choice! They tortured me until I brought them here."

"Tortured you?" said Mister White in a condescending tone. "I see. You don't have to tell me anything about it, Damon, I was expecting you. Allie came in last night. He told me everything."

"What?" Damon stammered. "That asshole! He lied! He lied! Whatever he said was a lie!"

"Really?" answered White. "You will have to ask him about that when you see him next."

Mister White cleared his throat then continued. "At the moment there are more serious matters at hand than foolish boys who let themselves get caught beating up little girls. I see that the preacher is there with you. The one whose wife and son you killed. As I recall, Damon, they were the ones you referred to as 'the preacher's whore and little son of a bitch.' Isn't that the way you said it? Damon?"

Damon cringed in terror. He refused to make eye contact with Mike. Farris ignored the terrified gangster on the verge of hysteria. He spoke directly to the shadowy image on the screen.

"You shouldn't have missed me, Mister White."

"Yes, well, good help is so hard to find in this line of work. Don't worry though," White said, "There's always next time."

Hogan stepped forward. "Speaking of next time. We are aware of your association with the illustrious Mister Usein and wanted to give you a chance to possibly redeem yourself Mister Vader…or White…or whatever you call yourself."

"I don't know what you are talking about."

"Oh, yes, you do," said Hogan. "We already of knew of Mister Usein long before running into Damon here."

Mister White didn't react to Hogan's statement.

"We also tracked the four vans you arranged for him and happen to know what he has in those vans."

"Really," came the response. White's hooded form didn't move at all.

"I am not familiar with this Mister Usein. Nor am I aware of any vans. I believe you are chasing the wrong squirrel, gentlemen."

"Au contraire," Hogan said, "You do know about them, although I am under the distinct impression that you may not realize what is in those vans, Mister White."

He moved closer to the screen and nearer the microphone holes embedded in its top edge. He lowered his voice as if speaking in confidentiality to the digital image of Mister White.

"You see, Mister White," Hogan continued, "Mister Farris and I happen to know Akbar Usein very well. He is a rather infamous terrorist. Now while you yourself have recently arisen in the local area as a slime bag of considerable depth, I do not get the impression that you are a mass murderer. Although I may be wrong. I mean, you are willing to dress up in a Halloween costume to address your employees so who knows?"

White did not respond. He only stared back towards Hogan from the shadow beneath his hood.

"Mister Usein, it seems, is intending to detonate a nuclear device right here in Columbus. Whatever payoff he has offered you is moot, because your customer base here in our wonderful city, and for that matter you yourself, will probably all be dead in a couple of days, if we cannot find him."

"How do you know this Mister Usein you speak of?" asked the shadowy figure.

"Let's just say that Mister Farris here had a very close personal contact with him as a representative of our government in Somalia several years ago. Since that time Mister Usein has spent his energies traveling the globe killing innocent bystanders by the hundreds."

"Who are you?" White asked. "CIA? FBI?"

"Something like that," Hogan answered. Hilde stood to the side of the television monitor with the handheld computer in her fingers. She pointed it at the back of the cabinet and read the display as numbers ticked across the screen. A progress bar slowly spread across the bottom of the display as she watched. When the bar became solid several rows of thirty-two-digit numbers representing IPv6 addresses filled the screen. The text "Route Trace Successful" flashed below them. She turned toward Hogan and nodded then stuffed the computer into a pocket of her jacket and backed away from the side of the TV.

"Well," said Hogan, "just thought you'd like to know who you have gone into league with, and by the way, remember since Patriot II anyone who knowingly provides assistance to a terrorist who commits an act that results in the death of American citizens will automatically receive the death penalty, if convicted. No matter how tacky their villain costume is…Darth."

Hogan turned his back to the TV and walked towards the door. The others followed. As they left the room, Farris turned towards the still lit screen.

"Sleep well tonight, Mister White."

The four of them walked back through the echoing warehouse and out of the building. Damon was just as nervous leaving as he was coming in. His eyes darted wildly over the buildings across the parking lot.

"You mean to tell me that that African dude is a real terrorist? Damn!" he said. "I thought he was just a drug dealer! I really didn't know. Shit! This sucks!"

"Yep, Damon. You are in serious trouble, because you just helped a known terrorist transport a weapon of mass destruction to your own home city," Hogan replied.

"But I didn't do it knowingly! You said, 'knowingly helps,'" answered Damon.

The group arrived at the car and Hilde unlocked the doors with the remote-control device on the keychain and went around to the driver's side. As they reached for the handles a shot rang out from above and behind the car. A translucent bright red mist blossomed above the rear driver side door. It spattered across the driver's side of the vehicle, making a mess of streaks and spots on everything, including Hilde, Mike and Hogan.

Hilde threw herself across the hood of the car and took cover next to Mike on the passenger side. The three of them crouched behind the protection of the steel vehicle. Weapons drawn, they pointed toward the sound of the blast but saw nothing. No more shots were fired.

Damon Clark wavered on his feet. His eyes wide with surprise. His mouth hung open in wordless shock. He dropped to his knees beside the car then fell over onto his side. A pool of darkening red fluid spread across the pavement around him as it ran out of the gaping hole a large-caliber bullet had punched through his back and out his chest.

CHAPTER 24

"Yes!" Andy Fleiss shouted.

He sprung up from his desk. The abrupt movement sent his chair spinning across the room. Its wheels clicked as it rolled over the joints between the raised floor's tiles.

"Yes! Yes! Yes!"

He grabbed the phone and hastily dialed Hildegarde Rottbruck's cell number. As soon as he heard the line click on he spoke fast and loud into the receiver.

"Hilde! We're back online!"

"What's back online?" She asked.

"The satellite tracking of those vans!" Andy replied.

"Excellent!" she exclaimed. "Do you have their locations?"

"Yes. I managed to kind of hijack a couple of GPS satellites and added our frequency to their grid. This gives me the location of each van to within about fifty feet."

"Outstanding!" she said, "Excellent work, Andy! We owe you big on this one!"

"I'll hold you to it," he said. His smile was practically audible.

"Roger that," she replied and hung up the phone.

She turned in the seat of the big SUV and faced Mike. Hilde would have taken her personal car home to change her clothes, but it was in the mechanic's shop that day. She had expected to get it back by mid-afternoon, but as they drove back to the office her, mechanic called to inform her that they had to order a part that wouldn't be available until the next morning, effectively leaving her stranded. She called the motor pool and tried to get a government car, but they were all checked out. The shooting had spattered both of them with Damon Clark's blood.

"Mike, I hate to ask this of you, but," she was surprised to find herself so nervous at asking him for a ride, "Could you give me a lift home?"

"Sure, of course," he answered without a second thought. "Where do you live?"

"Pataskala."

"No problem," he said.

"I know you live in Picktown though, and I hate for you to go out of your way."

"It's only a few miles," he said, "It's not too far out of my way."

In reality, her house was nearly twenty miles out of his way, but Mike didn't mind taking her. She really did need to clean up and change her clothes after what had happened. Few things in life are more traumatic that having someone else's blood or body parts splashed all over your pant suit. Hilde had been standing two feet away from Damon. His blood, propelled by what the investigator surmised had been a high-powered .308 caliber bullet, had exploded violently out of his body on impact. The red fluid had splashed on her face, hair, and clothes. It had been so forceful that it had even hit Mike and Paul on the other side of the vehicle. Hilde needed to wash herself of the afternoon's tragedy both physically and symbolically.

She hung up the call from Andy as they left the city beltway and turned onto I-70 in Mike's big white Denali SUV. Hilde told him about Andy's success in finding the signal. Mike suggested a change in plans to speed up their return to the field.

"Look, I realize this may be uncomfortable for you, but may I suggest that we just go to my house to clean up?" Mike said. "You are about the same size as Janelle, so I can let you have some clean clothes to wear."

"Oh...I...uh," she stammered, unsure of how to answer. "I'm not sure if...well...I mean, I'd hate to impose on something like that...I..."

Immediately after the words came out he realized the obvious discomfort such a suggestion carried with it. He cursed himself for not thinking that she might be uncomfortable with the idea of wearing a dead woman's clothing.

"I'm sorry. If you're not comfortable with it, I'll take you home instead."

"I'm not uncomfortable," she said. "I just don't want to stir up any bad feelings you may have. I mean, it is your wife's clothing."

"She's gone," said Mike in a quiet tone, as if he had only recently acknowledged the fact. "There's nothing I can do to bring her back. I have all the memories I can keep in my mind."

He paused then added, "I was planning to give the clothes to the women's shelter anyway."

Hilde looked at him then down at her watch.

"It will get us back to work faster," she exhaled. "As long as it is really OK with you, I'm alright with it."

He turned the Denali onto the exit ramp at State Route 256, and drove into the rolling cornfields and wooded plots of the semi-rural, suburban countryside. Ten minutes later, they reached his house across the street from Faith Presbyterian Church.

The sun was already low on the horizon when they pulled into the driveway at just before five p.m. They opened the doors and climbed down from the tall vehicle. Mike led the way as they crossed the short concrete sidewalk up to the front porch of the house.

As they approached Hilde stared at the holes in the siding and the splintered wooden posts of the porch, the damage done by the spray of bullets that had killed Mike's family and his friend. Most if it had been patched, but nothing had yet been painted. More than fifty rounds had peppered the front of his house.

The early evening sun was drifting on the downward arc of its daily journey, casting shallow rays across the wood of the porch. As they climbed the short steps toward the door, Hilde noticed the darker color of a large splotch on the wooden surface at the top step and several planks around it. Although it had been scoured clean, nothing short of sanding the wood down, maybe even replacing the boards themselves, would get rid of the stain of the blood that had pooled beneath the bodies of mother and child. A chill went through her body.

Hilde closed her eyes and tried not to imagine the scene. She tried not to see what was around her as they ascended the steps and crossed the morbid planks. She opened her eyes at the sound of Mike putting a key into the lock and opening the door.

He entered, flipped on a light switch, and turned around to face her. He swept his arm in a welcoming gesture, and she followed him in.

Hilde was surprised to find a very neat and tidy house. In her mind she had expected to find signs of a man emotionally broken, who barely held his life together and had let his home become a mess. She had seen it often enough before when she had been a regular field agent performing interviews with relatives of murder victims.

The families would don an outer shell of "keeping it together," but the private part of their lives would fall to pieces. Their homes would be disasters with clothes strewn about, open food containers lying on tables cluttered with dirty napkins. Unwashed dishes were usually piled in the sink, and the sour, sweaty odor of dirty laundry ebbed out of back rooms.

But Mike's house was not that at all. It was immaculate. No food containers, no clothes draped over the back of the couch, not even a used coffee mug sitting beside the comfy chair at the end of the living room. In spite of the fact that they had been so busy with the case, it looked as if he had recently vacuumed the carpet. She wondered if he had hired a maid to keep it so tidy.

As if sensing her thoughts, Mike said, "The church ladies have been coming in once a week and tidying up for me. They've all been a great help since the loss. Sometimes a few of them will even make some meals for me and put them in plastic snap-lock containers in the fridge, so I don't have to cook."

He reached out and took her jacket for her.

"You must be a good pastor for them to help you out like this."

"I've known most of them for nearly ten years. Until Janelle came along they were my whole family, outside of the Corps."

"What about your parents?"

"They died a while back."

"I'm sorry to hear that."

"They had been married more than forty years, since High School," Mike explained. "Mom came down with cancer and was gone within a month. She was fifty-eight. Dad missed her so much he just sort of faded away. He died of heart failure three months later."

"I'm so sorry," Hilde said. "It seems like they had a beautiful relationship."

"They did. Theirs was a model of what good marriage should be."

"Do you have any siblings?"

"A younger sister, Mary. Last I heard she lived in Arizona, but that's the only detail I know. I haven't heard from her in about twelve or thirteen years—since seminary. Mary hated the idea of my military career. When I joined the Marines, she pretty much disowned me. She considered me a hypocrite for claiming to be a Christian while at the same time going off to fight for my country. Like a lot of pastor's kids do, she totally rebelled against our parents and our religion and became a real, hard-core liberal. We've talked less than five times since I left for college. I couldn't even get a hold of her to let her know about our parents' death. She never met Janelle."

"So you have no other family?"

"Like I said, just my church now, and the Corps, and that amounts to quite a lot, actually." He glanced at the brown wool-blend jacket she had handed him. Damon Clark's blood was spattered across it in a random pattern of streaks and dots that nearly covered the right half of the jackets front and collar.

"Your jacket has some pretty bad stains on it. It looks like it might be ruined"

"Yeah, probably is. I'll take it to the dry cleaner, and see if there's anything they can do."

Mike led her up the stairs to the master bedroom. He opened the door and motioned her inside, but did not enter behind her. He stood in the doorway as if barred by an unseen barrier that prohibited him from coming into the room with another woman.

"The master bath is behind that door over there."

He pointed towards an open door in the back corner of the room. The bathroom vanity and mirror were visible. The mirror reflected back the image of an open walk-in closet full of clothing.

"There's a bottle of body wash in the little basket hanging on the wall inside the shower. There's also a new scrubbing cloth on the sink. You can open it. Help yourself to the lotions on the sink as well. I'm never going to use them myself."

He motioned with his hand as if he were pointing around the corner into the bathroom.

"There is a walk-in closet inside the bathroom as well, with a wide variety of clothes. Feel free to take whatever you would like from the closet. I know it may feel weird but don't be shy if you see something you like. You obviously can't wear that shirt back to the office."

He motioned to the smattering of tiny blood droplets spread across her white blouse. The fabric had acted to separate the various substances in the blood. Plasma formed a yellowish ring around dark brown spots of clotted red blood cells in the center.

"Like I said, I'm going to give it all away in a few days."

He paused, then hesitantly started to speak. His faced reddened as the words formed. He pointed to a small dresser that was visible through the bathroom just inside the open closet door.

"You may want to change your…uh…underclothes as well."

He blushed more as he spoke.

"There are a couple drawers of clean ones in that dresser. But…uh…well…you look like you wear about the same size underpants as Janelle did, but the uh…well…the other part… you're a bit…uh…bigger…than she was, so her bras probably won't fit…unless you wear one of the maternity ones…"

"Don't worry, Mike." She raised a hand to stop him from saying anymore. Her cheeks blossomed red too. "I'll figure something out."

"Look," she added, "really, if this is too much for you, maybe I'll just wear my own clothes until I can get home."

"No," he said. "you need to be comfortable. It's going to be a long night."

He abruptly turned and left the doorway, closing it behind himself.

Once he had left, Hilde entered the bathroom and started the shower. At the sink, she opened the plastic wrapper that contained the new body scrubbing cloth and laid it on the side of the tub.

She undressed, folding her clothes into a neat pile and laying them on a chair next to the closet door. She stepped over the side of the tub and rinsed off in the hot jets of steamy water.

From the mesh basket hanging from the shower head she took the tube of bodywash and squeezed some of its contents onto the scrubbing cloth. Its peach scent wafted through the air around her head like butterflies fluttering out of a mound of flowers. A rush of pleasure washed over her as she inhaled the sweetness. She wondered if Mike used this same wash on himself. Then she wondered about the woman who had last used it in that same shower, and she felt a twinge of remorse.

Within ten minutes Hildegarde Rottbruck felt clean again. She climbed out of the shower and stood in the middle of the room where she rubbed herself dry with a thick terry-cloth towel.

She picked up a hairbrush that lay next to the sink and leaned forward, bending over at the waist, allowing her long, thick auburn hair to cascade over her head and hang upside down until it nearly touched the floor. She slid the thick plastic bristles of the brush through it from behind, enjoying the tension of its course over her scalp and through the follicles. Hilde then stood upright, flinging the mass of silken hair back over her head where it fell in a neat flowing stream across her shoulders and down to her should blades.

Cool rivulets of water trickled from the ends of her hair, over her shoulder blades, and streamed down her naked body, forming tiny puddles on the floor beneath her feet. She brushed her bangs back and looked at herself in the waist-height mirror. On the counter top, a small picture in a frame caught her attention.

She picked it up and studied it for a moment. It was a picture of Mike's wife and son. Janelle held Mike Junior in one arm and they waved to the camera. Mother and son wore big smiles on their faces. As she stared at the picture, a lump formed in her throat. An involuntary tear rolled down her cheek.

"Poor Mike," she whispered. "Such a beautiful family."

Hilde gingerly put the picture down on the counter and tried to wish away the bad things that had torn Mike's family apart. She squeezed her eyelids shut, forcing the tears from her eyes and proceeded to finish drying off.

As she looked again at herself in the mirror she wondered if she would still be attractive to a man like Mike. She wasn't as young as his wife had been, but she was still very shapely. Hilde had never been pregnant, so her body was still smooth, and her skin bore no stretch marks. She was not past the age of having children. For that matter, she prayed fervently, as many women do, that she would not grow old without a baby. She just wanted to wait for the right man. She was beginning to wonder though if at the age of thirty-six, her chances for marrying and becoming a mother were quickly slipping by.

Hilde had only had one serious relationship in her life. She had expected the man to ask her to marry him, but the relationship ended with no such commitment. The boy-friend wanted to live together to see if it would work for them first. Hilde's strict religious upbringing would not allow her conscience to abide with the idea of living together without being married. When she rejected the idea, he got angry and abruptly called off the whole relationship.

She was devastated. He had been a prince charming to her while trying to woo her into bed, but turned out to be nothing but a sex-hungry jerk when it came time to make a real commitment. Since that time, from the age of twenty-two, Hildegarde Rottbruck focused solely on work. The hope that one day she would meet "Mister Right" gradually faded to a dreamy vision just beyond her grasp at the periphery of her reality. Now she wondered if, in the midst of this tragic situation, she had met him.

Hilde picked up a small bottle of lotion from the counter. It was the same brand as the body shampoo and had the same delicious peach scent. She squirted some of it onto her hand and rubbed it all over her body.

She moved to the closet. Due to the significantly more personal nature of the other items in the dresser, she opted to wear her own bra and panties until she could get home. They were freshly put on that same morning. She slipped those on and went to look for appropriate clothing for the evenings work.

In the closet she found and put on a pair of navy blue pleated slacks. They fit perfectly. Janelle had been more than just close to her size as far as the pants were concerned. She quickly glanced over the collection of tops and found a light-blue cashmere sweater. From the dresser she took a plain black silk chemise which she slid over her body and pulled the soft cashmere over that.

Once dressed, Hilde gathered up her own clothing and tucked it under her arm then stepped out of the bathroom and into the bedroom. She stood in the room and briefly looked around. She had been worried that she would have a feeling that there were ghosts watching her in the house. That somehow Janelle, or maybe even their son, would be accusing her of trying to steal another woman's husband, but she didn't have that feeling at all.

Instead, much to her surprise, she felt as though it were natural for her to be there as if she belonged. That feeling in itself was more disturbing to her than that of being accused would have been.

She tried to wipe the thought from her mind as quickly as it came. She was trespassing in another woman's domain. She was wearing another woman's clothing and had looked into another woman's underwear drawer. She was falling in love with another woman's husband, and she knew she couldn't resist it.

Is it wrong?

She glanced around the room, looked at the large king-sized sleigh bed, then squeezed her eyes shut. In her mind's eye she suddenly saw herself in his arms, an image she had not invited but that had pushed itself into her mind.

Oh, God! I've got to stop thinking this way. I can't fall in love with him.

A gentle knock on the door startled her. She opened her eyes and turned towards the door.

"Hilde?" Mike's voice called out, "Are you about ready?"

"Yes." She walked over to the door and opened it. "I was just coming out."

Mike stood just outside the door. He looked down at her with a tender gaze. She looked sheepishly up at him, embarrassed by the thoughts she had just been battling with. He scanned her up and down.

"Good selection of clothing. You look very nice."

"Thank you," she replied, "your wife was a very tasteful dresser."

"She was," he said softly. His gaze came back to her face and met her eyes. He paused there for a moment then abruptly spoke.

"Well, I'd better get showered too. There's some fresh coffee in the kitchen. I also made a sandwich for you, turkey and cheese on wheat bread. Hope that's OK with you. I'll only be about five minutes."

She turned her gaze away. The rush of blood in her cheeks glowed a radiant pink beneath her skin.

"I'll be downstairs then," she said.

Hilde passed him in the doorway and went down the stairs. She heard the door close behind her, followed by the sound of Mike's footsteps in the bathroom and the shower being turned on.

She got down to the kitchen and took a mug from a hook on the wall beside the coffee maker. She poured from the pot to the cup and lifted the steaming hot mug of dark brown liquid to her nose. The smell of the roasted coffee invigorated her senses. She took a sip, let it linger in her mouth and swallowed. Heat coursed through her body, warming her very core.

She exhaled through her nose and savored the smoky odor as it glided through her nostrils. She took another sip and glanced around the room. Neat and tidy. Everything in its place.

Everything except for the refrigerator door. It was plastered with a jumbled assortment of pictures of Mike, Janelle, and Mike Jr. There were what she presumed to be other family and church members or other friends. A birthday card hung from the surface by two laundry pins, which were stuck to the fridge by thin magnets glued to their back sides.

The pictures told the story of a happy family with many friends and a peaceful life: Mike and Janelle hugging, Janelle and Mike Jr sitting on the floor playing with a toy xylophone, Mike on his hands and knees with his son laughing wildly as he rides on daddy's back, and a glimpse of a church picnic.

One picture showed what looked like Mike playing football with a bunch of other men, but the ball looked funny, too round to be a football, and it was white instead of brown. Also, the way they were running didn't look right to her. She was no sports fan but knew this wasn't football. She scrunched her eyebrows and pursed her lips trying to recall what that sport was called.

"Rugby," she said quietly. "That's what it's called. Now that's a rough sport. I can see Mike in a sport like that."

She moved from the kitchen into the living room and walked over to the fireplace. At eye level were more pictures in frames and neatly displayed. Some were posed and others were candid shots. The kind of photos that made strong memories.

Hilde heard the shower turn off. She didn't hear anything for several minutes. As she looked into a picture of him and Janelle posing in front of a dark blue studio background, she noticed his reflection. Mike stood still in the corner of the room, staring at her. She turned and faced him.

Mike was clean, shaved and in new clothes. He wore a pair of loose fit denim jeans and a black polo shirt. Over this he put on a shoulder holster with his forty-five and two extra magazines of ammunition which he covered with a brown leather jacket.

"You had a beautiful family. I am sorry they were taken from you," she said. "It must be really hard."

"It is," he replied. "Harder than I can even say, but it is all in God's hands. He makes our path, and then leads us on it. Everything is for a purpose."

"But what is the purpose in letting an innocent mother and child die that way?" she asked.

"I don't know yet," he answered, "but eventually I will. Until that time, I have to accept it and move on."

"Accept it?" Hilde's expression tightened. She sounded irritated by his answer. "That's kind of cold, isn't it? I mean, your wife and son are dead. How can you say that you just have to accept it and move on?"

"If it had not happened this way," Mike said in response, "I would not have seen Akbar Usein at Cold Bones' house, and we would not know that there was a nuclear weapon about to be detonated in Ohio."

His voice sounded detached, almost cold. She looked at him incredulously.

"You're willing to just walk away from the memory of your family to stop this guy?"

"Look, Hilde," Mike looked down to the carpeted floor. "Janelle and Mike Junior are dead. I can't bring them back. Their death was not in vain. It caused me to see, and bring to your attention, a terrible event that we can now stop."

He paused. Hilde looked up at him. Small tears formed in the corners of his eyes. He inhaled sharply.

"My wife and son are in a better place. Of that I am sure. They are standing, right now, in God's presence. There is no more pain, no more hunger, no more fear for them. They are in paradise. I cannot bring them back, but one day I will go to them. In the meantime, there is no use in me trying to second-guess God's plan. Instead, I must do the work that is before me."

The tears welled up, overflowed and streaked down his cheek. They dripped in tiny splashes onto his jacket. Hilde's heart broke as she watched his pain rise to the surface. She reached up and gently touched his face with the palm of her hand.

Mike put his hand over hers and held it to his face.

"God, I miss them."

Tears rose and overran the corners of her eyes as well. She wanted to help him, to quell his pain. Hilde started towards him arms open. Mike stepped back.

"No," he said, "I'm sorry. I didn't mean to break down in front of you."

Hilde suddenly felt embarrassed and awkward. Mike's cell phone rang in the pocket of his jacket. They were both startled. He turned from Hilde and took the phone from his pocket. He flipped it open, looked at the caller id screen, and saw the number listed as private. He answered it.

"Farris."

"Mike, we found the vans," said the voice of Paul Hogan.

"Excellent."

"It's after six. When can you be here?"

"Give us thirty minutes," Mike answered.

"Us?" Paul asked, "Is Hilde with you?"

"Yeah."

"Good," Hogan said, "I've got Strategic Reaction Teams forming up now. We're going to hit all three of the known vehicles as soon as you can hook up with us."

"We're on the way now."

He hung up and repeated to Hilde what Paul had said. They moved to the front door. Hilde grabbed her jacket from the coat tree near the door. She started to put it on then stopped when she saw blood stains.

"Here." Mike turned and opened the nearby coat closet. He took out a different jacket, brown suede similar to hers, and handed it her. "Take this. Yours is ruined."

She put it on and Mike reached up to open the door. As his hand touched the doorknob a shape moved on the other side of the curtained glass window. The figure was reaching towards the doorbell.

His hand flew up to the butt of his pistol. Hilde backed up and likewise put her hand on the Walther PPK in the holster in the small of her back. Mike put his hand on the door knob, twisted it, and flung the door open. On the porch a small figure jumped in startled surprise.

"Oh!" a woman's voice said. "Pastor Mike, you scared me."

Before he could relax, Lenora Phelps, the thin, tight-faced church secretary, made eye contact with the butt of Mike's pistol as his jacket flapped back over it. Flowing from there her eyes fell on the form of the beautiful auburn-haired woman who stood a short distance behind him.

"I...uh...saw your Denali....and I, uh...I hope I'm not interrupting something."

"No, of course not Lenora. We were just on the way out."

"I see."

Her gaze was fixed on Hilde. Mike saw the question marks in her eyes. Worse than that, he could hear the assumptions starting in her head already.

"Lenora, this is Agent Hildegarde Rottbruck of the FBI. She is working on the case of the shooting."

Hilde lifted her badge from her purse and showed it to Lenora.

"FBI? How do you do, Agent Rottbruck?"

Lenora held out her hand in greeting.

"Nice to meet you, ma'am," Hilde replied shaking the secretary's hand lightly.

"My, I don't believe I've ever seen such a beautiful and young-looking FBI Agent before, except in the movies. Of course, they're all actors."

"Yes," said Mike, "Indeed, but we really have to get going now, Lenora. Agent Rottbruck's office just called, there's a break in the case. Is there something I can help you with?"

"Oh, yes. Elder Johnson said to give you this note, if I saw you. He sealed it in an envelope and made me promise not to read it."

Lenora seemed indignant at the elder's request, but the envelope was still sealed so she had obviously obeyed. She handed Mike the envelope and stared at him expectantly, waiting for him to open it. Instead, Mike put it in his pocket. The secretary's eyes shifted to Agent Rottbruck and ran conspicuously over the entire length of her body then back up to her face.

"Isn't that Janelle's sweater?"

"Uh, look Lenora," Mike said and stepped out onto the porch. His movement forced Lenora back. Hilde followed him. "We've really got to go. I'll explain it all to you later. Don't let your imagination take you too far. It's not what you're probably thinking. Nothing is as it seems."

The secretary stared open mouthed from the porch as Mike and Hilde walked to the SUV, got in, and left.

CHAPTER 25

Thursday October 27th
FBI Regional Headquarters
Office of the Ohio Valley Anti-Terrorist Task Force
Columbus, Ohio
18:50 Hours

Paul Hogan met Mike and Hilde in the rear loading area of the FBI building. He was dressed in an armored black assault suit, adjusting his side arm in a holster on his right thigh. Ten other men, similarly dressed, jogged past them through an open bay door into the parking lot where several vehicles waited for them.

"Mike, Hilde, we're heading out right now," Hogan spoke from the bent position.

"Fleiss has good solid tracking of the vans and they are moving at the moment. We're going to follow and hopefully catch up with them to get the drivers and the payload. Two other teams have already left. Mike, I've got a two-man team plus me. I have an assault suit in the car that you can change into or you can go as you are."

He turned to Hilde.

"You stay back here with Fleiss in the comms room. I got a strange email just a little bit ago. Believe it or not, it was from Usein. I'm assuming Kharzai sent it. Something about a case, codes, and half a million dollars. I passed it on to Fleiss who is tracing the original sender."

He rose from adjusting the thigh holster.

"I want full observation on what's happening with all three vans and the Loyal Street house. Andy's got them on satellite imagery now; let's make sure that stays up."

"Got it," she replied. "I'll be the communication liaison while Andy watches the screens. Keep your radios up at all times, so I can monitor you."

As they turned to go, Hilde called out, "Be careful."

She spoke to them both, but her eyes met Mike's. Mike faced her and smiled back with a nod. He walked out the door behind Paul Hogan.

Hogan led him to a row of identical Buick Roadmasters with government license plates. They got into one of the vehicles while the other two SRT agents on Hogan's team, John Goode and Phil Cooper, led the way in another car.

"Our target is headed directly west towards Newark," Hogan said as they pulled onto the road. "He's got about a twenty mile or so lead on us, but we should be able to catch up in a few minutes."

"So your man Fleiss locked right on to them, huh?" said Farris.

"Yep. He is one diligent nerd, that Andy. Hilde did well when she hired him. I guess quality nerds can identify each other," replied Hogan. "Speaking of nerds, is there something going on between you and Hilde?"

Farris gave Hogan an incredulous look.

"Something going on?" he asked. "Paul, my wife and son just died three weeks ago…less than three weeks ago. I don't think I'm ready for a new relationship any time soon."

"But it's happening, isn't it?" Hogan said matter-of-factly.

"What's happening?" Farris asked.

"I know she's falling for you. I've worked with her for several years and have never seen her look at another guy the way she does you," Hogan answered.

"Look, Paul, I'm not going to get into this right now. It's too soon for me to be thinking about another woman." Farris was shaken by the conversation.

"She's a good girl, Mike. Not to mention the obvious fact that she is drop dead gorgeous. She's also got one of the sweetest and smartest personalities I have ever known," Hogan said. "You two could get on well. And she's a Christian too—Methodist, I think."

"Are you trying to set me up with her?" Mike said. "Because if you are you need to stop. I'm not ready for anything like that, and probably won't be for a long time."

"Sorry, sorry," said Hogan, "I'll stop. I just thought that maybe, you know, you two would be a good match. When you're ready. I'm sorry, bad idea."

"Yeah," said Farris, "bad idea."

"I was just kind of surprised that you had her at your house," said Hogan, "and thought, that…uh…I'll shut up now."

A long uncomfortable silence followed the exchange. After several minutes Mike spoke again, "Look. I shouldn't have snapped at you like that. I can understand your assumption." He grinned. "I didn't think about it when I suggested she clean up at my place, but as we were leaving my church secretary suddenly showed up. Man, should've seen the look on her face."

Mike shook his head and nearly broke into laughter.

"I instantly realized that it was a mistake, but by then, of course, it was too late."

Hogan snickered. Mike continued.

"I was just trying to save time, being efficient, but now I am going to have a ton of explaining to the church deacon's board about why I had a female alone in the house."

"Yes, you are," said Hogan, suppressing a chuckle. "Especially a hot looking red head like Hilde."

Both of them let out a laugh as the hilarity of the scene came into full view in their minds. It took several minutes for their laughter to die down.

"If you think so highly of her, how come you haven't gone after her yourself?" asked Farris.

"I've got nothing to give her, or any other woman for that matter." Hogan replied.

"What do you mean?" responded Farris, "You're a great guy, Paul. You'd make a great husband. Back in the day, I thought you said you wanted a wife and a bunch of kids running around in a yard with a white picket fence and all. What happened to that?"

"Afghanistan," said Hogan.

Farris voice softened, "What happened there?"

"My injuries," answered Hogan.

"What, your legs?" asked Farris. "If a lady loves you, she'll get over the scars."

"It wasn't just my legs that got hit over there," said Hogan.

"Oh, I see."

Hogan drew in a deep breath, "Yep! Got no way to make those children for the wife to have in the picket fence house. I don't even have the parts necessary to give a girl a good time. To be quite graphic, my willie looks like it went through a blender. I can't imagine a woman who'd want to get married to a guy who could never satisfy her physical needs. Not only that, but my balls got blown off too. I couldn't even do the test tube thing."

"Wow, that is rough." Farris said then added, "but you never know. There are some women out there who would be interested, I think, and I'm not talking about the freaky ones. I've counseled probably a dozen or more women who would have no problem with a man like yourself. You'd be surprised how little some women desire sex, and yet could be totally loving wives."

"Yeah, well, we'll see about that. Maybe you could hook me up some day, with some celibate bride of Frankenstein chick." Hogan smiled an embarrassed grin.

The conversation ended abruptly. The two of them remained silent for rest of the drive to Newark.

Mike's mind filled with memories of the times and places in his life where the jarring damage of war had changed everything. He thought about how the violence of war changed everyone it touched for the worse. No matter how kindhearted the person may have been, no matter how physically strong they may have been, they always came out damaged.

Wounds like Paul's were horrible tragedies, physical scars that would change an individual's future plans irrevocably. No soldier goes to war with the expectation that his reproductive organs will be blown apart, and that he will be left alive as an asexual being, a eunuch. There are some wounds though that while invisible to the eye, can be much worse. Wounds Mike understood all too well. Psychological wounds took great amounts of skillful effort to keep from rising to the surface, to keep the different parts of one's life in the right places and context.

CHAPTER 26

Flashback
Jajce, Bosnia-Herzegovina
September 1998

In a vacant house across from the one in which they had dis-covered the sand-bagged position, Captain Farris and Gunny Johnson set up an observation point to watch that building as well as several others nearby. Hardt and the others finally got out of the traffic blockade on the far side of town by late in the evening. They put up in a hotel near the square and spent the night observing the area.

As the sun rose in the early morning hours of the small city's day, people slowly began to mill around the streets and sidewalks as the shops that lined them opened for business. By eight a.m, life bustled in the busy square near the check point. People scurried in and out of cafés and shops. They moved at various paces along the sidewalk towards their offices, homes, schools, or wherever they were going.

President Yeltsin was due to arrive in just over twenty-four hours. Hardt, Farris, and their men worked in advance to pre-empt any potential setup. Johnson and Farris were to spend the day watching the area of the sniper hide they had found. They were fairly certain that location would be the most likely for a shot to be taken from.

Staff Sergeant Hogan and Sergeant Flynn sat in civilian attire at the small café in which they had seen the two known members of the Sons of the Sword the day before. Over cups of coffee, they made small talk while unobtrusively observing the people who passed in the square and its adjacent shops.

"So, Paul, tell me," said Flynn, "how in the world do you Americans come off calling your game of football 'football' when in fact the vast majority of it is played with your hands and not your feet? Shouldn't you be calling it handball?"

Hogan glanced out the cafe window at the passersby on the sidewalk. He took a sip of his coffee and replied, "Well, my friend, it's like this you see. The first American football was made way back during the revolutionary war, you know, the one where we kicked England's butt for the first time." He winked at Flynn, who, although he served in the British SAS, was the grandson of Irish immigrants like himself. "You see, the troops at Valley Forge were getting bored and the cold weather necessitated doing a lot of movement in order to stay warm. They had gotten into the habit of running around in a big flat field in order keep their body heat up."

Flynn raised an inquisitive eyebrow at the explanation. He ran his eyes slowly over the patrons in the cafe. "OK, go on."

"So anyway, they were getting tired of doing jumping jacks and in place running or playing simple tag all day long. They wanted to change up their PT sessions a bit but couldn't figure out how. Then, low and behold, a patrol of US Marines detached to them gets ambushed by the redcoats. Naturally, the Marines kicked their collective lobster-back butts and in the process one of the British officers lost his boots, both of them. They had been blown off from his feet obviously because there were tears all over them but luckily for the British officer, no bits of foot. The Marines, upon securing the area of the scuffle found the boots and took them back as a trophy."

"I'm not sure where you're heading with this," said Flynn. An amused smile spread on his face as his eyes scanned the milling figures across the street, "But keep going."

"Well they get back to camp and that Marine Sergeant, an Irishman by the way, his name was O'Malley, in charge of the squad looks at all those Army and militia soldiers out playing tag in the field and says; 'My fellow leathernecks, it looks like those there soldier boys need something to make their game more focused and such, do we have a ball or some kind of similar implement with which they can play?' A very bright Corporal, by the name of Hogan, chimed up.

'Sergeant,' he said, 'we haven't got a ball, but we do have these boots from the English officer. We could make the leather into a ball of sorts.'

"The Sergeant looks at him and says, 'Well, you just see to it then, Corporal Hogan.' And the Corporal does just that, but it turns out that a bit of shrapnel had torn the boots up pretty badly and the Corporal, while being an incredibly intelligent young man, was not exceptionally skilled in the art of leatherwork. In the end, he came out with a ball that was egg shaped rather than round. It worked nonetheless, and the boys in the field had a great time."

Flynn shot a glance past Hogan at a pair of men moving toward the cafe, their expressions stern and their body language conveying alertness. He nodded in their direction and sipped his coffee as Hogan continued the story.

"'What shall we call this game?' asked one of them. 'Well, since the ball was made from the boot of that English officer, we should call it bootball,' said one of them. 'Ah! What are you thinking man?' said another. 'We should pay tribute to the poor English officer who lost his boots and had to walk across this half-frozen ground unshod, probably freezing those bootless feet. It should be called football!' and the name stuck.

"Oh, and as another note, one of the soldiers then asked as an aside, 'I wonder what kind of games them English play?' To which the Marine Sergeant replied, 'That officer has got nothing but his socks on, so whatever game it may be, the English will have to call it socker!' and that name stuck too."

Flynn chuckled over his coffee as Hogan finished the story, "You need to get out more man! You're daft!"

"Thank you, sir." Hogan nodded. Retaining his grin, he added. "GRU at the door."

"Yup," said Flynn.

Into the café door walked the two men Flynn had watched approach. One was blond haired, tall, and muscular. The other was short and stout. His head was completely shaved. The pair could not have been more conspicuous if they had "Russian Agent" in giant letters on the back of their jackets.

The GRU, *Glavnoe Razvedyvatel'noe Upravlenie,* is the agency that handles, among many things, the personal protection of the Russian president. One of the few remaining original vestiges of Lenin's empire, the GRU is one of the most powerful intelligence organizations in the world.

Much to the chagrin of many in Russian government, the GRU does not answer to anyone. Neither the KGB of the Soviet era nor the FSB of the current era had any power over them. They were above the Army or the Navy and for that matter did, not answer even to the President himself. The GRU was one of those powerful military entities that over time had become a self-serving creature to which everyone else bowed...or paid the price.

"They're casing the place," said Flynn, "looking for threats."

"Well," answered Hogan, "let's not look like threats then, eh?"

Flynn nudged Hogan's arm.

"Across the street…one of the tangos, he's coming this way."

Hogan turned to a passing waiter and asked if he could buy a bottle of water. As he waited for one to be brought out, he glanced over at the man across the street. He was a tall, dark skinned Middle Eastern looking man in a US Army uniform. The man crossed the street and entered the café. He passed close by Hogan and Flynn, the smell of cigarettes emanated from his uniform, wafting into their nostrils as he passed. He walked directly to the table with the two Russian GRU agents and sat down.

They rose and walked over to the counter to pay their bill. This brought them closer to within earshot of the Russians and their terrorist friend.

Flynn nudged Hogan again and said out loud, "Hey, I have to take a piss. I'll be right back."

"Man!" Hogan replied, sounding irritated, "You need to get your bladder checked out."

"Coffee goes right through me," Flynn said as he walked past the table where the Russians sat.

Hogan sat back down at a nearby table and pretended to read an old tourist brochure. He was close enough to listen to the low conversation taking place among the three men. They were all three speaking Russian, which Hogan understood fluently.

"You are set?" said the blond Russian.

"Yes, everything is ready," replied the soldier.

"He will be here precisely on time tomorrow," said the bald man. "You must be ready exactly as planned."

"There will be no problem. The site is prepared, and Hasan knows nothing. He expects to be a great hero by morning."

"The American," said the blond, "you will deal with him?"

"Of course," replied the soldier, "I have already planned everything. There will be no loose ends."

"Good. We will have the rest of your money when the job is completed, as arranged," said the bald one. "Has anyone been watching you?"

"No, we've been in the hotel across the square for three days and no one has taken notice. There are many soldiers who come here to see the waterfall and get some girls. We are just blending in."

"Good. We will have no more contact with you. You are on your own now," said the bald man. "Don't fail."

The soldier rose from his seat and walked away. He patted the blond man on the shoulder in a friendly gesture as he passed. Flynn came out of the bathroom just as the bogus soldier walked out of the café.

Hogan rose to his feet and said, "Are you feeling better now?"

"Yes, sir, I am!" Flynn replied, and they walked out the door.

Once in their car, Hogan told Flynn what he had heard.

"We'd better let the Captains know," said Flynn. "We don't need anyone walking into an ambush."

CHAPTER 27

The two unmarked 2010 Buick Roadmasters cruised heavily along the wide stretch of Morse Road until it ended at Worthington Road. Hogan followed the other vehicle as they turned east onto state route 16 and continued towards the city of Newark. The dashboard mounted LCD display set in the console next to the radio of the FBI vehicles showed the flashing dot of the homing signal moving ahead of them at a constant pace. Nearly thirty minutes after they left the headquarters building, the flashing red dot turned right on North 30th Street in the city of Newark, then left on Parkview Road. A few minutes later the driver of the van turned into the Mound Builders Country Club parking lot. Hogan and the others were two miles behind the van when the signal stopped moving.

They accelerated around the corner until they reached the entrance to the country club. The drivers extinguished the headlights of the vehicles and continued into the parking lot. Creeping in near silence they moved with windows down, alert and observant. The shadow of the van stood in stillness at the end of the large parking lot.

The flat asphalt paved lot was two hundred yards long and a hundred yards wide. The van was parked in front of a two-story building with a large sign above the double entry doors that read "The Club House." A high wall of glass windows set in a steel frame formed the front of the building. Like a giant mirror it reflected back the dark, shadowy images of the forest, sky, parking lot, and the van. Through the glass they could see that the interior was divided into a store and dining area. Racks of golf supplies filled one side, while a café with tables and chairs surrounded a high bar stocked with scores of bottles of liquor on a dimly lighted shelf behind the bar.

They kept their vehicles close to the trees on the side of the lot and silently rolled to within one hundred yards. Long shadows cast by the moon stretched across the paved area. Darkness concealed the agents as they crept closer. The drivers rolled to a stop and turned off their engines. Four men quietly opened the doors and got out of the Roadmasters. They rose smoothly and silently from the cars engulfed by the inky stillness and slid thermal sensing night vision glasses down over their eyes.

Crickets and frogs chirped a rhythmic symphony from the woods and the grassy expanse beyond the parking lot. The sound echoed hypnotically from every direction in the air around them. Nothing moved near the van. Through the night vision glasses the world was illuminated with a pale green light. The thermal optic sensors contained within the circuitry of the glasses lit up any objects that had a temperature over ninety degrees with an eerie glow. The metal engine block shone bright within the enclosure of the front of the van. A rhythmic tick sounded like a clock as the thick metal block gradually cooled. The exhaust system trailing under the carriage of the van carried the luminescence in decreasing intensity to the rear of the vehicle. The transmission glowed a dimmer shade than the tailpipe.

They saw no trace of human life there. No man shaped heat signature. For that matter, no other glow at all. They scanned the area around the van. The woods in the distance. The shadows and dark recesses around the building.

Nothing.

If there were any human beings, or mammals of any kind, in the area, their bodies were the same temperature as the cool autumn air around them.

The three agents and Mike raised their weapons and rushed towards the van. Their feet moved with fluid swiftness, silently crossing the parking area in short, controlled steps. They scuttled forward in a half crouch MP-5 submachine guns held at shoulder height, ready to spray a rain of ten-millimeter bullets into any ambusher. Their eyes scanned everything through the sights at the end of the barrel. The weapons pointed wherever their eyes moved.

As they approached they spread out in a wide arc to cover the flanks of the van. The fact that they had not seen someone in the area did not mean someone wasn't there, potentially hidden behind some barrier, waiting to charge them guns blazing. The fact that Mister White was such a technophile allowed for the possibility he could have robotics deployed to perform an ambush controlled remotely from a faraway site.

That's how the US military liked to do it in the War on Terror, and the gangs were seldom far behind in acquiring technology to make their crimes more efficient. One thing Hogan and Farris alike had learned long ago: never take anything for granted.

They kept several yards between each of them as they made their way forward so that multiple men would not be hit by a single shot or explosion. The soft rubber soles of their boots made almost no sound as they arrived at the vehicle. Still no sign of any human materialized.

Cautiously, they surrounded the van and closed in on it. Agent Goode stood at the driver's door. Agent Cooper stood at the utility door on the passenger side. Hogan stood at the rear double doors. Mike stayed back twenty feet to cover the passenger side and the rear.

Hogan whispered in a barely audible voice.

"One, Two, Three!"

All three agents simultaneously threw open the van's doors and thrust their weapons forward, ready to repel possible attackers.

There was nothing.

No one.

No cargo.

Nothing.

"It was a switch," called out Agent Cooper as he scanned the interior of the van from the passenger side doors. "They made a vehicle switch on us."

Hogan pressed the radio microphone button on the small transmitter box suspended from his assault suit.

"Hilde, this is Hogan," he said, "They've duped us. The van must've either been dumped here or swapped for another vehicle. There is nothing in it. Send a team to confiscate it for a deeper search."

"Paul, one of the other teams reports the same thing," she said. "The van was dropped in an empty parking lot, no cargo. No indication as to what was in it."

"Maybe the investigative teams can find something more on these," Hogan said, "Mike and I are going to head back. We'll leave agents Goode and Cooper here with the van until the CSI folks show up."

"Roger that, Paul," she said, "Oh, by the way, Andy is almost done with the trace of the IP signal from White's teleconference unit. It goes through a whole series of techno-hoops until it ends up at a computer lab in a Pittsburgh high school. From there it gets scrambled and diverted to a multitude of other signals. We think that's the last hoop and they're trying to find out which of those connections is legit and will take us to White."

"Good job, Hilde," replied Hogan, "Keep it up until we track that bastard down."

"Will do," she said. "Out here."

The radio went silent.

"Mike, let's head back," Hogan said. "John, Phil, you guys wait here. Field techs are coming to check the vehicle out. You may want to get back to your car and wait under-cover, in case someone else comes up later to get this thing. They may not be done with it yet."

"Will do, Paul," Agent John Goode replied and pointed to the tree line near their vehicles. "We'll walk back with you and move the car into those trees over there until CSI shows up."

As they walked back together, Phil Cooper looked over to Farris and asked, "So, Mike, I hear you were with UNSOCOM in Bosnia?"

Farris was surprised to hear UNSOCOM mentioned by someone he had never met. "Yeah. I did two tours there. One as an observer in ninety-two and one special ops mission later."

"Yeah," Cooper said, "The Yeltsin affair."

Farris and Hogan both stopped in their tracks and asked at the same time, "How did you know about that?"

"I was with the Defense Intelligence Agency as a human intelligence officer on the ground at the time. My partner was the guy who first saw Mathis in country and alerted UNSOCOM, who in turn called you guys."

"You were there? How come you never mentioned that to me before, Phil?" asked Hogan, "I was there too, you know."

"Yeah, well, I only met you a few months ago when I got stationed here, Paul," Cooper replied, "and there are a lot of Hogan's in the spec-ops world, must be an Irish thing. There were six Paul Hogan's in Bosnia in ninety-eight by the way, but there is only one Mike Farris, US Marine Corps who became an ordained pastor shortly after taking on Brett Mathis, the reincarnate Jackal, who tried to kill Boris Yeltsin and set off World War Three."

Goode looked incredulously at his partner.

"You know these guys from back then? That's incredible."

"What do you mean 'must be an Irish thing?'" Hogan asked.

"Glad you survived, gentlemen." Cooper replied. "That was some hard-core shit."

"Yeah, it was," Mike said as they reached the halfway point to their vehicles.

At precisely 7:59 PM the atmosphere around them erupted with a body crushing boom. The city of Newark shook from the force of a sound louder than any that had been heard in its entire two-hundred-year history. The glass windows of the country club's restaurant and pro-shop imploded in a shower of razor sharp slivers of glass.

All four men slammed violently to the ground as the concussion blasted past them. Jagged metal shards, some as big as man's head, screamed past like angry demons, zinging between them in a shrill death song. A ball of flame rose into the dark night sky from the skeletal remains of the van. The twisted mass of the steel frame cast long flickering shadows that danced crazily in the light of the flames. Bubbling puddles of black rubber that had been tires moments earlier oozed across the pavement.

Debris fell around the men where they lay prone, face down, hands covering the backs of their heads. As the last bits of the van drifted back to earth Hogan, Farris, and Goode rose slowly. They weakly pushed their bodies from the ground until they stood upright. They turned toward the flaming wreck. Cooper remained face down on the pavement, hands over his head.

"Hey Coop! Get up!" shouted Goode. "Danger's over!"

He kicked at his friend's foot. Cooper's leg flopped in limp response to Goode's boot. Goode dropped to his knees beside Cooper. Wetness seeped into the leg of his trousers as he knelt on the pavement. It was blood.

"Man down!" Goode cried out. "He's hit!"

A thin red sheet streamed across the back of Cooper's neck. In the space between his black Kevlar helmet and the thick ceramic shields of his protective vest a two-inch wide gash lay open at the base of his hairline perpendicular to his spinal cord. A pool of steaming blood spread on the pavement around Cooper's head. Goode flipped his friend over and sucked in a gasping breath of shock at what he saw.

The front of Phillip Cooper's face was split open from the inside. It blossomed like a nightmarish flower. Bits of white bone jutted from the periphery of the wound. His eyeballs, whole and unscathed, stared blankly at the sky. The two white globes sat at the top edge of the bright red pulp that had once been the face of Philip Cooper, victim of the randomness of shrapnel, the bane of every soldier's existence.

CHAPTER 28

The Crime Scene Investigations team from FBI Headquarters went through the widely scattered wreckage of the van in the Mound Builders Country Club parking lot with the absolute care of professional jigsaw puzzle addicts. While they meticulously scoured the area for clues as to what happened, paramedics inspected the three survivors of the blast.

The men watched as the medical examiner supervised a pair of technicians as they zipped Agent Coopers body into a black vinyl bag and carefully hefted it onto a lowered gurney. One of the technicians grasped the handle at the head of the gurney and together with the other tech lifted it until the wheels dropped to their full length. It locked into position with a loud snap that made Goode flinch. They rolled it into an ambulance that would take it to the morgue for an autopsy.

Hogan always wondered why they ordered autopsies on bodies that had been killed by obviously verifiable means. It was government policy, therefore it always happened. John Goode glanced over to Hogan and Farris. His eyes were moist as he spoke.

"I've served with Phil since Quantico. He was a really good guy, too good to die in such a random way."

Goode pressed the tips of his fingers into the lines that creased his forehead, trying to press the stress away.

"A God damned piece of shrapnel. Why didn't it find one of us instead?"

Farris looked at him sympathetically. He had counseled victims with survivor guilt before, both as a Marine Officer and as a Pastor.

"Did he have family?" Farris asked

"Yeah," replied Goode, "wife and two kids, boy and girl, five and eight. Cutest kids you'd ever meet, and his wife is one of those sparkly, bubbly types. I don't know how she's going to take this."

"No one ever takes it well when their spouse dies," replied Farris. "Not if they loved them."

Silence hung in the air between the three men. The medics quietly put away their kits. No one spoke. There was nothing that could be said to alleviate the heaviness of the loss. The silence was interrupted by the loud warbling ring tone of Hogan's cell phone.

"Hogan," he replied.

"Paul, this is Hilde."

"What's up?"

"We just got a report from the Worthington precinct of CPD. They picked up a speeder in whose car they found fifty pounds of heroin," said Hildegarde

"Yeah, so?" answered Hogan tersely. "We're not the damn drug squad. Turn it over to narcotics."

"Paul," Hilde said, "narcotics called me on it, because they found a GPS on the guy's front seat. When they asked him about it he mumbled something about 'that damn African' but other than that was totally uncooperative. They brought me the GPS and I gave it to Andy."

"Is it connected to our guys?" replied Paul.

"The guy was picked up less than five miles from the scene where one of the other vans exploded. Andy is trying to hack into the GPS. Whoever set it up seems afraid of getting caught. They have so much security on this thing that he…"

In the background Hogan suddenly heard Andy Fleiss' voice shouting.

"Got it!" Fleiss said. His voice was flat and distant in the cell phone's speaker. "Hilde! Talk about bait and switch!"

His voice grew louder in Paul's cell phone speaker as he walked closer to Hilde's phone. She switched to speaker phone as he spoke.

"The way this thing is programmed is crazy. It has locations that pop up at specified times between now and Saturday morning. I am manually pushing the time forward on the GPS and it is running me all over the map of Ohio," Andy said.

He continued, "It looks like he was to go tonight to an address in Dayton, then head out first thing in the morning where the programmed route was to lead him to an address halfway to Cleveland, then at 8 am Saturday he is to go to…" Fleiss voice tightened as he finished, "to Ohio Stadium."

"We were right," said Hilde. "Detective Martin was right then. They are going to try to bomb Ohio Stadium."

"This is like that Tom Clancy movie, 'The Sum of All Fears!'" Fleiss said, his voice quivering in a state of near panic. "The one where they blow up the Super Bowl!"

Hogan tried to calm Fleiss down through the phone. "Hey, don't worry. We've got a good head start. We'll get teams in there with radiation monitors and catch these guys. They won't get to set that thing off! The good guys always win, right?"

"Not in Clancy's book!" replied Fleiss, his voice rose to a higher pitch as his emotions elevated. "They caught the bad guys, but not before the bomb went off! You guys have to catch this bomb. There will be almost...maybe...I don't know...half a million people there!"

"Calm down, Andy," Hilde said softly, "we will catch them in time."

Her voice did not hide her own uncertainty very well. If a suitcase nuclear bomb were brought there, it would not be traceable until the person carrying it opened the case. Terrorists involved in this kind of work are suicidal; they don't use timers to let them get away from the blast. It's their ticket to heaven. Even if the FBI got the radiation signature, they would only have a few minutes to find it and capture the terrorists before they armed the detonator and set it off.

"Hilde, Andy," Hogan said, "figure out a way to track the other GPSs down. In the meantime, Mike and I are heading back in. We'll work it together once we arrive."

CHAPTER 29

Billy Z slipped the cell phone from his jacket pocket. He flipped it open with his thumb and scrolled through the contacts list. Names rolled up the tiny LCD screen until the name Jazzy Jeff was highlighted. He pressed the call button and put the phone to his ear. It rang twice.

"Sup?" said the voice on the other end.

"Yo, it's me," Billy replied, "I'm headed west out of Columbus but don't know exactly where I will end up. The African dude had us ditch the vans and switch the cargo to a different car that he provided. He said we were to continue to follow the GPS coordinates until the directions stop coming, then wait at the end until our contact comes to meet us and take the package."

"What kind of vehicle are you in now?"

"A white oh-five Impala. License Plates GLR-019," said Billy.

"Where is the GPS leading you?" asked the voice on the other end.

"Hell if I know," answered Billy. "It doesn't give the next coordinate until you pass a way point. I could end up in Utah for all I know."

"Just follow it," replied the voice, "and keep me informed of your whereabouts every few hours, until you come to your final stop."

"This is getting pretty tense," said Billy. "I don't like being led around this way. There is no way to get back up in here if it all goes to shit."

"Don't worry, Billy," answered the voice, "I've got you covered. Give me the MAC address on the back of your GPS. I'll see if I can pick it up on the grid, and maybe we can track you."

Billy turned the device over and read off the twelve-digit series of numbers and letters printed under the bar code on a small tag on the rear of the device.

"Got it," said the voice. "I'll put my IT guys on it. We should have you on our radar soon enough, and you don't even have to worry about carrying a bug."

"Man," said Billy, "when this is all over, you owe me a beer, and I am seriously going to take a vacation. Maybe Tahiti or something."

"Yeah, sure," answered the voice, "we're paying you enough for a damn good vacation."

He let a short burst of breath and said, "I've gotta live to collect it."

Billy hung up the phone. The semi-rural road on which he traveled in the moonlit night was at once peaceful and intimidating. He drove past a steady stream of fence posts and phone poles that beat a visual rhythm to the otherwise boring countryside. The tedium was occasionally broken up by high-price suburban housing developments that gradually encroached on what had been entirely farmland just two decades earlier.

"Yeah, baby," he spoke to the windshield and the stars beyond, "I gotta live to collect it."

CHAPTER 30

Jajce, Bosnia
September 1998

Captain Farris lay very still. So still that in the pre-dawn darkness of the chilly late-summer morning several mice had run over his back and scurried away, seeming to not even take notice of the presence of a living human in their domain. Beside him Marcus Johnson lay equally motionless. They had watched the sniper hide across the street all night long, waiting patiently for a sign of movement, something out of the ordinary that would indicate Mathis or some other person was setting up to take the shot at the Russian President.

There had been only one bit of movement the night before, not long after they had settled into their observation post. A family returned to their home almost directly across the street from their own position. A mother pulled her small car up to the two-story blue stucco house and got out with two young children, a boy about nine or ten years old and a little girl not more than six. The boy helped his mother carry in bags of groceries while the woman carried in two medium-sized suitcases.

"Must be returning from a trip or something," Johnson whispered. "I wonder where her husband is."

"In this place, most likely dead or in jail, if not with his family," replied Farris.

"You're probably right," said Johnson.

Once in the house, the mother went into the kitchen and cooked some food while the children played in the sitting room on the other side of the house. Farris watched them through the windows for some time as both rooms were at the front of the house. At ten o'clock the woman sent her children upstairs to bed. She followed behind them half an hour later and turned off all of the lights as she made her way up to her room.

The night had stayed very still for the most part. Twice packs of wild dogs made their way through the street sniffing and scratching about for anything they could find to eat. The dogs were more than just a nuisance as people were moving back into their old neighborhoods.

The dogs themselves had mostly been domestic pets before the civil war broke out. As the fighting drew nearer their owners had either fled the city or been killed. In either case the wide variety of dogs previously cared for by the mostly middle and upper-class residents of the cities had been abandoned, necessitating their own self-rule. The packs were a motley assortment of everything from Rottweillers to Shi-Tzu's. Sometimes the little one's actually ended up being the most ferocious of the pack. It wasn't uncommon to witness a Chihuahua or a Miniature Doberman Pincer leading a pack of larger dogs on forays through the neighborhoods.

Frequently there were cases in the local hospitals of children who had been mauled by wild dogs while out playing in their own yards or on the city streets. Sometimes, the children had even recognized their own former pets and gone to them with joyous expectations of reunion only to be savagely attacked. Throughout the night, those dogs were all that moved through the street.

The sun awoke slowly in the east, rising to illuminate the mist shrouded hills and valleys that surrounded the city. Its pale light moved the shadows across the streets and deepened the dark spaces between the houses as morning gradually kissed the landscape.

"I wonder if we are in the right place," said Johnson. "Maybe this was just a decoy."

"Maybe so, but this is the most likely spot in the whole city to hit him in that square," replied Farris. "It is only seven right now. Our shooter may be waiting for the last minute to take up his position."

From where they lay, they could see the inside of the house where the sand bagged position lay empty. They also had a good view of the side alley and part of the area behind the house. If anyone tried to enter that house through one of its doors, they would catch it. Even if not, they would be able to observe him once he got in position. At seven thirty the encrypted radio they carried vibrated silently against Farris thigh, he pulled it out and answered in a soft whisper.

"Farris."

"Thirty minutes to touchdown," replied Hardt's voice.

"Got it," Farris replied, "How are your guys situated down there?"

"Hogan and Flynn are in the square. Smythe is at the secondary location you mentioned. The target just passed my position on the highway. I'm making my way via motorbike on some back roads and hope to join them in the square before he arrives."

"Got it. We'll sit tight here. Nothing is moving out there yet," said Farris. "I'll keep you informed as things change."

"Roger that, out here," said Hardt, then he clicked off.

In the house across the street a light turned on in the kitchen. Captain Farris watched as the young mother prepared breakfast for her children. She was mildly attractive, thin, blond, and in her late twenties. Through his binoculars he could see that her life had been very hard. Her sorrow-etched face garnered an almost ghostlike appearance. She wore what looked like a wedding ring on her finger, so maybe her husband was still alive and just not home yet.

He scanned the area around the house, up the alley between hers and the next two then back to the woman. Farris watched her as she broke eggs into a bowl. She suddenly stopped and leaned against the counter with both hands. The young woman started to sob uncontrollably. Her entire body heaved with pain that shook to her very soul. Her long hair, damp and straight, shook like waves of a stormy sea under the power of her sorrowful convulsions.

Perhaps he was wrong. Maybe her husband was gone, one of the tens of thousands whose lives were snuffed out by the senselessness of civil war. The ring may have just been a symbol that she was trying to hold on to the one thing that had given her peace before hell surfaced on her part of the planet. She suddenly stopped her mourning, wiped her eyes with the palm of her hand, and attempted to straighten her hair. A moment later her son turned from the hall into the kitchen.

Life had to go on; Farris thought, regardless of what fate sent your way. And regardless of how each of life's steps fell, in his heart, Mike Farris truly believed that God had a plan in it all.

CHAPTER 31

State Route 16
East of Columbus, Ohio
Friday, October 28th
03:35 Hours

As Hogan drove them back to Columbus, Mike closed his eyes to rest. He drifted into a deep sleep moments before they got back onto I-70. While it lasted only a few minutes, it felt like hours. As the deepest point of sleep overcame him the dream crept back into his mind. All of the components were there again: his family's murder, Usein laughing, Mathis putting a gun to his head...falling.

The falling was the most frightening part of the dream. Fear burst through his veins as he dropped through a seemingly endless chasm, repeatedly passing the image of the child clutching his mother. They kept reappearing over and over as he fell. His chest was tight with anxiety to the point that he feared he might die of a heart attack in the middle of the dream.

And then, unexpectedly, in the midst of the terrifying descent he felt warmth, like a comforting blanket that wrapped around him, like a lover's arms holding him. This had not happened in the dream before. He didn't know what it was. He felt himself slowing down. His chest relaxed. The fear subsided.

Janelle stood in front him, smiling. She held Mike Jr. on her hip.

"It's OK, baby," she said. "It's OK. Move on, Marine."

"But I can't," he replied. "I miss you."

"We'll see you again when it's all over."

"Daddy, it's good here," said Mike Jr. He spoke with a clear sounding child's voice, not with the broken words of a toddler he had used the last time Mike heard him in this world, "I like it here."

"Mikey, daddy will come to you soon," he said.

"No, daddy," Mike Jr. said, "don't come here yet."

Janelle nodded at her son's words and added, "You have more to do, baby."

"But..."

Mike stood motionless in the dream. He breathed heavily but found himself unable to speak. A mixture of sorrow, confusion, and peace swirled in his spirit. Before he could say anything more Janelle and Mike Jr. faded, and he was left alone in a warm dark place.

"We're back." Paul nudged his shoulder. His eyes fluttered open and he saw that they had arrived at the FBI building. Mike sat up, He felt almost fully rested.

"Hey there, pal," Hogan called out, "You were seriously deep asleep there. Do you want to continue the trend in my office or do you want to go home for a few hours?"

"What time is it?" asked Farris.

"Almost a quarter after four in the morning," said Hogan.

"I'm good; that nap was all I needed."

"You sure about that?" asked Hogan. "You've been going hard for almost twenty-four hours, and you're not as young as you used to be, no matter how much Grecian Formula you use to hide the gray hair."

"We need to trace those bombs down, the sooner the better," Farris replied.

"Yeah well, I have radiation teams already on it. They'll be scouring the Ohio Stadium and the surrounding area, both on foot and via satellite, as we speak."

Paul Hogan looked at his friend with a serious expression.

"Mike, we can't do it all. I have teams out there working on it. Don't worry. We'll find them. I don't want you running yourself into the ground before we get these guys cornered. Go home, clean up, sleep two or three hours in your bed, and then come back here about nine. By that time Andy and Hilde should have something solid for us."

"Alright, Paul, I will," he replied. "I'll be back by nine."

He stepped out of the car and began to trudge heavily across the parking lot to his own vehicle. A few steps away he turned towards Hogan and called out, pointing to his own head, "By the way, this is my natural hair color."

Paul grinned back as Mike got into his Denali SUV and drove home. It was just before five a.m. when he drove through his neighborhood. It lay still and quiet at this hour. Frankie, the twelve-year-old paperboy wouldn't be up for another hour yet. Nothing stirred in the quiet suburban setting. He drove past the neatly laid out houses set on tidy half-acre partially treed lots until he came to his own street. He turned the corner and pulled past the parking lot of Faith Presbyterian Church.

Mike pulled into the parsonage driveway and got out of the SUV. He stood on the asphalt in the cool morning darkness and listened to the quiet for several seconds. Leaning against the side of the large vehicle he let loose a tension filled sigh that fled like a solid object from his lungs. Then he closed his eyes, leaned his head back against the glass window, and prayed in a whispered voice.

"Fathe,r God, help us find these terrorists."

Mike Farris rubbed his tired brow with the fingers of his hand and glanced towards the church across the street. As he looked up, something caught his eye. At first, he couldn't tell what it was. Something was not right about the church. Something was out of place. He stared closer, and then scanned across the parking lot. Towards the back of the church the education ministry's three vans were parked near the Sunday school entrance. Next to them sat a car, the immaculate, old Cadillac driven by Elder Harry Johnson.

"What is he doing there this early?"

A sudden pang of worry coursed through him. He rushed across the street. As he drew nearer the front of the church his gut knotted with worry. He realized what it was that had first caught his eye. No reflection came from the windows in the front doors. The light that illuminated the parking lot from tall poles was not reflecting back from the glass. The light didn't reflect because there was nothing to reflect from. The glass was not there. Mike broke into a dead run until he reached the doors. Shards of glass were scattered inside on the carpet. They had been shattered from the outside. Someone had reached through the busted window and opened the door from the inside. The building was silent. Mike pulled his pistol from the leather holster inside his jacket. He reached through and pulled the crash bar towards himself, opening the door.

Eyes wide and senses on full alert he entered the foyer and moved with silent, cat-like grace on the balls of his feet down the hall that ran alongside the cavernous open space of the main sanctuary. The side hall led past his office to the choir practice room. That room opened to the side of the stage just in front of the pulpit from which he had taught for the previous ten years.

Mike's mind buzzed like the computer circuits of a radar array as he used every one of his senses to scan the church.

Farris felt for vibrations that could indicate movement. His eyes watched for shadows or shifts of reflected light. He listened for movement through the walls. The building was silent. He inhaled through both his nose and mouth searching for scents or tastes that could give away an enemy's location: cologne or deodorant, body odor that smelled of garlic, onion, or grease, bad breath or flatulence, anything that could give up their position.

As he entered the choir practice room only a few feet from the stage of the church two unmistakable sensations wafted into his nose and slid across his tongue with a stinging, metallic, pungency: gunpowder and blood.

From the choir room he peered through the narrow-slit windows that provided a view across the front of the stage where the altar rail stood between the congregation and the pulpit. A form lay sprawled in the open space at the center of the steps that led up to the stage, between two sections of the railing.

Mike carefully opened the door. He kept his form low and weapon raised at the ready. His eyes scanned across the neat rows of padded chairs, over six hundred of them, that stretched to the rear of the large church. He moved slowly out of the door towards the figure that lay on the floor in front of the altar. Harry Johnson, the eighty-year-old retired CIA operative lay on his side. He was still breathing, but a sickly looking red froth foamed from between his lips. His face was pale gray. His lips were a ghastly blue and his hands quivered uncontrollably, a shattered cell phone in one.

"Harry!"

Mike rushed forward.

"Harry, what happened? Who did this?"

Harry's voice was weak.

"I was praying here late last night when several of those gang punks came in."

He took a shallow breath and added, "They wanted you, Mike."

Elder Johnson grimaced in pain. Once the wave of agony completed its course over him, he continued.

"You weren't home, so they came here."

"Where are they?"

"Gone. I got two…" A wet and painful sounding cough wracked his body, interrupting him mid-sentence.

He caught his breath and finished. "I got two of the punks dead on, Mike, and nicked a third just before he shot me."

Mike noticed a 9mm semi-automatic pistol on the stage several feet away. "Who were they? When did they leave?"

"I don't know who they were; it was dark…just before midnight." Harry's voice faded to a whisper. He closed his eyes until he gained enough strength to start again.

"I thought they were burglars or vandals, going to trash the place, but then one of them said Mister Usein knows who you really are and is coming to finish the job. He didn't talk like a gangster though. He sounded educated, intelligent. It was strange…he sounded like a military man…or a cop."

Mike grabbed his cell phone from his pocket, quickly dialed 911 and told the operator what had happened. They dispatched an ambulance and the police. He turned his friend onto his back and opened his shirt. Two dark blood-crusted dots, the thickness of a finger, stared back from the middle of his torso. One of the wounds was just below the heart. There were no exit wounds. The bullets were lodged inside the old man's body.

Farris looked down at the grandfatherly old warrior who lay before him. "Harry, don't talk. The ambulance is coming."

"It was like the old days Mike. But I'm not as fast as I used to be," said Harry. "Budapest in sixty-three. Did I ever tell you about Budapest?"

Harry shook his head slowly as the memory flooded back to his own mind.

"So much blood, young lives. So much for our country."

"Shhh," Mike said, "rest. The medics will take you to the hospital. You can tell me about Budapest when you get your strength back."

"Mike," said Harry, his voice lowering to a barely audible volume, "I'm going to die. I know it. I'm ready to go home to my Lord."

The elder smiled peacefully and his eyes closed with gentle ease.

He whispered. "I've always known what you were doing, and I've always agreed with it. I still do. You are like a son…."

Harry's voice faded mid-sentence. He breathed out a long sigh. It was his last. His soul left the shattered shell of his body. Harry Johnson's lifeless remains slouched across the steps of the altar.

CHAPTER 32

Hildegarde Rottbruck sat quietly in Hogan's office, listening as Mike Farris described to her and Paul Hogan what had happened to Harry Johnson at his church. Her throat tightened and a sick feeling roiled in her belly as she watched tears well up in his eyes as he explained to them how Elder Johnson had been like a father to him. Johnson had mentored him and always been there for Mike to confide in. They had been especially close since the death of Mike's own parents several years earlier.

He told them what the thugs had said to Harry about Usein's threat and that he had left that detail out when he spoke to the police at the church. To the officers on the scene Mike acted as though the two events, his family and friends murder and the attack on the church, were unrelated coincidences. Farris let the officers believe their assumption that it was just a burglary gone awry when the thieves ran into a feisty old timer with a concealed-weapons permit who went down fighting to protect what he valued most.

Hilde glanced up at Mike. "Your church secretary gave you a letter from him yesterday. Did you get a chance to look at it?"

"I forgot," Mike said, moving over to where his jacket hung on the back of a chair. He took the letter from the inside pocket and opened it, a quizzical look on his face as he scanned the contents.

"What is it?" asked Hilde.

"A list of names," Mike said. "There must be nearly a hundred."

"Do you recognize any of them?" Hogan said.

"No," Mike said, "there's some text at the bottom."

He paused, seeming unsure of whether to read it aloud.

"Can you tell us?" Hilde asked.

"I knew all of their names. Fifty years and I still see their faces. Some of them never knew what hit them, others looked into my eyes at their last breath. Mike, don't hold on to ghosts; they will suck your spirit and leave you hollow."

"Poor man," Hilde said. "What a burden to carry."

The men were silent, as if searching the chambers of their own minds, evicting the ghosts that haunted the places they had tried to seal off. Hogan broke the moment by rubbing his hands together and standing up.

"Alright, we need to get back to business. I'm assuming Martin wasn't there then?"

"No, he wasn't on it. A detective named Clay Dugan came in with CSI about an hour after the uniforms had arrived," answered Farris.

Hilde's face suddenly erupted in a look of surprise.

"Oh shoot! I forgot to tell you that Martin left a message on my cell phone this morning. He had gotten a call from his informant last night and was going to come by here about noon. He wanted to make sure you two could meet with him."

"Of course," said Hogan reaching into his pocket for his own cell phone. "but why the hell didn't he call me? You're not my secretary."

He flipped his phone open and saw a blank screen.

"Well, that explains that. Piece of crap phone. You know, it's been twenty years since these things became popular, and they still can't seem to make a battery that doesn't drop out on you at the most inopportune moment."

Hogan turned around to the credenza behind his desk and plugged the small phone into the high-speed charging cable that lay neatly rolled up on its surface.

"Hilde, what have you guys got so far on the GPSs?" he asked.

"Andy is trying to get a fix on all of the MAC addresses from about twenty or so units on either side of that same model," she replied. "No luck so far, but he only just got started on that idea a few hours ago."

Farris scrunched his eyes. "MAC address? You'll have to excuse my ignorance, but I can't remember what that is at the moment."

"The MAC address is the 'Media Access Control' address. It's a sequential number assigned from the factory for all network-attached equipment. It's a unique identifier for that piece of equipment on the Internet. No two pieces of equipment have the same address, at least not legitimately. Sometimes hackers and techno-pirates will 'spoof' an address to make their equipment look like someone else's for illegal purposes. Otherwise, the Internet governing body, IEEE, assigns sets of MAC addresses to each company that manufactures networking products. These numbers, like I said earlier, are sequentially hard coded into the equipment so that each device on the network will not bump into another or get the wrong responses back from their data source."

"Wow," said Hogan, "it's too early in the morning for my brain to crunch that much information. I think I get the basic idea though."

"That makes sense," said Mike. "If the numbers are sequential, and whoever bought the one that was captured bought the others at the same time and place, then the individual units may be in sequential order."

"Right," said Hilde, "As long, that is, as they bought all the same models. Andy did find out that the one we have was sold at one of the local Sam's Club warehouse stores about two weeks ago. It was hacked into though, and directly programmed, so there is a chance that we may not be able to trace the others accurately."

Hogan leaned back in his tall leather chair and stretched his back and shoulders.

"We have to," he said. "There is no room for error here."

Knuckles rapped on the office door. Before anyone could get up to open it, Andy Fleiss abruptly walked in.

"OK, here's the deal so far," he said breathlessly, not waiting for acknowledgement from the others. "Out of forty MAC's I scanned for from the GPS satellites eight of them are turned on right now. Three of those are in western Pennsylvania in the mountains sitting relatively still. They're probably deer hunting judging by their locations and the way they have moved in the past few hours."

"What about the others?" Hogan asked.

"One of them is located in a parking lot at the airport, it has been on for three days, but hasn't moved. Another is at French Run Elementary School in Reynoldsburg, it was switched on just a few minutes before I started the search and moved back and forth in a space of about thirty feet for half an hour, then became still again."

Farris said, "Sounds like a third grader doing show & tell."

"Probably," replied Andy. "I've already taken the liberty of asking the local police to check those two out, but I am pretty sure they're harmless."

"So what about the remaining three?"

"They are all within fifty miles of Columbus but in different places and moving in what seem to be random directions. Here's the thing though," he paused for a second, making eye contact with all three of the agents in the room, "they were all turned on at about the same time last night and all turned off at exactly the same time."

"If they turned off, how did you find them?" asked Hogan.

"They came back on at seven thirty this morning," he answered, "All three of them. They are only staying on for less than five minutes then not reappearing for two or three hours. That's how I caught them, because they all three came back on at 11:17 then went right back off at 11:22. When they came on each one had traveled more than a hundred miles in winding, circuitous routes that seem to be leading nowhere."

"Like a holding pattern," said Hilde.

"That's what I think," replied Andy.

"Alright then," said Hogan, "find them and try to get some satellite imaging on those signals once you do."

"I'll try to capture the programmed course from them," said Andy, "or maybe I can stop them from turning off so fast."

"What about that email address?" said Hogan.

"You're not going to like this," said Andy. "I traced it as far as a few hops into Georgia."

"Georgia? It's here in the US?"

"No, Georgia on the banks of the Black Sea. The former Soviet Republic."

"That likely confirms what the package is then," said Farris.

"Yeah," said Hogan, his voice grim with the realization.

Fleiss walked out the door. His footsteps scuffed the floor noisily as he shuffled back to the elevators.

After he shut the door Hogan asked, "Where'd you find that guy Hilde? He is good."

"Yes, he is," she replied. "And to think, he could have been working on a Nobel Prize in Nuclear Physics. Instead he's working overtime trying to stop a nuclear terrorist and will probably get no recognition for any of it."

"If you're in this line of work for the recognition, you watched too many movies," said Farris.

There was another knock at the door.

"Enter," called Hogan.

Dan Martin opened it and walked into the office.

"Hey," he said. "Sorry for so little contact over the past couple days. I've been running like crazy."

Mike Farris reached out his hand to shake Martin's. The Detective instinctively responded. As Mike gripped Martin's hand, the Detective suddenly winced.

"You hurt?" Farris asked.

"Yeah, nothing much," replied Martin, "I was in the middle of a remodeling project at home before this thing started. A nail was sticking out of the trim on my bedroom door and I caught it on the shoulder last night. I keep forgetting about it until something hits it."

"Oh, sorry," said Farris, "Have you seen a doctor?"

"No," he answered, "it's not that bad. I cleaned it up pretty good and put a decent dressing on it. I just won't be doing any workouts in the gym for a while, that's all."

"So what has your man on the inside told you?" asked Hogan.

"His handler called me a couple hours ago to say that he had switched vehicles and was now driving a...," he paused as he looked at the screen of his PDA, "2005 Ford Escape, blue, license plate GZA-019. The plates must be bogus, because it's not in our database at all."

Hilde wrote down the information and Farris asked, "Did he know where he was headed?"

"Negative," answered Martin, "He's following preset coordinates in a GPS that was left in the car, but he is pretty sure, according to his handler, that they are going to end up in the Ohio Stadium area since that was where they took Usein on a tour."

"When is he going to call you back?" asked Hogan.

"His handler told me that he was going to check in every few hours as long as he is not being watched," said Martin.

"Keep us posted," Hogan said. "Do you have any idea who this informant is?"

"Nope," answered Martin. "I wish I did, so we could put a tail on him, but he doesn't trust us. His handler is pretty good though and will keep us informed."

He turned to Farris.

"By the way, Mike, I heard about what happened this morning from Detective Clay. He told me all about it. I'm really sorry about your friend. That was pretty bold of Usein to come looking for you through your church like that. I really hope we put this guy down."

Farris nodded and said, "Yeah, well, I'm just a peripheral target here. I am sorry for what happened to my friend, but a whole lot more people are going to die if we don't catch him before he sets this thing off."

"Right," said Hogan. "Martin, you keep in close contact with the informant. Hilde, make sure Andy keeps moving on it but doesn't have a stroke before he figures it all out. Mike, you and I need to go check in with the surveillance teams."

Martin walked out the door as Hilde rose from her seat. Hogan turned to the credenza and checked his cell phone to see if it was charged yet. He called to Hilde as she reached for the door handle.

"By the way, Hilde," he motioned with his hand for her to come closer and continued in a lowered tone, "How is that trace on White's broadcast going?"

"Slow," she replied. "That guy really has a secure IT system. The last place we managed to trace to ended up taking us out on over a hundred diversionary lines and via the wonders of modern internet technology to no less than eighteen countries before we verified they were bogus routes. There are a few more lines yet to go but it is really time consuming. Each route takes as much as four hours, and we can only do a few at a time unless we want to take down the whole building network. "

"Do whatever you have to do. People here can live without email for half a day if necessary," said Hogan. "He may be the key to leading us to Usein, and by the way," Paul paused until they both looked up at him, "don't trust Martin. Don't give him any information that you haven't passed through me first."

"Why?" asked Farris.

"Because you said that you hadn't told the officers at your church about Usein's connection. Or that Harry Johnson said he was looking for you," he replied.

Hilde raised an eyebrow at the comment and said, "Isn't that a bit paranoid, Paul? He is a detective after all, and he is on the inside of this case. He probably just made some basic assumptions."

"Not only that," He continued. "That injury on his shoulder seems too coincidental with the shooting."

"That's a pretty heavy accusation," she said.

"Humor me on this, OK?" he replied. "Just humor me."

CHAPTER 33

Friday afternoon and evening were a non-stop buzz of hyper-activity in the area around the Ohio stadium. Hogan and Farris personally inspected the security. They walked the avenues of approach to the parking lots and the stadium. Hogan had meshed his forces seamlessly with local and university police to reinforce their emergency plans. Roadblocks were erected and barricades put in place. The roadblocks were normal for such events, but the additional security cameras and observation posts were placed all over the stadium were not. Nor were the snipers posted on the roofs and high places around and inside the stadium.

Hogan's FBI team worked over every scenario they could imagine for getting a suitcase sized nuclear weapon into the stadium. The surveillance and interception teams ran through multiple contingency plans. Over a hundred agents and another three hundred and fifty police and highway patrol officers scoured the stadium, the parking lots, the surrounding buildings and grounds.

Four radiation detection vans made circuitous routes through the streets of the neighborhoods surrounding the stadium, scanning for the tell-tale signs of fissile material hidden in homes or cars. At the same time two satellites had been redirected to positions above Ohio, to perform surface scans from more than two hundred miles above the earth's surface. Even with all of these devices, vehicles, machines, and people, not a single trace of radioactive material had been discovered.

In the area surrounding the stadium, tailgate partiers were already set up and had started the pre-game carousing. At one side of the massive parking lot, more than a thousand Michigan fans were massed around a large number of RVs and other vehicles drinking and having a generally good time. At the other side, a similar arrangement of Ohio State fans were doing the same thing. As they moved through the crowds, Farris watched the faces of the people they passed.

Men, women, and children of all ages and sizes milled about, going through the motions of their lives. An elderly lady walked past, wearing a giant red foam cowboy hat with a large letter O on the sides. She looked like she was in her nineties and was probably old enough to remember the first OSU Michigan game in 1935.

Like her, the rest of the crowd was oblivious to what loomed beyond the morning. They were mostly smiling, happy people getting ready for yet another great game between two historic rivals. To them it was just another day, standing around in blissful ignorance of the fact that they were at the edge of existence, at the cusp of a tomorrow, which may become a fiery hell for them and the tens of thousands who would be joining them soon.

He wondered why anyone would do such a thing to unsuspecting people—innocent people. The image of the Bosnian boy and his mother flooded his mind. A hard lump formed in his throat. It had been more than a decade since that incident, but the pain was freshly opened by the reappearance of Usein and the murder of his own family.

Ruthless men like Usein were the reason Mike Farris had kept coming back to the line of work he was so good at. They were the reason he could never quit taking leave from the pulpit to go slinking around in the shadows of foreign countries and hunt down men who seemed to take pleasure in killing women and children en masse.

Some men in this business dealt with the dreams and terrors that resulted from the job by running away from that life. Some ran to new careers, education, or counseling. Others ran to drugs and alcohol to deaden the pain. Farris ran back at his foes: the terrorists who continued to kill. Until the death of his family, he had seldom dreamed about the past.

The images of the past had occasionally popped into his mind when he heard news of terrorists attacking somewhere in the world. But for the most part he had kept it under control. Until the night of the shooting that is. Since that night, it had been almost impossible to close his eyes without those visions returning.

Usein laughing, Mathis sneering, and the young mother with her son quivering in her arms. He hated the scene; it made him sick just to think about it. He wondered how Mojo handled it. He hadn't seen him in the years since they debriefed out of Bosnia.

With that thought in mind, in an effort to change the images in his head, he turned to Hogan and asked, "Paul, have you heard anything from Mojo Johnson since Bosnia?"

"Actually, I have," replied Hogan. "I saw him at Pendleton in oh-three, he was headed to Iraq. He retired a couple of years ago and moved back to Alaska, to that farm he used to talk about. Harley Wasner called me from Coronado last summer and said he ran into him not long after he went home. Harley said they had one last adventure together before Marcus got married to some amazingly hot Korean chick who's a State Trooper up there. He runs a hunting guide business now."

"Is his wife the one who had jilted him when he was MIA?" Farris asked.

"I think so," said Hogan. "Harley said they seemed pretty happy too."

"Good for him," said Farris, "Mojo is a really good guy."

"What made you think about him?" Hogan asked.

"Well, nothing really," Farris answered. "Just curious."

"Seems like something's on your mind," Hogan said.

Farris glanced over at his friend as they walked across the parking lot towards their vehicle. "Since this whole thing started up, I keep thinking about Bosnia. How things turned out. If only…."

He choked up and couldn't continue. Tears welled up in his eyes.

"That wasn't your fault Mike," Hogan said. "There was nothing you could have done. You know that. That whole thing was just crazy."

Mike breathed deeply and cleared the lump in his throat. He regained his composure as they arrived at the car. They got in, closed the doors and sat in the dark.

"I wasn't able to save my wife and my son either," Mike said. "It's almost like someone is getting back at me by taking my wife and son in retribution for what happened there."

"Now come on, that's crazy talk, Mike." Paul Hogan turned his body to face Farris. Through the shadows he saw that Mike's chest was heaving. He could hear the soft sound of Mike Farris trying to suppress his sobs.

Mike laid the seat back and put his hands over his face. He spoke in a muffled voice through the space between his palms.

"I miss them Paul," he choked tears back. "God, I miss them so bad that part of me hopes I get killed tomorrow, so I can join them."

"Look, Mike," Paul fumbled for words to comfort his old commander, the one who had always had the role of professional comforter himself. "I know it hurts, but if God wanted you dead, you'd be dead. You know that. We have no guarantees in this world, and no guarantees that you won't die tomorrow. For that matter that we won't die tonight in a car accident on the way home, but every day that we wake up is one that has a purpose to be fulfilled.

"Now I'm not as religious as you are, but I do know this, you have a purpose. So don't give up on it. God has you here in these circumstances to save these people today. When that's done, who knows what may come next, but we have to trust that it's all in his hands and that he'll guide us to the next phase. Otherwise, we could all just throw in the towel now and let a quarter of a million people die in the morning."

Farris inhaled deeply and relaxed a little.

"You should have been a pastor," he muttered.

"Nah," replied Hogan, "too much stress."

Hogan's cell phone rang. He pulled it from his pocket and flipped it open.

"Hello?" he said into the microphone. There was a pause while he listened. His mouth turned down in a frown, and he looked over to Farris. He handed him the phone.

"It's Hilde."

Farris took the phone and put it to his ear.

"Hello?"

"Mike," said Hilde's voice on the other end, "I have some more bad news, I'm afraid."

Mike braced himself, unsure if he could take more. "What is it?"

"Li'l Mac died about half an hour ago."

CHAPTER 34

Billy Z., aka Detective William Coffee, had been an under-cover narcotics officer in Columbus for five years. Billy had started his life of espionage as a nineteen-year-old soldier in the Army, where his high intelligence and aptitude for lan-guages, especially his uncanny knack to pick up local accents and colloquialisms, quickly got him assigned to the Defense Intelligence Agency. He had lived for several years as a deep cover operative in Central America and the Caribbean along-side DEA agents who spied on drug dealers and their con-nections to communist and terrorist insurgency groups that posed a threat to US interests.

Although he never attended college, Billy spoke three languages in addition to English with native fluency. Within those languages (French, Spanish, and Portuguese) he could imitate dozens of local dialects and blend invisibly into almost any Caribbean or Hispanic culture he found himself. He could have made a lot more money as a Hollywood actor for the performances he put on, but the adrenaline rush of the real thing was something Hollywood could not offer him. Billy continued in the work for six years until, at the young age of twenty-five, he decided it was time to head home and see his family again.

Once home, it wasn't long before he realized that he would not be able to settle into something like the normal nine to five lifestyle his friends had made for themselves. Five years ago, he walked into the Columbus Police Headquarters to offer himself for specialized service.

At first, his offer was rejected because he refused to start as a patrol officer. He had requested to start directly as an undercover agent to avoid the risk of any of the street thugs recognizing him from the time he served as a patrol officer. After the personal intervention of none other than the Director of the DEA himself and a letter of recommendation from President George W. Bush, CPD reconsidered and brought him straight in as a detective, waving the requirement to serve as a patrol officer first.

Over the following years Detective William Coffee had managed to gather enough hard evidence to shut down four major drug rings in Central Ohio, leading to the capture and solid convictions of seven internationally wanted drug dealers and dozens of mid-level dealers and the recovery of over forty-million dollars' worth of drugs, weapons, and cash. He had done it all without ever pulling a gun himself and without blowing Billy Z's cover.

In the two weeks before Usein showed up on the scene he had been within sight of closing the net on the infamous Mister White, but when the African showed up, he was relegated to this driving job and had to stop his pursuit of the newest crime boss in the area for the time being.

The information he had gathered thus far demonstrated that Mister White operated a legitimate sales business on the north side of Columbus, and that he was really high tech. He had recently discovered that Mister White was more than just a serious technophile. He was heavily invested in the technology business which offered a very good opportunity to launder the money he made from drugs. Billy had pinpointed what he thought was the office where Mister White worked and was working on a scheme to get in to the secured complex.

Billy also learned that while Mister White offered very good salaries and benefits to those he employed in his underground operation, he was ruthless when dealing with failure or deceit. No less than nine of White's narcotics employees had disappeared in the past eighteen months alone. Only two bodies were found, and they were only identifiable by DNA.

Billy had been working with a detective on the west side as his handler for the first three and a half years. About the time he started investigating White he was transferred to a new handler. He had only seen him twice, but spoke with him on the phone often, keeping him abreast of his operations and filing regular reports of his findings.

His handler seemed to him to be a pretty good detective. He let Billy have a lot of leeway in how he performed his operation. He always seemed to act on the information given him fairly quickly. The only time he wasn't able to move on the information in time was a few weeks ago, when that pastor's family was shot up during the hit on LeRon.

Billy was quite distraught over the lack of action in that case, because it led to the unnecessary deaths of three innocent people who were trying to make a positive difference in the world, and that little baby. The way they did that baby just tore him up inside. He hoped to God that he would get the chance one day to smash Cold Bones' face for what he did.

At the moment though, he was confused. His GPS had been leading him in circles for two days. He had thought they would be heading in towards the Ohio Stadium by now, but as of three a.m. Saturday morning he was still driving in circles.

The last time he had checked in, he was told they were tracking his movements through the GPS, and that CPD and the FBI knew where he was all the time, but the whole situation made him feel uneasy like he was hanging out over the edge of a cliff. He felt all alone. He had a pretty good idea of what was in the case he carried in the car, and that it was not drugs of any kind. He was pretty certain that it was a bomb, most likely nuclear.

His handler ordered him to continue on as if he knew nothing. To draw the enemy closer to the trap and get more of them out of the closet before they came in for the kill. He had trusted the man so far and followed his order but was growing more and more uneasy as time went on.

Something just wasn't right. Something didn't add up.

CHAPTER 35

Saturday October 29th
Lima Tank Works
Lima, Ohio
04:10 Hours

Ronald Henderson was a train engineer extraordinaire.

"Most people think that being a train engineer is easy," he often told his wife Peggy, "because they think that 'hey, you know, there's tracks laid down, and all you gotta do is control the speed, there's no steering or anything like that,' but they only think that because they don't know all of the mechanics and science involved."

He would go on about the physics of pulling a two-mile long vehicle that weighed hundreds of thousands of tons carrying any number of different types of goods and cargoes. Always, he would end the conversation with his trademark phrase, "You know, without trains, this country could starve in only a couple of days."

To which Peggy almost always gave the same reply, "You sure do have an important job, honey."

Ronald's world revolved completely around trains, and not just in the sense that he loved his job, which he did, but he truly was one of the best in the business of driving trains. He was certified to drive almost every type of engine built since the 1930s. He was also certified to deliver every type of cargo that crossed the North American continent, including, in spite of his capacity to talk, top secret military cargoes.

Such a cargo is what he found himself hauling on that mid-autumn Saturday morning. He had driven a trainload of iron and steel sheets from A&B Millworks in Pennsylvania to the Lima Tank Works, in Lima, Ohio. He was well known at the military factory, which had been manufacturing tanks since 1942. The plant's products had included everything from the Sherman Tank of the World War II era to the modern M1-Abrams and its progeny.

Upon arrival, his crew disconnected the cars of steel, and he moved the engine through the rail yard to engine barn 3B. There he linked up to a single rail car that would be his sole cargo on the next leg of the trip. He would drive it to a quiet location in eastern Tennessee where he would turn it over to the authorities there.

While Engineer Ronald Henderson knew what he was carrying, and the heavily armed guards that rode with him knew, almost no one else did. The public's lack of knowledge of what Ronald's train car contained was primarily due to the fact that they did not know about the other product manufactured at the Lima Tank Works since the fifties.

Lima Tank Works was spread over three-thousand acres in the rolling green Ohio countryside. The edifice of brick and iron structures that comprised the sprawling active factory buildings covered something more. Three hundred feet beneath the surface lay a maze of tunnels, offices, and massive concrete walled rooms that contained the operating base of Project Fire Phoenix. Started in the late fifties it was one of the nation's few remaining weapons grade nuclear material processing plants. In that massive underground complex technicians and scientists used the technology that created and stored some of the purest and most refined nuclear fission material on the planet. In days past, enough material to destroy the world several times over had been created there. Since the end of the Cold War the mission had been redirected to that of decommissioning nuclear warheads.

Ronald's task was to transfer the fissile material to down-blending plants at the Atomic & Nuclear Services Corporation in eastern Tennessee where it would be reduced to energy grade nuclear fuel, used in power generation throughout the Midwest. Ronald had been making these runs once or twice a month for almost twenty years.

If anyone had tried to use social engineering techniques to get even the most rudimentary information out of Ronald's wife as to what her husband did for a living beyond being an ordinary train driver, they would have gotten absolutely nothing. She had no idea that in spite of her husband's well-known ability to talk non-stop for hours on end, he was also capable of keeping a secret—especially from her. She was totally unaware that he held one of the highest levels of top-secret clearance in the nation.

At shortly after four in the morning, Ronald and four secret service agents stood in the large driving compartment of Engine 426863. With only a lone triple-armored container, a small caboose containing eight more secret service agents and enough weaponry to hold off a small army rolled on the tracks out of the factory rail yard.

The train would skirt downtown Columbus on a circuitous route until they hooked up with the main southeast line again in Picktown at about eleven a.m. From there, they would head straight to the downgrading plant where they would offload the fissile material from ten fifteen-megaton warheads. It was enough nuclear material to wipe most of Ohio off the map and to render Eastern Indiana, Western Pennsylvania, and most of Kentucky uninhabitable for hundreds of years.

The container the material traveled in was extremely well protected. Multiple layers of lead, steel, titanium, and more steel surrounded the warheads. The space between each layer was filled with nearly a foot-thick layer of composite cement, which could absorb and dissipate the shock of a direct hit from a conventional artillery shell or rocket without affecting the warheads. It would take nothing less than an external nuclear explosion to rupture the container. Satellite tracking and high-altitude air cover provided by Wright Patterson Air Force Base prohibited the possibility of any kind of aircraft getting within fifty miles of the train itself, well out of missile range. Nor could a rocket be fired from seaborne craft that could reach this far inland, and there was almost no possibility that an enemy could get close enough on land to detonate a device without its radiation signature being picked up by satellite.

Just like the dozens of times he made the run before, there was nothing to be worried about Ronald thought as he rolled out of the rail yard. Expected arrival of the train and its payload was two p.m. Saturday. He would be home in time for dinner with his wife.

CHAPTER 36

Akbar Usein sat back in the office chair and smiled. He had received the email from his greedy contact in the former Soviet Republic of Georgia. Usein had expected such dealings from a communist. Russia and its former satellite states were overflowing with corrupt military officers, former KGB and GRU agents who would do anything for cash.

The master terrorist had pretended to balk at the thought of paying such a high price but in reality, had no problem meeting the additional demand of five-hundred-thousand dollars in order to receive the arming codes for the suitcase in Billy Z's car.

Usein grinned as he opened the email containing the codes. A series of six eight-digit numbers were the only text in the message. He clicked the "Reply" button and typed in a brief message.

Received, Spaseba.

He clicked send and in an instant the message vanished. Usein then forwarded the list of numbers to another email address which was then forwarded to a cell phone as a text message. The recipient of that message posted an almost immediate reply.

Got it.

"Yes," Usein muttered, pleasure rising through him. "Now they will feel the sword."

He selected all of the messages in his inbox and deleted them. Then he right clicked on the "Deleted Items" folder, its title had darkened to indicate it contained files. He chose "Empty Deleted Items Folder" from the drop-down menu. The files vanished from his system.

To make sure that all of the communications regarding his transactions were gone he opened the "Sent Items" folder and selected all of those files as well. His finger clicked the right mouse button and he slid the cursor to the word "Delete" in the menu. He clicked the button and the messages disappeared.

The "Deleted Items" folder again darkened to indicate there were files to be deleted. He slid the mouse up to the folder name and clicked on it. By mistake he clicked with the left button instead of the right. The folder opened to reveal the list of items marked for permanent deletion.

Usein clicked on the "Deleted Items" title again, this time with the right mouse button and slid the cursor over the menu until it hovered on "Delete." He glanced over to the list of messages about to be deleted. Messages that had been sent from his computer recently. In the split second before his finger twitched on the button that would permanently erase them from his computer something caught his attention.

The fourth message in the list contained a recipient address he did not recognize.

TO:AgentPaulHogan@fbi.gov

His expression immediately soured. Rage rose within his body as he opened the message, a forwarded copy of the email his Russian supplier had sent.

"Al Gul," Usein growled in a low voice.

He rose from the desk, slapping the laptop shut as he strode quickly out of the room. He went upstairs to the room where Al Gul had been staying. Usein kicked open the door and flipped the light on.

Al Gul was not there. The bed was empty. It had not been slept in. Usein stormed back down the stairs and into the kitchen. Cold Bones and one of his foot soldiers stood at the counter making a pot of coffee when Usein burst in.

"Hey, good morning," said Cold Bones. "You ready for this thing?"

"Where is Al Gul?" growled Usein.

The young man next to Cold Bones scooped a large spoonful of store brand coffee into the filter basket. He spoke without glancing up.

"Freak is out on the front porch with the guard, howling at the moon or some shit."

Usein tore through the house and out onto the porch. Al Gul was standing on the porch, leaning against the rail. He looked up as Usein burst out the door.

"Akbar Aga."

"You infidel traitor!" shouted the African.

"Huh?"

"Grab him!" Usein ordered the guard who stood between them.

The guard instantly obeyed and lunged toward the hairy wild man on the corner of the porch. Kharzai's leg flashed up. The sole of his shoe caught the young man squarely on the solar plexus. There was a loud crack and the man let out a whoosh of air. He tried to scream but could only gasp, his diaphragm torn by rough shards of bone.

Usein raised his pistol. The hairy Persian rolled backwards over the rail. The explosion of the shot shattered the early morning quiet as Kharzai landed ungracefully on his back on the hard ground. A loud "Oomph!" erupted from his lungs on the impact. Kharzai twisted himself onto to his knees and scrambled into a clumsy breathless run into the dark space between the blocky red brick houses. He tried to regain the wind that had been knocked out of him as he ran. Akbar Usein ran to the edge of the porch and fired two shots around the corner into the shadows toward which Kharzai had run.

"Ruh roh!" Kharzai mumbled to himself as he sprinted through the darkness. "Guess he found the email."

Shouts and curses echoed from the house. The sound of doors slamming and running footsteps echoed on the walls behind him.

"Where is that sumbitch?" someone yelled.

"He ran that way!" said another.

He charged from one house to another ducking under laundry lines darting around picnic tables and kid's toys. He paused in the shadow of the side of a house. His pursuers were not far behind. Kharzai could hear them coming. He leaned out from the side of the house to get a quick glimpse of where they were. A motion sensor spotlight suddenly flashed on at the porch high above him, illuminating his hairy face in a bright bath of light.

"There! I see the freak!"

"Ruh roh!" Kharzai said again. The trademark phrase and cartoon voice of Scooby Doo had once been something he did to make people laugh. Over time, it had become an involuntary reaction whenever he found himself in serious danger, and now it was all he could think to say.

Kharzai charged across the street and ran another half block, then turned left and sprinted through a dozen open backyards until a high wooden fence blocked his path. The other men closed in, gaining to within less than fifty yards behind him. He leaped up and grasped the top edge then swung his legs up and over like an Olympic gymnast on the pommel horse. He flung himself over the top and landed on the cold hard ground of other side with a solid, bone jarring thump.

"Oof!" he gasped. Pain shot up his legs from the impact of landing flat on both feet. The ground was even more solid than he had anticipated. There was no lawn in this yard, only dry hard dirt. Dirt and an odd ammonia smell.

Urine. Dog urine.

To his left he heard a deep throaty rumble. He slowly turned his head towards the back porch of the house and immediately recognized the source of the noise. A pair of golden brown pit bulls sauntered slowly into the light that flowed from a single bulb hanging from the remnants of a flood light next to the back door. Kharzai's eyes widened.

"Ruh roh." He smiled a wide grin. In the pale light that glowed around him his teeth shone bright white within the frame of his dark face and beard.

Footsteps and the shouts of men came from behind him on the other side of the fence. The pair of dogs jogged towards him, fangs exposed. Muscles rippled over their backs and shoulders as they moved. Vicious snarls curled at the sides of their noses.

"Nice doggies."

They growled back in response. His pursuers' voices were only a couple feet away on the other side of the wall.

"Get the son of a bitch!"

"Gimme a hand up!"

Two pairs of hands grasped the top of the wall. They pulled. Kharzai heard the grunts of two men pushing them up and over the wall. Their heads popped up over the top and the men saw him. The dogs turned their gaze from him to the new meat as it came vaulting over the wall. Kharzai sprinted for the fence at the far side of the yard ten steps away. The dogs leaped toward his pursuers. They were on them in a snarling, spitting tangle before their feet touched the ground. Kharzai jumped up and vaulted his own body over the far wall. Screams pierced the night as the attack dogs tore into the two gangsters.

"Better you than me, Alpo!" Kharzai muttered as he cleared the top of the wall and ran on into the darkness.

He made his way two more blocks until he was sure he had lost his tail. Kharzai came back out on the street. He slowed his pace and walked casually down the sidewalk. A taxicab sat at the curb, a short distance ahead and across the street. It was in front of a squat, gray, non-descript apartment building, the kind built with a government grant for low-income renters. Someone got out of the back seat and walked towards the building. The cab's light came on indicating he was ready for a new fare.

Kharzai sprinted up to it waving his arms and shouting.

"Hey! Taxi!"

The cab driver turned in his seat to see the thin hairy man running towards him.

"Taxi! Get me out of here!"

"Where you going?" The cabbie spoke with a Jamaican accent.

"OSU Campus," Kharzai answered, breathless from the run. "I'm late for class."

"Late for class?" exclaimed the cabbie. "Dude. Its four thirty in the frickin' morning. What class are you late for, man?"

"Music, Arts, and Anatomy." Kharzai replied as he jumped into the back seat. "It's a new double major. Really big with the chicks."

The cabbie shook his head, clicked off the overhead light, and flipped the meter lever on. Kharzai was flung back in the seat as they took off for the Ohio State University Campus.

CHAPTER 37

The phone on Paul Hogan's desk rang a loud warbling tone. The noise woke him with a jolt out of the two-hour deep slumber he had managed to find in his office chair. Mike Farris rose from the couch along the wall as Hogan answered the call, squinting at his watch. It was seven a.m. They had slept for two hours after spending the night checking reports and surveillance video of the stadium area with Hilde.

"Yeah," Hogan said into the receiver.

"Paul, its Andy!" Fleiss' voice sounded congested, like he had a cold. In spite of the flat nasal tone he was obviously very excited.

"The GPSs came back online a few minutes ago. When they hit, I also got a cell phone signal coming from one of the vehicles that was in a call at the same time the GPS came back online."

"Where are they?" he asked the technician.

"All three GPSs just received coordinates that take them straight to Ohio Stadium. They will all be coming into the area by around ten thirty, just before kickoff at eleven."

"All right then, here we go!" Hogan exclaimed into the receiver. "What was the cell caller saying?"

"I don't know, I couldn't get a recorder on it before he hung up. I am tracing the caller ID though to find out who he was talking to. I am also listening for that phone to come back online anytime."

Andy suddenly sneezed into the telephone speaker.

"Sorry. My allergies are acting up, and I ran out of meds last night." He sniffed hard then continued, "Anyway, I did get a little farther on the search for Mister White. I have narrowed the original signal to one of three possible locations. I'll let you know more later on that one."

"Thanks, Andy, does Hilde know this?"

"I'm calling her next."

"Don't bother, I'll go get her from her office."

"Roger that, chief."

Hogan hung up the phone and turned to Farris, who had walked over to the small bathroom at the corner of the office where he was bent over the sink splashing water on his face.

"Mike! The bad guys are all heading in to the stadium. Let's go get Hilde and get over there."

The two men walked into the hallway and briskly made their way down the length of the building to Hildegarde Rottbruck's office. Hogan knocked loud, then jiggled the handle impatiently. A moment later the lock clicked open, and Hilde pulled the door open. She pushed back at strands of hair that were askew from lying on her office couch for several hours. She rubbed sleep out of her bloodshot eyes as she spoke.

"Find something?" she asked groggily.

"Andy got their latest signal," Hogan answered. "They're all headed to the stadium now. Let's get over there ASAP. I want to be there with your surveillance teams when we nab these guys."

She instantly became fully awake at the news. She grabbed her purse and jacket and followed them out the door. They piled into Hogan's car and sped out of the parking lot on the way to the stadium. Twenty minutes later they walked into a trailer in the Ohio Stadium parking lot. The small rectangular structure was filled from end to end with computer and video terminals that were being fed images from cameras posted at every major intersection within a two-mile radius as well as most alleys and pedestrian areas.

Two different satellite images were also displayed. One was a standard video feed image. The other was a thermal imaging scanner set to find the radioactive material. More than a dozen technicians and agents stared intently into the monitors waiting for the alarms to buzz, informing them that one of the thousands of faces in the sea of humanity that would soon be flowing through the area had a hit on the facial recognition database.

At eight a.m. the sun was only just coming over the horizon but already hundreds of vehicles of every shape and size were making their way into parking lots for the big game. There was no sign of the Blue Ford Escape, nor was there any sign of Akbar Usein, Cold Bones, or Lucas Ring.

The NSA had parked a satellite in place over the area the day before to continue the scan for radiation from above. The search had been fruitless. Fleiss had managed to convince them to leave it there for the rest of the day to keep searching. Hundreds of FBI agents and police officers on the ground carried small handheld radiation detection devices. Teams of special units rode in vans containing much more sensitive scanning equipment. Nothing had registered so far.

Police and FBI dog handlers methodically scoured the lines of traffic that crawled through the checkpoints in search of everything from drugs and firearms to conventional explosives, but only the most routine amounts marijuana and a few small amounts of cocaine had been found.

"Man," said Hogan, exasperated at their inability to find anything of substance, "I wonder if we are wrong, if this is not the place."

"Could be," replied Farris, "but all the evidence points here. I am pretty sure this is it."

Hilde looked up from where she was seated next to a technician going over the live images from some of the surveillance cameras.

"I'd have to agree with Mike, Paul. Everything points to this being the place."

Paul Hogan nodded and added, "I know, but there is just this bad feeling I have in my gut that something is not right. Everything is not as it seems."

"As melodramatic as that sounds, you may be right," Hilde replied, "but we can only go on what we know so far."

"Well, let's keep our eyes peeled; if it is going to happen here, we will catch them."

"Ma'am!" called out one of Hilde's surveillance specialists. "We have a hit!"

"Who?"

"Ring! It's Lucas Ring. He got past the checkpoint, but I just saw him cross under our north facing camera in Lot 4E."

"Are you sure it's him?"

"Him or his twin," answered the surveillance technician.

"Send a unit to his location, ASAP!" Hogan ordered, "Mike, let's go!"

"Don't lose sight of him!" Hilde added to the order as the two men ran out the door.

Within four minutes a dozen plain-clothes agents gathered around Hogan and Farris. They half jogged through the parking lot to within sight of the last spot the techs had seen Ring.

"Where is he?" asked Hogan into the tiny radio microphone clipped to his collar.

The earpieces of the team members sounded with the answer, "I can see you guys. Ring just stepped between two RVs about a hundred yards ahead of you, Agent Hogan, on your left. I lost sight of him, so he may be in either of those vehicles, or he may have moved past them in my blind spot. A hairy guy with a thick beard followed him in there just a few seconds later and didn't come out the other side."

The agents and Farris moved slowly towards the RVs, discreetly drawing their weapons out of the holsters that had thus far been kept hidden beneath their jackets. The team approached to within twenty yards of the pair of RVs between which Ring had disappeared. One of the RVs rocked on its tires. There was serious movement going on inside. It seemed like a couple enjoying a morning tryst—or a fight.

Paul motioned, and they focused on the rocking RV. A crowd had formed around it. People in the crowd around them parted when they saw the guns in the agents' hands. Hilde's voice whispered into the earpiece.

"Paul, call me right away on your cell phone. It's urgent. Andy just called with something you need to hear."

Hogan nodded to Farris, and the pair dropped back from the rest of the group.

"Agent Clark, take over."

"Got it."

The two men moved about a dozen cars away before Hogan picked up his cell phone and dialed Hilde.

"Yeah, what is it?" he asked.

"Paul, I have Andy on conference call," she said, "Go ahead Andy."

"Paul, things just took a turn for the really sucky. I got three pieces of information that came in all at once and they are really blowing my mind."

"Spit it out, Andy! We don't have time to play."

"OK. First, the Nuclear Regulatory Agency just called to say that a train load of decommissioned warheads is being transported across Ohio as we speak. Two, I just picked up a call from the cell phone that was with the one GPS, he got a change of directions from the African."

"Shit!" exclaimed Hogan, "What's the third thing?"

"I found out who the guy on the cell phone is calling."

CHAPTER 38

Jajce, Bosnia-Herzegovina
September 1998

At five minutes before eight a.m, nothing moved at the house in which they had found the sniper position. Marcus Johnson and Mike Farris both remained motionless, observing in the silence for the slightest movement throughout the entire field of view.

The young mother with her two children was sitting quietly at breakfast in the kitchen of the house across the street. She smiled at the young ones as they told her something that involved exaggerated arm gestures and wide-eyed expressions. She laughed at what they said as she got up to pour a cup of coffee for herself.

As Farris watched the scene unfold a slight movement above the windows of the house caught his eye. One of the curved red roof tiles seemed to wiggle out of place, as if it was coming loose and being moved from the inside. The tile fell forward a couple inches, was caught by something, then pulled inside. The radio hissed briefly followed by Flynn's voice.

"Target's motorcade is slowly moving into the square. Several GRU are trotting alongside as they approach the checkpoint."

Farris eyes grew wide as the knowledge of what was happening dawned on him. "Marcus, he's in the other house!"

"Oh? Then who just went into the place we've been watching?" Mojo replied as a man who had just sprinted from around the corner ran into the house with the sniper position upstairs.

"Two shooters?" Farris said. "You take that one, I'll take the family house."

The two men sprinted out into the street, one towards each house. In the square, President Yeltsin's vehicle slowed to a crawl as a smiling, flag waving group of pro-Russian Serbs moved towards the car as closely as the armed American soldiers would let them. The limousine came to a complete stop a few meters in front of the checkpoint, and one of the GRU officers leaned towards it as the rear window slid open.

The officer that leaned into the window was the short bald man Flynn and Hogan had seen in the café. He motioned to the occupants of the vehicle and said something that Hogan could not hear over the din of the crowd. The GRU officer positioned his body towards the rear of the door and pointed to the people on the sidewalk with his right hand. President Yeltsin leaned out the window and raised his hand in greeting to the people beside the street, waving Serbian and Russian flags together.

High up on the hillside Farris ran with all his might and crashed through the front door of the house. The mother in the kitchen screamed in startled surprise as the tall armed man ran down the hall and up the stairs.

Farris made his way to the second floor and found the flight of stairs that led up to the attic. He charged up two steps at a time until he reached the doorway at the top. He expected the door to be locked. He quickly verified that the hinges were on the inside then jumped up the final steps with a high kick of his heavy military boot. The impact smashed the old wooden panels open and shattered the wood of the frame as the thick metal bolt burst through the jamb and the door flew open into the space. The form inside the dark room jerked as pieces of the door hit him. A shot exploded loudly in the split second before Farris dove down on top the figure that twisted toward him.

The bald GRU officer shuddered as a slimy red and white mass of blood, flesh, and bone smeared the trunk and rear window of the Russian President's limousine. He leaned against the back of the vehicle, eyes wide and staring up the hillside then slumped to the ground. A second later the loud pop of the shot caught up with the bullet. The crowd flinched in unison at the sound.

The uniformed American soldier who had spoken to the Russian agents the previous day leaped out of the crowd with a pistol pointed towards President Yeltsin. The tall GRU agent from the café moved forward and shoved the President back into the vehicle. The imposter soldier was surprised to see his comrade raise his weapon towards him.

The tall agent squeezed the trigger and shot the man in uniform squarely in the forehead. The crowd on the side-walks quickly degenerated into a panicked, screaming mass as they ran in every direction trying to find cover. In the confusion people trampled each other as they desperately sought safety. Their days of hell were supposed to be over with.

Yelstin's limo lurched forward towards the gated checkpoint where the real American soldiers quickly let him through, out of harm's way.

The fake soldier's friend moved out from the other side of the street, pointing his weapon at the Russian. Flynn and Hogan moved forward, weapons drawn towards that man, as more GRU and Americans drew weapons on each other all around the square.

"Freeze! Freeze!" shouted Flynn to the fake soldier.

The Russian glanced towards Hogan and Flynn. The would-be assassin pulled the trigger of his pistol and hit the tall Russian twice in the head, making a bloody mess of his face as the bullets punched through his skull.

Flynn and Hogan both fired into the soldier's chest. The rounds knocked him back against the window of a nearby shop. He slid in death to the ground, leaving a streak of gore across the glass that followed to where he laid slumped on the ground.

Flynn convulsed violently. Blood appeared on his shirt from the bullets fired by yet another GRU agent in the crowd. As he dropped to his knees with a look of surprise on his face, Hogan wheeled around and shouted in Russian over the screams.

"We're UN! We're protecting your president!" He repeated the phrase in English.

The GRU agent paused and Hogan raised his hands taking his finger off the trigger of the weapon. American and Russian soldiers and GRU agents who had their weapons raised at each other paused in confusion, then gradually lowered their weapons. Medics rushed forward to help the wounded in the square.

As the scene in the square decelerated, Farris and Mathis were locked in a deadly wrestling match on the attic floor of the house on the hill. They rolled across the wooden surface, boots and heads thumping loudly, as each man struggled to kill the other.

Both men grasped the other's wrists in a tight grip. Farris jerked his head back and slammed Mathis with a blinding head butt. He had aimed for the mercenary assassin's nose, but Mathis turned his face at just the right time. The blow fell hard on his cheekbone instead of smashing his nose where it would have blinded both eyes.

Mathis kicked with both feet, struggling against Farris's hold until suddenly he felt one of his legs release. With a sudden swift move of the freed leg, Mathis rammed his knee hard into Farris's testicles, sending him into a crumpled fetal position on the floor. Mathis swept his heavy soled foot out from where he laid and caught Farris squarely on the side of the head. The smashing blow caused Farris's head to whip back, and he laid on the floor stunned, eyes rolling, unable to focus.

Boots thudded heavily up the stairs of the house. The sound of Mojo's voice shouted from below.

"Stop!"

The woman and children downstairs let out another shriek of terror. A gunshot exploded in the hallway, followed by the sound of a scuffle that ensued under the floor beneath Farris and Mathis's feet.

In a room below them, on the second floor of the house, Marcus Johnson grappled with a man wearing an American uniform. He had seen him go into the house next door only to run out the back door when the shot rang out from the house in which they now stood. Marcus had made chase and caught up with him on the stairs leading to the second floor.

They wrestled over control of the MP-5 submachine gun the man in uniform was brandishing. Marcus had the man in an arm lock grip that held him in such a way that the man could not get the two-foot-long weapon around to fire.

In the attic, Mathis leaped to his feet, gasping for breath. The skin above his fractured left cheek bone turned purple and caused that eye to swell quickly. Farris recomposed himself and rose to his hands and knees but was still unable to stand. Mathis deftly grabbed the rifle that lay on the floor and chambered a new bullet into the barrel. He pointed the weapon at Farris where he knelt panting on the floor and took aim at his head.

"Sorry, Mike, but you know how this business is."

Farris's body tensed in preparation to receive the large caliber bullet that would soon shatter his own skull, ending his life on this planet. Below, Mojo and the other man struggled violently. The soldier dug hard into Marcus' face with the tips of his fingers. Marcus grabbed at his hand, not releasing his lock on the man's weapon arm. The man suddenly lurched to one side and threw Mojo off balance.

As Marcus tumbled the man got a good grip on his weapon and started to bring it down towards him. Marcus flailed out with his free hand and grabbed a handful of the man's hair. He slammed the man's head into the floor as hard as he could. The uniformed man convulsively jerked the trigger, sending off a long burst from the MP-5. Bright white flames spat from the end of the weapon

Ten feet above them, as Mathis's finger wrapped around the trigger in deliberate slow motion there was a sudden, unexpected chatter of loud staccato pops. The floor under his feet splintered wildly. Mathis jerked in pain-wracked full-body spasms as several projectiles rammed upward into his body. More bullets holes continued to appear, moving rapidly in a line towards Farris. He knelt, stunned by the unexpected turn of events.

The image of what was happening processed in his mind and he quickly came to his senses and rolled right, in a fast scurrying motion across the floor. Another burst of gunfire from below ripped up the wood of the floor where he had been.

In the room below, the MP-5 stopped firing as a round jammed in the breach. The assailant kicked Marcus off himself and struck him across the back of his head with the jammed weapon, then ran out the door headed downstairs. The Marine gunnery sergeant dizzily got to his feet and pushed forward in pursuit.

Mike Farris was coming down from the attic when he saw Mojo run past. He followed him down the stairs to the main floor of the house.

The sound of cars and men shouting outside meant that backup had arrived. A scream from the kitchen drew the attention of Farris and Mojo. They ran to the doorway of the room, barely ducking out of the way as the soldier fired two shots at them from a pistol.

As he passed the door, Farris looked quickly inside. The man had the young mother and her two children cornered in the back of the room. The mother whimpered in terror, her arms around the two sobbing children, where they cowered on the floor. The uniformed man stood over them with a crazed expression on his face, pistol pointed toward the doorway.

Mojo nodded towards Farris, and on the count of two both men leaped into the room. At the sudden motion the man reached down, moving much faster than the two Marines thought possible. He snatched the screaming six-year-old girl from her hysterical mother's grasp, lifting her by the hair until he held her in front of himself like a shield.

"No! No!" screamed the mother.

"Drop the girl!" shouted Farris, his weapon pointed at the man. "Drop her now!"

"Let me out of here!" said the man pointing his weapon back at them. "Let me out, or I will kill them!"

"My baby!" the woman cried out.

Mojo stood there silently, keeping his sights trained on as much of the man's head as he could. Waiting for a shot.

"Let the girl go, and we'll let you leave!" replied Farris.

"You drop your weapons," screamed the terrorist, "or I'll kill them all!"

Their shouts mingled with the screams of the children and their mother. It was a giant soul grinding noise of sheer terror. Heavy footsteps came running in through the entrance to the house. In a flash the man swung the pistol toward the mother and the terrified boy huddled on the floor behind him.

"Don't!" shouted Farris.

Before the word left his mouth, the man fired several rapid shots into the mother and her son, instantly killing the young woman and sending multiple rounds into the boy's torso. The boy's face drooped as his young life drained out slowly. He clutched helpless and weak at his mother's lifeless body. The little girl squealed in terror and started kicking and screaming with renewed ferocity. Her movement caused her to slip down in the man's grip. Mojo seized the moment and fired his weapon.

The shot caught the man in the side of the head, just above the little girl's blond hair. The terrorist slammed back into the wall then crumpled to the ground. The girl landed on the floor and spun towards her mother and brother.

Farris stood in shocked silence. He stared at the bloody forms of the dead mother clutching her dying child. Every bit of energy drained from his body. He felt like he was falling, tumbling through space.

"Why?" he whispered.

Mojo ran forward and grabbed the little girl, then took her out to the other soldiers who were running inside. Farris dropped to his knees on the floor. He slowly shook his head side to side.

"Why did you do that?" he asked the man, who was laying in a spreading pool of blood, a gaping expression on his shattered, lifeless face. "Why did you kill them? You didn't have to kill them."

Captain Hardt entered the room, put an arm around his shoulder and led him out to the street.

At the debriefing two days later, the mission was listed as a success. The President of Russia was spared, and World War III was averted, all with a minimum of collateral damage.

Mike Farris said goodbye to the men with whom he had worked for the past week and boarded a plane back to Pasadena. Classes were starting back up in a few weeks, and he had to get himself ready. He had to step back into the daily routine, back into the life of a seminary student and soon-to-be pastor.

A month later, at his monthly Marine reserve weekend duty, he was officially promoted to the rank of major in a ceremony lead by the commandant of the Marine Corps, General Charles Krulak, himself. In addition to the promotion, Mike Farris was awarded the silver star "for conspicuous gallantry in a classified operation, details withheld."

CHAPTER 39

September 29th
Ohio State University Campus
Near Ohio Stadium
07:30 Hours

Billy Z followed the route he had been given on the GPS unit. He had just turned from Olentangy River Road onto King Street when he was surprised to see a man flagging him down. He was about to pass him by when the man leaned into the street and Billy recognized him.

Cold Bones.

Billy slowed the vehicle and pulled to the shoulder behind another car that was parked up against the curb. He lowered the window. Cold Bones reached in and pushed a piece of paper towards Billy.

"Change of directions, Billy. Go to the location on this paper and wait, your contact will meet you there in thirty minutes."

"Does Mister White know about this?" Billy replied.

"Mister White is in that car, and he says to obey whatever Mister Usein tells you. Got it?"

"Yes sir," replied Billy.

He took the paper. Cold Bones walked away and got into the other car. The car pulled a U-turn on the street and headed back towards Billy. The rear passenger side window slid down as it passed. Akbar Usein smiled at him, his lips curled in a crooked snarl.

Billy looked into Usein's eyes as he passed.

Evil. That man is just plain evil.

He had seen that look in the eyes of many of the drug dealers and hit squads in Central America. Usein reminded him particularly of a Haitian pirate he had busted several years earlier, Michael Courtier.

The physical resemblances were cursory at best. Both were tall, thin black men, well-muscled and very dark, but other than those most basic of similarities they looked nothing alike. No. It was not the physical aspects that drew the memory from the depths of his mind. It was the unadulterated hatred in their eyes. Their souls were identical. Evil to the core.

Michael Courtier was a pirate in the traditional sense, not to be confused with the Jack Sparrow Hollywood version. Courtier was a real murderous thug who plied his dastardly trade on the high seas. He transported drugs, weapons, and stolen goods throughout the Caribbean. The drugs usually went from Central and South America to the Gulf Coast states of the US. From the US he picked up weapons and stolen technology for sale in the markets to the south.

To both sides of his trade zone, he proffered his favorite inventory: slaves. Kidnapped women, children, and young men of all ethnicities, skin colors, and languages were picked up and transported to clients throughout the Caribbean Islands and the coastal areas of all the nations that circled that sea, including the United States. The poor slaves found themselves in a variety of situations, none of them pleasant, depending on their skill and their looks.

The most handsome among them, male or female, were usually forced into sexual slavery, either in brothels or as the personal sex toys of wealthy magnates who already had everything money could buy yet still yearned for more. It was never a loving relationship. More often than not, those poor souls ended up dead from the abuses heaped upon them.

While those activities made him money, and lots of it, that was only his business. His personal pleasure was much more basic, much more insidious. Michael Courtier reveled in the torturing and the excruciatingly slow killing of his helpless victims, especially children.

In 2005 Billy was undercover in a drug ring that came into contact with the notorious pirate, Courtier. He managed to get aboard the pirate's ship with a group of dealers and their henchmen. The vessel was a converted two-hundred-foot-long cargo vessel that was part yacht, part container ship, and part hell.

Deep below its decks, within the dark and foul-smelling bowels of the ship, Courtier had built a torture chamber that would have made Vlad the Impaler, the real life Transylvanian sadist prince that formed the basis for the Dracula stories of a century ago, proud. It was a SS concentration camp Nazi's dream playroom. Courtier proudly showed off his torture chamber to Billy and two of the drug dealers with him.

In it he had imprisoned a group of young boys in a barred cage, deep beneath the cargo hold. The boy's sole purpose on his ship was to satisfy the beastly pirate's sadistic desires. The terrified children were chained naked to the bars of the cell like animals. They were forced to watch their peers tortured before their eyes. Some of the unfortunate souls looked no more than five or six years old. The boys were insane with the hopelessness of their situation.

In the center of the room a wraith of a boy hung from a chain suspended from the ceiling. The skin had been flayed from his back, belly, and thighs. Bright red sinewy muscles lay exposed in the dank light. A pool of blood had spread on the floor beneath him. The boy looked dead. At the sound of the men stepping into the room his eyes opened and the pitiful child started to whimper. An IV bag hung from a post nearby, its tube stuck in the boy's arm. The pirate was keeping the child alive to prolong the agony.

Billy fingered the iconic image of the Virgin of Guadeloupe that hung around his neck as he looked at the tragic sight. Courtier chuckled at the apparent fear in Billy's eyes, not noticing the tiny movement that clicked a concealed button on the oblong medallion. Unbeknownst to Courtier, Billy had signaled for help with the powerful beacon that had been tracked by satellite from inside the medallion.

When three coast-guard gunships closed in on Courtier's vessel an hour later, the pirate attempted to toss his torture victims into the sea. Billy intervened, with a bullet into Courtier's stomach. As the pirate captain laid on the deck of his ship slowly bleeding to death, Billy had kicked him viciously in the abdomen, causing his wound to rip open wider. The demonic torturer's body lost its hold on his intestines. Michael Courtier's entrails spilled out in a mess of slimy ooze across the deck of the ship.

No crew members moved to save pirate Captain Michael Courtier. Billy prayed he would get such a chance with Akbar Usein.

He studied the paper Cold Bones had given him. It was a map. In the top corner of the page written instructions directed him towards a new destination. He turned the car around and headed back the way he came. Billy picked up his cell phone and dialed his controller to let him know of the change in plans.

"The African just stopped me on the road and turned me around. Instead of using the GPS, he handed me a hand drawn paper map with directions back to Picktown. It leads me to a pull off and says to park next to the railroad just out-side of town. That's where I am to meet my contact."

"OK, follow the directions, I'll get right over there with back up."

"I don't like this, man." replied Billy. "You'd better have SWAT there with you, 'cause I think this isn't going to go very well, and I still don't know for sure what is in this case."

"Don't worry, Billy, I've got you covered." said the voice on the other end. "Go to the location on the map, and I will meet you there with more than enough back up."

CHAPTER 40

September 29th
Ohio State University Campus
Ohio Stadium Parking Area
08:30 Hours

Kharzai had told the cab driver to drop him off near the south dormitories where the medical students live. It was nearly a mile from the stadium. He took an indirect route, slinking through the shadows of the OSU campus as he made his way towards the stadium. He cautiously scoured the parking lots looking for Cold Bones' men. He didn't know which of the four vehicles the bomb would be in.

"They might have even switched vehicles again without telling me," he muttered to himself after more than two hours of searching. "Imagine Usein not trusting me with that information. What is the world coming to when a bloodthirsty, murderous terrorist can't even trust a deep-cover secret agent? Was my acting that bad?"

Speaking of acting, he continued his discourse silently in his mind, *I wonder if Hogan's people caught my thingy back there at the house, and if they did, did they tell him about it? Ooh! I hope he's not on leave or something. That would suck.*

Moving through the rows of parked RVs and vans, many with partiers still going at the previous night's revelry, he could see more clearly as the sun rose. There was no sign of the vehicles or of any of the men Kharzai had met in the past week. He wasn't sure what he would do when he met the men.

Something will come to mind by that time. Hopefully.

He had no gun. His had fallen from the back of his pants at some point during the escape. Most likely, it had dropped out when he tumbled backwards over the porch at Cold Bones' house.

The only weapon Kharzai still had was a two-inch polymer blade embedded in the leather belt that held his pants on. Its handle formed the buckle of the belt. While such a weapon could certainly be useful, Kharzai's thin build required the belt to keep his pants up. That meant that he could potentially lose his pants if he had to draw it out, or at best to fight one handed while holding his trousers up with the other.

The plan as Kharzai had been told was to have an RV parked in the southeast corner parking lot to which the drug deliveries would be made. Usein would take his "package" at that same point, and the initial large delivery arrangements would be made at that time. Mister White's personal assistant, Lucas Ring, would be in charge of the pick up and delivery of the various drug quantities, worth hundreds of thousands of dollars. The RV was to be marked, but Kharzai didn't know with what. He was originally going to be with Usein and was therefore never told what the marking would be.

The supposed logic behind doing it in this crowded parking lot was that no one would suspect such a massive transfer in such a public place.

That's why the bad guys always lose, Kharzai thought as he passed a group of police officers walking along the rows of vehicles with drug sniffing dogs quietly snuffling the air beside them.

They're constantly coming up with stupid plans like that.

He walked past several other large white RVs when suddenly a figure lurched out from between two of them. A mass of vomit exploded from a young man's mouth and splattered sickeningly on the pavement just two feet in front of Kharzai.

"Eeeyewww!" Kharzai exclaimed. "I see you really enjoyed yourself last night, eh?"

The man nodded weakly, his face was pale and his eyes vividly bloodshot. Red veins crisscrossed the sunken white orbs like spider webs.

"Say, maybe you can help me out there, old boy." Kharzai said in a friendly manner, "Have you seen a muscle-bound blond haired guy who looks like he was rejected from the world's strongest man competition because he was too big?"

The man looked at him with a stare that was somewhere between blank and barely aware. Kharzai was about to turn away when the man spoke.

"Yeah," replied the inebriated football fan, "about half an hour ago he pulled his RV in. He was a real asshole. Asshole honked his air horn at us when Bucky puked and passed out in the road. He got out like he was going to beat the shit out of us. Asshole was huge and meaner than a rottweiler. Scared us so bad Frank pissed in his pants. The asshole."

"That'd be him. Ugly as a rottweiler too, was he?"

"I don't know about that," replied the man, "I think rotties can be kinda cute. That asshole was ugly though. Asshole passed us and parked over there somewhere."

He pointed in the general direction of the stadium that stood across half a mile of parking area.

"Thanks mate. Have an Alka-Seltzer on me, and maybe you should get a thesaurus and learn some additional forms of your favorite pronoun. It'll make you sound smarter." Kharzai said, and he reached out to shake the man's hand.

The man reached up to accept the shake. Kharzai noticed vomit smeared across his fingers. He quickly retracted his own hand.

"You may want to find some sanitary wipes there, buddy."

The man belched loudly. Kharzai flinched in fear of more projectile vomit heading his way and quickly walked on leaving the man to deal with his mess.

"I wonder if Usein ever trusted me at all?"

He sighed.

Friendship is so hard to come by. Oh, well. I'll probably have to kill him anyway, so it never would have lasted.

Kharzai looked at his watch; it was nine fifteen already. He had to find Ring soon or things would be getting too close for comfort. He walked a hundred yards to the end of the row of vehicles, rounded it, and began to make his way back down the next aisle. He kept his eyes peeled on the variety of vehicles as people were beginning to rouse themselves for the game that would start in less than two hours.

Crowds had begun to form. The noise level steadily increased as the mass of excited fans made their way from the thousands of RVs & vans. First it was a trickle, which soon grew to a river and very soon would become a flood of rowdy supporters adorned in the scarlet and gray of Ohio or the blue and gold of Michigan.

A group of a dozen college-aged men bounced past Kharzai whooping and hollering. They wore nothing but gym shorts and sneakers, their bodies covered entirely in blue and gold paint. He ducked out of their way, not wanting to get smudged with the bright colors slathered all over their bodies.

His effort was useless. As he jumped between two RVs he bounded right into a half-naked fat man painted from the waist up entirely in a thick layer of bright blue paint. An equally bright "M" was painted over the blue on his face. The collision smeared the entire upper right half Kharzai's jacket and shirt in blue. In addition to the blue a streak of bright yellow ran across the right side of his face and hair.

"Hey, asshole!" bellowed the giant. "Watch where you're going!"

He looked like a fat blue Smurf with a bad attitude. His breath stank of hard liquor covered by what seemed to be a breakfast of beer.

"So sorry," replied Kharzai, quickly stepping aside from the man and passing him between the RVs.

"Asshole!" mumbled the fat man as he joined the flow of the crowd.

"Hmmm…strange. They all seem to use the same pronoun," Kharzai said to no one. "Someone needs to invest in thesauruses for the whole Midwest."

As he made his way to the middle of the row of massive vehicles resting back to back along the parking aisle a shape caught his eye just above his head. He stopped, turned and looked up to see the huge back and thick neck of Lucas Ring through the rear window of the RV next to him.

"Hot diggity dog!" he chuckled, "It's show time!"

Kharzai glanced at his watch. It was nine thirty-five. He went over to the door of the RV and turned the knob. It was locked. He shook it rapidly, sending vibrations through the whole vehicle. Ring threw open the door and shouted.

"What the hell!"

When he looked down at Kharzai, his fierce anger evaporated, and he burst into uproarious laughter.

"What the hell happened to you, asshole?"

"I ran into Sphincter Smurf. Whom I believe must have been in the same grammar class."

"Jesus H. Christ," laughed Ring.

"Well, can I come in?" Kharzai asked with a note of exasperation.

"What for?"

"What do you mean what for? Usein sent me."

"Did he?" Ring said jeeringly. "Well, I guess I'd better let your freaky little ass in then…asshole."

"Don't you Ohio people know any other derogatory names?"

"Huh?"

"Step aside, Mister Giganticus." Kharzai waved with his hand and let his eyes flair with a well-practiced psychotic glimmer.

"Or what?" challenged Ring.

"Or I will bite your testicles off and stuff them up your nose," replied Kharzai. He smiled viciously and pointed towards Ring's crotch, which, due to the height of step on which Ring stood was directly in front his face.

Ring's mirth dissipated, and he glowered down towards Kharzai then motioned him into the RV. Kharzai stepped up into the vehicle and closed the door behind himself. Ring tossed him a roll of paper towels as he topped the last step and stood in the tiny living room area of the RV.

Ring stood by the three-burner stove top in the equally cramped kitchen space. His shoulders were wider, almost by double, than the aisle way between the counters, sink, and stove top in which he stood. His hips nearly touched the counter tops on both sides of the aisle. Kharzai could not see past Ring, whose body completely blocked everything behind him.

"Clean that shit off your face, asshole. You look like an idiot."

"Thanks." Kharzai tore off a hand full of towels and wiped the greasy blue paint from his face. It streaked through his hair and burrowed deeper into his beard. Nothing short of a very hot shower would get it all out.

"So what did Usein send you to do here, Mister Al Gul?" Ring asked.

"To check and make sure everything was going as planned, and that you had not been careless," Kharzai mumbled with the towels over his face.

"That's funny," replied Ring. "because when he called me about an hour ago, he said that if I saw you, I was to kill your traitorous ass."

Kharzai froze, the towels still covering half his face. He peeked over the top of the paper towels. Ring grinned back at him spitefully. The giant raised his hands and tightened his fingers into massive fists that looked like a pair of medieval maces on the end of his thickly muscled arms.

Each of Lucas Ring's fists was almost as wide as Kharzai's entire face. The bulging muscles of his upper arms were bigger than Kharzai's head. His sheer mass outweighed the Persian-American secret agent by at least a hundred-twenty pounds. The narrow space inside the RV suddenly seemed even smaller to Kharzai.

Ring lunged forward arms outstretched. Kharzai jumped up onto the dining booth seat and stepped nimbly onto the small table. Its surface wobbled with his weight as he tried to leap over Ring. His body cleared the giant's head, but Ring caught the wiry Persian by his thighs in mid-air. Kharzai's flight abruptly stopped as Ring's thick fingers wrapped around and squeezed the cords of his hamstrings. Kharzai squished up his face in pain as the giant's vise like grip compressed the muscles and threatened to crack the bones in his legs. He struggled against the pressure but got no relief.

"What'd your momma feed you," he shouted, "iron shavings?"

Ring laughed a deep throaty roar. Kharzai pounded at the man's kidneys with his fists but found only a thick wall of muscle covering his entire back. His hands stung from the force of the blows, but Ring didn't react except to continue laughing. Kharzai felt a painful tingling in his calves as the circulation was cut off by Ring's tourniquet grip. He arched his back up and reached backwards with his hand towards Ring's face. He wanted to gouge his fingers into the giant's eyes but couldn't reach them. Ring's laughter rose higher in pitch, with an almost childlike gleeful sound. He was really enjoying himself.

Kharzai remembered the belt buckle knife. He arched his back up again and unbuckled the long leather strap. Ring countered Kharzai's movement by squeezing the Persian's thighs around his thick neck like the handles of a nutcracker, except that the giant's neck muscles resisted harder than any pecan ever would. The pressure was excruciating.

Kharzai let out an agonized screech as his femoral bones twisted against the hip sockets. He yanked the short black polymer blade from inside the leather belt. He raised it high in the air and drove it into center of Ring's back just to the side of the spine, right where the giant's kidneys should be. Ring's maniacal laughter ceased, and he let out a bestial roar of pain. Kharzai raised the blade and drove it down into the other side of his spine. Ring howled in agony. Lucas Ring had never experienced such pain in his life. He had always been the biggest boy on the block.

Kharzai felt the pressure on his thighs let up ever so slightly, and he continued to rapidly plunge the blade in and out of Ring's back. With every jab the giant's grip decreased in minute quantities. Ring started twisting and spinning with Kharzai still on top of his shoulders. He slammed the Persian side to side into the walls and furniture of the RV. The massive vehicle rocked violently with their motion. A small crowd gathered outside, not sure what to make of it.

Kharzai flailed with his knife hand, trying desperately to stop the giant from smashing him to death against the walls of the RV. Kharzai's head smashed into the door, flinging it open with a loud crash. He briefly saw people standing out-

309

side the RV, eyes wide, gawking at the fight. He was drawn back in and banged his head into the cabinet as Ring twisted violently. Kharzai raised the blade and drove it into Ring's thick right shoulder. He pulled it out and drove it home three more times.

The giant's movement slowed. He was tiring out. His mass and weight were designed for sheer strength, not sustained energy output. Kharzai stabbed the stubby blade under Ring's right armpit and ripped upward with it. Ring's arm released the Persian's leg and fell limp to the side of his body. The Persian swung his freed left leg down and behind Ring's back, spun his body as far to the right as he could until he was nearly facing the back of Ring's head. He spread his arm's wide and clapped them together on either side of the giant's head. The blade in his hand pierced Ring's temple. Blood burst in jets that sprayed bright red across the RV's window, the dining table, and the cloth seats.

Ring stopped moving. The giant's body swayed, then he crumpled to his knees. He relaxed his grip on Kharzai's other leg. The Persian quickly scrambled away from Ring not wanting to be pinned to the floor by the man's massive body as he toppled face down.

Lucas Ring was still. Kharzai backed away from his hulking body, twisted between the dining seats and the three-cushioned couch on the other side of the aisle. His foot twitched and Kharzai flinched. Lucas Ring was dead.

CHAPTER 41

Hogan ended the cell call with Andy Fleiss. He stuffed the phone back in his pocket. Shouts came from between the RVs where the team had followed Ring and seen the hairy man enter. The violent rocking of the RV had stopped. The agents rushed forward.

"Get out of the RV with your hands up!"

"Move it!" shouted another agent.

Kharzai Ghiassi moved slowly and deliberately out from between the RVs. His hands were behind his head, which was streaked with blue and yellow paint and speckled with red dots of blood.

"I'm one of the good guys."

"Shut up!" shouted the agent nearest him.

"Ring's dead," came a shout from inside.

"Search it for drugs and weapons. Get the dogs on it!" Hogan called out. "It's OK, he's one of us!"

Kharzai raised both hands and waved.

"Paul, you saw my signal?"

"Yeah, come with us," Paul shouted in reply. "Hurry up"

The trio ran the two hundred yards across the parking lot to the command trailer. As they ran, Kharzai stretched his hand in introduction to Mike Farris.

"Hi, I'm Kharzai slash Seirim Al Gul. You're the preacher, right?" Kharzai said.

"Mike Farris," Mike replied.

They reached Paul's car and got in. Kharzai sat in the back.

"You guys know that this is a bomb thing, right? Nuclear?"

"Yeah," said Paul. "Do you know if it is only one or are there more?"

"It's just the one, as laid out in that email I forwarded you. I don't think anyone else knows, except the dirty cop and maybe Mister White."

"You know about the cop?"

"Yeah."

Hogan sped to the exit gate and the police officers at the barricades stopped the other traffic to let them out of the congested area.

Kharzai looked around. "Where are we going?"

"I was just told that it's on the move towards Picktown and not here."

"Not here?" Kharzai asked. "Well that beats it all. That Usein never did trust me."

"You said White knows?" asked Paul.

"I think so. I overheard part of a cell phone conversation between him and Usein and the cop."

"Stop the car!" shouted Mike nearly jumping out of the seat.

"Its Usein!" he shouted to Hogan. "He just got out of that car. He's walking away! Let me out here!"

Akbar Usein was a hundred yards up the street, walking casually towards the stadium.

"Call for back up!" Hogan replied, "I'll go to the Picktown site."

Mike Farris jumped out of the car before Hogan had come to a full stop. Kharzai followed him, grabbing a Bengal's ball cap that had been left by someone on the back seat. He stuffed it down over his thick mass of hair in an impromptu disguise. The two of them jogged on foot towards Usein. Halfway across the distance Kharzai tapped Mike on the shoulder and split off. Mike spoke into his radio.

"Hilde! This is Mike. Send a team to the northwest parking lot, on Cannon Drive. Usein is on foot northbound on the west side of the road; I am in pursuit. The hairy guy, Kharzai, is with me several yards to my right."

"Wait for backup, Mike!" she replied. "They're on the way!"

Hogan's car disappeared around the bend in the road as he sped towards the freeway. Mike continued towards Usein. Kharzai vanished into the crowd that moved in a steady stream towards the stadium, along the sidewalk and from the parking lot beyond it.

The African walked towards a waiting car. He grasped the door handle and started to pull it open.

"Usein! Freeze!" Mike shouted from twenty feet away. Akbar Usein turned to see the retired Marine pointing a pistol at him.

The evil smile that came across Usein's face sent icy shivers of fear and long-forgotten hatred through Farris's body.

"You are too late, Captain Farris. Or shall I call you Pastor Mike?"

The scar on Usein's temple pulsed as he stared hard into Mike's eyes. The ghastly tissue seemed to take on a life of its own.

"Close the door, Akbar," Mike said calmly, "and put your hands above your head."

"It makes no difference," Usein replied as he raised his hands. "You will all die in a short while anyway. You will die and go to the hell for infidels."

Usein laughed.

"I will go to Allah as a martyr while you will join your pig wife and pig child in hell."

"Step away from the car," Mike said, ignoring Usein's taunts.

"What can you do to me, Captain Farris? I am not afraid to die."

The African stepped toward him. The sound of the boots of several police officers and FBI agents crunched on the pavement as they approached from between the parked cars. Weapons raised, they moved cautiously towards the confrontation from behind Farris.

They were still fifty yards away when a small child, five or six years old with nut-brown hair and huge brown eyes, unexpectedly ran out from behind a large SUV parked just inside the parking lot across the sidewalk. He was giggling and squealing gleefully as he escaped his parent's grasp.

The small boy was looking back towards his family, who were walking somewhere between the vehicles. He nearly ran into Usein before he knew the man was there. The terrorist grabbed the child and swung him up in front of his body like a shield. He simultaneously whipped his own pistol up and pointed it at Mike.

"Now you put your gun down, pig, or I will kill the child!"

The little boy let out a whimpering cry.

"Daddy!"

His parents came out from behind the SUV to find their terrified little boy being held by an evil looking man with a gun. Usein pointed the gun to the boy's head.

"Mommy!" the boy shrieked.

The mother screamed, a blood-curdling shriek of horror.

"Please!" said the father, terrified. "Please don't hurt my son; please don't hurt my son! Just let him go!"

"Put the boy down, Usein!" shouted Mike, his pistol aimed at Usein.

"You will die, pig," Usein replied, "and so will this child if you do not let me go!"

"Can't do that, Usein!" Mike answered. "Just put the boy down, and we'll talk!"

Police officers formed a wide circle around the terrorist, weapons trained on him.

Mike's head started to spin. He suddenly saw the house in Bosnia. The mother and boy. The little girl forced to be a shield. He knew he couldn't let Usein go. He did not want these parents to see their son die. He could not let the boy die.

"Put the child down, Usein!" Mike shouted.

A Police sniper positioned himself a hundred yards away. Mike heard the whispered conversation in his radio earpiece.

"I'm in, but can't get a shot," said the sniper, "He keeps moving the kid around."

"Wait for a clean shot," came the reply.

"Can't get one."

Mike looked hard at Usein.

"Put the kid down, and you will live!"

"Back off and let me go!"

"Put him down!"

"I'll kill him!"

"Mommy!"

The child's mother suddenly lunged forward, arms towards her baby.

"Please let my baby go!"

The father caught hold of her just as Usein turned the gun on them. Kharzai leaped from the crowd near the parents. He waved the bright orange Bengals ball cap wildly in the air.

"Akbar Aga!" he shouted and danced a flailing arrhythmic dance that drew Akbar's attention.

Surprised, Usein jerked his weapon towards Kharzai and pulled the trigger. The cap flew from Kharzai's hand. The bullet smashed into the windshield of a Winnebago parked a few yards away.

Everything took on an extreme slow-motion quality. The mother broke from her husband's grasp. Usein swung his weapon towards the fast-moving figure and fired again. Usein's bullet grazed the mother's cheek and hit the father in the flesh of his arm, then passed through him and shattered the windshield of the SUV behind them.

Usein swung his arm with the pistol towards the child's head. The little boy shrieked with his mouth wide open, tears streamed down his face. A portion of Akbar Usein's head came into view behind the child's flaring brown hair.

Farris fired a single shot from his forty-five. The round passed within an inch of the child's head and slammed into the edge of Usein's left eye socket. The inertia of the large caliber Hydra-Shock round fired from Farris's weapon exploded with such force against Akbar Usein's skull that the entire top half of his head was blown apart. His arms flung wide. The pistol spun through the air, and the child dropped from his grasp. Usein's body fell straight back onto the pavement.

The child collapsed to the ground, scrambled to his feet, and ran to his mother who grabbed him up in her arms. She clasped her arms around her son and wept mightily, tears mingling with the blood from the wound on her cheek. The boy pressed his shaking flesh into his mother's body as if he were trying to crawl inside her skin. Kharzai pressed the wound on the father's shoulder. Mike dropped to his knees.

"Thank you, Jesus," he called out breathlessly. "Thank you, Lord."

CHAPTER 42

Picktown, Ohio
09:55 Hours

Billy Z pulled the white Chevy Impala into a quiet area of Sycamore Creek Park in the quaint suburban city of Picktown. He followed a dirt road that led around a group of baseball diamonds to the back of the park. It ended behind a grove of trees in a small gravel parking area next to the railroad tracks. The spot was obscured, practically invisible from the view of casual observers who might be on the diamonds. He stopped the car, turned off the engine, got out, and stood in the quiet.

Billy tried to make sense of things as he inhaled the fresh autumn air deeply into his lungs. The sight of the red, yellow, and brown leaves on the trees and the fresh taste of the crisp autumn morning air invigorated him. This was his favorite season, one that he had missed during the years he had been serving his country in the perpetually hot, steamy jungles of Central America.

The park was calming. It could even have been relaxing were it not for the internal certainty that something bad was about to happen. He was not allowed much time to do any thinking. The sound of tires crunched on gravel and pulled his attention back to the road he had come in on. Billy got back into character and tried to look as gangster as he could while he waited for the vehicle to approach. He did not know whether the vehicle would be Usein's contact or his police controller and the SWAT team, and he did not want to not look the correct part for whoever it may be. A burgundy Ford Crown Victoria pulled into view. It was alone. The glare of the sun on the windshield made it impossible for Billy to see the driver's face or to tell how many may be in the car. The car came to a stop a few yards behind his. The door opened and out came the driver.

"You came alone?" Billy said.

"Yeah."

"Where's SWAT?"

"Right behind me."

Detective Danny Martin extended his arm and before Billy realized what was happening the police officer fired three shots into the undercover agent's chest. Billy quaked from the force of each shot. He stumbled backward, arms reaching in vain to grasp hold of something that would stop his fall. A confused look spread on his face before he slowly tipped over like a small tree cut down with an axe. He landed hard on his side in the dirt. Blood oozed from the wounds and slowly spread in a deep-red pool across the cold hard ground. His eyes slid closed.

Detective Danny Martin of the Columbus Police Department was in a good mood for the first time in many, many years.

Finally. I get to be my real self and do what I was trained for.

Detective Martin's birth name was unknown to anyone other than a small handful of people in the CIA and an equally small number in the KGB.

"Ulrich Heider Krieghammer," he said aloud to the dying young man in the dirt.

His parents, Werner and Anna, a humble cobbler and his wife, had immigrated to the US in 1973 under the auspices of political asylum. Their home country of East Germany had issued warrants for their arrests for aiding in the passing of state secrets to the Americans and participating in the anti-communist resistance.

The CIA helped them escape and expedited their name change. Krieghammer, the literal meaning of which was "War Hammer," indicated a warrior lineage in the family. Martin was much subtler and became their legal name before Danny's fifth birthday.

The CIA handlers who had charge of their case were totally unaware that Werner Krieghammer, the shoemaker, was in truth a double agent. The Easter German Stasi, in cooperation with the Soviet GRU had contrived the entirety of the story of the Krieghammer's involvement in the resistance in order to plant the family in America. The Martins' purpose in America was simply to act as what the spy industry called "sleeper agents." Agents put in place and kept in deep cover, living as civilians among the general population, until a situation arose that required their activation. Little Danny had no clue that his parents were actually Soviet spies until he was sixteen-years old.

One day during his junior year of high school, Danny's father sat him down and gave him a carefully worded lecture about the glories of the old world and how socialism would one day fully take root in America. All they had to do was get rid of that anti-progressive, fascist president of theirs, Ronald Reagan, and put a good socialist in his place.

Danny had been enthralled by his father's lecture. His heart beat heavily as he hung on the older man's words. As the diatribe drew near its end Werner abruptly stopped talking and stared deeply into his son's eyes. His voice lowered as he spoke in his thick East German accent.

"Danny. Do you know who I am?"

"Of course! You are my father."

"Do you know what I do?"

"You are a custom shoe maker."

"What would you say if I told you there was more to me and your mother than you ever knew?"

That day Danny discovered why they had really come to this country, and that his loyalties belonged to East Germany and the Soviet Union.

Danny "Ulrich Krieghammer" Martin relished the idea of being a spy. He had never been good at making friends in school and often found the other kids to be quite boring, even tedious to associate with. He had especially despised the fact that most of the families in their town in Illinois were, at least nominally, Christian. Almost all of them went to church every Sunday. They looked suspiciously on anyone who didn't. His parents of course were atheists, and Danny could not understand how anyone in their right mind could be anything different.

When his father asked him to join the struggle for socialism, Danny bit into it full force. By the time he was twenty-one-years old he had been thoroughly indoctrinated into communism. Danny spent five years attending several secret schools of espionage. He trained right under the nose of the American intelligence agencies.

Once he was fully trained and prepared for any variety of missions that may fall into his lap, he was ordered by his controlling agents to become a police officer. It would be the perfect cover. As a police officer, his job could allow him terrific levels of access once he reached positions of authority, however long that may take.

Communism was patient and would wait for an entire generation, or even two or three generations, to meet its goals. Unlike those greedy capitalists who want everything right away. They were always striving so hard as if life were a race. They would lie and cheat and steal to get rich on the backs of others. They would hold back things or knowledge that could help someone advance, keeping it for themselves, rather than share equally with their fellow man.

They called it individual success. Danny called it unfair, And now, after twenty-five years of waiting secretly, working his way through the ranks until he became a senior detective, Danny Martin had been called into action, and it was big.

After the collapse of East Germany, the Stasi was defunct. The GRU on the other hand, in spite of the supposed fall of the Soviet Union, had remained in full operation. When they sent him the message that he was to be activated to perform a mission of worldwide implications, he felt almost giddy with excitement, like a six-year-old on Christmas Eve.

Undercover Detective William Coffee lay in a slick of steaming red mud next to the Impala. Martin went over to his warm body and rolled him on his back. He held the back of his hand over Coffee's mouth and nose. He felt no breath. In Coffee's neck there was a pulse, but it was weak, brushing like feathers over the tips of his fingers. What life remained in William "Billy Z" Coffee would soon be gone.

Danny rifled through the pockets of Billy's jacket until he found the car keys. He pressed the button on the small black plastic remote. The trunk popped open with a click and the large lid slowly yawned at the rear of the car, exposing its contents to his view. A thickly-built, heavy-looking suitcase was the only item in the compartment.

Martin reached into the open trunk and drew out the case. It was indeed heavy. He had to use both of his hands to lift it out of the deep, spacious trunk. He waddled across the graveled parking area, carrying the heavy case with a two-handed grasp. It swung across the front of his legs as he took it through a narrow path between sections of a thick hedge of blackberry bushes that grew parallel to the railroad tracks.

A huff of wind escaped his lips as he set the case on the ground next to the gravel rail bed. His right shoulder ached. The wound from where the old man had shot him in the church was not deep, but it hurt like crazy under the strain of the case. It felt like a couple of the butterfly sutures he had applied to it had ripped open. A trickle of blood oozed from the wound. He would have to dress it again later.

He grunted from the exertion as he knelt in the rocks and tipped the case so that he could see the dials for three separate combination locks set in a row across the front of the case. He rolled the number wheels on each dial to match the combinations he had received in an encrypted email message from Usein that morning.

Once the number sequences were completed, he clicked open the latches. The case came open with a hiss as the thick anti-radiation seals released air that had been locked inside the case for almost twenty years.

The contents of the case appeared amazingly simple. The majority of the case's contents consisted of heavy foam padding surrounded by thick lead radiation shielding that kept the chaotic nuclear material out of view from the prying eyes of America's radiation detection satellites.

In the center of the shielding material in a padded indentation lay a metallic silver ball, heavy and menacing. It was about the size of a grapefruit. Affixed to the side of the ball was a small box with a brightly lit digital display screen. Five glowing yellow zeros blazed on the screen. The clock itself could have kept ticking for several centuries powered by the radioactive material next to it.

Six wires stretched to a black rectangular object that lay flush in the padding two inches to the right of the ball. The top of the rectangular box was filled with a keypad consisting of three rows of numbered buttons. Directly below the number pad were two key holes, one at each of the bottom corners. Between the key holes a square red button jutted from the box.

The keypad acted as the arming device. The digital timer display was set on the end of a simple detonator, which consisted of a rod extending into a thumb-sized charge of plastic high-explosive into which was firmly pressed thousands of microscopic shards of Plutonium.

The ball itself was a solid compact alloy of the hardening agent Beryllium and Polonium, a highly unstable radioactive element. On activation of the trigger, the shards of Plutonium would be thrust out from the core of the sphere at speeds measured in nano-seconds. They would smash like infinitesimal bullets into the Beryllium-Polonium inner core crashing against its nuclear structure and sending millions of electrons scattering about from the impact. This scattering would continue in a riot of light speed movement that would build a nuclear chain reaction that would reach critical mass in only a few millionths of a second.

Once that state of critical mass was reached, eyes hundreds of miles away would be drawn to the terrifyingly familiar form of a mushroom cloud rising from the gentle rolling hills of central Ohio. All of that destructive power lay before Martin, tightly wrapped in a smooth sphere of lead and encased in a thin layer of steel.

Martin looked over the contents of the case. The technology required to set the device was not terribly complicated. The suitcase sized bomb was designed to be triggered via the connected timer. This enabled the agent time to escape once the explosive was in place. Unlike modern terrorists who expect, even look forward to, death by triggering the bomb manually, this device was designed by Soviet KGB operatives who had families to whom they hoped to return upon defeating their enemies.

Martin anticipated escape. He expected to live and see himself grow old, but he would not be using the timer. His orders instead required arming the bomb and placing the trigger leads in such a manner that when the NRC train rolled over them, its weight would detonate the bomb. That detonation would in turn set off the one-hundred-fifty megatons of military-grade fissile material contained in the shielded train car being driven by Engineer Ronald Henderson as it passed through this small suburban town in a very short while.

The reaction of the combined explosions would at the very least destroy this small city of thirty thousand residents and poison the air for generations to come. At best, the hoped-for outcome, was that the explosion would trigger a massive chain reaction among the warheads in the train. If that happened, the cataclysmic explosion would be massive—destruction on a Biblical scale.

It would likely vaporize most of central Ohio and render Illinois, Kentucky, western Pennsylvania, and southern Michigan uninhabitable for millennia. Either reaction suited Martin and his employer, Akbar Usein, perfectly well. Martin smiled as he looked into the case and envisioned the awesome destructive power he was about to invoke.

He had a perfect plan for escape. Once the bomb was armed, the trigger set, and the timer zeroed, Martin would cross to the other side of the park to the small municipal airstrip where a single engine Piper Saratoga awaited him. Barring complications, Dan Martin would be nearly nine hundred miles away and safely out of the blast radius when the Ohio Valley became an uninhabitable wasteland.

To avoid suspicion, Martin had logged a flight plan with the local authorities for a personal trip to visit relatives in Quebec. He was not concerned with the thought that anyone would turn him after the fact, because any and all potential witnesses would have been reduced to a handful of charred remains and wisps of subatomic vapor by the time he crossed the border. The relatives in Ontario were his "uncle" and "cousin" visiting from Berlin. He and they would together disappear from the continent, spirited back to safety among Martin's true comrades on the other side of the planet.

Giddy with those thoughts in mind, Danny Martin ran back to his car to get the folding shovel he had brought with him. He retrieved it from the passenger seat of the police issue Crown Victoria and ran back through the blackberry hedge to the side of the railroad bed.

Martin scooped at the fist-sized stones that lay across the outside of the rail bed until he had cleared it down to the smaller tightly packed gravel that supported the rail itself. He created a space about a foot beneath the rail ties that was large enough to hold the suitcase. Just above the large hole he dug a smaller hole with his fingers that was just large enough for him to insert his flattened hand.

From the inside pocket of his sport coat Martin removed a two-inch-wide by twelve-inch-long rubber strap. Two-inch square copper plates were embedded at each end of the folded rubber strap. To each of these plates were soldered two lengths of insulated ten-gauge copper wire. The four wires were coiled together and hung along the sides of the contraption. An alligator clip was attached at the end of each of the wires.

He folded the strap in half, lengthwise, until the plates were approximately one centimeter apart. Into the gap between them he slid a square of thick, non-conductive rubber that was slightly larger than the copper plates.

Martin inserted the device snugly into the smaller of the two holes he had dug under the railroad. He uncoiled the wire and let it hang to the side of the larger hole.

He turned back to the case and pulled a small pair of wire cutters from his pocket. He snipped the two wires that connected the timer to the arming unit midway between the devices. With the small stripping blade at the crook of the cutters Martin stripped one half inch of the insulation off the four ends of the wires.

He then attached the alligator clips of the four wires that hung from the folded rubber device to the strips of bared copper wire on the bomb. He wrapped the clips loosely with small strips of electrical tape. He had no desire to let the wires touch each other and complete the circuit prematurely.

Just inside the lid of the case two keys were taped to the rim. He took the keys from their decades-long resting place and inserted them into their respective keyholes on the arming device.

He turned both of the keys simultaneously. The lights on the timer blinked three times then changed from zeros to a line of five dashes on the tiny screen.

Martin took a paper from his shirt pocket and depressed the buttons on the numbered keypad in the order shown on the paper. Sixteen digits. He hesitated before pressing the last two. Beads of sweat rose on his forehead, in spite of the autumn chill.

Martin's finger hovered warily over the last two buttons. He took a deep breath and pressed the next to last number. He touched his finger to the last digit. He could feel the indentation of the number, cast like reverse Braille on the square metal cube. Even beneath his light touch, he felt the spring under the button give from the weight of his finger tip.

The button was warm. It had been basking in the glow of the radioactive material for nearly two decades, almost half of Martin's life. He pressed the button fully until it stopped moving.

Something inside the detonator came to life with a loud metallic snap against the ball of radioactive fissile material. Martin's heart thumped two hard beats that felt like it had leaped into the center of his throat. His eyes widened with surprise.

Nothing else happened.

He recovered his composure quickly and wiped sweat from his brow. Wetness ran in a salty stream across the back of his hand. Steam rose from inside the open collar of his shirt, spreading like a mist around his head in the cool autumn morning. One more step. The final button to press and he could be out of here.

Martin took a deep breath and held it in. He reached towards the square red button on the arming device. His hand trembled.

What if this thing goes off without warning? What if I've been tricked?

He suddenly remembered an old movie he had watched years earlier, "The Fourth Protocol." Pierce Brosnan played the part of a Soviet spy tasked with setting up a nuclear bomb near an American air force base in England. Unknown to the spy, his controllers had ordered his partner to bypass the timer so that as soon as he turned the key to arm it, the bomb would instantly explode.

Danny Martin closed his eyes, pursed his lips, and pressed the plastic button. Part of him expected the world to suddenly become a bright flash of white light. He imagined being evaporated by the light-speed explosion of the nuclear device he was touching.

What would death be like? Is it really over at that moment? Would he instantly become nothing? Is there really a God? If so, would he see him?

No.

He forced the thought through.

There is no God. There is nothing. Death is nothing.

The button clicked solidly under his finger. The dashes on the timer's digital display blinked off and on. Then they changed back to a line of five zeros. That line now pulsed in a constant steady rhythm of two beats per second. The bomb was live.

Danny Martin gently closed the lid and carefully stuffed the case into the larger of the two holes he had dug. It fit perfectly into the recess. He had dug it out sufficiently that there was plenty of room for him to cover its face with a layer of rocks. The suitcase nuclear weapon vanished from sight, camouflaged in its new, yet temporary, home.

Martin reached up to the triggering device in the small hole above the suitcase and very gingerly pulled the thin strip of insulating rubber strap from between the copper sheets to which the wires were connected. The bomb was live. The trigger was armed. The safety was off.

It was an incredibly simple device. A basic booby trap with the potential power to kill three million people. Maybe more.

"Done," he said aloud and smiled to himself as he rose from the work.

He picked up the shovel and started back towards his car. He had fifteen minutes to get into the plane and take off. In just about forty-five minutes he would be across the border of Canada and more than half way to Quebec.

He ignored the pain in his right shoulder as he walked briskly through the blackberry hedge. His feet crunched on the gravelly dirt of the parking area. As he passed Billy's Impala he was startled by a sharp metallic click. Martin froze in his tracks. Slowly he turned to his left towards the source of the sound. Paul Hogan rose slowly from beside Billy Z's body. His weapon pointed at Martin's chest.

"I don't know what all is going on here, Danny boy, but I do know that I have never liked you." Hogan said. "Now put the shovel down and assume the position against the Impala. Keep your hands above your head."

"Paul, are you crazy?" protested Martin, "I'm on your side."

"No, I don't think so," replied Hogan. "Andy intercepted the informants call to you an hour ago. Now, get your God-damned hands in the air, or I will shoot you where you stand."

Martin gave up all pretense and puffed his chest out in a display of bravado.

"Go ahead and shoot me. At least I am dying for a cause."

"Oh," asked Hogan, "and what cause is that?"

"Truth!"

As he spat the word Martin flung the shovel towards Hogan. The move diverted the FBI agent's eyes for a split second. Martin rapidly drew his own pistol from the paddle holster in the back of his trousers. Pain stabbed through his shoulder as he thrust the gun forward and fired. Hogan fired at the same time. Both men shuddered violently. The bullets from both pistols slammed home into their targets.

The two men tumbled to the ground from the blast of the bullets. Blood spouted and bubbled from the right side of Hogan's chest. He rolled onto his side and tried to raise him-self to his knees but collapsed, gasping for air. A high-pitched wheeze sounded wetly through the wound in his ribs. He crunched his brow in a pain washed grimace.

Martin slowly got back to his feet. His left arm hung limply at his side. Blood poured from the wound that pierced through his left shoulder, just below the clavicle. It was a clean flesh wound that exited through his armpit. It bled like crazy, but he would recover. He walked over to where Hogan lay bleeding on the ground.

Paul Hogan's face was pal, white as a sheet. He blinked rapidly as air gurgled in foamy scarlet bubbles from the hole in his chest. Blood splashed out of his mouth, brightly con-trasted against the whiteness of his skin and the blue of his oxygen starved lips. The FBI agent struggled for breath. William Coffee's still body lay between them.

Martin stepped over Billy and stood directly above Hogan. His thin lips stretched in a spiteful smile, baring yellow coffee-stained teeth. Martin's face wrinkled at the edges of his eyes and mouth. His lips quivered with rage like a wild dog about to pounce for the kill. He raised his pistol and pointed it towards Hogan's face.

Paul Hogan stared up into the ten-millimeter-wide barrel of the gun. He slumped onto his back in the dirt and gravel and turned his eyes to Danny Martin's. Danny "Ulrich Krieghammer" Martin, communist sleeper agent, glared back at Paul.

"Oh, this is going to be so sweet. I've always hated you too, you little Irish shit."

Martin stretched his arm forward. He closed his smiling mouth, squinted across the sight post of the pistol, pursed his lips, and tensed his body for the shot.

Paul saw the tendons in the back of Martin's hand swell as the fingers tightened around the pistol grip. His index finger curled slowly around the smooth steel trigger. Paul stared up into the darkness of the barrel and watched.

ten-millimeter Glock. Why don't they just call it a centimeter?

The absurdity of such a thought at the moment before his own death struck him as funny. He smiled to himself and wondered if he would be able to see the centimeter-wide bullet as it came down the barrel. He wondered if his mind would register it before it blew his head apart.

His lips moved in a prayer he had often heard Mike mutter as they prepared for battles they had faced in the Marines.

Father forgive my sins, so I may be received in your kingdom.

Two explosions, like claps of thunder, ripped the morning calm. The air compressed around him with the force of a ten-ton hammer. Paul convulsed reactively. Death was on him for sure. He blinked in a rapid twitching motion then slowly opened his eyes and stared.

Danny Martin was still standing over him, smiling. He wavered on his feet. Hogan's mind whirled in confusion, unsure of what he was seeing. Martin wobbled; his cheeks fell slack then the detective's eyes glazed over, and he toppled straight back. He landed with a ground shaking thud on the gravelly dirt road.

Police and ambulance sirens sang their shrill song in the distance, growing louder as they drew close to the park. William Coffee lay flat on his back, his left hand clutched the still smoking pistol he had managed in his weakness to draw out. He had shot the man who had deceived him. It was the first time he had been required to shoot anyone since he became a cop; the first time he had killed a man since leaving the Army.

Seconds later, five police cars and two ambulances roared to the scene. Paramedics in blue jump suits ran to the three men laying on the blood-soaked ground. One of them bent over Hogan and spoke reassuringly to him. Hogan was barely conscious. He was unable to focus his eyes on the man.

"Alright, buddy. You're going to make it, just hang in there."

Hogan moved his lips. Blood trickled from his mouth. A deathly pallor colored his skin. He could barely hold his eyes open. He tried desperately to speak. Only foamy, blood soaked gurgles came out.

A second paramedic pressed a patch of sealant material over the bubbling lung wound on his chest. Hogan was finally able to draw in a breath. He whispered hoarsely, choking painfully on the blood that filled his mouth. The medic leaned down closer to him. Hogan finally managed to get the words out to the medic who bent over him.

"Bomb on tracks."

In the distance the air horn of a train sounded its warning as it began the approach into town.

"Dear Jesus!" shouted the paramedic. He shouted out to the officers nearby. "There's a bomb on the railroad tracks!"

"What?" a police Sergeant called back.

"This guy just said there's a bomb on the railroad tracks!"

The train's horn sounded again. It was only about fifteen miles away.

The half dozen police officers ran through the blackberry hedge and scrambled along the tracks.

They looked frantically for a bomb. There was nothing obvious.

"I don't see anything!"

"Me neither!"

"Look for something buried!" shouted one officer. "Like the insurgents did in Iraq."

The train's horn sounded again. It grew closer. Ten minutes away, maybe less.

"Over there!" called out one of the officers. He ran towards an area of the rail bed. "The gravel here has been disturbed."

"Careful, Manny, don't set off any detonators," said the police Sergeant.

The officer made his way towards the spot. Four wires jutted out an inch from the gray rocks piled alongside the rail bed. The gravel in the area was a darker color than the rest, it had been turned over recently and had not dried in the sun yet. Two other officers joined Manny and gingerly moved the rocks away from the wires.

"It's here! It's here!"

"What does it look like?"

"A suitcase, a big metal suitcase," came the reply, "and there's four wires going in and out of it."

"Alright, everybody get out of here. Manny, can you take care of it?"

The train's air horn sounded again, it was only a few minutes away.

"I hope so," Manny replied.

"Do it."

Officer Manuel Juarez, former army ranger with two tours of duty in Iraq, crossed himself, prayed a quick prayer, and continued to gently remove the rocks that hid the wires. He followed their path, to the spot just above the indentation in which lay the metal suitcase. The horn of the train echoed loudly from only about a mile away. He had only seconds left.

Manny pulled the last rocks out of the way and saw the trigger device where it was wedged into the rocks under the heavy wooden railroad tie. The ground began to vibrate around him. He glanced up and saw the bright head light of the train coming his way. The massive machine lumbered towards him on the tracks half a mile distant.

A great drop of sweat plopped heavily onto the rocks beneath his face. Manny saw that the copper plates were separated by less than one fourth of an inch of space. He quickly understood that if they even barely touched together it would trigger the bomb.

The train loomed large down the tracks. It was only a quarter of a mile away. Manny's heart beat so hard he couldn't tell which was louder, it or the train. The thundering vehicle would be blasting over him in fifteen seconds. The engineer leaned out of his window. He saw the policeman on the side of the tracks and pulled on his air horn. It blared hard and loud, splitting the atmosphere with deafening volume.

The ground on which Manny lay shook like an earthquake. He had to act. He scraped some of the gravel out from under the trigger with his fingers. The strap spread apart, separating the contacts further. The engineer leaned on the air horn. The morning air trembled with the blast of sound.

Five seconds. Manny grasped each end of the rubber strap with the tips of his fingers and yanked. He fell to the ground eyes tightly shut as he held the copper plates of the strap apart. If his own skin touched the plates he would complete the circuit with his body and the bomb would still detonate.

The world around him rumbled and shook as the massive train rolled passed. Engineer Ronald Henderson and several secret service officers stared wide-eyed. Curiosity turned to fear that spread on their faces as they passed and realized what they were looking at.

Five seconds later and the short train rolled out of sight around a bend in the tracks. The bomb squad arrived a few minutes later and relieved Officer Manuel Juarez of the device.

Manny walked over to the blackberry bushes a few yards away and puked his breakfast onto the dusty ground.

CHAPTER 43

October 31st
Wickersham Wholesale Shoe Distributors
Columbus, Ohio
11:45 Hours

Two days after the Ohio State vs. Michigan game, which Ohio State won by a single point in double overtime, Francis Beauregard Wickersham IV sat in his posh office at Wickersham Wholesale Shoe Distributors. Business had been brisk and quite profitable for some time. Both his primary and his secondary inventories had consistently improved for the past five consecutive quarters.

Additionally, well performing was his stock portfolio. The portfolio, which he managed himself, was primarily composed of network security companies and high-end encryption technology. This rampant financial success was, of course, no surprise to Francis. He had inherited the business from his father, who had inherited it from his father, and so on for six generations dating back to the 1840s.

In spite of the almost guaranteed success of his company, Francis Beauregard Wickersham IV hated the shoe business. He felt that it tied him down to the boring existence of a boring executive of a small, but stable, company. He had always wanted excitement. As a young man he had tried the military.

The Marines laughed when the diminutive and physically weak young man walked in. He was only five-feet three-inches tall, which in itself did not disqualify him, but he weighed in at a hundred-two pounds, which was five pounds under the absolute minimum weight limit for his height.

He had no interest in the army, so he went to both the air force and the navy. Their physical requirements were not as strict as the Marines, therefore he had hope. He did after all have a 4.0 GPA in college.

The air force at first accepted him, but just before he shipped out for officer school it had been discovered that he carried a rare form of hemophilia that had missed detection in the early part of the medical screening. While the disease was neither contagious nor imminently life threatening, it could, under the right circumstances, particularly abdominal distress such as one might incur during physical fitness training, cause him to bleed internally and die.

The government, not wanting a risky recruit who could land them in needless lawsuits for physical damage during training, barred him from enlistment on medical grounds. His hopes for high adventure were dashed because of flawed genetics.

Francis blamed god for his genetics and the US government for not giving him a chance. He decided from that point that he would get back at them both by becoming a success in his own right, without either of their help. Then he would rub it in their noses.

With the brain that earned him an MBA from Harvard, the use of cutting edge technology to streamline operations, and an amazing knack for understanding market trends he knew there was no way he could lose. Unless that is, someone beneath him failed to fulfill his orders.

Very early on the morning of Saturday the 29th, in the first year of the second decade of the 21st century, Francis boarded a flight to Florida. He left his vice president in charge of the business for the following week so that he could attend an international footwear exposition in Miami.

Shortly after his arrival in the Sunshine State, around lunch time, he was surprised to get a cell-phone call from that vice president stating that one of his senior-account managers had just lost a major contract and that his presence was needed immediately back at the office.

He returned on the next flight. Arriving in Ohio at just past nine in the evening that Saturday, a day and a time he had thought would not exist for the people of Columbus, Ohio, he rushed back to the office. He had to get the full details and to do as much damage control as possible.

At his desk Monday morning the diminutive Francis Wickersham sat straight up in his large brown leather office chair and sipped a steaming hot cup of chai tea. With a small mouse-like face, pointed nose, high forehead, narrow mustache, and round wire-rimmed glasses, Wickersham's features would have, at least to a student of history, reminded one of the Nazi architect of the Holocaust, Heinrich Himmler.

He rubbed a hand over his balding forehead and pushed the few remaining strands of straight brown hair back over his scalp, following through until his hand ended at his neck. He could feel the tension like steel cords tightly coiled on either side of his spine.

He rose from his chair and walked to the back of his posh office. Two doors hung on the back wall, one on each side of the credenza behind his desk. One led to a nicely appointed private bathroom, complete with a steam shower and massage bed.

The other door led to a soundproof private conference room. At one side of the room was a dark cherry-wood desk with a high-backed black leather executive chair behind it. A dozen high definition twenty-inch plasma video monitors covered the wall directly across from the desk and chair. These were symmetrically arranged around a single sixty-inch plasma screen mounted at the center of the wall. Above the large screen the lens of a video camera was trained on the center of the room, focused on the desk and chair.

Two of the small monitors were on. One displayed an image of the outside of a warehouse. The image was captured from a building across the parking lot and included the entrance to the building as well as all approaches to the warehouse. A black cross, like the cross hairs of a rifle scope was in the center of the screen. The second monitor displayed the desk in the room in which Francis stood. Its purpose was to ensure that the person behind the desk knew at all times how the viewers at the remote locations saw him. The wide, sixty-inch screen was also on. Across it was the shadowy image of the inside of the small room at the back of the warehouse. The interior lights were not on, but the dark shapes of the table and chairs in the room could clearly be seen by the illumination that came from security lamps that always stayed on.

On a hook just inside the door hung a large dark-gray hooded robe. The robe's shoulders jutted out stiffly as if already filled with a body. Likewise, the hood was expanded as if it contained a head of its own. A small shelf next to the robe contained a pair of thick black leather gloves. These gloves, if worn by a small man the size of Mister Wickersham, would make his hands look simply huge. In addition to the gloves, the shelf held a small wireless microphone transmitter that could be worn over the head. This transmitter worked in conjunction with a receiver that was set in a drawer in the desk and wired to the sound system for the video teleconferencing camera. On the receiver was a small knob that was labeled with a strip of white tape imprinted with the word

"Effect." Of the half dozen options for various sound filter effects, the knob was set to the effect titled "Vader."

In the drawer next to the audio receiver was a game controller, like the kind used for an X-Box or PlayStation system. It was wired to control the video feed with the cross-hairs, and the high-powered rifle on which the camera was mounted.

Francis glanced around the room and sighed deeply. His breath hissed out in a high pitched, almost feminine, wheeze. The insulated walls absorbed the sound of the breath, as if it had been sucked out of the air.

It was a technologically perfect studio. It had cost him a tremendous amount of money. It had been worth it all so far, but now....

There was a brisk knock at the outer door.

He stepped quickly out of the conference room and shut the door behind himself. He moved back into the brown leather chair in the main chamber of his office.

"Yes?" he answered. His voice intoned with a flat nasal quality that accentuated his generally nerdy appearance. It was the kind of voice one might expect to hear from a forty-year-old shoe factory owner who had a passion for technology. It fit his physical appearance very naturally.

The door popped open and Francis' personal assistant Joanna leaned in. Her face was contorted in an exasperated look of confusion and frustration.

"Sir, there is a man and a woman out here who claim to have an appointment with you, but I am not..."

Mike Farris and Hildegarde Rottbruck pushed past the personal assistant into the office.

Joanna protested, "Hey! You can't come in here!"

Hilde held a PDA in her hand as they walked into the room. She stopped just inside the door and raised it to eye level. She glanced at the screen and nodded.

"Yep. This is the place."

"Hello, Mister White," Farris said.

"His name is not Mister White!" said the secretary.

Hilde showed her FBI badge and Joanna's jaw dropped open.

"Mister Wickersham, I am Agent Rottbruck of the FBI. You are under arrest on charges of racketeering, money laundering, distribution of illegal narcotics, murder, and conspiracy to commit acts of terrorism against the United States."

"What is this?" Joanna mumbled in a dazed tone. "You must be mistaken. Mister Wickersham is a nice man."

"It's all right, Joanna," Francis said, trying to comfort his beleaguered assistant. "I am sure it is all just a mistake."

"Mister Wickersham, you will need to come with us. Place your hands on your head."

He straightened his tie and tugged at the collar of his suit jacket then slowly put both hands on top of his smooth head. A rivulet of sweat ran across his temple and dripped onto his jacket.

"Of course, I will go with you to clear this up, Agent Rottbruck."

Hilde approached and stood behind him. She patted him down for weapons.

"I am unarmed."

"So you say," she replied.

There was a metallic snap and Francis felt the cold steel of handcuffs clamp around his left wrist.

"Is that really necessary?"

"Yes, it is," replied Hilde.

Francis Beauregard Wickersham strode as gracefully as a handcuffed man could across the room towards the door.

Mike Farris towered over him as they passed in the doorway. He silently glared down at the tiny man who had ordered the death of his wife and son. Wickersham averted his eyes from the tall, muscular pastor. The retired Marine he had so despised. He said no words to Mike at all as Hilde led him out of the office and into the waiting FBI van outside the front door of Wickersham Wholesale Shoe Distributors.

CHAPTER 44

Columbus Memorial Hospital
January 18th, 2012

Hogan was aware of his friends standing over him, although he wasn't sure how long they had been there. For that matter, he wasn't sure how long he had been there. The right side of his body hurt like crazy. He vaguely remembered several images of being wheeled into surgery, but knew no details. A doctor spoke with Mike and Hilde quietly.

"Well folks, your friend here sustained a lot of damage in that single gunshot. It was a very dirty wound too. As you know we have taken more than half of his right lung, that is in addition to the rib that the bullet had totally shattered. The real problem though, and what continues to be a problem, is the infection and the damage it caused to some of his internal organs, primarily his liver and pancreas. It is finally under control now and hopefully will stay clean. Also, during the course of his surgeries several pieces of shrapnel from his old military injuries dislodged and although we were able to get them out, there is a bit of residual nerve damage that we were unable to repair. We finally feel comfortable taking him out of the induced comatose state he's been in for the past six weeks. He has a long road to travel before he's going to be back behind a desk, and he won't be kicking in doors again."

"Thanks, Doc," said Mike Farris. "Thanks for all you've done."

"So you two have known each other for a long time?"

"He saved my skin in Somalia back in ninety-three," replied Farris, "I just wish I could do more for him now."

"Well, your prayers are the best thing you can do for him at this time."

"Yes." Mike nodded, "Again, thanks."

They glanced down to where Hogan lay on the bed. Hilde leaned over Paul Hogan and gently kissed him on the forehead. His eyes fluttered weakly and he attempted a smile. The medication that had kept him unconscious for more than a month and a half was just starting to wear off.

"Hey, Paul, how you feeling?"

His eyes opened to narrow slits. They were glazed and unfocused. He parted his lips and managed to breath out a barely audible reply.

"Good."

"Hey, Gunny," Mike said, "doc says you've got a long road ahead, but you'll make it. You're going to be fine, Marine."

"How's Billy?" Paul whispered.

"Bill Coffee?"

Paul's head moved in a barely discernible nod.

"That kid is amazing," Mike answered, "not to mention blessed. Three bullets hit him in the chest but missed all of the major organs and ribs. He did nearly die of blood loss that day but has since almost fully recovered. He's itching to get back to work too, but then, he's about ten years younger than us old guys and still has a few lives left."

Paul smiled. His thin, bloodlessly pale lips stretched weakly across his face. He closed his eyes. He seemed to drift out of consciousness again then breathed out more words.

"Good for him. Me too. Gimme two months."

Mike smiled, "You're going to be alright, man."

"Start looking for that Frankenstein chick for me," Paul said. He managed a soft chuckle.

Hilde smiled down at him.

"Kharzai went back to whatever it is he does, but he said to pass a message to you when you woke up."

He looked up at her.

"What did he say?"

"Here's to saving the world…we've got a few more to go…now pass the Scooby Snacks."

Paul smiled and said. "We'll have to figure out what he meant when I'm a little more awake."

Paul breathed out a long, wispy strand of air that floated quietly from his nose. Then he drifted back to sleep.

Mike and Hilde stood over his bed for another minute then turned and quietly walked out of the room. They got on the elevator in silence and pressed the button that would take them down to the ground floor. The elevator's motor was the only sound as it carried them down its shaft.

It came to a stop and the door slid open to a lobby full of people. Some were moving about, with direction and purpose in their walk. Others sat impatiently waiting for rides or for news of loved of ones. A young lady, not more than nineteen, sat on a bench softly rocking a tiny sleeping infant, a newborn. Their faces were angelic and peaceful.

A group of doctors walked past them into the elevator, slacks and skirts fluttering beneath white lab coats. They were off to save another life, no doubt. None of them, not a single person in this hospital save Paul Hogan, Mike Farris, and Hildegarde Rottbruck had the slightest knowledge of how close they had all come to complete annihilation.

Mike and Hilde walked out the main doors of the hospital. Once outside, they made their way slowly up the sidewalk in the chilly winter air. The sky was gray with heavy, snow-laden clouds that hung low above the surface of the earth and deadened the sound of the busy city traffic that flowed like a steel and carbon river through the streets around them. Hilde glanced up at Mike. His eyes were fixed at some distant point far ahead of them beyond the hospital campus buildings and the structures. A trace of sadness seeped out of his gaze.

"Mike?" She asked.

"Hmm?"

"What are you going to do?"

"I don't know yet," he answered.

"How is your church handling everything?"

"They want me to stay on."

"Are you going to?"

"No. I put my whole congregation in danger by the way I did things. I think it is best for me to find a different ministry altogether."

"Look, Mike," she said hesitantly, "I saw a memo about a job opening at the FBI."

"I am done with all the secret agent stuff Hilde."

"Not as an agent, Mike," she replied, "As a Chaplain and Psychological Counselor. Our current one is retiring this month."

He glanced over at her.

She continued. "It covers the Ohio Valley Region, six states. It's right up your alley. You're the only qualified person I can think of who has actually experienced what some of these agents go through. You'd be perfect for the job."

"I'll think about it."

"The office is at the Columbus headquarters," she said, and then added in a quieter voice. "Just down the hall from mine."

"Oh, really?" he smiled.

"Yeah, four doors down."

He stopped walking. The leather sole of his shoes scraped lightly against the cold pavement as he turned to face her.

Mike wrapped her hands in his own and looked down into her eyes.

"Hilde, I don't know if I am right for you," he said tenderly. "I have too much baggage. You deserve someone fresher than this old war horse."

"If I was looking for someone fresh, I would have been married long ago."

He started to reply, but she put a finger to his lips to stop the words. Large, fluffy white snowflakes loosed themselves from the ceiling of cloud and drifted down from above as their heels clicked softly on the pavement.

Mike offered his arm to her and Hilde accepted it. She leaned into him as they moved into the gray winter light of the cold Ohio January afternoon.

ABOUT THE AUTHOR

Basil does not just write stories, he has lived a lot of what they contain. The backdrop for his writing started with his birth in rural Alaska. He spent his school years among the only slightly less rural, yet somehow slower moving, corn fields of Ohio, where he wished to be anywhere else, as long as it was exciting. He has lived in Fairbanks, Palmer, and Anchorage, Alaska, Camp Pendleton and San Diego, California. Washington DC, Baltimore, MD, and Baltimore, Ohio. He tried a career in the Marines, but injuries sent him home way too early. After that he waited tables, managed a family diner, worked at the NSA, owned a computer shop, was a carpenter, farmer, intelligence operative, actor, lumberjack, voice actor, EMT, network admin, helpdesk supervisor, Boy Scout leader, IT trainer, radio talk host, youth minister, and a sergeant in the Alaska Defense Force Coastal Scouts. Until a ski injury in 2008 he was an avid weight lifter and could bench press over 420 lbs. Now he's limited to a brisk walk each afternoon, hefting his laptop to his lap whilst sitting in his comfy chair, and curling a pint or three of stout each night. He lives in Anchorage, Alaska with his wife and sons, and Heimdall the Norse Dog.

PERMUTED PRESS
needs *you* to help

SPREAD (THE) INFECTION

FOLLOW US!

f | Facebook.com/PermutedPress

🐦 | Twitter.com/PermutedPress

REVIEW US!

Wherever you buy our book, they can be reviewed! We want to know what you like!

GET INFECTED!

Sign up for our mailing list at PermutedPress.com

PERMUTED
PRESS

KING ARTHUR AND THE KNIGHTS OF THE ROUND TABLE HAVE BEEN REBORN TO SAVE THE WORLD FROM THE CLUTCHES OF MORGANA WHILE SHE PROPELS OUR MODERN WORLD INTO THE MIDDLE AGES.

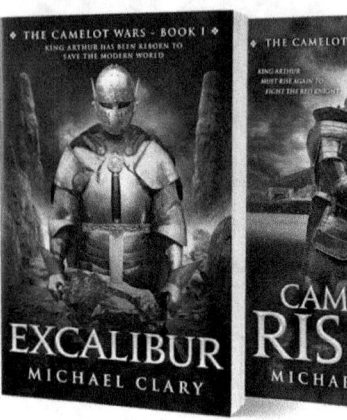 

EAN 9781618685018 $15.99   EAN 9781682611562 $15.99

Morgana's first attack came in a red fog that wiped out all modern technology. The entire planet was pushed back into the middle ages. The world descended into chaos.

But hope is not yet lost— King Arthur, Merlin, and the Knights of the Round Table have been reborn.

THE MORNINGSTAR STRAIN HAS BEEN LET LOOSE—IS THERE ANY WAY TO STOP IT?

An industrial accident unleashes some of the Morningstar Strain. The doctor who discovered the strain and her assistant will have to fight their way through Sprinters and Shamblers to save themselves, the vaccine, and the base. Then they discover that it wasn't an accident at all—somebody inside the facility did it on purpose. The war with the RSA and the infected is far from over.

This is the fourth book in Z.A. Recht's The Morningstar Strain series, written by Brad Munson.

PERMUTED PRESS

GATHERED TOGETHER AT LAST, THREE TALES OF FANTASY CENTERING AROUND THE MYSTERIOUS CITY OF SHADOWS... ALSO KNOWN AS CHICAGO.

EAN 9781682612286 $9.99   **EAN** 9781618684639 $5.99   **EAN** 9781618684899 $5.99

From *The New York Times* and *USA Today* bestselling author Richard A. Knaak comes three tales from Chicago, the City of Shadows. Enter the world of the Grey–the creatures that live at the edge of our imagination and seek to be real. Follow the quest of a wizard seeking escape from the centuries-long haunting of a gargoyle. Behold the coming of the end of the world as the Dutchman arrives.

Enter the City of Shadows.